THE NOTES OF DR. NEWGATE

ALAN FRANKS

MUSWELL PRESS LTD

First published in 2013

by Muswell Press Ltd
6 Pinchin Street
London E1 1SA

ISBN 978-0-9572136-4-7

Book design by Bewick Abel Thompson

Printed and bound by Shortrun Press Ltd.
Sowton Industrial Estate
Bittern Road
Exeter
EX2 7LW

www.muswell-press.co.uk

For Ruth

May 25th 2010. Serena Miller in again. What to do about that one. I have the sense that something dreadful is going to happen to her. We're all out of our depths with her. She's one of the bright, canny ones who would play all the members of the practice against each other if she got the chance. All that intelligence, all that charisma, but in such hands. Like a gun. It was all there when she was a girl. Ten years ago now? More? That mischievous face pressed against the window of the squash court while I was losing to her father. That ghastly man. He must have something to do with her present state.

I do wonder whether she's decided to play the instability card because it makes life so much more interesting. And because she is clearly a gifted actress, whom I expect to see on the West End stage one day. A month ago I referred her to Martina Lubasz, whom I've got to know much better since coming through my own recent troubles. Well, not so recent now. How the time goes. She's not just a very experienced psychiatrist but also – more importantly in my book – a kind and perceptive woman who is better than most at spotting an antic disposition. But now young Serena is back with us, telling me it didn't work with Martina. I ask her why and she shrugs and says, 'Because.' I suggest she gives it one more try, and this time goes along with a more positive approach. She pouts in resentment. Sometimes I don't know where to start. Nearly twenty years in general practice and still clueless on a regular basis. Quite good at hiding it though, I think.

May 28th. Imogen going through another biting phase. At least I hope it's only a phase. I wonder whether these phases only become apparent when you, in this case I, go looking for them. I see her this morning from the bathroom, through the crack in the door. Technically, yes, I am spying, and am not proud of myself. Nor ashamed enough to stop. She is my wife - and I am a doctor. Also, I have good reason to believe she has spied on me in the past. For all I know she has taught Inez and all the previous au pairs to do likewise, going back however many years it is since Imogen was expecting Ricky. Twenty-two. So we're in a climate of mutual surveillance here. Very polite on the outside. Habitually polite to the point of formality these days. But spying away like hell on the inside. As the whole world is now doing. While we were all waiting for Big Brother to install himself, Little Brother slipped in by the back door.

Today is the longest biting session I have witnessed. So, longest since records began, as the weather people say. I'm positioned in the bathroom so that I can see her through the slightly open door. She just sits there in the bed with her hand up at her mouth like something you eat - a sandwich, drumstick, corn cob. But something that never gets consumed. It just oscillates across her mouth and back as she works her teeth against the finger nails. Technically, you can't really call it nail-biting since that has already been done. So, it's a kind of ongoing after-sales service, ensuring that the nails will never grow back to the length they were when she started biting them.

May 29th. Same again. Me in the bathroom, looking back into the bedroom; her hand moving hard against her mouth like a harmonica. It would go on for as long as yesterday. As far as I can tell, it would only stop if someone else came into the room - i.e. me at the end of the day, after surgery.

So today I do that - I walk back in from the bathroom to see if the action stops. It does. As her hand goes down, so her face comes up and gives me a neutral acknowledgement. I suppose I've become more aware of it since other doctors at the practice – well, one other doctor really, Maurice – decided he was an authority on compulsive and repetitive behaviour of all kinds.

Because of his intensely rivalrous nature, I am sure he has only become an expert in this field to let me know I do not have a monopoly on knowledge of the addictive personality. There are many things he will not forgive me for. One is my apparent recovery (caution here, Newgate) from alcoholism. Another, of course, is my wife.

I don't know if Maurice is aware of her habit, although I couldn't help hearing him drop the word Onychophagia (technical term for nail-biting) into a phone call the other day. Nor have I missed his recent references to the role of behavioural therapy in Impulse Control Disorders. I remember the time when HRT stood for Hormone Replacement Therapy. Now it stands for Habit Reversal Training. But then I'm hardening into a dinosaur, I know. When I hear LSE I think London School of Economics when I should be thinking Low Self Esteem.

May 30th. Maybe the Onychophagia should be telling me something. Probably something like: 'Your wife is exhibiting symptoms of stress or anxiety or both, Dr, Newgate, and it is almost certainly your fault.'

Or not. This two-word riposte stands me in good stead when anyone, including me, comes up with a cocksure explanation, particularly one with a little twist of blame thrown in. Arrogant to see yourself as the origin of another's symptoms. Easier to fall back onto the Anglicans' secret friend, agnosticism, and accept that your only certainty is that you are uncertain.

Henry Gordon-Venning (HGV to the other three of us as he is as slow and bulky as a Heavy Goods Vehicle) likes to put these fringey conditions down to *accidie*. Pompous old toad. When stumped, reach for classical archaisms. The ancient marble of authority. Although maybe I did sense something of that sort in Imogen, right from the start. Again, maybe not, since in those days my diagnostic skills were so lacking that I would have needed to see a right angled bend in a thigh before suspecting fracture

9

of the femur. Anyway, pretty soon Imogen was so overjoyed at having Ricky, as was I, that everything else vanished.

So it's possibly no coincidence that her mood has been slumped ever since he started at Oxford, which is now three terms ago. I go back and back in my mind to the time before she was pregnant. Those two years we had in Hastings, before coming here. I try to remember how she was then - pretty low is the answer. The damp little cottage, her psychotic department head, what was his name - Derek - not to mention my terrible houseman hours. All grim stuff, yes, although fairly run-of-the-mill for the doctor and the teacher who are so early in their careers that they've still got one foot in adolescence.

June 4th. Co-dependence. That's the other new Maurice word I was trying to remember. Actually quite dated now in California, its birthplace, but pretty big in certain parts of the Richmond and Barnes areas. I'm fed up with it and its glib reduction of relationships to the status of harmful drugs. Giving myself away here but what the hell.

June 5th. If I'm going to do this, then I must try and keep the entries regular. Six in ten days and already I'm feeling virtuous, professional, candidate for Great Diarists of the Twenty First Century, nonsense like that. The fact is I've never been a diary sort of person, partly because I've never had the energy. Also, when you read the things, they are so clearly for publication -which this one is absolutely not - that you can't quite believe what their authors are saying. An opinion is an opinion, but it becomes something else, like rhetoric, when it is being given with a sense of audience. So, I'm my own reader. I am one hundred per cent of my circulation. I shall write it for me. I shall peer over my own shoulder and try to exert some quality control.

June 6th. That resolution has hardened overnight. I knew this to be the case just a moment ago when I sat down and read the

May 28th entry, my second. The one about Imogen and the biting. I appreciate the fact that the author, while hardly a Charles Dickens, is at least doing his best to be forthright and to hold the attention of his reader, i.e. himself. The handwriting could be better, but I'm trying to get it down fast, and if you're a victim of the teaching fashion for italics, as I was, you have to abandon the aesthetic of the line in the interests of pace. This is my sixth entry in the space of a fortnight. I've surprised myself by getting even this far.

June 11th. Even with this small number of entries and tiny passage of time, I can feel something beginning to shift. One other person, says Clive, my lovely, lumbering, Bible-bearing sponsor in AA. That's all you need; just take one other person into your confidence, and the poison of secrecy is bled from you. I think Clive would like that other person to be him, and if that is the case then he has every right to expect it. After all, it was me who approached him at the St. Stephens Saturday morning meeting.

A doctor, he thought, and his eyes lit up. A real live doctor in Alcoholics Anonymous. And not as an observer but a punter, a full participant. People's eyes often do light up - the cliché is an accurate one - when they realise that even medics, who are meant to know about addictive disorders, can fall prey to such conditions themselves. God, if only they knew. And I suppose we're good to have aboard. Like priests, or lawyers or teachers. They leaven the fellowship with that fetching English brand of professionalism. Devout, but not too much. Serious but sociable. It is a similar spirit to the one which has helped hold the afflicted body of the C of E more or less together through its own well-practised frailties.

June 13th. When to do this, that's the next question. It doesn't matter, seems to be the answer. I'll do it when I can. When I think how busy we all were at St. Thomas's, how we sometimes never slept properly for days and yet found the time to study. If you can live that life, you can live any life. That's the theory, isn't it? Weed out the ones who can't hack it, early doors. So thank you, horrible, sleep-deprived, verge-of-madness, keeling-over-in-theatre St. Thomas's for your invaluable practicals in pluralism. This scribbling, the black biro and the big notebook, the crossings-out and the notes in the margin - they all remind me of those days. Mixed feelings about them; on the one hand the sense of usefulness and the fruits of a profession; on the other hand, all that future stretching ahead with its infinite caseload of the not-yet-sick.

June 18th. Another biting morning and nothing to do with the weather. Me peering back into the bedroom through the crack, and wishing that I weren't. I ask myself if I am experiencing revulsion and the answer is no. Curiosity perhaps, nothing worse than that. To my great relief. Imogen has never repelled me, quite the opposite, and I hope that remains the case, whatever the state of our relationship might be. I am probably in some form of denial about the way she looks. No, not her, that's wrong; about the way I look. That's where the problem lies, or stands, or walks, whenever I catch my reflection in a public surface. Or rather, whenever my reflection catches me, since it's always that way round. I never go looking for it. Then, as I decide I'm looking old enough to be my own father, I draw a similar conclusion about her, and it sends me hurtling back into the time of our youth, our first knowledge of each other. I try to stay there, in the scent and danger of it, but I can't hold on. It slips from me like soap in the bath.

I shall have to come back to this subject later.

June 20th. All right then, now. Of course you don't see your own alterations as dramatically as the rest of the world. Yes, you do get the odd shock from the cruel refractions of a mirror-lined lift - how dare they make you look at the back of your own neck without prior warning - but if you want a consensual view of what is going on, watch the expressions on the faces of people who have known you well but not seen you for a while. This happened the other day in the High Street, when a little group of what used to be The Young Mums from the NCT classes walked straight past me without recognising me. The Young Mums, for Heaven's sake, still looking remarkably pink-faced and springy-haired in their Pilates and au pair lives. Only yesterday that we were all going distant with unutterable love for our beautiful, perfect, world-saving, tottering little creatures, wishing the other parents and toddlers well but not so well that their own perfect ones had calculus nailed by the age of six and were premiering a Tippett concerto at the QEH by seven. Now I've reverted to being a stranger to them.

No, one of their gazes did meet mine questioningly. There was shock, as if to ask me was I playing a joke of some kind; she was thinking about saying something but we passed before she could put anything together. There was the unmistakable be-hind-the-eyes glint of *schadenfreude*, never as good at suppressing itself as it fancies. What was her name? Megan. Yes, I'm sure it was Megan. Imogen was forever Round at Megan's in those days, with Ricky totally edible in his Osh Kosh dungarees or whatever the latest kids' fashion statements were meant to be.

June 21st. Pre-sleep sounds from upstairs. The water leaving the basin and a few seconds later rattling down into the drain at the foot of the house. Imogen padding across from the bathroom, and the bed whining slightly as she transfers herself onto it and then into it. The muffled sharpness of the Radio 4 beeps as the ten o'clock news comes on and she listens distantly to the usual stuff about bankruptcy and earthquakes. Maybe down here is where I'll do this. It's worked so far. We always said this should be my study since it is directly below our bedroom and so wouldn't be disturbed by a noisy boy or a late-returning au pair.

I find that I have sympathy for us; for Imogen and me, singly and together. Like I have sympathy for some of the people coming through my door at work, playing their losing hands and heading towards sure defeat with such gameness. What to do with that sympathy for the Newgates, William and Imogen, is another matter.

We are always being told to beware of pity. Someone even wrote a book of that name. *Beware of Pity*. Stefan Zweig. Mila is horribly good on all this. At least she is certainly better than the other three of us at the practice, all white middle-class males. Maybe the Czechs, and the East Europeans generally, have a much more direct approach to certain diagnostic areas - less cluttered with misguided correctness.

Of course a beautiful person experiences loss when they believe that beauty to be gone. This is Mila talking, and I'm only paraphrasing slightly. She wasn't discussing Imogen, but a friend of hers in Prague. Still, she might just as well have been talking about Imogen. Or rather, Imogen's opinion of herself. She - says Mila of her friend - was rich in beauty. In her case literally so; the men who wanted her were always rich in money and allowed her visual form of wealth to make her their social peer. But such an arrangement could not last. The men tended to hang onto their money, unless they were reckless or unfortunate; many of them made their money beget more. Her friend, however, was bound onto a course of diminishing returns. It meant that a kind of bereavement was inevitable - a beautiful woman trapped inside one who was no longer beautiful; the equivalent of an oligarch reduced to living in a hostel.

Leave it there. There's some conclusion forming in my head but I'm too tired to nail it.

June 22nd. Still not there. What I'm trying to say is that Imogen's certainty of her own decline is making her act as if it's an acknowledged truth, even though it's no such thing. This in turn makes me feel I must be at least partly responsible. And so I get on with the business of being repelled by my own behaviour; the peering back into the bedroom, the breaking-off to splash water about in the basin in a nonchalant, shaving sort of way, giving her no chance of thinking that she might be watched.

When we were young… no. No time for that today. Already running late.

June 22nd. When we were young, I was obsessed by her. Even before I had got to know her, she occupied me all through the days and nights. I mean literally; she took up residence in my head and heart. I would write her name down on a piece of paper, carry it around with me, open it up to surprise myself with the dazzle of it. In the street, at Thomas's, any time of the day or night, or those long shifts when you lost track of the time and the date. Even the digits of her phone number - her family's phone number - carried a force that was beyond me. Just a handful of ordinary digits, turned into a kind of drug by their association with access to her. Imogen, from the Celtic for maiden, used by Shakespeare in *Cymbeline* but probably misprinted in the Folio or whatever. Her father's favourite name; not because of anything as arty as that but because he was a fan of the American comedienne Imogen Coca. Image, imagine, Imogen.

Her by Pen Ponds in Richmond Park very early one autumn morning, after a medics' all-nighter on some boat at Teddington, in a silver gown, looking through the mist at the swans. When we'd not been able to get home, and just walked through the small hours, oblivious of where we were heading. The light on her shoulders, the curve of her back, her completely perfect figure. Her name definitely played some part in intoxicating me. I don't think I would have lost my reason, which is definitely

15

what happened, if she had been called, I don't know, Cheryl. Names are unfair like that.

I can't write any more of this, not about Imogen. Not about her when she was young. And yet I know I will have to. I haven't thought about these things, let alone tried to express them, until now. These entries are starting to organise themselves, as if they don't really need me. Like I'm getting in the way. Not that I can remove myself.

June 29th. Imogen much better today. No more of the Onychophagia routine this morning, at least not while I'm watching her. Which isn't very long at all, me having decided that it's not really on to stare at someone when they don't know they are being observed. My profession doesn't give me the automatic right to do that. How would I like it if someone kept doing it to me? As my mother used to say. Poor Mum. Also, I realise there's a danger that I'm willing her to do the biting so that I've got ongoing evidence of her strange compulsions. What am I thinking about? Physician heal thyself. As my mother never lived to say.

The *Guardian* is rumpled on the bed, much more so than when she's only read it for the crossword and the sudoku. I might even hear her humming when I come home, although she stops soon after. Two reasons for her improved morale stare me in the face. One is Inez, who is now back from her week in Bilbao. There are Spanish delicacies in coloured wrapping paper on the kitchen table; something called kokotxas, which I am told comes from the jowls of the spider crab; Chorizos and Manchega cheese and bottles of Sangria on the sideboard; a stack of classic CDs by Narcisso Ypes, Andre Segovia, Montserrat Caballe as well as the singers and players from Bilbao. They have faces of magnificent passion and heroic abandon. I look forward to hear them in the house, to play host to the sound of them, even though I know they will make me feel thin and constrained. Some of them she knows personally.

The second reason of course is Ricky himself, who will be back from Magdalen any day now. He's managed to stay in Oxford for a fortnight after the end of term, either in college or in the spare room at a friend's lodgings. He's using the libraries and generally enjoying the town until it gets overrun by tourists and he finds himself turned into an unwilling attraction. The weather always brightens on Imogen's brow when he's due, just as it did twenty-two years ago. Every return he makes is like a smaller version of that first, great expectation. How will he be this time?

You change like a foal when you are a student. Being a late developer, as I was - am, he looks like a variant of himself after every gap of eight weeks; you blink and he's put on yet more inches. Surely he had enough already. His face is half-hidden behind a shoulder-length tumble of Merry Monarch curls. Blink again and it's vanished; he's as jar-headed as a G.I., with his shoulders made huge and muscular from rowing in the college eight. The culture and the politics keep pace with these wild style swings. Now he's a classic economic liberal with whole chunks of *The Wealth of Nations* committed to memory; then, just as suddenly, I've nothing to lose but my chains (at least this carries the acknowledgement that I do actually work for a living), and Uncle Karl is his virtual godfather.

So I am waiting to be slain like Oedipus, in the full knowledge that this is the natural order of things and therefore not just good for Ricky but a growth opportunity for me as well. I don't yet know what form this necessary killing will take, nor what percentages of the literal and the figurative will be there in the mix. I love the boy. Unconditionally, I'm sure, in that if he felt the need to trample all over me, or ignore me, or use his friends' cyber skills to void my current account in his favour, I would be rooting for him. Smarting a little perhaps, but fundamentally on his side, infuriating him yet more with this show of self-denying liberalism. If it's any help to him, I do manage to annoy myself just as much as I must annoy him.

July 4th. Ricky duly back from Oxford and Imogen visibly improved. Surely no reason to look any further than Empty Nest Syndrome for the source of her apparent anguish. The real question is what will happen when he's gone for good, in the sense of married, own home, own children. I can hear Clive's voice in my head, going 'Day at a time, William. Day at a time,' all flat and safe as a mattress. Right as ever. Dull but right.

Ricky's hair is sticking out in batches. There is a hint of orange which fades as it gets to the root. I deliberately don't comment on it. I can remember something similar happening to my hair at about that age, when the man in Ginger Group pulled it into swatches which he then wrapped in tin foil until I looked ready to pick up signals from Saturn. For some reason he took it into his head - or rather, onto mine - that this was My Look. I managed to keep my eyes off the mirror until he'd done. It cost me about a third of my grant for the term, and I went straight to the public baths at Kensal Green to wreck it in the showers. No such problems for Ricky, who obviously went clear-eyed into the operation.

I approach him in the kitchen with my arms out a little so that they could just be greeting him or else ready to turn into a full hug if required. Instead he shakes me by the hand in a quaintly formal way and says 'Hello old man all right.' Hugs must be for friends only. He smiles very openly, as he always did. There's the slightly crooked mouth - amused, yes, but with the possibility of reproach as well. It's a look that tells me I'll get dealt with before too long. Not destructively perhaps, but with the attention of a younger, stronger, more battle-ready intellect than mine. Than mine ever was.

Inez comes in, surly as ever. Is it only me who sees her like this?

Possibly. She hardly acknowledges me before greeting Ricky, who practices his limping Spanish in reply. They laugh, both enjoying his lack of competence. Her face is split across by that frighteningly big mouth with its tight rows of pearl tombstones.

I hear myself say 'How's tricks then?' and sound distressingly old. He and Inez giggle. I guess they've found a shared joke in my mannerisms. I don't really mind. At least I don't think I do. Imogen gets busy with the tea things, shooting little glances at our big, almost finished son. Our undoubtedly handsome son. They contain love, of course, and a softness which I find myself envying. But there also, unless I'm over-reading her face, is the certainty of imminent loss; the half-formed question of how and who to be in the still-long future; how to relate with this man across the kitchen once their beloved charge is no longer that thing and the shared project of his development is terminated.

Inez helps her with the tea stuff and the three of them sit at the table. There is no fourth chair. It's not actually a pointed exclusion of me; I don't think. The other chair's gone somewhere else, and besides, it's coming up to two thirty and afternoon surgery.

Later on, when I get back, they're still at it. A bottle of Inez's Sangria must have come out because that unmistakable slurpy swinging quality has got into the conversation. Even Imogen who had come in is animated, as she hardly ever is with me. One voice interrupts while the other, the interrupted one, pays no attention and carries right on so that the exchanges are not so much antiphonal as simultaneous.

Everything is the fault of the Baby Boomers, seems to be the gist. Yawn, frankly. Not that it's not true of course; just that it seems to be the only song on the juke box. They, the Boomers, rolled through the post-war years like a mighty wave and now the children are having to pay for their parents' indulgences. They got free higher ed, for heaven's sake. Not loans but grants. Grants. Where do you hear that word these days? They danced till dawn to the best bands the world had ever heard; they smoked grass which bore no more resemblance to the murderous skunk of today than does Babycham to raw poteen; they saw history's window of opportunity opening between the pill and AIDS and clambered on in. Some never came out again. Others had the high and left their kids the hangover.

It's a fashionable enough argument, verging on received wisdom. Which is not to say it's a wrong one. Or a right one. Loads of socio-economic underpinning of the kind which is probably second nature to Ricky and his fellow PPE students: illusory wealth of house price inflation; long-term student debt; decline of the employment market; growing divide between rich and poor. There've been whole books about it. Whenever I read the reviews, I feel personally targeted by the argument. I expect the net to close around me, and to learn that I alone have been responsible for the decline of the manufacturing base in the East Midlands. 'Most culpable of all in the great plundering of the nation's youth to fund the continuing ease of the greediest generation in our history is Dr. William Newgate of 127 Elm View Crescent, Richmond, Surrey. At a time when longevity is taken for granted and the Boomers' lives turn into a monster-fade of hypochondria and ruinous state provision, Dr. Newgate truly is the *Hey Jude* of licensed scrounging.' Imogen seems to have been given a free pass, but that must be because Inez and Ricky see her as an ally by virtue of her opposition to me. My enemy's enemy and all that.

If I loiter long enough in the hall, I feel sure a line of *ad hominem* attack will become audible from the kitchen. I imagine Ricky twining his hands magisterially beneath his chin and rounding up the excursions of the seminar with an admirably plain form of words, as in: 'Basically I blame Dad.'

Instead I can hear Inez taking it international with an indictment of the English colonial legacy and then Imogen, to her credit, saying that Britain wasn't going to take any lessons from Spain on the exploitation of overseas possessions. I always loved that forthrightness of hers. It was dangerous and principled, such a welcome change from well-schooled diplomacy. She never knew how to stand down. Ricky says 'Actually, Mum's got a point,' and Inez makes an odd, disconnected noise like a cat getting caught in a closing door.

I don't think I know anyone else who has children in their twenties and is still keeping an au pair. Certainly not round here, and yet round here is precisely the sort of place where you'd expect such behaviour. For some reason we never stopped. Before Inez, it was Agnieszka from Poland, and before her Marie-Claude from Lyons, and back and back in almost apostolic succession to the original Inez, also from Spain. Not Bilbao though. Valladolid, I think. I called her Saint Inez because of the miracles she worked with our unusually demanding baby and his seriously depressed mother. Like she'd experienced something similar at home.

We just went on replacing them as they left. As Ricky grew towards his teens they stopped being au pairs in the usual sense and turned into hybrids of cleaners, shoppers and general companions for Imogen. Someone once suggested to me that she clearly wanted a daughter without the trauma of bearing one and bringing her up. A therapist who'd turned up at a Pfizer drug lunch in Putney. He even asked me how their presence impacted on my relationship with Imogen, and looked pleased when I said I hadn't thought about it.

It never seemed to matter that the au pair's conversations were hampered by language barriers. The conscientious ones took it as an opportunity to improve their English. The rest just spoke in their own language so that by the end of their time with us our Spanish had improved remarkably while their English had got even worse. Ricky always helped out if they wanted slang.

He sent the very straitlaced Limoges girl, Francoise, round to Cyril Pegg's, the family sweetshop, to ask for a Bum Bandit, which he said was the name of a chocolate bar.

This present Inez is no saint. I can't work her out. But then I could never work any of them out. They always belonged in Imogen's province. And Ricky's to a lesser extent. Particularly Agnieszka, who was after him, and endeared herself to us all by getting her plumber cousin to come down from Luton and fix the rebel toilet at the top of the house. A huge saving, unless you take into account the flooding and the cost of the new carpets. If I were twenty-five years younger, I would probably be very drawn to Inez, as Ricky clearly is. I wish him better luck than I would have had. The ratio at Oxford is still so much in favour of the girls, never mind all the secretarial colleges and language schools that flocked there in the hope of some reflected standing.

God I'm exhausted.

July 5th. Still exhausted. I've had the Underground dream again. Or part of it at least. The bit where the train's actually coming into the station and I know what's going to happen.

Then I must have woken up, or else the rest of the dream must have gone underground, so to speak - carried on in the dream section of my head without alerting the other section which records and memorises the action. When I wake, I'm aware of straining after the sequence of now-familiar nightmare events, almost as if I am following the train into the tunnel against my better judgement. Back to this when more time. Too big for now.

July 13th. Serena Miller in again. Last patient of the afternoon. She must have phoned and got the temporary receptionist, Gill, who then must have slotted her in at the end of normal surgery without letting me know. It's happened before, although this

22

is the first time with Serena. My fault really. I've always said I'd rather see them than not. She's a welcome sight, why pretend otherwise. With her tossing hair, all full of springtime and youth, and, in utter defiance of her life-style, the figure of an athlete. A swimmer perhaps, sinuous but fluid. Well, she was once, wasn't she, when she was about seventeen. Long-legged and broad-shouldered, without being remotely manly. You can't help noticing these things, particularly not after an afternoon's procession of the folded-double and the frame-assisted insects. The depression which brought her back here seven weeks ago has led to her taking a term off her drama course, with the college's agreement. They clearly think she is exceptionally talented, and will achieve great things when she sorts her present troubles out.

Serena - I should say Ms Miller but find myself preferring to say Serena - single-handedly brings down the average age of the afternoon's clientele with a bump. She is only the second under thirty. Almost all the remaining fourteen patients were maintenance jobs; old cars still kept just about roadworthy through replacement parts and medication. And that undoubted sense of entitlement that the ancient and ageing seem to have acquired in the last few years. The entitlement to life on a permanently renewable basis. Like a club subscription that no-one is authorised to cancel. On the few occasions when I try to tell them in the kindest and most diplomatic language I can find that the Reaper is getting restless, they look at me as if there has been a mistake and all that needs to be done to rectify it is a second opinion or a new part and a different tablet. Some of them have seen off so many terminal onslaughts of this or that that I can quite understand why they've decided the Maker has lost interest in meeting them, and resent the suggestion that he's sniffing around again.

The Underground is passing through my head as Serena

23

comes in and takes a seat. This must be making me furrowed or distrait because she asks me if I am all right. Enough emphasis on the 'right' to make me think she suspects I am not. Which is presumably the idea. I hate it when patients do this. Just because I ask how they are does not give them the right to ask how I am. Information about them is my stock-in-trade, not a component of social exchange. I am aware of being and looking immensely tired. All day I have tried to avoid a mirror or any remotely reflective surface in the certainty that there's nothing in it for me; just the dark crescents under the eyes and the stubborn outcrop of slept-on hair.

I must look startled by her. I am. She notes this, sniffs disapproval and then pushes her hands out like buffers, reversing out of the question she has just asked. I say 'Fine. Thank you. More to the point... '

She laughs and nods and says: 'Not fine, actually. Not fine at all.'

'It's a lazy word, I know,' I go on. 'I do rather wish I could come up with a better one.' I don't add that one of the many mantras of the fellowship is that fine really stands for fucked-up, insecure, neurotic and egocentric. A bit glib, a bit tiresome but, as ever, not that far from the mark. In her case, bang-on, I'd say. 'So... '

'If I were fine,' she says, 'I wouldn't have come again so soon, would I.'

'No. I suppose not. So. The same, is it? Broadly, the same as... '

I call up her entries and start scrolling down for my notes on her last appointment.

'The same, yes,' she goes on, 'but at the same time different.'

I am aware of her studying the side of my face and being amused by what she sees there. It must be something I give off, the same something that made Ricky and Inez exchange their giggling faces when I was talking to them.

'You saw Martina,' I say. 'I mean Miss Lubasz.'

'Yeah,' she replies, bored and impress-me. 'I told you.'

'And?'

'And what.'

'Can you just refresh my memory. Some of the issues that seemed to be preoccupying you when we spoke before. I presume you raised them with her.'

'Not particularly, no.'

'I see. Not particularly. Why was this, if I may ask.'

'Didn't come up.'

'Didn't come up?'

'With talking, right? It takes two, yeah. Martina didn't really want to engage.'

'No. I see. Well, you know, the thing is. People doing what she does can only be effective if the patient, that is if the other person, will, as it were, well, speak to them. Were you able to say anything to her?'

'No. Not really.'

'Nothing at all?'

'Nothing of any interest. Well. She seemed quite interested in music, and so that was OK, but then it dried up. I'm not very well up on Mahler.'

'Ah yes.'

'And she wasn't into Indie bands.'

There is a silence. She looks at me with her chin slightly up and a what-next challenge in her eyes. She looks a lot better, a lot happier than she did when she walked in a couple of minutes ago, just as I must look a lot older, a lot more tired.

'Of course,' I say, 'there is no compulsion for you to see Miss Lubasz. All I am suggesting, as I think I did when you were last here, is that it is strongly advisable for someone in your situation to open and sustain a dialogue with a qualified professional.

That is what they are there for.'

'I did try,' she says with sudden emphasis. 'I did.' She is almost shouting. 'I mean, I don't like it when people are awkward. You know, just two people, so they have to talk. Not like now, which is fine. But with her, right, the truth is I just didn't know what to say to her. I didn't want to offend her.'

I laugh slightly, which in turn offends her. I shouldn't find it funny, but I can't help it - the plain comedy of someone not knowing what to say to the shrink. Having to make stuff up, even. Hardly the first time. Perhaps Martina was not the right choice. Perhaps I made it hurriedly because I like and trust her. I apologise for laughing and am about to try and explain why I was doing so when she gives out a big, rather bawdy laugh of her own and agrees that it's got its funny side. This strikes me as progress, although what direction we're moving in I'm not sure.

I resume the scrolling through her notes and find that on her first appointment with me, five months ago, she was talking of something in her life that was too big (her words) to tell anyone. I also see that I asked her whether that secret was responsible for her having used cannabis and amphetamines at various times in her past - she insisted it was all in her past, although I wasn't convinced. I'm still not. She answered that that could well be the case, although, she claimed, it was surely for people like me to find out. Already evidence of what I hear again today - some desire to get our profession to show its metal, sing for its supper, something like that.

The screen picks this moment to freeze. Maybe it's the whole practice going down, as has happened before. More likely just mine. Our technology's like that. It only has to see me seating myself before it and it comes up with a package of humiliations. Like anyone whose soul is stranded in the mechanical age, I respond to the freeze with more and more clicks and key strokes. To which the screen responds by having nothing at all to do with me. It will not trade with someone quite so disrespectful. I am an embarrassment to the lovely virtual salons of e-speech.

My hands close on either end of the keyboard as if I plan to use it violently against its own computer. The lines and page borders are beyond instruction. They are decomposing and jumbling so that they look like the remains of a crow on a windscreen. Then my glasses help the anarchy along with a stand-by routine from the low tech days, and fall off my face onto the desk. I comment urbanely on the strange march of progress from the radiogram days when you had to wait for the valves to warm up, to this present time of intelligent people unable to switch a TV on, but she is leaning forward with a hand across her eyes and her face almost covered by the curtains of converging hair.

She is shaking, and I realise that while I have been busily losing my latest computer war, she has been overcome by these unmentionable troubles of hers. This is good, in a way. Painful of course, but better than letting them burn her inwardly and in silence. Perhaps we should persevere with Martina after all. Another mighty mantra from the fellowship falls into my head - Remember, William, you're as sick as your secrets.

You're also the world's worst diagnostician, Dr. Newgate. Those aren't tears, but the heavings of hilarity. Her turn to apologise, and she would if she could get the words out. No chance. Whenever she draws breath to speak, the air is hijacked for the laughter, whose need is great. 'I'm sorry,' she manages eventually. 'It's just that… it's just that… .' But she only has to try and explain why she is laughing (very simple: me) and it makes matters even worse. Toxic Mirth Syndrome. Recovery is slow. She and the computer are level-pegging on the road back to normal function. I can hear Gill in the corridor. Gone closing time by several minutes and she is checking the place for left items and lights still on. She passes slowly by my door and I can almost hear the curiosity in her tread.

'Well, ' I say to Serena, who now looks every bit as tousled and blotchy-eyed as if she had just weathered a major emotional hurricane. 'I'm glad I've been able to, erm, entertain you.' Only the truth. I'm delighted. And goodness how her face catches fire when she smiles.

I decide to carry on. 'Listen, if you were going to apologise for laughing, there's really no necessity.'

She looks at me anxiously, expecting some but-clause to come in, some reminder that we have to trade in the adult world and cannot hide behind the diversion of laughter. It doesn't come, and this surprises her. 'Actually,' I say, 'I'm very glad if I make people laugh, even if I'm not at all sure how I do it.'

The anxiety gives way to the warmth of relief. 'Thank you so much,' she says.

'Not at all.'

'No, I mean, thank you for seeing me today. I didn't think you would.'

'What made you think that?'

'Oh, you know.'

'It's what we're here for.'

'Yes. But people don't.'

'Don't what? See you?'

'Yes. It's not easy, is it.'

'What is not easy?'

'Any of it.'

'No. I suppose not. You mean, being well.'

'Yes.'

'No. Not easy at all. But worth it surely. Worth it in proportion to its difficulty.'

She nods ruminatively. Her face is much as it used to be all those years ago when she and her sister pressed their noses against the squash court window while I played their father, by far the most aggressively competitive member of the club.

They would breathe on the glass, then write things on the mist with their fingers and dissolve into helpless laughter. The spasm which she has just had takes me back to those occasions. Brian Miller steeling every sinew for the next point, me affecting languor and complimenting him on his strokes, the girls up in the window falling about at their unaware father. Or was it me? Beyond these scenes, I knew nothing of them or their father. Brian himself was so focussed on victory that he never had the inclination for a drink in the bar; just a shower in silence followed by some elaborate routine with embrocation and bandaging. The nearest we got to conversation was him doing a rigorous critique of his own backhand boast shots.

There was a mother. A mournful, slight woman who only very rarely came to join her family at the club. I saw her on a handful of occasions, each time looking more spectral than the last, nursing a drink as if it was an injured bird, right over in the far corner of the bar while the girls watched their father on court.

I remember that she was admitted to The Priory for depression. I think it turned out to be one of those conditions which mask an addictive disorder. In her case it was plain old alcoholism, which of course was exacerbating the depression while posing as the cure. She was referred by old Dr. Montague, whom I knew a little.

Since then I've realised how impossible it was for me to discuss such addictions dispassionately as I was suffering from one myself. I would go through the motions, nod liberally at the praise - the sometimes grudging or patronising praise - bestowed on AA, and wait for the topic to pass. Physician heal thyself indeed. Eventually she just vanished, as I remember. I suppose everyone just vanishes in the end, but Mrs. Miller seemed to diminish, physically, to the point of transparency, as if she had no wish to be seen. She relapsed and died. Alc and barb, but an open verdict at the coroner's.

There is little of that poor dead woman in Serena, who has the broad frame and athletic face of her father. I wonder how she coped with her mother's death - whether her present troubles are a result of her not dealing with that loss and its implications. Open verdict maybe, but, as I never stop hearing in the rooms, alcoholism is nothing if not a long suicide note.

I've never worn the idea that people can read each other's minds. Synchronic initiatives perhaps, based on the laws of probability, but actual reading, as if the face is a page of print, no. Which is why Serena's next remark alarms me so much. 'You could have gone the same way as her.' She says it matter-of-factly, as if she has been running a cursor along my lines of thought and has now reached exactly the same place as me. I am aware of looking startled, and try to counteract this with an innocent 'Who? The same way as who?' Serena laughs to indicate that she knows who, but then comes to my aid with the information. 'My mother, of course.'

So Serena knows about my alcoholism - and my recovery from it. Does it matter? Do I mind? I haven't time to interrogate myself fully on this. No reason to worry though, surely. Sick as your secrets and all that. The healing powers of glasnost. I do know doctors who go to elaborate lengths to keep their addictions - their past addictions - secret. Like travelling thirty miles to go to meetings in neighbourhoods where they won't be recognised. The wrong policy surely. If this programme of recovery is good enough for a middle-aged, fairly conventional family doctor, shouldn't it be good enough for anyone? And shouldn't this fact be known?

My thoughts run back to her father and a particularly unpleasant, ill-tempered three-setter we once had. Again she appears to have stalked me in this shift of concentration from one parent to the other.

'You know he fucked us,' says Serena.

I hear myself replying quite coolly - something about Philip Larkin putting his finger on the inevitable harm caused by the parenting process. As I do so, I'm aware that it might be the wrong answer. Or an inadequate one. But then, when people, young ones mostly, say someone screwed them, they usually mean screwed up. So the f-word might also have shaken off the 'up.'

'No, no,' she says. 'Me and my sister. He fucked us. You remember Charlotte.'

'Yes. No. Not really.' True. I don't. They had the better of me, looking down through the wire-meshed window. To me they were two young, rather spirited girls. There was barely more than a year between them, and I doubt I could even tell them apart. They hunted as a pair and were a single entity. They may have watched me banging about the court after their father for forty-five minutes on end, but I hardly saw them, except briefly, in the family room. I simply didn't know them.

'That was a terrible shame,' I hear myself say. 'Really awful.'

'Oh yes, that,' she replies, realising that I'm referring to the tragic death of Charlotte in a skiing accident in the Bernese Oberland, eighteen months after their mother had died.

'More than a shame. Much more than a shame.'

There is another a silence, a really long one this time, for the good reason that I can't think of anything to say, and she is apparently happy not to. I try and weigh the moment just gone. The patient appears to be telling me that her father committed incest. Not just with her but with her sister also.

Any hope I had that she was speaking figuratively seems to have gone. She has also raised the skiing accident which, I remember, shocked this community to the heart. Not that it's really a community, just lots of private and comfortable houses, but the word always gets pressed into service for such tragedies.

You can't really shock a suburb, or a district. She pronounces the word accident with a mild inflection, as if she is saying it in italics or quotation marks, and so withholding endorsement of it. The patient appears to be waiting for my response. There are still no more words coming from her but her face has gone questing, defiant almost. It is saying: 'Go on then, medicine. What you got?' She has hauled from her insides a big bleeding gobbet of information, and what are you going to do about it, Dr. Newgate?

In my mind I am once more reaching for the name of Martina Lubasz, but I suspect she has guessed that too, and so I don't mention her. I break the silence - someone has to - by saying 'Look.' It sounds heavy and paternal, and I can almost hear it thud on the carpet between us.

'Yes,' she replies, ready for whatever is to follow.

'You need help,' I say. The words sound even older and more unoriginal than they are.

'I'm so glad you say that,' she replies.

'Are you?'

'Yes.'

'Well, that's good. Sometimes, you know, people take it as a criticism. As if they're defective or something, and it's all their fault.'

'That's a pity. To see it like that.'

'Listen.' This sounds even weightier than the 'Look.' But she fields it just as adeptly, with a similar Yes. I can hear Gill passing down the corridor and the sound of the mortise closing in the big front door. Before I say anything else, Serena carries on: 'The reason I'm glad you say I need help is that it confirms what I have come to think. It means that I agree with you, which is in itself very reassuring to me.'

She gives another smile, this time the smile of a warm and balanced young woman. It looks incongruous at first, like a borrowed garment, but it quickly becomes her own and she wears it plausibly. 'Thank you for helping me.'

I protest that I haven't, while being glad that she thinks I have. She pushes my denials back at me and says 'There's time, there's time.'

'Listen. Miss... '

'Serena.'

'Yes. We are going to have to get you together with the proper person, someone who understands you and your, your experiences.'

'Definitely,' she says, now quite breezy. She is gathering her bag, standing up, smoothing down her skirt with a hand. Bringing the appointment to an end, in fact.

'I'm sorry to have taken so much of your time,' she says.

'That's quite all right,' I reply. 'The important thing... '

'I can be briefer next time. Honestly.'

'No. No.'

She is at the door. Before leaving, she remembers something else that she needs to tell me. 'You know, I really hoped you'd win.'

'That I would win?'

'Yes.' Seeing my confusion, she smiles again, and just for an instant I think she is going to touch my face with the palm of her hand.

'Charlotte and me. We really hoped you would thrash our father.'

Then she's out of the door, leaving the light scent of herself in her place. As if she has musked my surgery.

July 16th. The Underground dream again. Still not playing by the rules. For me, this one rebuts the theory that dreams are essentially the liver and kidneys of our psychological produce, disposing of stuff that would go toxic if left inside. Here is a dream that simply re-runs an event which happened three

33

years ago, refining its graphic skills at every outing. So it's not a matter of me waking up and pulling myself clear of some vivid, overcoloured world full of people and places that turn out to be symbols of something else and then graciously fade from view like a hoarding by the road. No, when I wake up, I am further in its domain than I was before I fell asleep. This dream is not in the business of waste-handling. On the contrary, it locates the worst baggage it can, and then dumps it in the doorway of me.

It always starts the same way. The train coming into the station with a great boom. Even writing it down like this makes me feel I'm encouraging it. So what. It's on me all the time as it is. Like everyone else, I've seen thousands of tube trains come booming out of tunnels. For some reason this one sounds louder, angrier than normal and of course I react with raised anxiety. Even though I reckon it is my anxiety that is upping the volume.

What anxiety? Well, the old one, the one that I have diagnosed, right down to its cleverest symptom of denial, but cannot treat. I am anxious because it is one of the days when I am hollowed out with alcohol. Even now, with three years of good solid abstinence behind me, the sensation is shockingly real. There I am in the old condition, the old paradox: you fill right up on the stuff and it leaves you empty. You have the interior of a famine cupboard. The acoustic in my head is as cavernous as the tube station.

The train is doing the same speed as always. The line, and therefore the platform, curve quite sharply to the right so that the view facing the driver is a crescent of people packed right up to the edge. Catching the train is so important, so competitive, that waiting for the next one, only two minutes away, is not an option. They can't afford to think like that. I can't imagine why all the lines haven't done what the Jubilee has, and put glass barriers in. These people are so packed that they remind me of the arcade coin games that Ricky used to love as a boy. You would

34

only need a fresh surge of more coming in from behind and the front row would start teetering and peeling off the edge and onto the live rails.

People would scream; of course they would. But you wouldn't hear them above the train noise, you would just see their faces doing some screaming expressions and their hands reaching up to the sides of their heads as if they are going to pull their own ears off. People do go on the lines. You hear stories of blood being thrown up out of the gaps and splattering everyone; of drivers seeing someone start to fall forward out of the tight line - a City chap or a young girl in high heels - then going on falling, frame by frame into the horizontal. Then the head down and a dive starting, the briefcase or the handbag flying up wildly. The driver slamming the train to a halt but not until it's well beyond the point of the fall and the dead person - must be dead - is hidden underneath. The train has eaten him or her, and he or she is no more to be seen. It happens. The only surprising thing is that it doesn't happen more often.

When the dream opens, I keep expecting something of this sort to unfold. It is like a standard introduction. Then it doesn't occur. The train comes in and stops without incident, and this comes as a surprise to me every time. Because of what does happen next, I do wonder whether I know, at some subconscious level, that a dreadful thing is about to take place, and that I have been alerted accordingly.

Nonsense of course, but just the kind of theory that some of my colleagues are happy to entertain. Well, in fairness, not so much entertain as refuse to write off entirely. Maurice, for instance, with that silly face he does whenever such ideas come up; the kind of wooh-wooh-wooh expression grown-ups pull when they want to share their children's credulity at a ghost story. Except that Maurice is using the face to forestall everyone else's scepticism. It's generally followed by an open-palmed gesture of modest ignorance and the *Hamlet* quote about 'more things in Heaven and earth, Horatio.'

He's not being modest at all, but just letting the rest of us know that he at least is boldly open-minded when it comes to New Age enlightenment. The arrogance of the agnostic. How he gets on my tits.

Enough for now. Thinking of Maurice grinds me to a halt. And I can hear Imogen in the hall. More of the dream when I've a couple of hours.

July 17th. Maurice. I'd better get this down now, and then back to the dream. Saturday, and everyone seems to be out. I suppose there have always been people who flaunt their alternativism but are fundamentally ambitious in a conventional sense. Hippie squares. Good girls and boys who download a safe sort of radicalism into their approach in order to look fearlessly modern. Not so much at Thomas's, but before that, at Cambridge. And not just in medicine. I remember Mark Ludlow and his disciples, the young English research fellows who were natural conservatives - Leavisites, I suppose - but found room for a fashionable pinch of structuralism in their lecture hall gigs.

Just as Derrida and Saussure became their heroes, so Maurice has decided that the ultimate diagnostic wisdom is to be had from a professor working in the division of addictions at Harvard. Under the name of Samuel Shem, he wrote a satirical novel called *The House of God* which became required reading for young US medics.

As I understand it, the book is basically a series of riffs on the core belief that the best medicine consists of doing as much nothing as you possibly can. I say 'as I understand it' because I have only managed to sneak the odd glance at it when he has left it under his *Guardian* at the surgery. In the margin he has scribbled notes which I then recognise when he inserts them with artful casualness into our conversations.

This for example, when I mention a patient of mine with early onset Crohn's Disease: 'I suppose we are all in danger of overlooking the centrality of narrative in the life of an illness.' Or this, on the inconclusive evidence of an MRI on a suspected meniscal lesion: 'Strange that having studied quantum we can still find it hard to embrace uncertainty.' They are the kind of remarks which you're not meant to question, only admire. Like unreturnable squash serves.

July 22nd. If I have a problem with Maurice, it's fair to say he has one with me as well. It has to do with me being in AA, hence - technically at least - in a spiritual programme. The recoveries I have seen are the kind of thing that are understandably described as miracles, however incorrect that word may be. I'm thinking of hopeless cases who really do the modern equivalent of picking up their beds and walking. In the cases of tramps, this truth can be literal. Old men with faces like bruises, once fine young lads who came to London as McAlpine's Fusiliers and drank their way to dereliction; executives' widows who anaesthetised themselves with gin until they could not function without it; girls about the same age as Serena (of whom I should not be thinking), fast-tracking their way towards a lethal dependency. On and on, more than I can begin to count, a sprawling, classless range of cases who discover this strange and wonderful way to secular (I would say) salvation. They then find that though the meetings may be held in the least glitzy of premises, the organisation itself is fashionable to the point of cool. Some start calling it The Firm. Naturally it's been this way for years in the States, particularly on the West Coast. There's the bit at the end of *The Player* when Tim Robbins is driving to an AA meeting. He says as much to the person he is talking to on the phone, who commiserates and says he didn't know he had a problem. I don't, says Robbins; I'm going there because that's where everyone from the movie industry goes.

37

And when was that made? Must be nearly twenty years ago now.

Although I've made no secret of my AA membership to any of my colleagues, I don't talk about it all that much. For a start I feel I have to honour the famous Yellow Card that is displayed at every meeting and reminds you not to say who you see there and what you hear. They know that I belong to it, that I do so with complete conviction, and that I believe this has been the saving of my life, no less. What they can never know is the strange reality of belonging to such a fellowship – the slogans on the wall inciting you to Let Go and Let God, the mantras of A Day at a Time and Easy Does it But Do It; the photos of the founding fathers Dr. Bob and Bill W. with their Eisenhower haircuts and tough-love smiles; the indestructible and weirdly beautiful language of the wartime literature, still surviving un-altered in a world changed past recognition. A kind of Author-ised Version of addiction recovery, made by man but powered by divine afflatus.

Maurice, inevitably, is enticed by it. Enticed but excluded. So of course, being Maurice, he reads up on it, as anyone can if they have a mind to, and then, being Maurice, drops in some more of his casual-but-competitive references. For example: 'Jung's endorsement of the twelve-step programme was perhaps the turning-point in its early development.' Thank you, Maurice.

July 24th. Squash with him horribly soon - another of those dreadful occasions where that competitiveness finds legitimate expression. I keep meaning to call a halt to our matches. I could do so on the grounds of age, except that I am not a day older than him; or injury, except that I haven't got one and besides, what a miserable prospect, to have to go on trying to fool a fel-low quack with a feigned limp; or quitting the club, except that I'm not, and he would only see me there as usual. No, what I've got is chronic Mauricitis, with all the attendant symptoms of resentment, boredom and fear. It's a dreadful package of effects but as there is only one case (mine) on the database, it can't be said to have developed anything like a recognisable narrative, yet.

Underground dream upstaged again. Thank you Maurice. Tomorrow late evening perhaps. I'm getting quicker. Longer too. The two are linked, obviously.

July 27th. So. To finish with it (the Underground dream). Perhaps I'm really in with a chance of expunging it by getting it down on paper like this. Maurice I can't expunge, but even with him, the evidence is that writing about the subject makes the problem more manageable. I really do feel I am talking to someone, even though that person is only me. I don't know why I should be so surprised. The whole purpose of 'sharing' in AA is that it bleeds the isolation from you. I should have started before.

Where was I. The new passengers are funnelling towards the doors. They are always trying to barge in before everyone has got off, as if they are worried that the train will leave without them. What a bovine tide. Incredible how they do this every time, apparently never learning from their several thousand previous experiences that they are actually slowing down the process of their own boarding.

Then comes the instant that definitely sets an alarm off in my head, there's no denying it. As the carriage fills up, I see the young mother struggling on with her two children. One of them is a toddler, asleep in a buggy. The other is her older brother. He must be about six. He and the mother have the same beautiful, big-eyed faces and lustrous fair hair. She is having trouble pulling the tiny-wheeled chair up after her onto the lip of the carriage. A man is trying to help her, but he needs more room to bend down and lift the thing by its front axle. He is unwittingly separating the boy from his mother and sister.

Eventually the man does get the buggy on and the doors start closing. They are slicing together along the back of his jacket. The boy is being shut out. His mother is peering out anxiously, straining her neck round to one side of the man. The boy pushes at the man's back, but he is too little to have any effect, and there is no give in the passengers. The doors have shut and the train is moving. So is the boy, although he is still on the platform.

He is going along at the side of the train, picking up speed as it does, but then starting to lose his footing as the train gets to running pace and more. Something is pulling the material of his anorak tight across his back. When he falls forward and seems to be going along in a grotesque, sprinting kind of crawl, I can see that the cord of his jacket is being held in the grip of the doors. I thought tubes couldn't start if there was an obstruction in the doors, but the cord must have been too thin to register. And his weight must be insufficient to activate the automatic brake. Whatever was on the end of it, a toggle or a knot or something, was too big to be tugged out.

Now he has stopped the flailing at the ground with his hands and is pushing and kicking at the side of the train. He is being dragged into the gap and would go down if it were wide enough. In about twelve or fifteen yards he will run out of platform and either smash into the side of the tunnel's mouth or else, if there is room, which looks unlikely, be pulled into the tunnel with the train. The time has split into two, as it must do on such occasions. On the one hand everything is happening so fast that the people on the platform can't make sense of it; the cord is holding, and he is crashing into people's legs. They shout and shout, like victims of an attack by a strange animal. I have a head's start because I saw this developing - the struggling mother, the back of the well-intentioned man. On the other hand, the world has gone so slow that it is almost stationary, each frame of the reel so vivid and permanent. I want to hold it there, halt it, rewind, start again with a different set of images. Surely you can do anything with visual material these days.

The boy duly hits the front of the tunnel. The impact must

at last have broken the cord because he lies there on the end, the very end of the slightly tapering platform. The train does him the unknowing favour of bashing him with the front ends of its two final carriages so that he is shoved back clear from the platform edge. At least now he won't fall onto the rails for good measure.

Apart from that buffeting, there is no movement from him. Nothing autonomous. There is the loudest noise it is possible for a train to make without crashing into another oncoming one. It is made of tearing brakes and the desperate sheering of steel on steel. Even the small amount of speed that the train had accumulated is proving a devil to shed. Sparks throw a brief light into the base of the tunnel. These are the noises and the sights of an unimaginable wrong. Why did it take so long? Why did no-one pull the emergency lever earlier?

Maybe they couldn't reach it in the crowded carriage. Maybe no-one noticed. So hard to see out of their own lives. Maybe they did notice but were too shocked to do anything. Or too tightly packed to manage anything but yelling. Maybe, on the contrary, not long at all, but all over in a few seconds. About a third of the back carriage is sticking out of the tunnel. A knot of people is forming around the boy.

There are two currents of people, one of them moving forward to help, the other moving away with the energy of shock. For two or three seconds I have been part of the first current, and came close enough to notice the angelic cloud of fair curls on the top of the boy's head, bright on the black of the platform. Now I find I am part of the counterflow, the one moving towards the exit. It is as if I have stepped sideways and walked into an oncoming wave. But that makes it sound involuntary, which it is not. I could have gone either way, could have rushed to get through to the boy, clearing the way by proclaiming that I'm a doctor. Only the truth. It's amazing how those words cause seas of people in public places to part. This is what I should be doing, but am not.

Instead I am succumbing willingly to the pressure of the stream making for the exit, the escalators and the street. I start to think of the mother in the carriage, the train eventually reversing painfully into the station (that always takes an age); her losing her mind on finding her son vanished, worse than vanished. I do start to think of her, but it is debilitating and I have to abandon it.

Out on the street, I might start crying and so I do what I always do whenever possible on such occasions. I breathe deeply, comically deeply, getting enough puff into me to leave no room for anything else - no grief, no indecision, no re-think. It's the only way. This is not the first time I have been at an emergency and opted for flight. No point in interrogating myself on the reasons for doing so; it's all very straightforward. I am technically drunk, as I am for a great deal of the time. I say technically because I'm not acting it necessarily; people aren't going to point at me in the street and say 'Look, that man is so pissed he can't stand up.' But that is because I am well practised and can be three or four times over the legal limit without totally giving the game away. It's called compliance and is an extension of the great English art of being what people want you to be: you want me to be a safe and conventional doctor? OK, I'll be a safe and conventional doctor. You want me to be a regular family man who loves his wife and children? Sure, no problem. You want me to be sober, I assume? That's fine, I can do sobriety as well as anyone. I defy you to spot the cracks.

But if I let myself loose on that poor boy, that poor dead or dying boy (there was a dreadful thud of bone on brick as he hit the tunnel, and the noise is only now registering in me, minutes after the event), I'd screw it up, yes, fuck it up even, get something dreadfully wrong, be seen to be unsteady and stinking of liquor. It would be a disaster.

I go into a pub, get a stiff Scotch in the public bar, then straight round into the saloon (different barman) for another. I can see the mouth of the tube station through the big ground-glass window. I didn't mean to, but I can't help it. That's the view, and I needed a pub. A team of paramedics is hurrying a light-looking stretcher to the waiting ambulance, which is whooping and flashing blue. How rich to think that one of my regrets about general practice in the safe suburbs is that there are only the chores of managing degeneration; no dramas or emergencies, and everything being handled by other agencies.

Not long afterwards another knot of people surfaces. Among them is the mother, with a WPC at her side, trying to calm her. She is roaring in pain like a billion poor women on TV being led from a wrecked home with everything and everyone lost.

Double Scotch, single gulp. Already it has stopped burning. It just goes down as if it is something far less serious - beer, wine, even water. Then I'm out and onto the pavement again, doing a sharp right for no particular reason and finding myself in that posh network. Can't remember the street names.

Nearly done. Finish this tomorrow.

July 28th. Cavendish This and Devonshire That. I've had to use the A-Z to be reminded. I'm not navigating the streets so much as blowing around them with the illusion of purpose that you try and pull off with a brisk stride. They make me sick, these streets, which is quite funny when you think how packed with medics they are. Broad, quilted valleys of plenty, worked by those plausible men and women - Heavens, I know a few of them - who specialise in the diseases of the terminally wealthy. Huge sod-off doors and brass plates. Property magazines on the waiting room coffee tables.

My internal compass is having a laugh and veers me back round in a big U-turn until I'm in the tight little streets around

Portland Place. Foley, Riding House, Titchfield, that sort of thing. Into a couple more boozers, same thing there, dark old panelling, bar girls with East European accents; then another one with some huge wrestling spectacular from America. A Hispanic man with a narcissistic swagger, trying to conduct applause from the crowd but causing a bowlful of jeering. An overweight blond American with a square jaw comes on and starts flinging him around. The crowd loves this.

It's when we go back to a giddy aerial view of the ring that I notice the band of breaking news scuttling across the bottom of the screen: Boy Dies in Freak Tube Accident. A few minutes later someone behind the bar flicks the channel and we're watching a reporter at the same tube mouth I was looking at a while ago. He's wearing the sensitive newsman face, but I can't make out a word, and anyway don't need to. Then we're back in the wrestling, and the referee is being tossed out over the ropes like a hay bale.

Even though it happened three years ago, the dream has stayed with me all this way into sobriety. It hardly seems right to be visited again and again by the sequence when there is surely nothing I could have done for the poor boy, who was declared dead on arrival at UCH. But there I go with the excuses. The fact is I behaved disgracefully. I would raise the subject with Clive, which of course is exactly what you're meant to do with your sponsor, except I know what he would say. It would be stuff about the Lord finding His own way of reminding me what I should be taking notice of.

July 29th. I didn't know Clive was quite so Lord-based when I asked him if he would take me on. That was back in the strange, really very thrilling days of my early abstinence, when you're so desperate to do exactly what the programme says that your social antennae go all to hell and you're hanging out with people you'd normally never look at twice. I suppose I should have told Clive that it wasn't really working for me, this sponsoring thing, but it would have felt as if I was jilting him. Too cruel to contemplate, when I consider how he was ringing me every day of the week to see how I was, making sure I was getting myself to meetings, offering to take me to coffee with some other members I might like to meet.

You couldn't fault the man. Plain decency and humanity. No blowing his trumpet, no reminding you all the time of his twenty years sober time, just being plain and practical. And loving - definitely loving. And me coming over all difficult because he takes the God parts of it more seriously than I ever could. So seriously that whenever I talk to him for any length of time, I start feeling he's brought this enormous, powerful friend along with him, who for some strange reason I'm unable to see. When I think about it, I suppose that's exactly what he has done, each time hoping that he can manage to bring the enormous, powerful friend into view for me.

August 13th. Serena again. Not in my surgery now. Far more serious than that. My bed. That is, in my sleeping head and then in my not-sleeping head, my very waking-up head. But in bed too, in the sense that she is reminding me of Imogen as she used to be nearly thirty years ago; as she used to be in that very particular, charged time between my first meeting her and my then getting to know her; when there was absolutely no purpose in going for rational thought as it was instantly laughed out of court by sexual desire. I do try to engage myself in conversation as this situation clearly won't do. To say the least. I even try to turn the picture on its head by saying that since Serena is raising in me the same sensations I had in the very early days of Imogen, she (Serena) is evidence of my continuing feelings for my wife. I look across at her sleeping form, six inches away and an incalculable distance from me, yet she meanwhile is reasserting her appeal by resembling the absent and much younger woman.

August 31st. Squash with Maurice. Oh God. One of those commitments that looks harmless enough in the diary, until you run out of days and it's on you. We go to the Town Club. Or what used to be the Town Club but has renamed itself several times, whenever a new owner gets it and decides it has potential. Some of the identities have been beyond parody. First it was Soles, with a Sole Food Bar, where the billiards and tennis used to be; then Courts (toilets labelled Courtiers and Courtesans, but scrapped after complaints), and now something that I can't read because the sign is an over-athletic flash of neon italics.

In the changing room I can see Maurice's clothes on a peg. It's the beige linen suit and one of the shirts with a man's name on it that is meant to impress me. Well, not me, but people who know about these things. It's not Tommy Hilfiger as that would mean he would be gay - according to some article that was lying open in the practice waiting room. William Smith, maybe. Or Ted Baker. I forget. It looks competitive, even without Maurice inside it.

What a grim little compound this still is, stuck out on the dual carriageway and surrounded by the warehouse shapes of the new stores. It has that determined ugliness that can see off any number of facelifts. If I ran it, I could call it Bypass View. Good for a doctor. The smell down here has remained constant, unimpressed by the identity shifts around it. Wet male towels, dispenser soap and a suggestion of drain.

On my way down the corridor to the court I can hear Maurice warming up. He is grunting and talking to himself in a goading manner. There is a crash of wood and shoulder as he hits the door, then some nasty expletives. If you didn't know he was alone, you would think it was someone else's fault. He is already breathing quite hard when I get in. He's all smooth and brown from, I've forgotten where, I always switch off when he tells me - I think of it as Costa del Mauricio, a resort you can find almost anywhere in the southern hemisphere, full of Maurices. I suppose if one of us has a coronary in the next hour, our survival chances are better than average, given we're so close to a doctor.

I've spent twenty-five years, ever since Thomas's, pretending that I like Maurice, and trying to act as if I do. It was just easier that way. I felt he was daring me not to. The trouble is that once you've gone down that route it's hard to turn back. Your friendship is official. My mistake was to say nice things about him to the others when he applied to join the practice. Particularly to HGV, who knew we'd studied together and asked me what I thought. Maybe I should have pissed on him then, but, as ever, I was afraid I'd be found out and something horrible would happen. The same when he asks me to play squash with him. Actually, he doesn't ask; it's more of a statement: 'Squash' without a question mark, leaving only the details of time and place to be sorted out. I'm better than him, which is why he always wants to play with me. Someone told him the way to improve your game is to play regularly against someone better. This means I am always playing against someone worse and so my game is deteriorating. These days, if he tries his hardest and I try slightly less hard, we're quite evenly matched.

'William,' he says.

'Hi Maurice. Sorry I'm a bit late.'

'You're not actually.'

'Slightly overran. Again. Sorry.'

'Pill?'

Meaning ball. Nothing more sinister than that. One of the indelible public school ways that has survived his own overhauls. It's not exactly alternative, like his conversation elsewhere strains to be, but I guess he thinks that since there's no such thing as a New Age squash player, you may as well get on with the time-honoured business of smashing the opposition.

'Warm-up,' he states, no question mark.

'Whatever,' I say, with a nonchalance that surprises me.

We carry on hitting the warmed-up ball, which is already bouncing generously up onto the racket, repaying flicked boasts against the side-walls with big looping flights into the opposite corner and generally flattering the hitter. Then we're off. No coin-tossing, just him saying 'Want to Start,' me replying 'No, you, honestly,' him knowing I was going to say that and serving straight away from the right-hand box. I can see there's something odd about the serve immediately the ball has left his racket.

While it's going through the air towards the front wall, I find myself wondering again whether Maurice ever got anywhere with Imogen when we were students. He had met her before I had, and since it was impossible to meet her and not be attracted by her, maybe he tried. As she never talked about men who'd wanted her (there wouldn't have been enough time), and as I never wanted to hear about them, there was nothing ever coming from that source. And as he just about denied any knowledge of her after she and I started going out together, it's quite possible that I'd bested Maurice in love without really knowing it. In which case one could see the mean and cunning serve that now reaches the wall as the latest shot in a long slow campaign of revenge.

It slaps grudgingly off and then just about clears the red centre line to fall dead in front of me like a dropped flannel. Because I'm waiting at the back for the nice bouncy ball, there's no way I can sprint forward - not these days - to spoon up some kind of return.

'Bad luck,' states Maurice and marches over to the left box for the next serve. No need for anyone to say one - love. It's clear he's put the warmed-up ball into his pocket and is using a cold, slow one instead. The next serve makes a similar journey, with the noise of a smash but the soul of a lob. I still can't get used to the sheer deadness of it.

Although this time I stand forward and just about reach it as it pitches, my stroke is still reflexively the stroke for a ball with the grace to lift itself off the deck a few inches. Only my frame-edge connects and hammers the ball straight back down onto the floor. Two-nil and Maurice strides back to the right-hand box.

There's a face up at the viewing window. I can't help noticing it as I walk back to receive. Or fail to receive. It's familiar. A man about my age, heavily built head and shoulders. There's a sideways smile on him, not so much at me as about me, to someone else just out of the picture. He stays for a moment, takes a couple of swigs of his beer, then vanishes. It's not till he's gone that I realise it was Brian Miller. Serena's father. That's the same window she used to press her nose against when she was a girl, then doodle with her finger in the steamed glass. She and her sister. Was Serena here again, now, with her father? Surely not, given what she told me at the surgery.

'You all right old boy,' says Maurice, rightly diagnosing an absence in me. The words are yet another statement trying to pass itself off as a question. He has a bunch of these court gambits and they need sub-titles to convey their proper meaning. So, 'You all right old boy' is not an inquiry after your well-being but a way of saying 'You're rattled.' 'Concentrate Whistler' means 'You may have taken that point but only thanks to my unforced error. Don't start taking credit.' 'Played' or 'Shot' means 'Never let it be said I am a graceless opponent.' 'Sorry' after a rally won by a fluke stroke means 'Tee-hee.'

It's five-nil to him before I make any contact with the ball that could be called meaningful. Though I say it myself, it is a remarkable shot, an overhead backhand while I am running towards the back wall to stop the ball dying alone in the corner.

A little warmer now, it whams back off the front wall with enough air in it to head for certain death behind the two of us. Maurice is standing three feet to my left. He has no hope of reaching the ball, but he launches himself into my left shoulder as if I am obstructing him. He awards himself the point and pretends not to see that my face is querying his decision. I say 'actually' half-heartedly, and he replies with 'obstruction.'

Serena Miller's father has re-appeared in the window and is now sitting down on the little carpeted bench for spectators. He catches my eye and motions apologetically in Maurice's direction to let me know the rally was his.

There's an unofficial code at this club, and at others too, I imagine. If a fellow member adjudicates in this way, he is assumed to be impartial and the players abide by his ruling. No matter. I've written the first game off anyway. But the ball is warming up and I've got a match on my hands. This is good. No need to patronise him with easy returns. He takes the first by nine to love, and steps briefly out of the court to towel his face and swig some water.

I say 'Well played, Maurice,' all easy and generous, and he counters with 'Cheers. First fixture situation.' This is a reference to the first match we ever played, when it was me who took the opening game to love. By mentioning this he is getting on record the fact that the tables are already turned, no matter what happens next. He is the self-appointed archivist of our encounters and somehow remembers all the scores of all the games with the precision of a cricket nerd. Brian Miller is settled in and on the job. He motions us to play on when we are ready. It's the imperiousness of a man with his own building firm. Not a particularly big firm, but his nonetheless.

Surely Imogen never did anything with Maurice. Although. There was that week, Rag Week in fact, when he was dressing up as Dr. Kildare and going round the Circle Line with a collection bucket. Wasn't she involved in all that somehow? It was the Saturday of the week after that one that I spent my first night with her at Devonshire Place when both her flatmates were away. I wish I could let go of these useless autopsies of the past.

I take the second game nine points to six, setting up the decisive third with just fifteen minutes of our court hire left. Next time I look up at the window I seem to see Serena there with her father, as she sometimes used to be. Once again she is breathing on the glass and doodling in the mist. Then she giggles and wipes it all out. She is eleven or twelve years old; her father has grown stern with her about something. But it is the sternness of fear as much as authority, as if he knows she is about to explode and pass from his possession, and that nothing will ever be the same again.

How can I be seeing this? Serena is twice this age and was in my surgery only the other day. By herself. A young woman. An independent young woman, sitting facing me, like any number of other patients. I blink to clear the picture and then keep my eyes away from the viewing window in case I have failed.

Maurice gives himself a team talk for the crucial third, which looks like the last one we will have time for. 'Squash, Whistler, squash,' he says, clenching his non-racket fist and punching the air in front of him. Twice in succession he balloons his service over the red line on the side wall. He carries on as if the ball was in, readying himself for my return, and defying me not to make an Out call.

Something else has caught Brian Miller's attention and he has gone from the window. So we are back to self-adjudication. Most members err on the side of the opponent - anything not to cause offence. All very English. Get the cheating done at work in the manner evolved by your profession over the centuries. At play however, silly levels of polite self-denial are the order of the day.

Except for Maurice. He has now anchored himself to the

T, from where he can launch more of those obstructive little two-step manoeuvres in the certainty that I won't complain. Most of the time I'm happy to go along with the arrangement as he's so much nicer for the next few days if he has won. Yes, the magnanimous post-match analyses are sickening, but better that than a week's supply of sulks and resentments.

Late in the match I find I'm totally engaged. A few properly weighted returns arc up and hug the side wall so that Maurice has to scurry and truffle to keep the rallies going. I'm enjoying the sense of power and control that I can exert over his movements, and wish I were more ruthless.

By the time the next players are tapping their rackets on the outside of the door, I've pulled myself back to five points, just two adrift. He seems to be interpreting this as a victory rather than the draw which it technically is. I find myself doing nothing to stop him. 'He says 'Bad luck, William,' and I reply 'No no,' without knowing quite what I mean. He says 'Good game though,' with his voice set to breezy generosity.

One of the players taking over the court from us is Brian Miller. As I'm leaving, he says 'Long time' and suggests we get together for a game. It's hard to make an invitation sound quite so hostile, but he manages. I nod and say 'Great,' as flatly as I can. Not rude, but not encouraging either. Close up, I see the nasty chill in his eyes, the cruel readiness of his lower lip to shift from leer to sneer whenever the need arises - or even when it doesn't. I wonder if he has any idea his daughter has been seeing me as a patient. I also wonder whether he has any idea about her. About what the matter is. Because I haven't.

September 5th. To the St. Stephens Sunday lunchtime meeting with Clive. He makes the tea there and I agree to go early and give him a hand. There's just the two of us in the funny little wooden hall that squats at the back of the church. It was his idea that we should get together today. He phoned last night with his quietly insistent voice and said he'd be falling down on his sponsorial duties if he let any more time pass before we got together.

He's as soft in his voice as in his middle, but both hide a fearsome tenacity. His suggestions to meet don't go away, but stick to you like a burr on a jersey. 'Then you can tell me what is really happening in your life.' As if all previous contacts have been shallow or evasive. Which they mainly have been. My fault entirely.

That's the maddening thing. Because I accepted him as my sponsor, it seems I have to tell him everything that is happening to me, plus the details of my responses to those events. Otherwise the accusation of isolation, or else of 'not working the programme' hang in the air like an axe. That's how it goes. You join the fellowship, undertake the famous twelve-step programme of emotional housekeeping, and start to confide your innermost secrets to inquisitive strangers.

This is a grossly unfair caricature of course, and even as I write it I can recognise all too clearly the cause of my anger: the process works. It is the inspired product of lay ingenuity, naif determination and, admit it, faith, and when it comes to alcohol it shames the weasley incompetence of my profession.

Clive fills the big old urn from the tap, puts it next to the literature on the table, and plugs it in. He focuses on me and says 'So.' It's one of those heavy, round sounds, giving you an awful lot for your two letters. It means nothing less than Tell Me Everything, William. He sees me think about it, then falter. He's horribly acute like that. He comes towards me and puts a big soft hand on my arm. Another prerogative. I am aware from his expression of chronic goodwill that he has asked the Lord to join us and the Lord has gone and obliged.

He may stifle and embarrass me, but He infuses Clive with so much current from His mighty grid that he can divine trauma, turn lost cases to temperance and make tea for thirty people, all at the same time. The urn begins to rumble and I busy myself with getting the cups from the cupboard to the table.

Transparency is what we seek. Or are meant to seek. I seem to have it in quantities, but in the wrong sense. That is, not in the sense of being an open book, but of being seen through. It's a serious difference, even if the same word is involved. Clive can see there is something on my mind. I wish my mind is all that it was on. He can see this as clearly as Serena (the something in question) could tell, as she sat before me, where my thoughts were going and my words were about to follow.

The urn's innards begin to rumble, and he says: 'What kind of a week have we had?'

'Good actually,' I reply, trained to avoid the use of Fine. 'Yes. Very good. You?'

He smiles again to show that the last word was superfluous. I suppose my asking after his well-being is as irksome to him as my own patients asking after mine. How pride plays with us. It is here, right here, that I should be saying: 'Well, Clive, actually, I'm in quite a bit of trouble. It's to do with a young woman who comes to my surgery and seems to think I have answers for her that I don't in fact have. Worse than this, Clive, she's getting into my head in a most inconveniently erotic way and so disturbing my days - yes and my nights, let's not forget the nights - more than they have been since I was young enough to be my own son, if you follow me. More than, well, basically more than anyone since Imogen. I'm so sorry to lay this on you, Clive.'

Instead I say: 'Cracking game of squash.' Which is not just diversionary but also a plain old lie. It was a horrible game of squash. And Clive should be sharing back at me, saying how hard it was for him in the years after Madge had passed on; when he found himself being attracted to inappropriate women; trying to think of Madge all the time, but being frail, being fallible, being - in a word, William - a man like any other, with the usual range of appetites and a few years left in him and still, if I didn't mind him saying, not completely out of luck when it came to the admiring words from members of the gentle sex, and recognising that these blessings were responsibilities also, and therefore doing what we all have to do in sobriety, William, sooner or later, handing it over to The Man Upstairs and saying, Lord, do with me as You will.

Instead he says: 'You don't want overdo it with the squash, William. None of us is getting any younger.' I swallow the resentment which this remark is bringing me, knowing it could haemorrhage at any moment like a smuggler's condom. The thing is, I did start doing the Steps with Clive. Round at his house, with photos of Madge beaming from every wall and every surface, giving us her benediction, urging us on, virtually offering us tea. We got off to a roaring start, me admitting my unmanageability, my powerlessness over alcohol, my need to change, even making an inventory of my defects and a list of the people I had wronged, pledging to make amends. Difficult in the case of a patient whom I have reason to believe I killed, and whose case I can't bring myself to write about, not even here. Maybe some day.

I was a model sponsee, although I can't stick that word. That was two and a half years ago, when I was five or six months off the drink and so desperate not to relapse that I would try anything. At those sessions with Clive that's exactly what I was doing - trying anything. But it was the willingness of Toad to confess in captivity. 'Oh in *there*! Yes, of course I apologised in *there*!'

Since then the current has dimmed in my own confessional impulses, the old liberal scepticism has already spotted an opening and is feeding itself back in. Just another compulsion doing its opportunistic thing. However I choose to mock the process, now or in the future, I can never deny that it worked.

If someone came to me and said they were presenting symptoms of something potentially terminal (in which category I place alcoholism very firmly), and I was able to say to them, well, all you need do is sit in draughty church halls and community centres for a few hours each week with God-filled but harmless slogans on the wall, and people telling you how brilliant it is to be free from the bondage of their addiction, and to put just a quid in the pot when it goes round at the end, and to hang out with well-meaning if slightly dull people like Clive and tell them what's really going on in your life, and that if you do all these things you will win an open-ended reprieve from your condition, I would feel that I had pioneered a form of psychic dialysis which was in its own way as revolutionary as the discovery of penicillin or the mapping of the genome.

I feel my voice mustering from me the best available intentions and saying: 'I'm sorry I haven't been more available, Clive.'

'That's really OK, William,' he says. 'We all.'

But again, availability is a jarring choice, the word of the dispenser rather than the receiver. Clive's word, therefore, not mine.

'Perhaps we can do a lunch some time. Usual place and my treat.'

I'm still too much the initiator for him, and he replies: 'That would be grand, William, but I think you should commit yourself to carrying on with the steps. We were doing so well. I know life is busy.'

'We.' Me as a joint project, with him as senior partner in the development programme.

'I agree with you, Clive,' I say. 'And it's really kind of you to be so conscientious. To give me so much of your time.'

He opens his palms and says: 'You know what they say.' What I know is that in this fellowship 'they' always say something. 'They' are never stuck for a well-used form of words to summarise the addict's predicament or cap the gushing well of his or her self-pity.

The maxim Clive has in mind here is that 'you give it away in order to keep it.' Yet again I can't quibble, however much I might want to.

I agree to go round to his house in the next couple of weeks and do some more work on the steps. The alternative would be for me to slide out of the process and in effect sack him as my sponsor.

These things do happen, and they are as painful as any jilting. Worse in a way since the parties go on bumping into each other in the same round of meetings. Then one of them takes up with someone else and the Green-Eyed Monster starts gorging on the reject. I could no more sack Clive than I could knock a child down at a crossing. That is, I could, but the consequences would be unbearable for everyone.

So, Clive and I are back in business. Whether I start talking to him in the exacting emotional detail he thinks necessary is another matter. He gives me a big hug, which I reciprocate. I find myself incongruously thinking of Serena Miller. The urn picks this moment to orgasm with its usual gurgle and the green paint on the walls goes moist.

The door opens and in comes a woman with the hair of a country spaniel. It is Spiritual Sally, the acting secretary. With her is Anne from Rivermead, who does the literature. We all embrace and start putting the chairs out. Then it's the slogans onto the walls with Blu-Tack. 'I can't but He Can.' 'Let Go and Let God.' 'Easy Does It But Do It.' A few more minutes and it fills up, like it always does just before the off. There's a run on the tea urn and the metal chairs scrape and settle.

Spiritual Sally opens the meeting and gives me the pre-amble card to read aloud. 'AA is a fellowship of men and women who share their experience, strength and hope with each other that they may solve their common problem and help others to recover from alcoholism.' Etc. Someone called Ronnie is down from Enfield to do the chair, which is a terrifying hurtle through bankruptcy courts, near-miss suicides and boot camp clinics in California.

Doctors know nothing about this illness, he tells his approving audience. If you want to get well, don't look to the medical profession; there's more wisdom in this room than the whole of Harley Street. Who'd have thought it would come to this? And what would Maurice say? Actually, to hell with Maurice.

September 20th. I bump into Ricky. This should not be worthy of note, seeing as he is my son and this is my house. Yet on most days since he has been back from Oxford, seven weeks now, I never catch sight of him. He has been a creature composed almost entirely of rumour, like the Yeti. True, there has been evidence of his passing through the room - the tideline of stubble in the basin, a fallen shirt, burger boxes from the small hours, new CDs that I'm surprised he can afford. But no sighting by me until now.

He looks gaunt and angry. There is a muted smell of sick, and I can see quite a big crust of yellow sauce low on the back of his shirt. It makes me think he has been on the wrong end of a passive vomiting incident.

I find myself saying 'So,' just like Clive. I can see him responding as I did, so I follow up with 'You're looking ever so well, Ricky.' He smiles thinly and asks me how the practice is going. His tone is slightly formal, and I wonder if this is the result of contagion from his parents' manner with one another. He doesn't know quite how to be. This fills me with disproportionate sadness and makes me think how it was only the other day that he was launching his tiny self into the air and flying, really flying into my arms from the step on which he is now standing - the sixth.

'Well,' I answer, 'it's in rather good health, really. Better than the people who use it. Shall we have a coffee?'

To my surprise he says Yes and we go into the kitchen. Inez is strangely coiled around herself on a stool, clasping her thighs to her body by hugging her shins. The sound of Carlos Adorno is coming from the speakers. He is providing perfect musical sub-titles for her mood, which is bruised but defiant. This, I think, is the singer who is a friend of her parents. The CD cover is on the table and his fine sultry face, lived-in but still up for it, is giving the ceiling its full attention.

Inez darts a surly look up at, I think, Ricky, but it could as well be aimed at me. Ricky looks awkward and I say 'If you'd rather... ' to anyone who might have some use for it. Inez dismounts from the stool and leaves the room with her muscular glide. The air feels full of some indistinct but very recent trouble.

I can't remember how long she has been with us. Nor exactly what she does, if anything. Nor whether any money changes hands, in either direction. She is always impeccably dressed, goes out a great deal - opera and ballet mostly, I gather - and smells of the expensive scent that Imogen used to love me buying for her when I started being able to afford it. Obviously any duties she might have don't run to looking after my son. Still, Imogen seems glad to have her around, which is the main thing. She has even started learning Spanish from her.

'Working hard,' I say, but he isn't sure if this is a statement about me or a question about him. 'Those are mighty tomes,' I go on, referring to the enormous textbooks he has brought home. 'The Baumgartner looks particularly daunting.' Venerable too. I'm sure I remember that very book, *Private Liberty, Public Cost; a brief history of regulation and the international markets from 1795 to the present day*, lying heavily on the desks and on the lives of the PPE students of my year.

If that is the brief history, I'd hate to see the comprehensive one; old joke. But then my knowledge of economics is lamentable, and my interest in it is not much greater. I wouldn't admit this to Ricky, who is probably looking to the dismal science for his living, but I'm always quietly glad whenever some very public forecaster is spectacularly wrong and the discipline is lumped in with Nostradamus or Michael Fish of the Met Office on the evening of October 15th 1987 ('There will be no hurricane.')

I try to show willing by asking Ricky if Ricardo - very popular with my two school friends who turned Marxist at Wadham College - was still thought important. He goes 'Yah up to a point,' in that timeless student way, but is not buying my feigned interest.

When I say 'So' again, I realise it is turning into a bit of a tick, offering itself as a filler for even quite brief silences. He senses a line of questions marching his way and he's right. But it's too late for me to stop myself sounding like a distant uncle and asking him if he has any idea what he's going to do after he's graduated. Still more than a year to go, but you know how time flies, and all that.

He mutters something about research and the Labour Party and I can't quite work out whether they are separate ideas or a linked aspiration that will see him joining those ferociously bright young men you sometimes catch at the shoulders of senior politicians. Billed as special advisers, and familiar with the true rather than the perceived workings of the national machine, they look as if they have yet to leave school. If Ricky is to be of their number, I would be more than happy.

Then I ask him if he has made any new friends this term. He lists a few names, some of them already familiar to me, none belonging to a female. His heart isn't really in it. I feel intrusive and abandon further lines of inquiry about budgeting and laundry, possibly for life. No more efforts at solidarity based on my own past (yes, and present) hopelessness in those areas.

There's something in his face, right back behind his eyes, which is waiting to declare itself. It's a look I know from patients who are functional enough in conversation but have yet to get round to disclosing the true purpose of their visit. 'Oh yes, sorry, Dr. Newgate, just one more thing before I go, I think I might have caught motor neurone disease.'

We'll get to it, I expect, in the course of the vac. But not right now. I've a feeling it concerns Imogen in some way. She comes into the kitchen, looking better, less plain sad, now that Ricky is home. She puts the kettle on and asks him if he'd like a cup. He says yes please. I'm not included in the round, so I make some excuse and leave the kitchen. It's not quite that I've been cold-shouldered, more that they want to be alone. Fine.

September 24th. I had a feeling I would receive another visit from Serena around now, and so it turns out. She seems to have worked Gill out as a soft touch, and must have discovered what days she's on reception. She (Serena) can give the impression of being so reasonable that it would make no sense to refuse her request, in this case a request to be slotted in late in the afternoon. Fortunately (for her) there has been a cancellation. In she comes, all tall and confident. I can feel my glands deciding to set up a blush, and I have no more control over this than I did thirty-five years ago. You would have thought that ageing at least had the compensation of sparing you from these internal assaults and external symptoms, but no.

Now I can feel myself flex my musculus buccinator - both of them but I've forgotten what the plural would be - in order to try and marshal my face. If it has to redden, then I will assert myself by keeping it firm. But firm is happening elsewhere, also of its own accord, as the glans penis insists on doing its party piece yet again. Quite clever the first time, yes and the thousand-and-first, but please.

I sit down and cross my legs to try and contain the crisis. I don't know how much she has noticed. My guess is somewhere between quite a lot and everything. Her smile has become cryptic and magnetic. It is managing to do vulnerable and masterful at the same time. She's waiting for me to say something. I reject So in favour of Well, with the tiniest interrogative upturn at the end. At least, that's what I think I'm doing, but I'm aware of it coming out more like a frog opening a conversation. She smiles again, this time to reassure me. She knows this appointment has now gone over into the territory we all call inappropriate; but as no-one has mentioned this and nothing has, as they say, happened, there is no reason to leave that place. Or this place.

She takes her coat off, puts it on the back of the patients' chair and then says 'May I,' all in that order. I motion to her that that's all fine. She sits down and pulls the chair a little closer to mine. Not provocatively so, just a few inches, like nothing more than a side-effect of the sitting-down process. She is wearing a short dark silk skirt. That is, it didn't look particularly short when she was standing up, but now that she has sat down it has ridden up to, I would say, just short of the middle of her thigh. That's what it's there, or not there, to do, I suppose.

I try not to look at her legs, but they are so evident, taking up so much of my immediate view, that it would be impossible not to. Odd as well, as I'd have to look in the opposite direction. With some of my patients I'd be happy to use that arrangement, but not with this one. Even though she is the one I should most be using it with.

They are quite magnificent legs, perfect without being predictable, strong and used but with fine long contours that are as smooth as they are sinuous. In the right hands, or legs, the quads, the biceps femoris, the tibialis anterior, the whole lot of them actually, can align themselves in repose with such astounding grace. The stuff of great sculpture. Hers is the figure of a Steffi Graf rather than a Venus Williams.

I'm aware of closing my eyes fleetingly as I raise my head to face hers, so that I don't find myself looking at the middle of her. My head makes the journey just about intact, but there is no safety in her face as it is wearing such a pleasant expression. This was the very same agony that I got into over Imogen. Let her not be nice into the bargain.

I'm about to say something - not sure what - when she says: 'I've really just come along to say thank you.'

'That's very kind of you,' I reply, 'but really not necessary.'

'Would you perhaps have preferred me not to?' She follows the question with a little tinkly laugh.

'No.'

'Ah. In that case I'm so sorry.'

'No. No, I mean. That's not what I'm saying.'

'That's good then.' Back to the default smile.

'It shouldn't take long,' she goes on reassuringly. 'I know how busy you must be. Goodness, I bet this is a harder job now than it ever was before, with people just getting older and older, and all the health services coming under these terrible pressures.'

Bang on. I let it run. Her voice is more honeyed and a little deeper than when she first came.

'Do you think we're all sick? A little bit sick? I mean, collectively. Sicker than we would ever care to admit to ourselves?'

I make an equivocal motion with my hand to admit the possibility.

'I do. I think we all take too much of what we don't really need. And don't take the things we really do need.'

I can't quibble with that, and I tell her as much.

'That's why I'm so grateful to you for seeing me,' she goes on. 'Because you gave me what I needed.'

I protest that I can't imagine I did any such thing, but am of course delighted to have been of some help. I am also flattered beyond reason, but I keep that to myself.

She carries on: 'You may not know why you have been of such immense help, and I'm not sure I can tell you why. Or rather, I do know why, but I'm not sure if I should tell you. You're looking uneasy.'

'No no,' I lie.

'What I can say is that it will probably become apparent. Thank you so much, William. I think we should express gratitude when we feel it. Just as we should apologise when we have a reason to. And I'll see you again soon. There. I promised I would be brief.'

She stands up and so do I. She is not wearing a bra and appreciates the fact that I have noticed. I am not sure whether I am standing in order to make her going smoother, or to say something. Possibly something big. While I am wondering, she steps towards me, puts her right hand up against my left cheek and pulls my head slightly forward so that she can... so than she can what... kiss me on the other side. It's not an improper kiss, but definitely on the high end of social; the kind an uncle might get from his niece. A special uncle though.

My head goes a little too far forward and the kiss goes off in my ear. It is intimately loud and has the fragrance of a bursting bud. The whole of my right side feels as if it has taken it intravenously and turns to fur. It feels numbed and heightened, all the way down the nervous conduits, still astonishingly effective, into the far reaches of my toes.

I say 'Yes,' which is laughably inadequate for anything here. Yes that was nice? Yes that was beyond nice? Yes I'll see you again? Yes you're on your way and thank you for coming in? Yes I've been a help? Yes we take more than we need? I've no idea. Nor has she, and she reaches up the register again for one of those tinkly laughs. It's her space-filler, just as 'Well' and 'So' are mine. But it is intoxicating, there is no other word for it. The laugh is accompanied by a slight throwing of her head. This has the effect of a swung pomander, flinging the scent of her hair out into the space between us.

It is only when she repeats the words 'Again soon' that I can feel Dr. William Newgate stirring inside, getting his shit together, being the really quite convincing, even formidable family doctor that his repertoire runs to. I have seen him before, of course; I have rolled him out to patients who I believe are overstepping some mark. This mark may be a blurred old scratch of chalk, but I do know when it's been gone over.

The Dr. Newgate who then emerges from the container of his bumbling liberal custodian is lean and mean, like the Matryoshka within. He is the young ideologue fresh out of St. Thomas's, with the precedents of great mid-century men of medicine still defining his moral course. He gives short shrift to the canny slacker with his load of unreviewed US campus data on lumbar contusion from off the web, and his perfectly sound back. He identifies the benefits scrounger straight off and feels a young man's rage at the threat to Beverage's great legacy. He noses out the faux-depressives and the weak compulsives, never more so than since acquiring the honest testimonies from AA's infinite vernacular pool.

He spots games-playing and ulteriority in all their forms, and he sends them on his way, saying to the young woman who now stands statuesquely before him: 'Serena. Miss Miller. I am grateful for your kind words, and I repeat, I am very glad if I have been of some assistance. However, I have said to you already that I believe you require the help of a qualified professional to deal with some of the matters of a more personal nature which you have raised with me.

'I appreciate that Dr. Lubasz has not in your view proved to be suitable, but there are others whom I can recommend to you with confidence. As to your no doubt well-intentioned suggestion that you will see me again soon, I think it might be better for you if you were to seek the advice of a general practitioner other than myself. I do hope you don't take this personally, but I feel I would be failing in my duty to you if I were not to say what I just have.'

She is looking at him - at me - as if I have changed into someone else, which of course I have. At least, I have tried to. My anger was not simulated. I directed it at her because I truly found her behaviour out of order. But I also directed it at me because I was shocked by my susceptibility to her. My weakness. I keep coming back to that word. Or rather, it keeps coming back to me. The more I try to avoid it, the more it pursues me, stalks me, comes up close to me and hangs itself around my neck.

She begins to laugh, rather as she did on a previous visit. The laughter suggests that she is not taking me seriously. But when it subsides, she too has altered. The smile is gone from her eyes and there is a jut to her chin. She asks whether I am in effect sacking her as a patient, and I hear myself answer: 'Not as such, no. I am just saying.' To which she says: 'And I am just saying that it would be inappropriate for me to stop seeing a doctor who seems to know exactly what is wrong with me. Because I don't think there are many like that.'

Then I say 'Very well, very well,' aware of trying to roll the whole conversation back up, take it to a depot and dump it. It is too late. She is huffing and rallying, and saying: 'But then, if someone doesn't want to see me, for whatever reason, then I'm happy not to see them. So thank you for your honesty, Dr. Newgate. I hope everything goes well for you, here and elsewhere.'

There is a darkness about her last few words, as though she thinks she might have a say in how everything goes for Dr. Newgate, here and elsewhere. I wish I had not taken the conversation in this direction but simply done as AA urges you to do; take things a day at a time; stop projecting; live in the moment.

So easy to mouth, so hard to practise. I even find myself wishing I had taken advice, both from within the practice and from within AA.

The trouble is that this would have meant either letting Maurice in - about as wise as handing matches to an arsonist; or HGV - too straight, too bygone, ultimately too unimaginative to sympathise with me on this one; or Mila - beyond inappropriate to confide the truth of the matter to a female colleague. And the final, extra-mural option would have been Clive. Enough said.

The young woman looks at me. I am aware of my shoulders heaving slightly and my face contemplating the floor. She says 'Bye' in a light voice, gets to the door of the surgery and adds the words 'For now.' I look at her more questioningly than I intend and her face changes again. She gives a big, broad wink, no doubt about it, and is gone.

September 26th. A call from Dad. He has nothing in particular to say, but it is an everything sort of nothing. He says the weather's not been up to much for the time of year, there's big new potholes opened up in the back road to Highmoor which no-one's doing owt about, and there's more of the buses out of Newcastle being laid off. I listen to his voice going past like a man in the rain, and I make the odd Mmm sound to show that I'm still on the other end of the phone. He says Dr. Cowgill's going after forty years and won't be replaced but no-one's doing owt about it as there's no-one left in the village but weekend folk in fancy gear, all with their own doctors.

So now there's only young Cowgill, the son, who's reckoned to be no better than his father. Dad assumes I know the Cowgills as we share a profession. Like me assuming he knows Clive's uncle because he too was apparently a Bevin Boy who went down the mines. The older Cowgill I do remember. Of course I do. And because of Dad's conviction that his lack of vigilance led to

Mum's death, I've never been allowed to forget him.

Dad says the Pitman's Arms has gone very strange, with food written in chalk on a blackboard that you can't read. He says you'd've thought that in these days with so much in the way of technology they could have come up with something better than that. He says it's run by two young men from Manchester and you never see a woman behind the bar.

These calls may have the odd variation, but they can all be translated as: I'm stuck on this moor at the top of England and the village is dying around me. Just as your mother died twenty years ago this winter, or twenty-one years ago this winter; nothing comes here any more, and that includes my only son who is too busy with his London life and who could do nothing to save her despite him having become a medical man himself; high time he came up; all the houses in Upper Level Row have got subsidence; there's builders after the allotments; old Douglas Garside is back in the Queen Elizabeth in Gateshead with the canker and likely won't be coming out; my chest is rattling again and there's nowt…

September 28th. A man with an enormous bunch of flowers at the door. So big it hides his face and he has to peer round the side to check this is the right house. I can see pink chrysanthemums and purple carnations and maybe some peonies and magenta as well. Dad would know. It must be for Imogen. Oh Lord, let me not have missed her birthday. Who could they be from? The Interflora man reads out the name, Miss Freers, and I tell him he's come to the wrong address; we are Newgate. He shows me the name on the accompanying envelope: Miss Inez Frias. I thank the man, sign for the flowers and take them indoors.

They brush against the passage walls and I have to manipulate them through into the kitchen. Imogen and Ricky are sitting at the table. He's got his Baumgartner and she's got her *Guardian*, but they are chatting and drinking tea. This is good. He must be holding forth about Oxford in the way she craves as he is in the middle of telling her something about the deer park at Magdalen, always a popular emblem of the place's alleged magic.

She looks up at me, and through the bright and waving blooms I can see her face lift in disbelief. Ricky is looking at me too. You couldn't not be looking at me if you were in the kitchen. He has an expression of similar amazement, which is amazing in itself as it takes a shock to pull him from his coolness. They look to me for an explanation: have we forgotten something important? Has William lost it? Is this a massive amends for all his defects?

'It's for Inez,' I say, and they deflate.

'She's not here,' says Imogen. 'What time did she say she'll be back, Ricky?'

'She didn't. She tends not to.'

'Here, you'd better let me deal with them,' says Imogen. She sounds as she used to when Ricky was tiny. He would be in my arms, something would go wrong, he'd start to wail tragically and she would say: 'Here, you'd better let me deal with him,' and I would hand him over, and we were both happy.

Now, with the flowers, she goes over to the sink, lays them on the draining board, then fetches the two big vases from the dresser shelf. Standing there sorting out this sprawl of brilliant colours, she could be a vet suddenly finding herself with a Bolivian Macaw on her hands. Although she is so much larger than she used to be, her movements are still full of grace. I am aware that the image of Serena is about to slip into my head like a slide into a projector. The readiness is no prevention.

She asks whether Inez knew the flowers were coming, and Ricky and I enjoy a second of unity by swapping search-me faces.

September 29th. I decide to go up and see Dad for a few days in a fortnight's time. A good moment actually. All of the other three have had their holidays, and I've got a bit owing. I'd better use it up or I'll lose it. I find myself relishing the trip north, the plain elsewhereness of it, even if not the prolonged exposure to him. We'll see.

I get the Underground dream again, or bits of it, a few hours after talking to him, and I can't dodge the conviction that they are linked. My reasoning, if you can call it that, goes like this: that dream was, and is, about my failure as a doctor. As an individual too, but as a doctor specifically. A boy is dying on the platform and I walk the other way because I am drunk. A certain rationale there, you could say; an understandable caution not just for myself but also for the boy. Perhaps, but only in the service of my sickness.

Now, when Dad says those things about Mum dying and me being powerless to stop it happening, the same self-reproach kicks in. The same assault-based introspection starts up, looping round in its own Circle Line, and back comes the dream like a red light on the panel.

Sept 30th. Imogen perfectly OK about me going north. She seems almost happy, what with all this Ricky time. Strangely for a student he hasn't any plans for backpacking to Lhasa or getting kidnapped in a former Soviet republic. How I love Ricky. How I fear him too. But how I love him for the memories of his childhood and for this ability of his to take Imogen out of herself, as they say. She is the one who is taking a holiday from her usual emotional location. I did not intend to devolve the responsibility for her welfare to him. But nor have I tried to stop it as I saw it happening.

A release from the bondage of self, or however those relentlessly spot-on American words describe it. Isn't that what I should be facilitating in her? As a doctor. As her husband. Doesn't ecstasy come from ex-stasis, standing outside? Nice line of inquiry, this, but a dangerous one too since it would bring us to liberty's toxic counterpart, getting out of it.

October 2nd. Well, I do get it in the neck from Ricky, after a fashion. This too happens in the kitchen, or mostly in the kitchen, which has become a fashionable area. Strictly speaking, it's a split-site bollocking as there's a second bit across the hall and into my study, after I think we're done. The whole thing divides neatly into two sections: the public sector and the private. If he structures his essays on Keynes etc. as rigorously as this, it would be an injustice if he didn't get a starred first. On the public front, the gist is this: Dr. William Newgate, whom we shall call the defendant, has bankrupted the ensuing generation by his rapacious self-indulgence.

Of course the jury will be aware that he has not accomplished this single-handed, despite his best intentions; rather, we shall take him as the representative of the generation known as the baby-Boomers. Why? Because he is making tea for himself in the kitchen of Number 127 Elm Park Gardens, Richmond, Surrey and it is Sunday morning so he cannot slip off to the surgery.

The defendant has glided through the years of post-war prosperity, taking lavish and non-repayable state hand-outs for the entire period of his education; he has benefited from the purchase of cheap housing which has since increased in value so exorbitantly that today's would-be purchasers are priced out of the property market and trapped in a rent vice which further enriches the landlords; he has adopted a hegemonic position over culture and society, enjoying a prosperity made possible by the very inflation which impoverishes his children (although he only has one); he has further benefited from the influx of migrant labour in the past two decades, which has kept the cost of services low while depressing the wage economy in which these said children must function; he will in the course of his life take from the welfare state 118 per cent of what he has put it, thereby, M'Lud, violating the inter-generational contract. He is, in a word, a thief, stealing from the very parties he should

71

be assisting.

This is a brief precis of the charge-sheet, but not, I think, inaccurate. It is underpinned with a wealth of statistical data. I have trouble with this, just as I have trouble with the financial reports of the practice manager. I am aware that there is a blizzard coming at me, so I set my face to patient and wait for it to pass.

Today I do, briefly, try the other way, listening carefully to every decimal point and percentage estimate, and nodding to show that I'm getting it. But that's like trying to catch machine gun bullets in your teeth. Better to let them go through your neck and out the other side, and to hell with it. Yes, very Boomer, I'm sure, but you may as well be hanged for a sheep as for a goat, or whatever it was that Dad used to say. As the numbers come at me from Ricky, my main thought is of admiration for him; that and plain optimism for the future of someone who can marshal his data so well for the making of a case.

I think it's a bit rich, for want of a better word, but I don't say so. I don't say anything. Not now at any rate. But inside I'm reckoning he's got the wrong man. Doctor, for Heaven's sake. All those knackering, grinding early years before you could even get started; cheap labour if ever there was. And Boomer? *Moi*? Surely not. Whenever I hear the term, I think of people who were teenagers in the Sixties, once so glorified and now so trashed.

In the Sixties, I was far too busy being born to get into all these bad habits like nicking the nation's future. If it's 1945 to 1964, then yes, technically I squeak in by a year. But with my body rather than with my spirit. Like Larkin and the Sixties. I mean, I was born on the day Kennedy was shot. He must have been making room for me. I don't think I've ever mentioned this to Ricky, although I'm tempted to do so on some future occasion, just to see what his analytical machinery comes up with.

Surely the people he's after are the druggy *flaneurs* of the

Flower Power days. (Even using a term like that makes me feel like the historian of a vanished civilisation.) The Beatles were heritage to me and my crowd; the Stones were already wrinkled curios, dirty old men even, long before they got that endless second wind as monumental survivors. Glam Rock was embarrassing. We were punk. Pistols, Elvis (Costello), Police - though we were always suspicious of Sting and how right we turned out to be; a bit of New Romantics but then into the Smiths when they broke in Manchester.

Actually, the bands for me were ones that not everyone knew about in the north of England; Bad Religion and Dead Kennedys. I hadn't made the connection with my birthday, but you never know. East Bay Ray on fire with his guitar, Jello Biafra just tearing down everything at the mic and beyond, for as far as he could. I remember Mum's face after she'd chanced on a copy of *Give Me Convenience or Give Me Death* ('What's this then, William?') and seen *Too Drunk to Fuck* on the track listings.

She looked like people look when they are just about to die, which she did do the following year. That's not a death I have on my conscience. I just can't afford to have it there, although there probably was some vague connection, in the sense of her not understanding the world any more, and then, so to speak, getting out of it. But me a member of the Boom? Mistaken identity surely. Only the very end. Only the m sound after the Boo.

I've got to hand it to Ricky though. If this is the new way of going Oedipal, I think I'm in favour. He's working at it, bringing his intellect and research to bear. Like he's had a team on my case. Strangely flattering, and definitely better than the stuff I found myself meting out to poor old Dad, which was basically neglect, lack of interest and virtual loss of contact. He deserved better than that, but I just couldn't raise my game. That's what not being grown-up is about. Early twenties by then, yes, but far from adult.

He could have given it a bit more of a go himself, but he couldn't raise his game either. Couldn't say anything to me at all, absolutely not a word for days, about any subject other than that my shirts weren't shirts but blouses and made me look like a woman; couldn't find any way of coping with Imogen on our one trip to Highmoor. Kept staring at her as if she wasn't real, but then so did all the other old boys in the Pitman's Arms. Just didn't know what to do with himself, or how to be. Something which I picked up from him, or which must have come down in the genes.

At least he didn't try to medicate himself with alcohol, I'll say that for him. But he could have tried harder with Imogen. When I told him I loved her as much as he had loved Mum, something inside him went, like an organ haemorrhaging, and it was never the same. We couldn't get back from it. I'd given him an insult. In the medical (generally American) sense, as in 'Dylan Thomas suffered a fatal insult to the brain.' What Dad got from me was an insult to the soul. Comparing my wife to his; the nerve of the boy.

Imogen is the subject again, all these years later, as his grandson - his bright, scary grandson with the whole world awaiting his instructions - turns to the private section of the indictment. His opening question on the subject is stark and simple after the economics stuff. As I write it here, it all looks much more aggressive than it really is. There's something polite, almost deferential in his manner, as if his head is after confrontation while his heart is wanting to keep channels open with the conciliation services.

'What's up, Dad?'
'With?'
'You know what with.'
'Me?'
'No.'

'Ah.'

'Imogen.'

Why did we ask him to call us Imogen and William instead of Mum and Dad? When he uses her name now, like that, it flings everything all over the place, like someone kicking the underside of the dinner table. If he wants to rebel, challenge, maim, unhouse, cannibalise, then fine, but he should return our names to us before he gets stuck in. It's all wrong because it gives him the status of a peer group member, which he is deliberately not being. What is he being? Imogen's representative and my interrogator.

'It's all wrong, isn't it.'

'I don't know.'

'I mean.'

'Go on, Ricky.'

'Well. Look at her.'

'I do. I do.'

'And what do you see, William? What do you see?'

'I see your mother. I see your mother and my wife.'

'Sure. But.'

'But what?'

'You know.'

'I'm not sure I do.'

'William. Dad.'

'Tell me then. If you say I know. Then I can tell you if you are right.' This is both convoluted and childish, not a good combination.

'The way she is.'

'Which is?' I try to put a little steel into this, to show that if he is about to say something derogatory about his mother, he will have her husband to contend with.

'Well... '

I wait, nursing the faint hope that that's all he's saying; that

75

she is well.

'Well,' he repeats. 'Sad. Basically.'

'Sad.'

'Yes.'

'I see.'

'You sound surprised.'

' No no. I mean, if that is your view, then it's right that I should hear it. I mean... '

'Actually... ' He is hearing my Reasonable Manner and it is irking him. It always has. I give way.

'The question is: why.'

'You mean why she is... what you say.'

'You got it.'

'Yes. I see.' He puts his head to one side, raises one hand to support his chin while the other cups his elbow. His watching posture. I've seen him do it while looking at *Newsnight* and seeing politicians crash in flames on Paxman's floor.

'Have you ever tried asking her?' I say.

He answers with something about not divulging the opinions of others. I think the phrase 'protection of sources' comes into it, but the sentence loses me. I observe that she's not his source but his mother and he replies that his point still stands. While the initiative is bobbling about between us I manage to grab it and say that since he raises the subject, Imogen seems to be rather happy at the moment.

'I see,' he says without conviction.

'I mean, I think she's very glad you're here, Ricky. As I am too of course.'

He nods at this. I can see it pleases him though he is at pains not to show it.

'You mean when I'm not here she's worse?'

'Well, worse implies bad; that it's bad otherwise.'

'So. What is it?'

'What, Ricky?'

'You know. I'm asking what the matter is.'

'Yes. I gathered that.'

'You must talk.'

'I suppose we must.'

'I don't know what that means.' Nor do I, as it happens, but I hoped he would let it go.

'Well, Ricky, I suppose it means that yes we do talk, but also that it's private.'

'But she's my mother.' This he says with a touching passion. Nothing about my right - no, my responsibility - to protect my sources; they are to be trampled underfoot by filial prerogative, I suppose.

'Oh very much so, she's your mother,' I say clumsily.

'Well then,' he declaims, like a delegate carrying the conference.

'But she is also a woman,' I say. I can feel pride and gallantry puffing their chests out through the words. I used to love defending Imogen against her critics, real or imagined; I assure myself I'll do the same now, even if the person on her case is her own son; and even if he claims to have her interests at heart. I invoke the bigger picture with a plea for privacy itself; the great social ideal of it rather than the scandal of hacking into David Beckham's love texts.

'... because, I mean, it is no less under threat, would you not agree, than the rain forests of Latin America or the ice caps of the... the Larsen Shelf.' The slight hesitation is caused by rust. I just can't remember if it was the Larsen Shelf or something else, possibly the Weddell Sea. Ricky senses I'm trying it on and he makes a rubbery, Paxmanesque horse face as if I'm just a Rent-a-Spart put up by the Student Union. I plough on: 'For all the miracles of communication, Ricky, we forfeit privacy at our peril. And your mother has a right to it as inviolably as the next woman.'

Ricky looks angry at this, as though I've stolen his clothes literally as well as politically.

'My mother has the right to her son knowing what the matter is.'

This sounds oddly parochial and self-seeking. I chance my arm and say: 'Ah no. There I think you're wrong.'

'In what way'

'In confusing your rights with hers. What you are advancing, Ricky, is your right, but you are, with respect, presenting it as hers.'

There is a silence, the first for a long time. I expect him to ride over it on a bridge of theory, but in fairness to him he stops and nods, chewing this one in his head.

I carry on. 'You've every right,' I begin, aware at once that my reasonableness will irk him again, but too late to turn back; 'You've every right to be concerned about your mother. Well, either of your parents. And I think it's to your credit that you are. Do you think that I am not?'

'I wasn't saying that.'

'Perhaps not,' I reply. 'But I am asking you whether you are thinking it. Whether you are thinking that it is somehow my fault, my responsibility. Because if that is what you think, Ricky, I'd actually be quite grateful if you would let me know.'

I really would.

'Since I seem to be responsible for the impoverishing of the young and the cancellation of the inter-generational contract, I feel I should know whether I should be adding this one to my list of transgressions.'

Another silence, a major one.

'I wish,' he begins.

'Go on,' I say.

'I just wish…' Then he tails off uncharacteristically and looks

78

at the floor. I think about taking it on from here; talking candidly about what has passed between Imogen and me; our discussions of the menopause and its management; my suggestion that she, that we, look at the pros and cons of HRT (not Habit Reversal Training); the bleakness she feels about her longed-for and adored baby Ricky growing up and fleeing the coop. I also consider talking about depression, since I am convinced no assessment of her would be complete without acknowledging the presence of that condition. But the mere contemplation of them makes me re-affirm their absolute privacy.

And so Dr. Newgate takes possession of me and makes sure I watch my words. I am grateful for his intervention, for his taking over from Ricky's father. Patient confidentiality; that's what Dr. Newgate brings with him, and I am glad of it. Not just because it gets me an exit visa from this difficult country, but also because I happen to believe in it. I am a doctor. Whatever else I am - father, husband, bloke, ex-drunk, future-thief - I am a doctor. And as such (where does that come from?) I believe in my obligation not to discuss the conditions of others. This is only the restraint of proper doctors.

But then Dr. Newgate, having done his bit, steps back out of me and leaves William. Me. I look at Ricky's downturned face and of course see the six-year-old looking down inconsolably at the body of Rab, his rabbit, who died an hour after we bought him; the nine-year-old cradling the corpse of his crashed glider on the common, and so on.

Since the prosecution seems to have rested its case, I decide to change tack and go Dad. Not my Dad, but just Dad as opposed to William. Father of a young man, fellow occupant of adulthood's estate. 'You know how it is with women,' I say, with what must be a candidate for World's Clumsiest Gambit. 'In fact' - self-deprecating here - 'you probably know much more about that than I do.'

He looks at me with despair rather than contempt. Perhaps there is even sympathy in there too. Ricky doesn't know how it is with women. He can't know, unless he is keeping all his research intensely private. Always possible, except that there are still no signs of girlfriend activity. There was a 'friend' called Celia, a fellow economist and member of the university mountaineering club, but she turned out to be more interested in other women. I realise that even as I have been asserting the rights to the privacy of others, I have invaded his own.

Ricky doesn't look remotely reproachful. If anything he looks rather soft and doe-eyed. He takes a step towards me - just one step and the whole picture can change - and says: 'You do love her, don't you.'

I say 'Absolutely,' and mean it.

'You do love Imogen.'

'Of course, Ricky. Of course.'

As I hear the front door open and the sounds of, I think, Imogen and Inez coming in, I realise that his face has turned heavy with sad thoughts. I put my hands on his shoulders, firmly and lovingly but stopping well short of a hug. I tell him that everything will be all right as if I believe it with my whole heart.

October 4th. Lunch with the other three, plus the new practice manager. Was dreading it. Terrible precedents of Maurice showing off and tipping out his latest swottings from the *BMJ;* HGV acting emeritus and seen-it-all-before; me not really wanting to engage with either of them and trying to keep Mila for myself. Not as bad as I'd feared. At least, not to begin with.

New practice manager turns out to be delightful. Joan is her name. Used to be a nurse, then brought up three boys, then became a pub landlady somewhere in Kent, but saw the business go under when the smoking ban came in. 'I shouldn't be saying this to you,' she says with a smile,' but smoking would have kept us alive.'

I think she'll do very well. I've always been sceptical of the role, probably because I am nostalgic for the days of management by partnership. I don't know why, as it meant dealing with Maurice as a partner. Just the notion of it, I suppose, with at least an appearance of democracy. But Joan's got the measure. I look at her and I don't think it's the medical bit of her history that's significant, but the pub landladyship.

That's what you want; someone welcoming and egalitarian, the same as with receptionists. The longer I'm around, the more I realise that those simple human qualifications are better than any diploma. That's why Gill's good, even though she lets people in when perhaps she shouldn't. Or perhaps because she does do precisely that. Serena walking through the door of my head again.

We'll all speak to Joan individually when she starts next month. This is just the hello lunch. We're in the Jamuna as usual, because it's always empty. Instant service and no noisy neighbours. Just the wavy line of a sitar playing against a busy tabla. Very nice. We go round the table and say a little about ourselves. HGV assumes she is already familiar with him, as she might be with a landmark which happens to be called Harvey Gordon-Venning. Mila is full of her customary modesty, apologetic if ever she is sounding a little feminist, but not so apologetic that she will change her tack. Very fond of Mila, and would trust her in a crisis. I think I would say the same of our new practice manager.

HGV gives a lofty overview of General Practice in Britain: The Last Five Hundred Thousand Years, with particular reference to the Elm Park surgery at the start of the third millennium AD. This he finds in rude health through its enlightened stewardship and its admirable blend of calm experience and open-mindedness. I see Joan's eyes do a lightning poll of our reactions. She is so fast that I'm sure she catches me wincing.

HGV locks into four-wheel drive and does his usual pitch

about the besetting ills of the day: doctors' readiness to over-prescribe; lazy diagnosing, particularly in the area of depression and related disorders; patients getting very adept at faking it. All this delivered with the air of a man who will not make too much of how lucky we are to have him. I tune out as best as I can while he's going on. Two or three times I hear him say 'for my sins,' which is always a signal that he is about to brag while pretending not to.

He takes a few routine swings at self-help groups, and I realise that he probably has no idea of my AA membership. No idea and no interest. For some reason he's particularly drawn by the subject of malingerers today. As he has never had an original medical or social thought for the forty years of his working life, he must have been at a dinner with an influential bigot whose views on the widespread feigning of depression he has now been parroting.

'Not so sure with respect,' says Mila. 'Depression very serious and going unrecognised for long time. Hiding behind other bits and pieces.'

'I must say,' I put in, 'I'm with Mila on that.'

'You see, these people,' says HGV as though we hadn't said anything, 'they get onto a good thing.' I think he's referring to patients, but then he mentions the name of Lewis Wolpert, whom I've always thought is very strong on the subject, partly because he has suffered from depression himself and gives a truthful account of it. I doubt whether HGV has even dipped into the pages of *Malignant Sadness*. Not that this prevents him saying: 'Now, I mean, I have no doubt that Wolpert is a thoroughly decent, well-intentioned man as well as being one of our most eminent embryologists. However, on the subject of so-called depression, I fear one must take issue with him on certain fundamental points of medical fact. Then of course we have such popular 'experts' as... ' - further benefits of his overarching knowledge coming up… 'as the Australian woman, very fashionable these days, Margaret Rowe.'

'Is Dorothy,' says Mila.

'I think you'll find… ' says HGV.

'No no with respect, is Dorothy Rowe. *Way Out of Prison, Courage to Live*, many other books. Very good. Margaret Rowe is nail care specialist in High Street. Also very good.'

'I think… ' says HGV.

'Is perfectly understandable mistake. I know Dorothy a little bit. Was clinical psychology head in Lincolnshire. Personal construct theory very good. Very helpful. I find.'

I think about putting in my bit about how I tend to try and establish whether there's any substance abuse going on in cases of depression; how skunk is so powerful these days that it can, and does, trigger psychotic episodes; how it is an entirely different substance from the cannabis of our youth. Some of our youths. But I don't proceed. It would be heading towards the subject of drink, and I don't trust Maurice with it. Not where I'm concerned. Joan however; I look at her and think, yes, pub landlady, you've seen a bit. You'd know where I'm coming from. Another time maybe.

Maurice has been silent for too long and comes in with some of his rubbish about the narrative of illness. Well, maybe it's not all rubbish, but he just makes it sound like it is. 'Stories with recurrent plotlines and unexpected twists. Careful reading is the key.'

Strange how both he and HGV, faced with this new woman, get bragging. Even if they try and mask it with the language of modesty. There's more where it came from. I should be enjoying it, I suppose, but I find myself feeling inconveniently sorry for Maurice. This is the social equivalent of me not hammering him to ignominious defeat on the squash court.

'The important thing,' he goes on, 'is that when we hear hoofbeats, we should think of zebras.' Joan nods gamely at this.

Mila too. HGV remains impassive, eating, as if a conversation is not taking place.

'And of course,' Maurice adds, '*Primum non nocere.*'

We all go rummaging for the scraps of Latin that we still have somewhere. Firstly, do not harm, I think. Maurice is enjoying our moment of doubt. Joan helps out by offering 'Don't knock it,' as a translation, and we all laugh. HGV as well, to show he knows the real meaning, even if he wasn't able to come out with it just then.

There's one more flurry from Maurice as he attempts a final riff on the sickness-as-story theme, but it lapses due to lack of interest and there is a pause with the makings of a nasty silence. He feels it coming and nips it in the bud himself by saying across the table to me: 'Squash.' Statement rather than question. I'm about to say Yes with the hope of conveying No when the door of the Jamuna swings open and four or five big men come in. This is very unusual. Maurice looks across at them and I see recognition forming on his face. He says to me across the table: 'There's the man from the club. You know.'

I do indeed. The biggest of the men, the one seating himself at the head of their table and summoning the waiter, is Brian Miller, Serena's father.

I say 'oh yes,' flat as I can. A chemical trigger causes discomfort to enter my bloodstream and surround me from the inside within a matter of seconds. Whatever mechanism has been activated – I should know but don't – it is in excellent working order. As effective as you would find in a man thirty years younger.

'Are you all right, William?' asks Maurice, rather energetically. 'You look a bit, I don't know.'

That's one way of describing it. Perfectly accurate as far as it goes. I pretend a grain of the pilau has gone down the wrong way, in the hope it will explain my sudden reddening. This has happened as quickly as it did the other day when the man's daughter arrived in my surgery. I just don't seem to have an antidote for it. This is guilt, I suppose. Plain guilt, even for something that I haven't done. In no way have I done it.

Joan offers to slap me on my back and I accept for credibility's sake. She wallops me three times, so hard that it knocks my breath about and makes my head do a minor whiplash. I say thank you and feel the colour going down again, just like mercury in a capillary. Maurice has sensed something. Blood, you could say; at least the effects of a surfeit of the stuff in my face.

'You know him, don't you,' he says.

'Not really,' I say, truthfully.

'There's a connection though.'

'Well. The club.'

'Ah.'

'We played. Years ago.'

'Ah yes.'

'Quite good as I remember.'

'He's coming over.'

He is. Brian Miller has noticed me and is approaching our table. He is looking bluff and raw-boned. He has the large gestures of someone who is dispensing the hospitality today. Forcing it on his chosen recipients. This is the bonhomie of the bully. One of the old rumours about him was that he bribed one of his daughters - not sure which - to say nothing after she had seen him taking her mother's best friend Deborah into the bedroom at home. I wouldn't put it past him, though I'm aware of having to keep my imagination under control where this man is concerned.

Looking at him now, he is built for rugby rather than squash. He is probably two or three stone heavier than he should be, but the extra weight merely enlarges his swagger. He frightens me physically, there's no denying it. It's the figure of a man who's always first out of his car in a traffic dispute. The facial glint of a dog whose owner swears he's safe but who is then found with his jaws locked on your face.

'Don't mean to interrupt,' he says, like people do when they're interrupting. 'William isn't it?'

'That's right,' I say.

'From the club.'

'Yes.'

'Recognised you. Dr. William.' He looks across at Maurice and says

'You too. Good to see you both.' He shakes us by the hand - dear God that's a powerful grip - and apologises to the other three. 'Good game. Mustn't keep you. Fancy one sometime?'

I try the same self-refuting Yes. The result is no better.

'Also, and won't go into it now, something I'd like to ask you about. Hope you don't mind.' A demand rather than a request. Followed up with a quick glare.

'Of course not,' I lie through my fibres.

'Give you a bell.'

'Yes.'

'Know where to get you. Cheers.'

October 9th. At the kitchen table with Imogen. Anyone seeing a photo of this would take us to be another perfectly functional professional middle-class couple. As I try to place myself beyond its confines, like a man in a Raymond Carver poem, I could almost convince myself that this is the case. We are both reading the paper, me the news bit, her the review, music coming out of the speakers. This is Carlos Adorno, and not for the first time, full of articulate agony, fighting back against love's injustice. The CD case is lying open on some article about how to take your clothes off with style. She must have been perusing the leaflet with the lyrics and the singer's biog.

Our furniture is looking dated; the blond wood units, the Kohler sink and the Bella Cucina stuff. I can almost see Little

86

Ricky in his room playing with his Lego or its electronic successor, or round at friends. Same as now really, but him a quarter of his present size.

Imogen is looking relaxed, pleasant, pretty. She is carrying herself with the new civility. Well, new in the context of our twenty-five years. I date it back to just under three years, when we were both so rapidly on the change, each in our own way; she hormonally, me just as radically, in the manner of newly zealous abstainers through history.

There is nothing resentful in her routine, no sharp little asides, just the settling and the sipping, and the safe distance that formality can provide.

The ratio of the silent to the spoken in our conversation is about twenty to one. For me at least. For her I can't speak. Her composure seems so total that she might well be untroubled by interior dialogue. How would I know? It's a matter of privacy. My gambits die in the mouth like a generation of young men before they're out of the trenches. In these never-to-be-made exchanges I am asking her if she might feel like working again one day. I am putting it to her gently and solicitously. Not that we need the money. GPs are doing more than fine these days. Just that she seemed to like the world of children's publishing, and was a wonderful editor. Might she want to go back part-time? I'm sure Barbara and Tim at Tiny Tales still miss her.

Then I'm suggesting that we should go away for a weekend, maybe longer actually, but nowhere near Alston and those moors, don't worry, I got the message on our one and only time there, and besides, I'm off up that way any time now to see the old bugger. No, I'm suggesting The Swan or The Crown at Southwold; good memories there surely after those tremendous evenings at Snape and Aldeburgh - that unforgettable *Peter Grimes* - and days out at the Minsmere reserve in our brief but keen period of birding.

I'm suggesting, not for the first time, that if she likes, we could go and see someone. Capital S See. Someone other than the marriage guidance counsellor whom I rather liked but she didn't. But only if the thought appeals to her. Just to, I don't know, make contact again. With each other. Sometimes these things do take an intermediary, and we shouldn't hobble ourselves with pride. We - I mean we as in practice - know some very good people. I know they're good because the patients come back and tell me so, and we could just give it a try, see how it feels, nothing to lose. I know we've tried it before, sort of, but we could give it a better shot. There's someone very good I've got in mind. Very sympathetic, very high (no better way of summarising it) emotional intelligence.

I'm saying - but still without a word spoken - that it must have been so hard for her. Not just when I was doing the drinking and being so comprehensively unavailable, although that must have been worse than if I'd been having an affair. Which I was in a sense, with the bottle. With Ethel, was my not very amusing joke. As in ethyl alcohol. I mean afterwards, after The Priory, when I was all clean and perky and getting on with it and relentlessly positive and undergoing whole ranges of seismic alterations. This must have been even harder for her. Everyone saying how well William is doing and her having to nod supportively, self-forgettingly.

I'm saying how sorry I am for my sheer neglect of her, also how sorry I am for having said sorry in what must have been a stiff and impersonal way when I was going through the amends part of the step-work with Clive. Sodding Clive. How sorry I am for having broken something and not being able to repair it. As if I'd trodden on one of little Ricky's gliders and walked out of the room.

Carlos Adorno tries to help out by saying that yesterday love was such an easy game to play but that now he needs a place to hide away. His English, obviously, is much better than that of the Spaniards we normally have in the house. He is giving it a go, and this fact alone fills his voice with a vulnerable nobility.

Imogen hears him out for just one verse, then smiles as if it is not really her thing, and switches over to the news. More progress reports about the trapped Chilean miners. 'Isn't that incredible,' she says.

'Out in ten days. And it was going to be Christmas originally.'

'Incredible,' I agree. 'One of the best stories there's ever been. I wish all the news was like that.'

'Do you think they really talked about eating each other?'

'Well,' I reply, 'I thought that was just a joke.'

'Now it is,' she says. 'But I mean in those first seventeen days, before the probe came through and they thought they were all going to die, and having a spoonful of tuna every forty-eight hours. Do you think they were going to eat each other?'

'I don't know, love.' After it's out, I realise this is the first time I've called her love in years. Maybe seven or eight years, in a different time. I can feel it shock her with its casual intimacy. Her look lets me know I have transgressed. She pushes on, quite animated now:

'We were discussing whether it was leadership or democracy that saved them. I was saying leadership because of Luis Urzua, who is obviously a terrific man.'

Obviously; a titan-spirited hero when nothing less would do. Considering him now, I am summoning the Underground once more, and with it my own shabby and fugitive behaviour on the platform.

'Urzua was the foreman,' she continues, 'when the mine collapsed. It was he who worked out the food rations and got them to rig some headlights so that they could simulate the hours of day and night. Said he was in charge of the shift and that's how it would stay. What a guy.'

She's got all the names, all the details. She knows there's a former pro soccer player among them. She knows the youngest is nineteen and the oldest is sixty-three. She even seems to know about their families. There is one who turns out to have had a mistress. His wife only found about it when she saw this Other Woman weeping over a photo of him. I must say, that case - narrative? - made me uneasy. The man may have done wrong, we just don't know. We are in no position to judge him. He is not a celebrity, his private life is no concern of ours. He has been trapped in a hell-hole two thousand feet beneath the Andes and therefore must surrender his rights to privacy along with his liberty and, very likely, his health. Something amiss here, surely.

Imogen carries on. The disaster animates her. A welcome side-effect.

'Ricky was saying that it was democracy and that all the important decisions had been put to the vote.' I say I wonder how he knew that and she says he just did, in the way he always did just know things. 'He said they were favoured by being an odd number so that, as long as they banned abstentions, there would always be a decision one way or another. But Inez, you see, Inez was saying that democracy and leadership were all very well, but what really brought them through was their faith.'

The Man Upstairs again. In this case a very long way up. She gives me a look as if she is asking me where I stand on this one. Democracy, leadership, faith. Major players, all of them. I think about it and of course I immediately find myself triangulating, or whatever the right word is. I mean, trying to find a way of squeezing them all onto the winner's podium.

Then she says something unexpectedly direct: 'I'd have thought you were with Inez on this one.' Clearly a reference to me being, whether I like it or not, a member of a spiritual (I'll have to come back to that fraught word some time) fellowship (that one too). My wife has me down as a believer.

As if on cue, Inez can be heard coming down the stairs and along the hall, laughing throatily into her mobile. What is she doing here? This is just another of the questions I never put to Imogen. And this in turn goes to show how little idea one has - this one at least - about what is going on in one's own household, and why. (Probably less idea than one has about what's been going on in the home of the errant Chilean miner.)

It might be quite straightforward. Imogen was very happy when Ricky was little, once she'd got over the post-natal horrors.

Far from being possessive with him, as I feared she might be, she loved sharing him with helpers. She had a strange lack of confidence about the thought of managing without support. And we were lucky with the au pairs.

They were good company, helpful but also needful. The combination suited her. Linguistically and financially, they were guaranteed to be subordinate, which she liked, I have to say. If I were more into the relevant jargon, I could easily find myself declaring that Imogen's au pairs habit is a symptom of infantilism. A favourite word of Maurice's, that, which is another reason it doesn't find favour with me.

Economically, Inez appears to have broken the mould of the cash-strapped girl from abroad, and I'm not at all sure what's going on there. Just another question which I'm somehow unable to raise with Imogen.

Inez looks surprised to see us sitting together at the table without the bonding agent of our son, and I wonder what Imogen tells her about us. She says 'Cheers,' which has become her favourite greeting, and asks Imogen if Ricky is about. She replies that she thinks he has gone to the library. For some reason Inez is not happy with the answer. She goes to the sink and starts doing the washing-up. I tell her rather half-heartedly to stop and she takes absolutely no notice.

October 10th. St. Stephen's lunchtime meeting. Off north this week and thought it would be a good idea to appease Clive first. We still haven't made our sponsoring date, but my coming to this meeting, his home group, should make him conclude that I'm still working the programme to the best of my abilities. Which I am. More than that, I'm realising that the principles are not there for show. The more you're up against it, the more they come into their own.

The green walls of the little kitchen are sweating, and there's Clive at the urn, dispensing tea, biscuits and faith in the Lord. I take a seat at the back of the hall. Participating, but not too conspicuous. That's the nice thing about this one. You can keep yourself to yourself if you're so inclined. Not like the big glamorous meetings up in Chelsea, where everyone's rubber-necking to catch sight of the celebrities, most of whom I haven't heard of, and to be caught sight of by them. The tension and anxiety of it. Worse than drinking. Seeing how those poor hunted faces from the small-hours tabloid shoots look in the flesh. Dreadful usually.

Only about fifteen of us here today, which means that everyone will be expected to share. That's OK. Of course you can pass if you don't feel like saying anything, but I hate doing that as it makes people think you're hiding something. And that makes you think they must be right.

Spiritual Sally is still acting secretary. She's looking at the clock on the wall, and checking it against her watch. Her Chair hasn't turned up. She shrugs and says something to Clive. He points directly at me and she nods and comes over to talk to me.

'William, isn't it.'

'Yes. Hi Sally.'

'So sorry about the eleventh hour, but my Chair hasn't turned up and I was wondering if you'd mind stepping in.'

Behind her I can see Clive nodding and smiling assertively. Thanks Clive. I say I'd be delighted and move up to the chair next to Sally's, at the table at the front. She bangs the pot on the table for silence and we're off. A minute's silence to reflect on why we're here and to spare a thought for those who have yet to make the rooms. Teddington Ted reads the preamble, Phoebe with the houseboat reads from the Big Book, Spiritual Sally is saying the format of the meeting is round-the-room sharing after the Chair and then she is giving a big welcome to William who has come to share his experience, strength and hope with us today. And that's me off the springboard. Or right at the end, waiting to launch. The colon, the opening quotation marks, then the gap that waits for me to fill it.

I try not to look at Clive, who is wearing his encouraging face. I only have to say 'I'm William and I'm an alcoholic' and he nods vigorously as if he has just heard a statement of the most penetrating wisdom.

I do a bit of autobiography. About being a doctor because that's what my mother wanted me to be. And then sticking to my studies after she'd died because my father wanted me to do what my mother had wanted. About feeling guilty from since I could remember because I was an only child, horrible term, and assumed that the experience of having me had put my parents off repeating it. About never, ever in any circumstances, feeling that I could discuss it. About it being easier to eat my foot than broach such subjects generally, and so becoming private and diffident and, of course, finding that alcohol relieved the discomfort. About the bingeing at Thomas's but no-one thinking anything of it because that's just what you did if you were a medical student, and it was only if you didn't do it that people would think you were odd. About feeling, at some time, maybe even as early as Thomas's, that there was a special compact between me and drink. A very simple arrangement really, in which I drank it and it made me feel proofed and powerful, and both of us hung onto the secret.

Much nodding here, much murmuring of assent. I even do the gag about the affair with Ethyl. It goes down well, although I think there are two or three who don't get it. Mustn't show off. Mustn't patronise.

Then stuff about it getting out of control; sweats and shakes kicking in; dreadful remorse; lost hours; trying to make strangers and shits like me through the shared pursuit of getting pissed; still thinking I couldn't have a problem as I was a doctor and then despairing as my life started to overturn this assumption.

About guilt, guilt and more guilt. Toxic levels of the stuff. Guilt for my mother's death. A sense that Dr. Cowgill had probably missed it, but then his failure, if that's what it was, passing to me because I hadn't queried it, even though I was qualified by then, as my father has continued to remind me. Clive clenching with pain here and no doubt thinking of Madge and wondering whether he too had somehow let the greedy cancer come sneaking under the radar. Me too thinking of Madge now, and my sessions at Clive's, under her gaze from all angles, and wondering if I'm now throwing him a sufficient chunk of sponsorial meat.

I do the rock-bottom stuff, the shaking to pieces in my own surgery, the confusion and sheer incomprehension of my partners, except for Mila (I don't name her obviously) who was calm and brilliant; the capacity of this illness for bamboozling not just its sufferers but the health professionals as well. Speaking as both. The breaking-down in catastrophic tears for no reason and yet for every reason. The world just opening up and throwing you into the void of itself. Witnessing your self-murder. Being bereaved by your own hand. Becoming a corpse in the container of your body, your somehow-still-living body.

I even do the vision in The Priory, when for days I've got nothing before my eyes but this picture; a rectangle, no frame, the top half a burning sky, the bottom half burning sand, and nothing else in it except a tiny green plant. It keeps trying to grow. I focus hard on it, as if my life depends on it. Which it does. Then a boot comes down and stamps it flat. Like a Monty Python boot. Comical but terrible. Uncompromisng.

These are the green shoots, I say. The green shoots of recovery. You hear economists talk in these terms (although in fairness to Ricky I've never heard him use the phrase, but that's probably because he doesn't see a recovery.) Well, it looked like recovery, or my attempt at it. Little darts of growth, then crunch, then growth again, and more growth, amazingly, until the leaves start to broaden and the cartoon drops of rain fall on it and it grows and grows until the desert is gone and the whole rectangle is a tangle of lush green. And not a single drink, not an alcoholic one, since then. Clive is, well, Clive is drinking it in. The *X-Factor* judge who was always rooting for this act. He looks proud and proprietorial, and I find this very moving.

About ten minutes to go and I catch myself sharing about the Underground dream. Or rather, the events on which the dream is based. I just tell the story of what happened that day in the tube station. One of the exhibits in the nadir of my drinking, and therefore quite justified here. The crowd packed onto the curved platform and the train booming in. The mother struggling on with her buggy and the young boy getting stuck on the platform. The train moving off, the boy having to run, and everything that happened next. The bang and shake of the little blond head against the tunnel mouth. The crowd converging and me going the other way, again and again. Out into the pub, then the next and the next, forever. Spooling through nights until time's dismantling.

This is a new one for Clive, and he looks pensive. A 'why haven't I heard this before?' face. I brace myself for the interpretation that will surely follow. Since Freud it is always open season on other people's dreams. Anyone can play: Jung, Adler,

Frankl, Fromm, Clive. I privately think he (Freud) was way off the pace a lot of the time. There's none of his censorship, distortion and so on happening in this dream of mine. It simply recurs and is very accurate. There is nothing remotely metaphorical about its imagery. It matches what I saw. That's why, when I'm in it, it doesn't feel like a dream but a replay.

Imogen. My history with her. My feelings for her. Her present situation. These are the next concerns to present themselves for possible inclusion in the closing stages of my Chair. It seems wrong, disloyal, to bring her into this, in spite of the Yellow Card right there in front of me on the table, reminding us all of the need for confidentiality: Who You See Here, What You Hear Here, When You Leave Here, Let It Stay Here.

All the same, people in this room know who Imogen is. They have seen her around, just as they have seen me around, and we them. I could talk about love, obsession, compulsion and the other easy abstracts of the emotional collection. Not easy to live through, merely less difficult to discuss than the small and particular details of the behaviour which they brought about.

I go towards the subject. I start describing how I would stand outside her window all the way through the small hours and wait for a sign of her moving inside; the sway of a curtain's skirt; a light going on in another room; basin water, better still bath water, running out into the drain. The utter need for it. This would be called stalking today. Perhaps it would have been called stalking back then, if anyone had caught me.

This gets a decent laugh. How I scribbled her phone number on the back of my hand and let myself be intoxicated by the erotic power which that pattern of numerals released. Pornography by numbers. I think I might be on a limb here, but not a bit of it. Much nodding and identifying; the women as well as the men. On I go. How I came to see my other excesses with terrible clarity after I put down the glass. How I still try

96

and see a particular woman as she was twenty-five years ago. 'A particular woman.' So mealy-mouthed, and in such an English way. From the same origins of superstition and diffidence that have given us *The Scottish Play* for *Macbeth* and Another Place for the House of Lords, or indeed the House of Commons. Depending on which one you're in.

It is at this moment that I do believe I see her - the particular woman. Imogen. It is mildly comic. She is silver-scaled and vertical, like a fish walking upright. Mist coming off the lake behind her, that scene. I manage to eradicate it. All this talk of dreams and visions, that's what does it. I leave the subject, try to get grounded and head into the final straight with my theory of why the fellowship works. Speaking as a doctor. Yes, I really do say that. The arrogance of it, passing itself off as helpfulness. For shame, as my grandmother used to say.

I talk about it as the breaking of a tyranny through democratic action. It's a plain enough thesis, and although I'm speaking for effect, I also happen to believe its analogy holds. Alcohol becomes the tyrant. It does what tyrants do. Kills, maims, tortures, impoverishes, drives mad, sends into exile, you name it. Alone we can't topple him. Join forces though, making our combined strength greater than the sum of its parts, and see how vulnerable he becomes. Pathetic even.

So we're back with that trinity that was with us in the kitchen: here's Leadership (the founding fathers); Democracy (the structure of the meetings); and Faith (God's everywhere you look. You can't miss Him.) At last I approach my ringing conclusion, all about the only way back into the servitude of the dictator alcohol being down through the neck of the bottle into the dark hell below. A quick reference to the Chilean miners here to spice my argument with topical reference and heroic outcome.

I have often savoured the ideal of narrative as healing agent, even if this pushes me into bed with Maurice, but now I savour the conviction of it too. I wish he could see this, while also sticking to my wish that he never ever sets foot in my AA space. I make such an impression on myself. I seem so passionate, so convinced, so given over to this life. I would go along with me if I were someone else. I don't often think this.

It's a wonderful sensation. Dangerous too, naturally. Didn't we all catch Blair in the act of convincing himself of his own goodness? And didn't we all want to throw up as the piety settled compliantly on his features? I expect that something unspeakable, like moral smugness, is assembling itself handsomely in one of my recesses. And yet I believe what I'm saying. I do, I do. Just as I have no choice but to believe that I have become part of a powerful and under-known movement, as full of its own beliefs, commitments, mythologies, texts and martyrs as Christianity on one side and Marxism on the other.

Imogen is not going away. On the contrary, she is entering the hall from the back. I never thought she would do this. She is always scrupulous about letting me get on with my fellowship commitments as I see fit. She never interferes, let alone turns up to my meetings. It would be unthinkable. Except that she just has, and is exactly as she was twenty-five years ago - the walk, the clothes, everything; the same demure carriage and down-turned head. As if she is apologising for her presence and trying to draw a minimum of attention; therefore drawing a lot.

It is only when she looks up that I can see it is Serena. She catches my eye and gives a tiny shake of her head to indicate that she's not really here and that I am to carry on as if nothing has happened. Others are looking round to see who the new-comer is. No-one recognises her. They wouldn't, unless they knew her in a civilian context, which happens, naturally; a familiar face from the streets, the shops, the pubs. But no recognition here, as it surely is her first time. Surely. I do what I did at the Jamuna and in the surgery. Or rather, it does it to me, and I redden. It's automatic, like the traffic lights.

I take in her presence as best I can, and I try to process it. But it is too big - a mouthful that would choke you if you had to take it down in one. This has to be broken up and chewed small. The Serenity Prayer begins chiming in my head. More of that relentless good sense from across the pond. That carbolic right-headedness. It plays on the deck of my inner ear: God grant me the serenity... ' Tall order that, at the best of times. '... to accept the things I cannot change... ' OK. Serena Miller is sitting in the room and there is nothing I can do about it. '... the courage to change the things I can... ' Meaning myself, I suppose. My demeanour.

Be relaxed, be cool. Fat chance. OK then, fake it to make it; look relaxed, look cool. You mean lie? When the whole point is transparency? Well, that's a harsh way of putting it, don't you think? Harsh situation old boy. OK, I hereby embrace the imperatives of perjury. Good. Except that it doesn't work. I feel as if there's an unspeakable item, excrement probably, caught in my throat and it's making my face go sloppy-stupid. Only two choices: cough it out and disgust the world, or swallow it and die. This is true paralysis. '... and the wisdom to know the difference.' The Prayer keeps its toughest suggestion until last. While it is reciting itself to me in the disturbed room of my head, my voice, far below, is delivering the final sentences of my Chair.

I experience the mild, welcome coolness of relief for having done all the self-disclosing stuff; so all that Serena will witness will be my run-in along the home straight. I even find myself thanking the Lord, so either I'm taking deception to its next level and hoodwinking myself, or else I am going the way of Clive. I'm also pleased to have avoided the temptation of saying how many drunks and junkies there are in my trade, deep in denial and sicker than their patients.

I wrest back the reins of myself for the last few yards, and am aware of going over the finishing line in one piece. 'I believe that we have become connected to an enormous grid, a powerful field of energy, the force of one another and of ourselves, and that this force has the strength to overthrow the tyrant of alcohol and return to us the lives which he did his best to take. Thank you.'

Something like that. The thank you is a mistake. I know this even as it is coming out, but am powerless to stop it. It makes the whole thing sound like a performance, hence an act. My eager self-critic is at my ear before you can say turkey. A bit ringing, he says, a bit showboating. I admit to having got carried away - to imagining how a politician must feel when he has brought off a barnstormer in front of a home crowd. I could have halted on a sixpence, unhorsed myself and gone flying into the crowd. But I didn't. The room does a big collective exhale, as often happens at the end of a Chair.

Clive's posture slackens in approval, or is it relief, and he beams. Spiritual Sally makes her gracious response to the things I have just said, singling out my honesty and fearlessness and a few other qualities which I could have sworn belonged to someone else.

The sharing starts and I nod as the spectators identify with what I was saying, then take it on from there, into their own lives of blackest chaos, near death and recovered balance. I smile a serious and grateful smile and feel the kind of pride that doubles as humility.

Am I Blairing? Please God no. The fact is, I love these people. I may not know them very well, and in almost every case I don't know what their surnames are, or their lines of work. I mean I love them in their combined presence, their plurality. I also mean what I say about the overthrow of tyranny. The rhetoric is from a different planet than that of my own professional life, but this is the very reason I feel so at ease with it.

After a while the words go by like a long train and I can't see the joins between the carriages. I become increasingly aware of Serena sitting at the back on the right, and of the ninety minutes being almost up. The big hand is just past the IV. It is crawling, just as it always did in the Priory as the sessions neared the end and I would compute my chances of not having to say anything. There are only two more people left to share before it would be Serena's turn. What will she say if it comes to her? 'My name is Serena and I am an alcoholic'? If so, that's more than she's told her doctor. If not, what is she doing here? Don't answer that.

Without exactly catching her eye, I can see that she is looking at me and smiling. Innocent rather than guileful. And pleasant. Inconveniently pleasant. Before her, there is only Janet and Douglas to come. Planet Janet because of her always talking of having been spaced out, and DIY Douglas because that's the subject he tends to dwell on.

My immediate thought is that I am being stalked. As nothing like this has ever happened to me before, I can't be sure. I certainly never expected to be the object of a stalking. Yet look at the facts, Dr. Newgate. Here is a young woman who played the system at the practice in such a way that she could get to see you when you were not expecting her. What she is doing now is consistent with that approach. She has simply broadened her field of operation.

But then another thought breaks over this one like a following wave. She might genuinely be seeking help for an addiction which is still so early in its development as to be invisible to anyone else. It happens. The rooms are full of such stories. Perhaps hers is one of them. If so, I should feel some sense of pleasure that she is getting involved with the fellowship before her life slips further beyond her control. Heaven knows the genetic predisposition is there; look no further than her parents. In seeking help from a doctor (this doctor) who has a personal knowledge of the conditon, perhaps this is not the act of mischief or provocation that I took it to be. Perhaps it is plain wise. Goodness

There is a sudden noise like a burst of drilling. It comes from Janet and is either an isolated accident or the first shot in a major snoring campaign. She keels over slightly towards Douglas, who props her back up. Rather than wake her, he gets into his own share, which is a harrowing account of his failure to fix his leaking toilet. It has been blighting his life. In case anyone doubts the relevance of his testimony - and there's no reason to think they do - he explains this was just the kind of crisis he used to drink on and then smash the entire bathroom with a lump hammer. 'Battered the bugger till there was nothing left.'

He is still going strong as the minute hand moves across the foot of the clock face. When he's finished, we're five minutes over. Sally taps the pot on the table and we're done. Serenity prayer, pot going round, tradition seven about being fully self-supporting from our own contributions, usual rolling of credits for greeters, literature, treasurer, washing-up and Intergroup, and then we're stacking the chairs back against the wall and leaving the place pristine for Toddlers Group tomorrow morning.

Sally and Clive are onto Serena like wolves, naturally. Big, cuddly, totally well-meaning wolves. I can hear the usual small-arms patter of persuasion going at her point-blank. 'You're in the right place,' 'Keep coming back,' 'It works if you work it.' Plonking but irrefutable truths. She's absorbing it all with patience and goodwill. The crook of her elbow is filling with pamphlets.

Now she is shooting the odd glance across at me as I stand by the table talking to Frankie The Fish (he used to drink like one) and High Street Ken. I can't tell whether she has pointed me out to Clive and Sally as her contact with AA. I consider getting out as quick as I can, with some excuse about Imogen. Always good for excuses, Imogen. Not a good idea. Clive would smell a rat. Instead I decide to move towards the sound of gunfire and join the three of them. Play normal.

I say 'Serena, isn't it?' and she says 'That's right. Dr....I mean William. Hello. I was going to say, what are you doing here, but I suppose that's rather a dumb question.'

She is wearing her don't-worry face for my benefit, as if to reassure me that there is no out-of-order behaviour coming up. Not just now. She gets talking to Sally and I to Clive. I can hear the sound of my worlds grinding together like the bones in an arthritic joint; the space between them down to nothing and the cartilage all gone. He asks me if I know the newcomer and I say no, not really. True. But then I suspect nobody does. The time runs off with me and I ready myself for the altered settlement, where Serena is a vibrant and visible part of this community which I had thought was mine, and was safe.

I think back a bit. I remember wondering whether she had a drug habit of any sort (never forgetting that alcohol is a drug). I also remember reminding myself that GPs should routinely check on the possible role of drugs in patients presenting with depressive symptoms. My hobbyhorse these days, of course, but for good reasons. Did I do this in her case? If so, did I do so thoroughly enough?

I make a polite excuse, only loosely related to Imogen, and go. A quick peck on Sally's cheek, and a 'Speak soon' to Clive. Serena could not be more polite. 'Good to see you,' she says. I don't look at her for long enough to see if there is some other activity in furious play beneath the surface of her beautiful and unravaged face. A terrible beauty, to rip Yeats off.

Outside, walking home, I remember our last exchange in the surgery. The cryptic confidence with which she let me know she would see me again before too long. What were her exact words? I should remember. It was barely more than a fortnight ago. 'Bye for now.' Something like that. So she was planning this, even then, perhaps earlier still. The usual story with alcoholism is that people who've got it try to hide it. Futile of course, but concealment and denial are to the condition as spots are to measles. The lying is a symptom. Rarer, much rarer, is the opposite phenomenon - people claiming to have the disorder when they do not. They have their reasons, usually related to the need to draw attention to themselves.

I wonder whether Serena is one such, and whether she might be about as much of an alcoholic as Miss Piggy (bad example; food issues). I don't think so. I somehow believe her to be genuine, even though I still have a long way to go before I have faith in my diagnostic skills. Now the noise I begin to hear is not so much a grind as something pitched high with tension; the weird noise of that great string, or whatever it is, about to break at the end of *The Cherry Orchard*. The sad severing of old certainties. Enough. Day at a time and all that. Sleep. No concentration left. All snatched by the projections spooling away beyond my control.

October 12th. The bus out of Hexham crawls up into the moor like the last wasp of the year. The driver bangs it down to second and then first gear on Brownheads Hill, with the game old engine coming back in higher and harder after each pause. A matter of life and death. The pressure starts clicking in my ears as the road curves up to its first point of serious elevation. No trees up here, and the bareness gives a beautiful slow line to the long slantings of the land. We're in the middle of the top of England - Lakes away to the west, old coal country to the east, Dales to the south and bits of wall and debatable lands to the north. This is a place that people pass through on their way to other points. Things that stay fall slowly apart - the old workings, the roads, the houses, my father - and few people know they are here. That's how the residents like it, although here I'm generalising from a sample of one. He may complain about lifelines vanishing and the world forgetting, but the offence of that is nothing compared to the outrage of The Pitman's going gastro. I can't wait to see it.

I've looped up England the long way that makes no sense other than visually. East Coast mainline Kings Cross to Leeds. Anything to avoid Branson's mean little Pendolinos out of Euston. Then Leeds to Skipton and the Settle-Carlisle Line, the one they tried to kill through negligence but now vaunt as a lovely old strip of heritage.

This time I break the journey at Dent, partly because I always wanted to see the village that lies four miles down the valley from the station bearing its name, and partly so that I can get to the little Quaker meeting house at Briggflatts, just the other side of Sedbergh.

I once met Basil Bunting, who wrote the great poem called *Briggflatts*, through the parents of my school friend Oldroyd. Father was a sports sub, or something like that, with Bunting on the *Newcastle Journal*. Old tweed jackets and pipe smoke; anecdotes in pubs. I read the poem and became haunted by it.

> Brag, sweet tenor bull,
> descant on Rawthey's madrigal,
> each pebble its part
> for the fells' late spring.
> Dance tiptoe, bull,
> Black against may.
> Ridiculous and lovely
> chase hurdling shadows
> morning into noon.

The meeting house is everything I'd hoped it would be - a sort of counter-industrial space where concentrated silence has been manufactured for centuries. It houses conciliation. The only other place I have experienced this is in the AA meetings. There is some common ground between the two bodies. You sit there and stuff happens. Take the body and the head follows, as they say. Perhaps I should be a Quaker. Perhaps that's the place to be if you feel you should go a bit religious, only not too much. Heaven knows they have produced some fine medical men over the years. Lister, the antiseptic surgery man, Hodgkin the pathologist, Newman the public health reformer, and so on.

The room has the beautiful smell of cared-for wood. I sit on a pew and go as blank as I can. Clive would say this is a spiritual moment, and I would not want to see it that way on account of my problems with that word, which I still regard as the property of the self-aggrandising and publicly good. I am not happy with this attitude, and should have the courage to change. Still, for a few moments the worlds of Clive, and Maurice, and Imogen, and Ricky, and Inez, not to say Serena, all park themselves outside and give me a breather.

Then it's north again, Dent to Carlisle and Carlisle over to Hexham on the Newcastle line. Ridiculous route, but so beautiful, so empty. Apart from Carlisle, nothing in the way of big towns. You can still do that in England, if you know how to go. Now, knackered by the moor-top's never-ending brow, the bus hunkers down to about twelve mph. As if it is saying to anyone who will listen - there's only me and a woman about Dad's age, whom I half-recognise - 'It's even steeper than I remembered.'

Up the narrow street that is Knarrsgill, straight out the other side and then nose-down into the dent of Highmoor, which the hills cup like a basin. Into the tiny square, more of a triangle. Why have four sides when three will do? After every absence I forget how small it all is. Like a boy returning as a bigger one. Nothing going on except the benches and the war memorial. For such a little place it supplied an awful lot of Fallen. But then they all did.

The place has shrunk with age, just as people do. Like them, it bears its own baggage, seen here in the foundation traces of the pumping houses and the washing floors. Strange that Dad, pressed into the collieries as a boy, should have ended up in a long-dead lead village. I think he and Mum came here because the Garsides had already done so. Mining country, but without any mining going on. Something like that. I don't think I ever asked.

Never too late. There he is. He's seen the bus from his front window and come down to the foot of Upper Level Row to meet it. He's poised to ask if I had a good run through. Or 'good run through then did yer?' Since he mentioned subsidence, I look to see if the brief line of cottages has visibly tipped. No sign yet. Dad is wearing a look of mild triumph. 'Highmoor man spies bus.' He waves to the vehicle and its driver as if he's the official welcoming party and he wants us to know this is a remarkable thing we've done. Never mind the hills, it's the cuts in services we've had to overcome. And we've done it. We'll be in need of some refreshment.

He shakes me by the hand and looks up into my face. He's too old to become a hugger; wouldn't know quite how to do it. He was designed for the shaking generation and goodness he still has a vice for a right hand. Mine turns to twigs in his and there's a really quite severe pain in the extensor digitorums. Strong as Brian Miller in the Jamuna the other day.

I was wondering if there was something wrong with Dad, and he'd brought me here for one of his announcements. 'Just thought yer should know that young Cowgill's given me six months top so I'll not see eighty-six.' Far from it. On the evidence of his handshake he's in the rudest health and I should be finding space for him in my will. There's been a change of some sort, though. I can't yet be sure what. But he even sounds different than he did on the phone.

'Did you have a good run through then, did you?' he asks.

'Very good, thanks Dad. And lovely to see you.'

'Aye. Rum old route though.'

'Yes. As I think I said on the phone, I wanted to see Brig-gflatts.'

'And so you did.'

'I did, yes Dad.'

'I've heard it's grand.'

'Have you now?' I'm as surprised as I sound. Not because of it being called grand - it is grand - but because it's being called grand by him. Anything being called grand by him.

'Of course they were big up this way and all, y'know.'

'Who's that, Dad?'

'Well. I mean. The Quakers.'

They were. In fact, without them there would have been no Upper Level Row, no mines, no Highmoor, not so much as a once-a-millennium bus service. It was the Quakers who founded the North Pennines Mining Company back in the eighteenth century and their legacy is everywhere you look; in the little parade of street lamps once powered by gas and now used for displays of hanging baskets; in the reading room for the benefit of its employees, now converted into a solid home with a freshly installed loft as the upper storey and the figure 1702 embellished with gold on its road-facing gable; in the road itself, now being gouged back to the roughness of the ground by no repairs and high hard winters.

He gives a wave, part hello and part goodbye, to the woman who was on the bus with me. She walks across the square to her cottage in the lane behind the Pitman's Arms, while Dad and I go along the Row to number seven. There are scones out and the smell of just-made tea. There's the brown spout of the old round pot sticking out from its grey woollen cosy. Mum still in evidence of course, the big photo of the two of them at Dove Cottage standing in front of the books on the dresser shelf.

Yet there's less of her than there used to be. Unless I'm mistaken. Unless I'm comparing it to Clive's house, where you can't look anywhere without running into Madge's face. There is the lifelong ticking of the mantel clock, the treasured Edward Harriman piece that came down from her grandparents in Workington.

We sit and he pours.

'Milk no sugar isn't it.' It is. First time he's remembered.

'It's good to see you, William,' he says.

'Likewise, Dad, likewise.'

'I do appreciate you making the trip.'

'Not a problem, honestly. I should have come up a long time ago.'

'No shoulds.' This is the kind of observation you are more likely to hear in the rooms than in number seven Upper Level Row, Highmoor.

'How've you all been? Young Richard at college and taller than you as I understand.'

'Yes, Ricky is… Richard is…' I dodge 'fine' by force of habit and settle for 'doing very well.'

'Taking after his father, I don't doubt.'

'I'm not sure about that, Dad. He might be taking after his grandfather. After you.'

'Get away.'

'No, really.'

'Planning on going down the mines of West London then, is he?' A bit more like the old Dad, this. And not a bad gag; sharp in its own right as well as setting up a move towards his default setting of how the Bevin Boys gave their youth for the war effort and got bugger all thanks for it. But more of that later.

'Clever lad though?'

'Yes. When he puts his mind to it.'

'Now you're sounding like your own father.' Not quite. With Dad it was always a matter of putting your back into it.

'What I meant,' I go on, 'was the economics and so on. You were good at all that.'

He waves it away and says 'Oh that stuff.'

'No Dad, you were. And remember you were entirely self-taught. It's quite possible Richard got his enthusiasm for it from you. I remember the times you took us round the old workings when he was, what, eleven or twelve.'

Dad nods in recollection. A reversal of roles here. It's normally him who handles the remembering side of things. 'And he asked you who owned it and you said it was the company, more's the pity.'

'Did I say that?'

'Yes. And how it would have been better if the men had managed to get a co-operative off the ground, and… '

'Ah yes,' he says, 'that would have been me. So what are you telling me, William? That I've made a Marxist of him?'

'I'm not sure about that. But you made him think. I remember you telling us how the domestic lead industry had been undercut by the cheap imports from Spain.'

'I don't know about that. I'll tell you what, though, he'll be wanting a share of your house next.'

'Funny you should say that, Dad.'

'And proper representation in any decision-making processes with regard to the distribution of its operational profits.'

'There aren't any.'

'That'll not stop him.'

We both laugh. There is the noise of the bus's engine coughing back into life in the square. It takes two or three panicky whirrings of the starting motor, but then there's the old shake and growl of resurrection. Dad stands at the window as it pulls away entirely empty, past the immovable block of the old winding house, then back up and out for Hexham. We hear the revs climbing with the first gradient, and then nothing. Like the old seams, we are overgrown by silence and left alone.

I look at Dad. After all the years of looking at patients sitting opposite me, it's a habit I can't break. You listen for what they're not saying, look for what they're not doing. Now, with him, as with so many others, I begin to sense the something else, the undeclared agenda which the talking, although pleasant, masks. Perhaps I should disable my doctor function when I see him - and many others I can think of - but I don't know where the switch is.

There is a knock on the front door. It is Mrs. Garside from up the Row, come to return a Pyrex bowl. It is the big one I remember Mum using for the apple crumble. I can almost taste cinnamon on the roof of my mouth. He asks if she'd care for a cup, but she sees me and turns shy. She says hello from the doorstep and I'm expecting her to tell me I've grown.

'Another time, Jack,' she says. 'Another time. But thanks. And for, you know, everything else.'

'Oh that,' says Dad. 'It's a pleasure. And you'll let me know how he's going, won't you. And if he wants owt, for when I next go to Gateshead.'

'It's such a way, Jack.'

'Nonsense.'

'It's the whole day. I can't thank you enough.'

'Then you should stop trying. He's my pal.'

'I know. I do know.'

She turns and goes. She is of course the imminent widow of Douglas Garside, who Dad was saying would not see beyond the insides of the Queen Elizabeth Hospital in Gateshead. Old Duggy, or Young Duggy as he was at the other, vanished extreme of their lives when they had both found themselves crouched and homesick at the Easington coalface.

He sits down again and I say it must be hard for her.

'That's right. Poor lass.'

I find myself going over our usual boundaries of personal observation and tell him she's lucky to have him as a neighbour. I'm surprised to hear the words come out of my mouth. He hears them, but he goes on:

'Can't get out.'

'There's something the matter with her too?'

'Aye. There's things you can't see.'

This could be a reference to my own myopia, my profession's blindness (a favourite theme for all these years) or a general remark about people who aren't well: there's things you can't see. I'd go along with that. So would Maurice, who would embellish it as a new and expensive theory. But I don't want to think about Maurice, and I wish I hadn't allowed myself to.

'Take those poor young men down there.'

'You mean you and the other boys? Back then?'

'No no, William, we're done, us ones. No, them, and their poor wives waiting. Oh by the way, she phoned.'

'Who's that, Dad?'

'Yours.'

I guess Mrs. Garside is making his mind run to wives. I don't think I've ever heard him call Imogen by that word.

'Phoned here?'

'Yes. Imogen.'

Her name sounds extraordinary coming from him. As if there has been a major broadcasting blunder and an unscheduled programme is going out. *Top Tits from Thailand* on the Parliament channel.

'Oh, what did she want?'

'Her husband.'

'Did she say anything?'

'No.'

'Is she all right?'

'She didn't say anything. Except she'd ring back.'

'Oh. OK.'

So what is going on at home? An incident with Ricky? Or Inez? All three of them? God knows. Dad goes out to the kitchen to make a fresh pot. I try to explain the improvement in his demeanour. I do what I do at work and quickly run up a mental list of the possibilities. 1) He has been unwell but is so no longer. 2) He has got fed up with his own grumpiness and is trying a different tack. 3) He has come through. Almost all his contemporaries have gone away, mostly through reasons of death, and he is proud of being one of the last men standing. 4) He has become useful. Mrs. Garside is clearly grateful to him, and this in turn has affected him. 5) He has found love. Or it has found him. 6) He has let go of all the resentments which filled him with that sustaining bitterness. 7) He has finally come to terms with his own widowhood, twenty-five years after the event. He has even forgiven Dr. Cowgill Sr., and me, for the great diagnostic failure. 8) A miracle has occurred.

Thank you, Dr. Newgate.

'Them and their poor wives waiting,' he says again as he comes back in with the teapot.

'I'll tell you this though. It's not the triumph that they're painting it. All very well the President of Chile waiting at the pithead to glad-hand the lads as they come up, but they should never have been trapped down there in the first place. These mines were being kept open on the cheap. Just waiting to fall in. Owners should be taken for every penny.'

The phone rings on the sideboard. Dad picks it up, listens, says 'He's here now, I'll pass you over,' and does so.

'William,' says the voice.

'Yes,' I reply, realising straight away how easy it was for Dad to have mistaken Serena Miller for Imogen. I knew their voices were similar, but this is the first time I have heard Serena's over the phone. They are not so much similar as identical.

'How are you?' she asks. There is an edge of concern that makes me feel I have to give an account of myself.

'I'm fine,' I reply.

She gives a light laugh and says 'I thought we weren't meant to say that.'

How on earth did she know I was here? How did she get Dad's number? I would ask her, but then he would wonder, very understandably, why I was asking Imogen such a question. Perhaps I should quickly stop pretending, for his benefit, that it is my wife. But this is a tiny window of opportunity. The meanest of skylights. If I'm to say 'Oh, it's you,' I must do it at once. But I don't. In the time it takes me to consider this option and not take it, the chance has passed.

It's not even as if Dad would mind, or disapprove, if he knew it was someone else, another woman. For all his old-boy ways, there's a social liberal in him. I sometimes wonder how it got there. Maybe it was always present, like the seams in the ground. But the seconds go on and I am bound on the path of pretence. What would Maurice say? I don't want to know and I wish I would stop plaguing myself with such questions. 'Like life,' he would say, dazzling us all with his flair for plainness.

The trouble with lying, even lying by omission, is the after-sales service you lumber yourself with. So, by letting these seconds pass without saying 'Oh, Serena. Yes,' I'm stacking up an unguessable quota of later obligations. To say nothing of the present. Dad's not exactly earwigging. That's not his thing. But it's a tiny cottage, there's only one room with a phone, and we're both in it. It's like being a teenager again. Single phone tethered to the wall so you can't move round the house; everyone listening in when she calls, whoever she is, even if they're pretending not to.

I have, naturally, gone double red. Once for it being Serena, and once for the deception that I've taken on. She guesses the query in my voice and decides to let me off lightly. 'I bumped into your lovely sponsor - Clive, isn't it - and he mentioned that you were up seeing your father near Hexham. Newgate, Hexham, directory inquiries or whatever they call it now, only one Newgate. No problem. Unique. But how lovely for you to be seeing your father. I bet it's absolutely gorgeous just now. It's not an area I know, more's the pity, but my mother had an aunt in, I think, Bampton, would that be right. Bampton?'

'Yes. Quite possibly.'

'And she used to say how completely divine it is up there and how people still didn't really know about it, in spite of England being really quite tiny when you compare it with other places. And the mines. That must be, goodness, that must be so, I don't know, romantic.'

'In a way, yes, I suppose they are.'

'Although heavens, when you look at those poor Chilean miners on TV. Not romantic at all. Incredible to see that little space capsule thing peeping down into the cave and then next thing it's peeping up out of the ground. Oh, but the poor things. Apparently, you know, in the first seventeen days, when they were only having a tablespoonful of tuna every forty-eight hours, and a glass of water strained through a lorry's radiator or something, I mean, can you imagine. Well, of course you can, you're a doctor and actually, despite being incredibly modest, a very brilliant one who can see into people just as if you've got x-ray vision which, I suppose, in a medical sense, is exactly what you've got. I wonder if it's true that when they all thought they were going to die, they started talking about, you know... '

'Cannibalism?'

'Yes. What do you think? I mean, now they're saying they only meant it as a joke, but honestly, I bet it must have been so tempting for them to look around and start calculating, you know, who was the plumpest, who was the greediest, and stuff like that. Well, of course the plumpest would be the same one as the greediest most likely, so they would have been the obvious candidates. How are you anyway?'

'Really very well. As you seem to be.'

'Yes. Very well. And, as I say, incredibly grateful to you.'

'Well, that's extremely generous.' The word 'Serena' is practically jumping out of my face of its own accord. It would lend a certain serious intent to what I say, or want to say. Instead I am stuck with a blank where the name should go. I try and think what I might be saying to Imogen, and the best I can come up with is 'Everything OK at home?'

She finds this rather an odd one, and replies: 'It's as well at home as it is with me. As there's only one of me. Home for me is nothing to do with my father, which I'm sure you would agree is a good idea. Wouldn't you?'

'I don't know. It's very hard for me to say without… '

'Without more details?'

'Yes, basically.'

'Well yes, I totally understand, and will give you all the details you want when I next see you. When are you back actually?'

'Oh, the next few days.'

'We all miss you enormously. Do you know that?'

'We all?'

'Yes. Clive, obviously, who clearly dotes on you. Can't think why. Joke. And Frankie the Fish, who's fascinating when you get to know him a little. You'd never guess he'd been a stripper, would you? And Spiritual herself, who I love to bits and who I'm thinking of asking to sponsor me as you're meant to get a woman, aren't you.'

'Generally, yes.'

'I mean, if you're one yourself.'

'Quite.'

Hearing her talk about these people who are new in her life

but quite established in mine, I wait for the resentment to hit me; the envy, the awkwardness, the fear of being invaded by her in a place of safety that was my own. But these feelings don't come and don't come. Nor do I want them to. Who am I to say who should or should not come into AA? The general wisdom is that if you are unsure whether you have a drink problem or not, come to the meetings, listen to other people's stories, see if you relate to them. And this is precisely what Serena has been doing. I'm all for it. The only problem for me is how I deal with this particular phone call. It is taking me back to adolescence and the agony of personal phone calls made with people listening, in the pre-mobile world of family landlines. How did we survive?

Here I reach for an old trick, and have no idea if it works. With my back to Dad, I put my hand hard down over the mouthpiece so that Serena can't hear me say: 'All right, love, well, great to hear all the news. Give Ricky a hug, and my best to Inez, and really looking forward to see you again in a few days, but obviously will ring again before then. Mobile useless as ever here of course.'

While I'm doing that, Serena is saying 'Are you still there? William?' Good. I remove my hand and say: 'Yes. Still here. Bad line I'm afraid.'

'You don't mind my calling you, I hope.'

I reply: 'I don't know,' which is the truth catching me unawares.

'Better go now, though.'

'If you think it's inappropriate, although sorry about that word.'

'I didn't say that.'

'No, but I was going to say that if you ever did, ever do think that it is - inappropriate - I don't actually think you'd be right.'

'Oh. OK.'

'For reasons that you don't yet know, but which I will go into when you're back. OK?'

I say 'OK', and then round it off with one of the least organic (yes, and least appropriate) *Ciaos* I have ever done. Silence in the room again. I am learning to love the way it comes back in when the time is right. Unconditionally, like forgiveness. I try to formulate something about the beauty of the late afternoon sun on the tops in the middle distance. Nothing comes to mind, so I go along with the silence. Interesting that we use a word like break to describe the way we end it. As in breaking something of value, like a family plate.

I try to work back through the conversation, but from Dad's position, wondering how it would have struck him. I reckon he must have heard a few phrases separated by long gaps: 'Yes, quite possibly; really very well; very generous of you; cannibalism,' and then the oddly formal sign-off with best wishes to Inez and so on.

Eventually, after he's poured again and we're back facing each other, he looks at me and says with a definite twinkle: 'They do go on, though, don't they.' We both laugh and then he turns to Mum's big round shiny pre-cancerous face and says

'Nothing personal, love.'

October 13th. I stay in the Pitman's Arms. Dad was so disparaging about it on the phone that I thought it can't be entirely without merit. He offered me a spare bed, but that would mean setting up in the downstairs room, and us getting in each other's way in the mornings. Much better to stay somewhere else and then meet up later in the day.

Graeme and Josh, who run the pub, are delightful. They've been friends from St. Martin's Art College and did very well from an interior design partnership for pubs on the upgrade. There's a framed cutting in the hall, from the *London Evening Standard*, about how their company, called Inn, were without equal in nurturing the inner restaurant of the pub without.

They do a whole range of dishes which Highmoor probably

never saw before their arrival: goats cheese soufflé with puy lentils and basil foam; Prawns Piri-Piri and brown bread; ham hock terrine with onion chutney and sour dough bread; pigeon breast with butternut squash risotto and wine sauce; and more. How can it not offend Dad? I now remember that the place, while it was still just a pub, was run by another ex-miner from Chester Moor. Graeme and Josh have tastefully left some of the old photos on the walls.

Graeme does the cooking and Josh is front-of-house, all bonhomie and welcome, and boundless enthusiasm for their new venture. They both refer to it as The Project. 'Wonderful people here,' says Josh. Perhaps, but who are they? And where? The saloon and restaurant area are completely empty. However, through the retained feature of the old serving hatch I can see the signs of indigenous life - the profiles of two leathered old faces with grey wisps growing out from under their flat caps.

They are supping beer (there's a Durham Brewery tap) from pint tankards and concentrating on their card game. From the matchsticks on the table, I guess it must be the famous local version of cribbage. Famous because of its being incomprehensible to anyone beyond this handful of men. It will vanish when they do.

The walls of their snug are nicotine-yellow, untouched by the improving tide which has washed through every other pocket of the old building. There are about four or five of them in there. One of them is offering token recognition of the smoking ban by standing at the open side door and puffing out. Then one of the others tells him to close the door as there's a draught, and in he comes with his roll-up still going.

The smoke curls and hangs and even wanders through the hatch. No-one complains. You might have expected them to, but that's not how it goes here, where ethnic style is reckoned to be better for business, and for community relations, than health 'n' safety. There is a real coal fire which they are replenishing from their own supply, and a pin table in the corner.

I remember it from when we stayed near Alston for weekends and came here as a 'treat'. I used to fling the weight wildly around the pole and get hearty cheers for making it come to a standstill without having managed to knock a single skittle down. I thought that was the idea. It was a central entertainment of the pub in those days, but it looks so tiny and irrelevant now. I can also remember the two men's faces, now three decades heavier, but when they turn to see who the newcomer is, I can see that this is not mutual.

They sit there like the remnants of an old army that has made an accommodation with the new occupying forces. These duly arrive, and by eight o'clock the dining room is almost full. Just as the minerals once came out of the ground, so these new people have come in from the hills. You can't quite see how they have got here, but there's no denying that they have appeared.

I lack the social ornithology to define them by their plumage, but I would say there's some Fat Face sleeveless quilting going on. Maybe not Fat Face, but up a bit from your Blacks and your Millets. Cordings possibly, plus some very clear signs of Jack Wills among the younger men with their dated preppiness - Hugh Grant voices and floppy forelocks. Common in its own way, Ricky would say. But then he says the same of the 'arriviste' (he loves that word) Windsors, with their bogus tartans and showy houses.

From the talk, which is so loud it could make eavesdroppers of the most incurious souls, I gather that one of the groups is from Bunkhouse, the famous (i.e. I've heard Ricky mention it) recording studio in the converted block I passed in the bus just outside the village. Another is from one of the many film companies who find in the empty landscape the perfect setting for their werewolves or aliens or young lovers on the run.

One of the men at that table looks like Steven Spielberg. He even sounds like him, although there must be any number of bright, bearded Americans travelling in the comfort of late middle age. The woman next to him, who is also American and famous-looking, is calling him Steve. Maurice told me at the practice the other day that he and his wife had definitely seen the great director walking by the river at Richmond and making a square with his fingers in front of his face as if it was a camera lens.

Josh sees me looking, and confirms that it is indeed Spielberg, but says that he and Graeme have a policy of not bothering their famous customers. They treat them as any others, and only one or two have taken exception. There is a retired solicitor and his wife who have come up from Middleton-in-Teesdale for the food. They look as happy as honeymooners, everything paid off, kids totally done, no interest in the globally famous, no discouraging murmurs about anything from the GP, happy to discover they still like each other now that the distractions of thirty years have gone.

Everyone takes their time over the menu, coming across even more options on the other side. One of the old boys from the snug breaks cover and goes for the Gents. As he is crossing the restaurant floor he manages to burp and fart simultaneously - great rattling reports from another world. No intention to abuse, as far as I can tell. Just what he does. Always has, and damned if he's stopping now. I'm expecting shock, but there's none.

A woman on the American table starts laughing uncontrollably, and Spielberg says: 'Now Meryl, that's rude.' Which only makes her laugh harder. The man re-appears, pulling his fly back up as though it's a great weight from a deep hole, and heads back to the snug. The laughter has got to Spielberg now. He takes himself off to the far wall to collect himself by pretending to look at the Historic Highmoor photos. I can see them drawing him in. It's the one with Dad in that he is concentrating on. He reads the caption aloud: 'Bevin Boys Reunion, 1993. Easington Pithead 1993.'

'Well,' he says, 'Mr. Bevin sure put himself about. There's thirty or forty of them here. We know the guy, don't we; health service reformer, yeah?' A young man in tailored tweed goes over to join him. I guess he's an academic of some sort. A researcher. He says 'That was Bevan with an a.' 'Oh yeah,' says Spielberg. 'Welsh guy who made all the speeches.'

'Yes. Easy error. We all still make it over here, assuming we have even heard of them. No, this was Ernest Bevin, the war secretary. He was responsible for the recruitment drive for the young men to work the pits when the experienced miners were joining the armed services.'

'OK.'

'It was conscription by ballot. Every month his assistant would draw two numbers from a hat. If your national service number ended in one of them, then you were bound for the mines. Called up but sent down, so to speak.'

Not an original line, but the young man would not disabuse Spielberg if he thought it was. 'There was a degree of resentment from those who felt their own contributions were inadequately recognised. And many stories of disability benefit being refused because the injuries were not incurred in combat.'

He sounds a polished performer, probably another of the TV historians whom I've missed. 'Many of them were hardly more than schoolboys. They knew nothing of the mining industry and would rather have gone to the front with their pals.' His voice is carrying clearly through the hatch and into the snug, where the men listen impassively and carry on with their game.

'Over here,' he goes on, indicating another photograph of smiling men of a certain age, 'we see the first of the Boys' reunions. Nineteen eighty-nine, at the Chatterley Whitfield Mining

Museum. Why so late? It's an interesting question.'

Not to mention, his own question. I'm taking one of my irrational dislikes to this young man. It happens with patients from time to time, and falls on me like a bag of quick-drying hatred. Terrifying. I hope to God they never notice. It can be brought on by a look, a posture, a phrase. In such cases I try to rein in my alarming contempt, for professional reasons. No such constraints here. I have him down as a confident contrarian who, when it comes down to it, is just another grim little toady.

A bitter diagnosis, but there we are. 'The records of their service had been destroyed, as a result of which many felt that their work had been officially de-recognised, as it were. Indeed it was not for another six years that they were allowed to take part in the Remembrance Day Service in Whitehall.'

Spielberg is nodding gravely and the young man is forging on: 'Here, in the back row, we see some familiar faces. Well, very familiar to an Englishman.'

'And to an American too, I can assure you,' says the Hollywood legend, pointing to a man with a full head of grey hair and an energetic smile. 'That's, you know, the guy who did the comedies. Pants coming down all the time. You just said the place.'

'I did?'

'Sure. Whitehall. Whitehall Farces. Brian Rix. Well I'll be.'

'It is indeed,' says the young man with an astounding ability to sound patronising to the world's most successful film-maker. 'Sir Brian Rix.'

'Right,' says Spielberg. 'All that work for the sick kids. What a man.'

'And this is Jimmy Savile, whom you might remember as one of the early, ah, dee-jays. And the comedian Eric Morecambe, one half of the comedy duo… '

'Morecambe and Wise. Sure. And unless I'm mistaken, that's Shaffer right there. Not Tony. Peter. *Amadeus, Equus.*'

'Indeed so. And Stanley Bailey, chief constable of the Northumbria Police, who, I believe, used to come this way a fair amount.'

'And these are all Bevin Boys,' says Spielberg. 'And they all got forgotten?'

'For a while, yes.'

'That's some story.'

'You ought to film it, Steve,' says the woman at the table.'

'Sure. Any women involved?'

'Not really, no.'

'You know, irrepressible matriarchs, that kind of thing.'

'Hey Steve, there's not need for that,' she says.

'I'm just trying for you, Meryl.'

'You're always trying for me, Steve.'

'I like to help my friends get work.'

'Yeah, like offering me *Warhorse*.'

'I know people who'd've jumped at it.'

'Horses too.'

He makes a take-no-notice wave with the back of his hand. They have a lively double act going.

Suddenly Josh says from behind the bar: 'You know his father was one of the Boys.'

'Whose father?' asks Spielberg.

'His,' says Josh, pointing at me. 'I hope you don't mind, Dr. Newgate.'

'Not a bit,' I reply truthfully.

'Well there's a thing. And is he, may I ask... '

'Still with us, yes. Very much so.'

'My name's Steven.'

'I'm William. Or Bill. It's a pleasure to meet you.' I deliberately don't say how I've enjoyed his films as he must be sick of all that. Besides, I could easily make a gaffe and mention one that wasn't his. *Goodfellas*.

'Yes, he was in the mines. Joined in the war and then stayed on.'

'And he lives here?'

'Yes. In Upper Level Row. Just across the square.' Then I hear myself saying 'You can meet him if you want,' and him replying 'That would be an honour.' One of the serious males at the table gives a cautionary 'Er' in a loud baritone. He looks exactly like Al Gore, living on the border between being heavy and being fat, but he can't be. I know his political star has waned and he's done some film-making of his own, but surely not. 'Early start, remember, Steve.'

The food comes and they all fall on it. The heavy man is distressed by the unAmerican portions and orders the same again. I think it was a pork tenderloin in honey and grain mustard sauce, but it vanished too fast to be sure. Its final seconds were a blur. Spielberg gives me a DreamWorks card and scribbles his own number on the back. 'So give us a call, Bill.' He sounds as if he means it. 'And my best wishes to your father.'

The bedroom smells of rich woman's soap. How do I know? I don't. It's just a guess. All beautifully done up. Looks very Laura Ashley to me, but I'm out of my depth here. It must be classy though because you can always judge the quality of a hotel or a B-and-B by the performance of its shower mixer. Mostly they either freeze or scald and there's nothing in between except the tiny temperate instant as the thing yaws off to the other extreme. Like people in the permanent grip of mood alteration. This one settles beautifully in the middle ground; all sensitive and obedient in the pressure department, too.

I hear the phone go in the bedroom. Long single rings of an internal call. Must be Graeme or Josh. What time would I like breakfast. Or Steven Spielberg. No, it's Serena. 'Oh, William, it's me again, hi. I'm so sorry to ring again, but I felt I had to apologise for ringing earlier, when you were at your father's.

You know how we're meant to apologise promptly if we've been out of order, and so that's what I'm doing.'

No need for me to ask the 'how' question. 'I googled accommodation in the Highmoor area and there's not a lot is there. There's one called Moor Lodge, which sounded a bit more you than the Pitman's Arms, I hope you don't me saying that because it's absolutely not meant as a criticism, in fact if anything the reverse. It looks lovely from the photo, with those incredible hills behind it. Anyway, the woman at Moor Lodge knew who you were, and we chatted a little about you, and your father, I hope you don't mind, it was actually she who wanted to talk much more than me. So sad about your mother, I can quite see why your father was so upset, even though it would obviously be wrong to blame it all on Dr. Cowgill, as you probably know better than anyone.'

There is a silence, which is nothing more than my failure to say anything, and her running out of words, for the moment.

'Are you there, William?'

'Yes. I'm here.'

'You sound a bit… are you all right? Probably very tired.'

'Yes, that's certainly true. I am very tired.'

'Poor you. I really feel for you. Very hard seeing your parents. Well, look at me. I basically don't do it. Well obviously I can't see my mother although I would love to. Poor old thing. Passed down the illness to me, didn't she. That's what happens, isn't it. I've been reading.'

Oh Lord, another patient kept more up to the minute than her GP through days and nights of net-trawling. 'There is quite often a genetic predisposition, yes,' I say. 'I think that's generally accepted.'

'I hope you don't mind me talking to Clive, and Sally, and the others.'

What others? My mind can't track all the possibilities of who she has befriended. I lie that no, it's perfectly all right.

She carries on: 'It occurred to me since we last spoke that you might mind. Just because they are your friends, and people can be quite funny like that. Actually, I don't mean funny because it's perfectly understandable. But then again, when I thought about it, I realised that you're far too aware to fall into the trap.'

'Trap?'

'Of minding.'

'Aware?'

'Yes.'

'Of what?'

'It's meant as a compliment.'

'Thank you. I suppose one shouldn't inquire what people mean by compliments. I'm sorry.'

'We are apologising a lot, aren't we?'

'I don't know, Serena. Are we?'

My first direct use of her name. Even to have said it feels like a transgression. Dr. Newgate and I are working to separate agendas. I say it again. 'Serena.'

She senses something difficult coming down the line and gets in quick. 'Before you say whatever it is you are going to say, can I just tell you something. It won't take long, I absolutely promise.'

'Go ahead then.'

'Just that, you don't have to worry.'

'I see. Thank you.'

'What you said to me in the surgery, when I was last there, you were absolutely right. You probably know you were but are too modest to say so. I should be looking elsewhere.'

I prepare myself for hearing that she will never contact me again, and I wonder how I will react to that. Relief and regret probably, to use words that are far too mild for the emotions in question.

'So anyway,' she continues, 'I've left.'

'How do you mean?' I understand only too well.

'I mean I'm no longer your patient. Isn't that good?'

'I'm not sure about 'good'.'

'You're not sure about anything, are you?'

'What.'

'I shouldn't have said that, I'm sorry. I mean, aren't you a little bit relieved, even though you're too polite to say so, that I won't be coming into your surgery any more, saying the things I say, being the things I am? You don't have to say anything, honestly.'

'Well. That's good then.'

'I'm going to leave you in peace, but before I do I want to say that I think you are the most marvellous man. Also that you judge yourself far too harshly and prosecute yourself more cruelly than you would if you were a serial killer in the dock. Also,'

'That's an awful lot of alsos.'

'No, let me. I want to say that if doctors are meant to be in the business of saving lives, then you, William, are a living demonstration of that job description. There. I think you understand me. I only wish that I could find a way to repay you properly.'

I want to say 'But I've done nothing,' and find myself again prevented by the ambiguity of the words. So nothing is what I say. The silence grows and spreads as it does in rooms and chapels. We both know the other is still there at the end of the line. Silence as conversation. They come to an end simultaneously, her side and mine, and when we hang up we do so because we know the other one is doing the same. A stranger might take it as an ending.

October 14th. Back over to Dad's after breakfast. He's sitting at the table and his eyes are wet. In the low morning sun from above Bunkhouse Hill they look as thick as bottle bases. Then I notice Mrs. Garside across the room in the easy chair. She is also moist about the face and I assume her husband must have died in Gateshead and she has come down the Row to give Dad the news. But I am running on too far. I think she is quite regular here. It's barely ten in the morning and she almost says as much.

'Your father's been so good to me, you know.'

She offers to go back to her house and leave us with each other.

'A man and his boy need their time together.'

Dad and I both object and she happily stays. As neither of them are talking about Douglas, I don't ask after him. Same as usual, I'm guessing. On the way out, in other words. No, the reason for their tears is on the little screen in the corner. It's one of those TVs that have seen the information revolution conduct a wholesale transplant of the planet's nervous system, without offering a nod in that direction. It seems to have been there since *Hancock's Half Hour* and *On The Buses*, looks black and white even though it's technically colour, and is longing to show the restful stillness of the BBC test card.

Right now though, it is running footage of the Chilean miners coming out of that scary shaft from the San Jose pit. Some time in the small hours the foreman, Luis Urzua was the last man up, and Dad and Mrs. Garside have been watching it as if it were live. 'Sixty-nine days,' she tuts. 'Sixty-nine days, and the first seventeen of them without a peep from above. The poor loves.'

'Aye,' says Dad. 'Must have felt they were dying alive.' You couldn't put it better than that. Dying alive. Perhaps only someone who has spent days and years in the cramped enormity of the earth's crust could coin that form of words.

'Spoonful of tuna every forty-eight hours,' she goes on. 'Glass of water strained through the radiator of a truck. I ask you.'

'Well now, Mary, we'd best take note as we'll all be living like that after young Mr. Cameron's through with his cutting. I say, what a disgrace.'

Sensing politics and the old anger, Mary Garside comes up with a witty deflection towards me: 'I hope they managed something a little more appetising for you at the Pitman's.'

I assure her they did, without singing its praises too much. For all I know, her husband might have been one of the players in the snug before he was taken ill.

'Many people in, were there?' asks Dad. I assume he'd be happy for the place to be blowing tumbleweeds, but again I'm wrong. He sounds interested and asks me who I met.

So I tell him Steven Spielberg was there and said he would like to meet Dad. No point in embellishing a plain fact like that.

'Oh,' says Dad with a flicker of recognition. 'From the garage out back of Slaggyford. Nice lad. How's he going? Hoping to set up in Haltwhistle as I remember.'

'No, Dad, not that one. Another Steve. Makes films.'

'Oh very good,' he says, more polite than interested. No assistance coming from Mary Garside, who observes that we're not great ones for film folk round here, wouldn't you say.

Their attention is grabbed back by the little screen, which is re-running the pictures of Luis Urzua being hugged by President Pinera. The miner looks quite unruffled by his sixty-nine days in the nearly-morgue of two thousand feet below.

'Two thousand's deep,' says Dad. 'When you think, that's two-thirds of the tallest mountain in England.'

'Scafell,' says Mary.

'Scafell Pike as it happens, but we'll let that go.' They laugh at something. His reasonableness, I think.

Pinera is looking joyful in his solidarity gear. Manly red overalls topped off with the inevitable white helmet. These always give executives the look of pushy tourists, even when it's just architects on building sites. Dad's onto it. 'More's the pity he didn't turn up when the mines were rotting on account of the inspectorate taking back-handers.'

'Oh Jack,' says Mary. 'You and Douglas. You see back-handers everywhere.'

'Maybe that's because they are,' says Dad. 'Look at him, with his smooth hair and his millions of pounds.'

'I think you'll find it's pesos, Jack.'

He pretends not to have heard her and carries on: 'Look at him. Next he's coming here, you know.'

'Get away.'

'It's a fact.'

'To Highmoor?'

'No no.'

'Only joking.'

'England. See the Queen. I ask you. You run the mines down so's they collapse on the men inside, then you get your engineers to haul you out of the doings and say the heroes of the mines are the true wealth of your nation and then it's off to Buckingham Palace for tea with Her Majesty. Probably Downing Street and all so's young Mr. Cameron can get the benefit of his wisdom on cost-cutting in essential services.'

So he hasn't gone, the old Dad, he's just been resting. Maybe I get the grouchy version on the phone because he's had a couple too many before calling me. I do wonder. The camera cuts to a Catholic priest who is hailing the miracle of Los Trente-Tres as the work of the Lord. That makes three or four of them, all from different faiths, claiming the rescue as the product of their own proprietorial brand. I expect Clive will be doing the same at St. Stephen's Sunday, and meaning it too.

And the clever one - Barney, I think - who used to be a curate in Devon but who now manages a hedge fund ('I wanted to do something useful'), will now be mining the Chilean imagery for one of his secular sermons on escaping from the darkness of our own incarceration. Harmless, I suppose. And human. I did it myself just now. 'Mining the Chilean imagery.' As for Auden, whom I revere, goodness how he plundered this very ground for metaphor.

The scene grows mesmeric and oddly timeless. These men and boys - sixty-three down to nineteen - coming up out of the ground in the Chile-coloured pellet. Then the bottom of the thing reappearing through the roof of that dreadful cave to pick up the next man. There's the dated modernity of the space age, a Wallace and Gromit contraption being inched up from its nightmare basement with the freeze and flicker of the webcam.

The real story is not the men, lion-hearted though they must have been, but the women on the surface who created hell to stop the company allowing the men to, well, as Dad said, die alive. I expect Mary Garside knows this, being a miner's wife and having lived with daily apprehension as her diet. I expect Dad knows it too, but it's not something they're intending to talk about. There is a hazardous old seam where domestic politics and the pit butt up against each other. Plenty of silence there.

Mary Garside's eyes start to well again. She apologises and says it's because one of the young men looked like Douglas at the same age. The Chilean boy, with his fine and beautiful face, is clearly traumatised by what has happened to him. I try to imagine what it must have been like to lie dying next to all these men who have had so much more of a go at life than you, and who are old enough to be your father. The sounds and the smells of them. I come nowhere near it.

Now he is being swallowed into the bottomless embrace of his mother and two big sisters. They look magnificent and unbeatable, all got up as if they are going to a wedding, or a birth. Over the hubbub around the top of the hole, I can hear one of them say something about *nascimento*.

Dad looks for a tissue. There's none about so he goes and gets a couple of sheets from the toilet and hands them to her. They both laugh again, this time at his *gallante*, I guess. She dabs her face, apologises again and says she'd best be going. I say not on my account, which is what I feel. Just as Mum and Dad used to talk openly about certain friends who were 'good influences' on me, so I would now say the same of her effect on him.

He gets up to escort her back to Number Thirteen. I go to shake her by the hand and say how much I've enjoyed seeing her again. She reaches up at me with her face and plants a kiss on my cheek. 'You're a lovely boy,' she says. Then, looking at Dad: 'Both lovely boys.'

He comes back in a moment later, sits down and shakes his head. I say 'Are you all right, Dad?' He nods and says he's fine (no rules against him using that word), but that he's been fretting about Mary Garside. Douglas, whom he's known for nearly seventy years, is down to six stone. Mary misses him dreadfully but breaks down whenever she sees him, which of course makes Douglas feel even worse.

Besides, her back is crippling her, though she's too brave to let on, and it's a total of nearly five hours on the buses there and back. So Dad's taken to making the visits, taking her pies and pasties with him, trying to feed him up and keep him going with the same things she gave him for down the mine. Douglas always looks at them lovingly, but they stay uneaten at his bedside.

For a while they thought it was only emphysema. *Only*, even though it makes you drown alive. Dad says they wished they'd picked it up sooner, but that's... I think he's going to say 'That's doctors for you' as he has done on previous occasions, but I'm wrong. What he says is 'That's Douglas for you. Wouldn't see a soul. Knew there was something up but didn't want to know. Mary tried to get him to see young Cowgill, but Douglas said 'Look what his father did to Jack's wife.' Did to your mother. Which was most unfair seeing as Mum was the same way. Wouldn't see anyone in case they found something and told her she was ill, which she just hadn't time to be. Oh William.'

I've never heard him say those last two words together. Certainly not with such a passionate sadness in the delivery. For a second they upstage the revelation he is making - that Mum was as stubborn as his friend Douglas when it came to consulting doctors.

'We're the problem,' he goes on. 'sometimes it's us. Wouldn't you say?'

'We?'

'The patients. I know I've been hard on your trade all these years, I should say your profession, and I'm sorry for it, I really am. I don't know. It must have been me fastening blame for what happened to your mother. I read somewhere that we do find little tricks for pinning blame on other people when we should be keeping it for ourselves. What d'you reckon to that?'

I reply that what I reckon to that is he's very modern and well in advance of many of my colleagues and my patients. Perhaps it is Dad I should be sharing with. Perhaps the solution is very literally staring me in the face.

So off I go, projecting along these lines, imagining that at last, late in my life and very late in his, I am confiding deeply in him - everything: the confounded Underground dream; how it keeps coming for me on the coat-tails of worthlessness, like the militant wing of poor self-regard; how I have particular problems just now with, well, with so many people: Maurice, Clive and their respective suspicions; Ricky and Inez and their behaviour, which I am very far from understanding, even though I am physically very close to it through living in the same house; Imogen herself, though where to start; Brian Miller and his air of menace towards me. Serious menace. To say nothing of his daughter. To say absolutely nothing of her. I spool through these people, these places, these presences until they blur into a single impossible image.

I take Dad in. He is motionless, taking me in, more doctor than patient.

'How is it all?' he inquires.

'You mean?'

'Aye. The doctoring. And Richard. And Richard's mother.'

Still only the oblique reference where Imogen is concerned. As if he really can't use the syllables that make up the sound, 'Imogen.' Tried but failed. Poor Dad. Poor both of them.

'I expect you've your hands full. Specially these days.'

'I have, Dad. That's true. I think most of us have. But we've a wonderful new practice manager, who we're hoping will make a lot of difference to the running of it.'

'Well that's nothing more than you deserve. Are you glad you went into it, are you?'

'Yes. It's a good practice. The others… '

'No. I mean doctoring.'

'Yes. Well, I don't know what else I'd have done. After all those exams.'

'I was hard on it, William. I shouldn't have been, and I'm so sorry for it. It's a little late for that, I know, but there we are.'

'It's OK Dad. You felt as you did. I understand. Who's to say I wouldn't have felt the same way myself.'

'Her and all. I was hard on her. On Imogen.' Goodness. Again it sounds strange to the point of foreignness, but he's said it.

'Oh I don't know,' I lie.

'No no, I was. And I wish I hadn't been. It was like I couldn't help myself. When I should have been pleased for you. And when she rang, yesterday, I felt, well, I don't know, but I felt, bless you, you're not one for grudges. Sounded just as she used to and all. I wanted to say something but it didn't seem like the time.'

'No.'

'Your mother, you see. Not that I'm blaming her. But she loved you so much that another woman could never have done.

And then, when she died, I suppose I just took it on from there. And I wish I hadn't, William, and I am so very sorry.'

I find myself wanting to hug him. Still not an easy thing to do, although he looks less forbidding than he used to. I also want to tell him that I love him, and see what happens. The idea scares me now less than at any time I can remember. But the phone goes and I make a mental note not to leave Highmoor without doing these things.

'It's for you,' he says, and hands it over.

'Dr. Newgate?' says the American voice.

'Speaking.'

'Oh hi again. It's Steven. Steve. From the Pitman's Arms. Well. I hope this isn't a bad moment.'

'Not at all. How are you?'

'Yeah, we're all good. It was such a pleasure to meet you and talk about those Bevin Boys.'

'You too. My friends won't believe me, you know.'

Bad line. Slipped out in error.

'Aw now.'

'That was my father. Was it him you wanted to speak to?'

'I didn't want to presume.'

'That's very thoughtful of you.'

Dad is gesturing that he'd be happy not to speak to anyone. He underlines this by leaving the house and turning right up the Row, presumably going to check on Mary Garside. I think a good deal of his life now consists of checking on Mary Garside.

'I just called to say we're off on a brief vacation, down in Moustique. And then we have to go back to the States, unfortunately, for an opening. It all gets a bit crazy, I'm afraid.'

'I'm sure it does.' I'd love to express a little more solidarity here. Mr. Heaseman's waterworks problems would prove stressful for anyone, I'd say, but that's not really in the same league as a Hollywood premiere.

'I hope he didn't mind my calling. I got the number off Josh at the Pitman's. Aren't they just swell, those guys?'

'Very much so.'

'And when we're next in Europe, then maybe we can be in contact again. Any excuse to come back to this part of the world.'

'Yes, of course. Well, please get in touch again whenever you feel like it.'

'Well thank you. You know, one of my guys was so fired up about the Boys that he even came up with a title. *The Underground Warriors*.'

'That's very good.'

'You reckon?' No, but I've committed myself. 'We'll get there.'

'I'm sure you will.'

'Great to talk with you, Bill.'

'You too Steve.'

'Bye for now.'

'Bye.'

While Dad's still gone, my eye browses along the bookshelves. All the old walking books which seemed so rugged and forbidding when I was a boy; *Keep Out* by Tom Stephenson, whom my father knew. I really thought the title was a way of telling you not to enter the book, whereas it was a history of access rights to the countryside and campaigns of organised trespass; *An Account of the Mining Districts of Alston Moor, Weardale and Teesside* by Thomas Sopwith; an early edition of the Pennine Way guide published by HMSO, with the pages all scuffed and ragged between Dufton and Greenhead; a book with an AA logo. What's this? It's the other AA, the Automobile Association, publishers of the *Field Guide to the Birds of Britain and Europe*. Some poetry books: a Lakeland anthology, Wilfred Owen, a collected Auden, Palgrave's *Golden Treasury*; a newer anthology, *Staying Alive: Real Poems for Unreal Times*.

Then there's an incongruous bright spine at the end of the shelf. I associate its pattern more with my world than his. Not surprising; it is the *Oxford Book of Clinical Diagnosis*, an old edition which I must have left here one time. Yes, here's my signature at the front, which dates it to student days, when stuff was always going missing. Scuffed pages here too, but the areas of highest usage are quite close together, too local to have been caused by a student. These are the thumbprints of an interested party.

The first leads to Cancer, on which Dad must have boned up, albeit too late. The volume was protruding a little from its neighbours on the shelf, and I guess he has been revisiting these pages for the sake of the Garsides, but not wanting such a book to be hanging round too conspicuously. The second much-read cluster of pages leads to Depression. Someone - I'm assuming it to be him as I'm sure it wasn't me - has run a pencil line down the margin to denote an important passage.

It's the one detailing the symptoms of major depression: change in appetite or weight; psychomotor agitation or retardation; insomnia or hypersomnia; sense of worthlessness or guilt; fatigue or loss of energy; recurrent thoughts of death; poor concentration; and last the literally killer signal that something's amiss: suicide. What was going on? Was he self-diagnosing? Was it for someone else? Plenty of candidates here, though perhaps not the most eager for treatment. I hear his steps outside the window and put the book back on the shelf.

'Everything all right?' I ask.

'Oh, you know. Poor lass. Queen Elizabeth's been on. From Gateshead. It's not looking too clever.'

'Oh Dad. I am sorry.'

'Aye. Tea?'

He makes and pours, and down we sit again. We could have

been here for decades. He's ruminating. Something particular on his mind. This visit is going well for both of us. He knows it and he looks as if he wants to ride this wave of goodwill between us. I could never have guessed that he would do so in the way he now does. Laid across the books on the top shelf is a beige file. He takes it down, leafs through the loose sheets and pulls out a piece of A4 with some typing on it. Old manual characters; splodgy corners on some of them, missing arms on others. An O that needs help from a biro.

'Here,' he says, and hands it across. 'Nowt special, but I thought it might be of interest, given everything.' Then he goes into the kitchen to be out of my way. I can tell, just by the set of his shoulders and the back of his head, that he's wanting my good opinion but would rather eat his foot off than ask me for such a thing. I can almost see his anxiety standing silently in the little low doorway.

It's a poem, and it's called *Seamster*. Nice title. Please be good.

> Some men, as I've been given to understand,
> Interrogate the land,
> Sending their sharp inquiries into the seams
> And so enrich their dreams
> With schemes enabled by their gilded rubble
> They think to buy out trouble.
> And yet, my pet, my cause for pining,
> You're the one who's past divining,
> Gold beyond the power of mining.

Something hits me in the chest. It is just like a thump that is coming from the inside. It will have an effect, but I can't yet tell the full extent of it. Already though, there is a sharp alert behind my eyes, a calling-up of tears that might or might not be used. It was this single word that did it: pet. What he called Mum. The only application of the word that I have ever known. There was always a peculiar softness about the way he said it to her, a sort of caressing sound. I have never heard it since he said goodbye to her, softly and privately next to me at the funeral.

Now there is this thump about it - that's the only word I can use - as if it has put on a boxing glove and jabbed me with my guard down.

He must have registered this because he says 'You right with it?' very solicitously. He is not asking whether it's OK - although yes, that too - but whether I'm all right with it. I nod and say 'Yes Dad. Thanks.'

There's a second page, and a second verse.

> Love, I'm done with darning up the scars,
> The wages of those wars,
> For, as you know, I never had the skill,
> And see, I lack it still.
> You'd tut to see the wayward stitches fall
> Beyond my poor control.
> And yet, my pet, our time and teaming
> Lights me in my darkest dreaming,
> Steers my single-handed seaming.

The same thump again, and at the same point. I'm ready for it this time, but still it gets through my defences.

'Oh it's not up to much, William. I'm very aware.'

'I have to disagree, Dad. I think it's beautiful.'

'Well that's very kind.'

'Kind be blowed.' With those words I'm aware of sounding to him as he has often sounded to me. 'I mean it.'

'A bit rough, like, and you know something, I do feel a bit sheepish, on account of the rhyming.'

'Why? It's very well done.'

'Well now, when I started, when I tried my hand at this,'

'At writing poems?'

'Aye. Yes. When I'd done a few of them, I went along to these

140

meetings. Highmoor Writers' Group. At Jim Charlton's house. You remember Jim. His wife Anne is published in the maga- zines, and is very smart. So she runs the thing, you see, and when I mentioned to Jim that I'd taken to scribbling, he says to come along. And I did, William, and I was so nervous and, you know, they couldn't have been kinder. I felt a chump, mind, as none of the smart ones seem to have much use for rhyming and that. But it's just the way it settled in my head. Oh, and I meant to tell you. That book.'

'What book?'

'Used to be yours. College book. When you were thinking of going that way and not medicine, you remember. The Meta- physicals. John Donne and those ones. And it was you who told me to look at how they were made. Their anatomy, you called it.'

'I said that?'

'Yes, William. You did. We'd been talking about the ground around here, with the shafts and the workings, and you said it sounded almost human, like an anatomy. Then we were on to those poems, I can't think how, and you used the same word. I took your advice and looked them up. And I've an admission to make, which is that after you'd made your mind up about which way your studies should go, I hung onto it. I still have it upstairs. I'd have told you, of course I would have, if you'd asked after it. But... '

'But I never did.'

'No.'

'Well, Dad, I'm glad it's come in so useful. I think it found the right home.'

'I can't thank you enough.'

I wave this away, like I've seen him do in the past, and I feel his presence in me just as I sometimes feel my presence in Ricky. I tell him I am proud of him and his face begins to clench in grief. I put my hand on his shoulder - difficult, knobbly territory - and say I owe him one, after what that poem did to me. He smiles at this, and can't hide his pleasure that it had the effect it did.

October 15th. I say goodbye to Dad in the morning. We don't talk much. We've done that. He's concentrating on Mary Garside, who's already round. Just the one cup and then off. We can hear the bus arrive in the square, switch off and go silent. Mary says 'You've a nice day for it,' and Dad says 'I hope you have a good run through.' I'm at the door and she comes to give me a hug. She's got the habit now. Dad's hand is reaching out for his usual formal gesture of parting. But she nods him on to something more, and he too embraces me. I feel the lean firmness of his back, and the rasp of his chin as it knocks into my cheek. Then we're done and I'm off.

The bus doesn't go all the way to Hexham. On its destination plate it says it will, but then has second thoughts in the course of the journey. The buses do that. Just to let you know they're not going to be second-guessed, not even by a clever medical chap from the south. This one decides to call it a day at Brownheads. If this were somewhere else, I suppose I might take issue with the driver, but the fact is I can't be bothered. Besides, the driver's a lovely, chatty bloke. Bob is his name. From Longtown, just north of Carlisle. Also, I hate the sight of myself going into the character of consumers' champion or anything of that sort. Clive says this reluctance is the people-pleasing side of me, 'which we need to look at.' His view is that I should learn to be more assertive. And I thought there were no shoulds, Clive.

Brownheads is a beautiful limestone village that once thought itself a town. Market cross, cobbles, Bull's Head, White Horse, dead post office, Copper Kettle tea room, little Londis store with a cash machine, big old church at the top of the street, set-back Methodist hall at the foot. That's about it. Plus, of course, the handsome hills back beyond the roofs, standing there like the senior boys in the school photo.

Passing the last of the buildings, I see a group of people down by the side door. Guilty tang of outdoor nicotine, steam rising from polystyrene cups. There is something universal about the sight, and I think I know what it is. Curiosity barges my diffidence aside (OK, Clive?) and I walk along to join them. Inside is the reassuring presence of twelve-step banners hanging from the walls. 'Came to believe that a power greater than ourselves could restore us to sanity,' and so on.

There are about fifteen people here. They nod warmly at me as if they know me. Which, in an essential way, they do. Two of them shake my hand and introduce themselves. Something is strange and different. It is not until I look again at the table, with its Yellow Card and literature, that I realise I have walked into a meeting of GA. - Gamblers Anonymous. Gambling - thank the Lord, or the Higher Power, or the Man Upstairs - has never been a problem for me. I just don't do it, so I never get into trouble with it. Like Cliff Richard with sex, I suppose.

Before I can call myself an imposter and throw myself out, the door has shut, the chairs have scraped, and the secretary has banged the pot on the table for silence. And then, to borrow from the punter's vocabulary, we're off. Just as in AA, we introduce ourselves in turn around the room. Not everyone follows their name by saying they are addicted to gambling. Some just say 'addict,' so that's what I do. It doesn't feel like perjury. The problem will only arise if it's sharing round the room and it gets to my turn.

First though, there's a powerful Chair. The man's name is Mark. I work out from some of his references that he must be about the same age as me, but I choose to think he looks older. His story is so chilling that it freezes the room. At its core is the terrible simplicity of powerlessness. It started with mild flutters and low stakes. Then it just grew from there until there was no room in his head for anything else.

143

It was never about the money, he says. Not really. Nice to have a big win of course, and kid yourself that you were doing well, staying ahead, forget about all the losses that are the true and ongoing proof of it being a mug's game. No, he says, the real buzz was not even watching the horses on the home straight, but something apparently much more mundane - the completion of the betting slip at the William Hills or wherever.

While he was at it, he never knew why that should be the instant of the hit. Now that he's been clear for five years, he recognises what was going on. It was the surrendering of control to the forces of chance, the placing of himself in jeopardy. That's where the action was, right there in the scribbling and the handing over.

I'm an innocent in this country. I've never known any serious gamblers. While I'm sitting here in yet another church hall, I do remember a patient coming into the surgery and complaining that he couldn't stop gambling, no matter how hard he tried. This must have been seven or eight years ago, long before I'd had dealings of my own with the fellowship. He told me he had symptoms. I asked what they were and he said shaking and sweating, constant anxiety, feelings of self-loathing, was that enough?

I have to admit I was sceptical, although he insisted that when he placed a bet, or knew that he was about to place a bet, they vanished. As he was one of those patients I didn't take to, I had to raise my game and avoid the temptation of telling him to bog off and get a life. Also, I was deep in drink myself, and was identifying uncomfortably with the condition he was describing. Perhaps I started wondering, even back then, about the possible link between these apparently disparate compulsions. And yet here we are, listening to Mark and the unfakeable power of first-hand testimony: 'I did it and did it and did it. And every time I did it, the feelings got worse and worse, and the only way to feel better was to do it again.'

There it is. You use the very thing that is bringing you down in order to restore the illusion of balance. That's the vicious circle into which all addicts are condemned to slide like water circling the drain. The substance or the process we use is almost incidental - drink, drugs, food, no food, shopping, sex and, if you want to make it a thorough inventory, love, religion and God itself.

Mark describes his rock-bottom, which is the fellowship jargon for your lowest point in addiction. He bet his house - he can't even remember what on as he was in a kind of black-out. He lost it, of course, and had to tell his wife, mother of his two young children and a third on the way, that they were about to lose their home. He had a breakdown; the marriage went, and the job, and of course the house. The parallels are too clear for anyone but a fool to ignore. For mild flutter, read occasional sherry; for serious habit read daily bottle of wine; for out of control, read vodka before breakfast. So, yes Maurice, fair play, a narrative.

What saved this man, this kind-looking, balanced, decent and once-bedevilled man? Well, there was the matter of being so disgusted with himself that he started thinking solemnly and rationally about suicide. He phoned GA. A man came round and suggested that suicide was a form of murder, with all the terrible consequences of bereavement. He was, in the fellowship's form of words, sick and tired of being sick and tired. Ready to surrender.

He went to the meetings, hung out with other reforming gamblers until that abstinent company became the rule rather than the exception. And - big And - he found the Lord. Or the Lord found him. He got a sponsor, went through the steps, tried to make amends to those he had wronged, got on his knees and prayed for his defects to be removed. Long, hard road, but oh the sweet freedom from the gambling addiction. Peace talks with his wife, tentative moves towards reconciliation. Hope. Above all, hope, and trust, and even the unthinkable possibility of happiness. Well, contentment then.

Silence, the collective exhale, the chairs. The secretary responds and then throws it open. There is a pools gambler and three machine gamblers and two casino gamblers and more and more horse and dog gamblers. The longer I listen, the more I realise that the variations between them are like the variations between drinkers who pursue their habit in bars or clubs or at home. Same product, different packaging. It's not round-the-room sharing, but raised hands. So I don't have to say anything if I don't want to. But with twenty minutes still on the clock, everyone else has spoken and there's only me left. The others are too respectful to cajole, but there is a certain pressure in the silence itself.

Quickly I reach for a, well, for a narrative. I could easily cobble together a gambler's past, a sort of identikit based partly on everything I've heard and partly on my own recovery from another addiction. Then, just as quickly, I bin the notion and opt for the deceptively difficult lure of the truth. I get off to the most honest possible start by saying 'My name is William.' The room responds with a loud and welcoming 'Hello William.' I say that I owe everyone an apology - always a wise move - as I mistook the meeting for AA and that therefore I don't meet the essential requirement for membership, namely the desire to stop gambling.

They laugh sympathetically. They couldn't be more understanding. Some are cross-addicted, meaning they have moved from one bad habit to the other, and are members of both fellowships. Moreover they get the point that has only just dawned on me - the one about the close kinship of the conditions. I carry on, telling the plain truth about the progressive deepening of my alcoholism, making as many respectful links to Mark's Chair as I can.

I let drop that I am a doctor. I do, I think, check my motives here. Unless I'm fooling myself, I'm not out to impress but rather the opposite, to let them know that when it comes to a knowledge of addictive disorders, I consider medics to be the laity and us, in these rooms, to be the professionals. Sucking up, I'm sure, but true as well.

As I wind it up, I am aware of being like one of those patients of mine who can't or won't get to the point of their visit. In other words, the Serena question hangs in my head like a big, beautiful, daunting, imminent storm, magnificent in its disruption. If not here, then where. If not now, then when?

What a strange experience to find myself here, in this organisation. So open in its internal dealings and yet decidedly Samizdat in its profile. A non-toxic masonry. Having always thought that clubs and societies were for people other than me, I'm surprised and delighted to belong. As a doctor, I'm starting to feel particularly blessed in this belonging. Not only do you have the benefit of an almost infinite research base, you also have access to the hidden wiring of a society made sick by desire but finding in its own numbers the gift of healing.

I stand at the edge of the board. Yes, there is water in the pool, surely. I lean forward so that I will pass the critical point and override caution. I leave the board and am in the air. I might open into a swallow, but instead I ball up and hit the water in a niggardly posture. I even seek safety in third-person generality: 'Sometimes, even when things are going well in recovery, one can be faced with a situation in which all the old unmanageability comes bubbling back up to the surface.' And that, I'm afraid, is as far as I go. Thank you for your honesty, William. Or what we could see of it.

There's nothing else going out of Brownheads today. The

147

bus must have gone native and found a fold in the hills to over-night unobserved. There's always taxis, but they feel like cheating. Taxis are what you do in London, not over the big hills of the north. I stay in the Bull's Head, sit at the desk by the dormer in my bedroom, and scribble this. Now, when I'm done, it's nearly dinner time. Plainer menu than the Pitman's, but a third of the price.

I phone home. Imogen answers and we talk pleasantly about I'm not sure what. There's a comparative study of our weathers, and a little about Ricky's movements. I think I can hear in the background the noise of an animal which I didn't know we had. Or more likely this is coming from somewhere in the road outside the pub. I'm aware of wanting the call to pass without incident. She says 'Thank you so much for calling', polite as a good receptionist, and I say 'Not at all', just as impeccably.

October 17th. Although she has made it her own, Serena's room reminds me of so many others. But which others? It's not as if I've spent years of my life voyaging through the rooms of young women and then committing them to memory for purposes of comparative study. Student rooms, that's it. The kind that Imogen and her two best friends - what were their names? Sophie and Gabby - used to have in the halls of residence. The room is your own but the building is someone else's. Someone or something that is absent - a landlord or an authority. No point in trying to make your mark on the communal areas, the corridors, the stairs, the fire doors; you are a bird of passage here, and all the nesting is confined to your little box. One day you will have a house of your own, and a professional profile, and little children in their own bedrooms, but for the moment this cube contains and is contained by the boundaries of your domain.

I am dozing off again, looking up at the walls and the posters she has fixed to them. There is a rule against drawing-pins, so she has used Blu-Tack. A corner of the Michael Jackson is peeling down on itself. He seems an unlikely choice. But then again, Ricky was mad about him as a boy. Serena is, what, only three years older. Perhaps Jackson represents an old certainty for her. Stop it, Dr. Newgate, you're not on duty now.

These last words are spoken by her, but they could as easily have come from me. She delivers them lightly, and with a spring in her step. She is over by the kettle. It is steaming and she is whistling. Apart from some Degas dancers and what I think is a Landseer print, there are more stars of song or screen. It is a higher icon quota than I would have thought likely for the young woman of independent mind I take her to be. Hendrix, Joplin, Cobain, Morrison. You don't need to be a pub quiz hero to see that they share a significant detail; all made the ultimate career move and died young. Stop it, Dr. Newgate. These words, internally spoken, are mine this time, though could as easily have come from her.

'No milk one sugar?'

'Yes. Thank you. How did you know?

'I didn't. I was just asking.'

She brings the cup over to the bedside table and sits down with her own on the edge of the bed. 'So,' she says. The world of meaning that can be found in that sound. As 'So's' go, this one is friendly rather than nosey. Her bedside manner is good. As I pull more duvet onto me, the smell of her wafts up from my front. It is a beautiful, rich, dark smell and I feel the beginnings of hardness again.

I say something about the number eleven bus - nothing all year and then two in a row. She enjoys this and gets back into the bed. Because it's a single, intimacy comes as standard. She puts her head on my right shoulder and my chest. Her Venus Mound is around my right hip, and her right leg lies across my thighs. Conversation available upstairs, hard partying down below.

She arranges herself as if she is going to mount me. It's a

thrilling idea. We visited this position briefly about twenty minutes ago, between longer periods of me on top. The thought of pulling her down onto me repeatedly by her behind as I lie here again is topping out my erection. There is a certain entirely bearable pain, right there in the business section. Dr. Newgate reminds me that this is bound to happen to any part of the body that has not been properly exercised for a while. The structure feels permanent, locked in: this is the shape of you here from now on.

I am so longing for her to surround me again with her self that every second in which she withholds her clasp becomes a long punishment. Time is all over the place. But even as this is happening, or not happening just yet, I am anxious that it will, in case my performance is found wanting, the blood drains from my foundations and I collapse.

I am expecting her to say things. Lots of things. If she was garrulous on the phone, how much more so will she be on the pillow. It doesn't work out this way. Instead there is silence. A lot of silence punctuated by her now saying 'Thank you William' softly into me. It sets up the same sprinting along my nerve tracks towards the finishing line of my toes that my body hosted once before, vertically, in the surgery, when her kiss went off in my ear and I felt as much appalled as thrilled.

She strokes my chest with her right hand. I can't think of anything original to say, but am wholly untroubled by this and don't try. As a result, out comes the crude, fish-hooked response of 'For what?'

'For curing me.'

'I haven't cured you, Serena.'

'Oh great, you mean I'm still sick.'

'I mean that I can't take credit for you being cured. I mean, you left me.'

'Oh technically, yes. In a sense. But not when you think

about it. In fact, when you do think about it, it's quite the opposite. Nobody could have done what you have. And don't say 'oh but I haven't done anything.' (a horribly plausible imitation of me - am I really that nasal?). You have. Just by being you.'

Well, Maurice always says it doesn't really matter how we cure our patients, and I suppose I'm on his side. Except that I don't want Maurice with me now; when I think about his possible form with Imogen. Which I absolutely mustn't do. So I think instead about the present, just as AA says you should. Or rather, I think about the brief piece of time I passed through to get here.

I spool through it again with even more speed than its reality: the arriving of the agreed time; not a moment early, not a moment late; catching the pips on the radio in my mobile, to be dead right; nervous at my visibility between the bus stop and her house; who will see me? will it matter? I am a doctor; these are my streets; so nervous at the nothing happening in my crotch that I think it will be nothing for ever; my manner, shifting down through the gears and wrenching itself into neutral as I reach the top of the front steps, just as I have to do with patients who, for whatever reason I find challenging; pressing the bell, the correct bell and hearing it cause a dull rattle on the first floor; her coming down the stairs, her shadow enlarging into the frosted glass panel; she being relaxed and reassuring; going silently up behind her; the room, the smell of it, like powder shaken from her hair; her essence in the air; her drawing the curtains and doing that little silvery laugh; facing me; my heart sending the blood up to hammer my head in time; her pushing the jacket back off my shoulders; the kiss starting automatically; the kiss without which nothing else could happen; no talking, eating, thinking, being, without getting to the other side of that kiss.

It is a long, long passage. We stay joined at the mouth while we are starting to kick and scrape our bodies free of clothes;

the unseemly snorting as my nose bears the brunt of the air-getting; then onto the bed, and into it, and her; gasping with the shock of such tension and such relief, and in such quantities, all at the same time; the rightness of it driving the wrongness out; not the other way round, please not the other way round; disbelief certainly; plain incredulity, despite this highly persuasive evidence; disbelief that she could want me, twice her age and her father's contemporary, in this way; disbelief that I am doing what I am doing; disbelief that the illicit footage which has been reeling through my head for all these months should now be so trumped and so upstaged by the live version; then the afterness, this unexpectedly easy afterness, which doesn't feel like an afterness at all; the guilt; ah yes, I wondered where he'd got to; just biding his time in order to make the most damaging raid into the soft tissue of my emotions; why should he waste an opportunity like this, knowing my unguarded angles and my Sentry Asleep openings as well as he does;

But he (the guilt) doesn't come and doesn't come; there's something the matter with him, and about time too; what next? What now? The drowsiness tugging down at my lids; seeing things in the half-dark; Imogen by the lake and the mist rising; a much younger Serena framed in the viewing window of the squash club while her brute-father slugs and sweats on the boards below; the Underground, mines, miners, Dad, the nearly widow, sleep falling on me heavily; this changed condition; the knowledge that life can never be the same again; the thrill of that, and the terror.

October 18th. An atmosphere in the house. As if they know something. And yet they can't, can they? It must be me. I must be imagining suspicion in their faces. Projecting again, I suppose. Oh God, how I hate this awful jargon. I must stop using it or it will wrap me up in itself.

Inez surly. Nothing new there, but there is a fresh charge in her pout. The place has that slightly sick smell of flowers on the turn. Like public mourning. Two or three more big bunches have arrived and been divvied up around the hall and the drawing-room in vases I didn't know we had. Imogen blank and neutral again. I haven't really seen her since I got home from Dad's. First day back, i.e. yesterday, I was straight round to Serena's. Then not here till past eleven, after she suggested I should go. Then a bath, which I should have had at Serena's. Except that there wasn't one, only a shower room for general use, down the corridor, and there was someone in it. I wanted to get out of the building without being seen.

So a bath at home; the warm water reheating the scent of Serena, here in the house, then leaving through the plug and being replaced on me by home soap. Camay, I think. It smells of plain prettiness and simple contentment; the England of its own dreams. Imogen stirs half-awake and asks me what I smell of. 'Just bath,' I say, and she replies: 'Oh yes. How nice.'

October 20th. The front-door bell. I'm just getting ready to go to work. None of the other three up yet. Another big bunch of flowers, with a man's face peeping round behind it. Not an Interflora man but a gent in a City suit. He asks if he might deliver them personally to Miss Frias. I tell him she is not here, a white lie which I justify by being far from certain she would want to see this man. Whoever he is, with his chalk-stripe suit and his Burberry (I think) overcoat. He is disappointed but polite. I put him in his mid-forties, a little younger than me. I think he is about to ask me who I am but then decides against it. I say I will tell her he called, if he would like to give me a name. 'Oh, just say Geoffrey. She'll know.'

I take the flowers into the kitchen and do my best with them. We seem to be out of free receptacles, so I feed some of the tulips, beautiful waxy crowns on slender stems, into the spout of the kettle. The remainder I lay on their side in the big wok and fill it up with water. Very postmodern. Better this than letting them die straight off.

October 22nd. At Serena's again. The agreed time on the agreed day. We have been as good as our words and not phoned in the interim. Huge effort of will on my part and, I now gather, on hers as well. Instead of being at each other's ears the whole time for post-match analysis, or reassurance, or what Maurice would call validation, we've decided to go for mature restraint and emotional continence. Or at least the outward show of it. In this we have been so successful that we have convinced one another the thrill of the affair has already worn off. What are we up to? Demonstrating to each other, and to ourselves, that we are not really addicts, while bingeing self-righteously on romantic abstinence? That's a possibility. I keep it to myself for the moment.

She admits to having worried that I'd had second thoughts and wanted to call it off. I can match those fears precisely and I tell her so. What I don't tell her is the frequency with which thoughts of her father have been claiming my attention. All through these past few days, there he has been, like an over-social clubman inserting his big red face between me and my newspaper; or a garish pop-up getting in under the computer's radar and occupying the screen.

I suppose he has been there for a reason; making me sift and ponder what Serena said about him, back in the surgery. What he did to her and her sister. Allegedly (that necessary spoilsport of a word.) Whether it had a literal truth or existed in some other wing of memory's manor. Whether I should raise it with her, ever. Or just wait. Whether I was wanting to retain my identity as a doctor, her doctor, even though I had moved into another persona, that of lover. But what an inadequate, oddly impersonal word that one is.

I also keep to myself the guilt of transgressing the AA protocol which says, basically, hands off newcomers. In fact I hide it so deep in myself that I have probably reached the condition of denial. Clive would give me hell - the kind of hell that only benign, morally certain god-fearers seem able to dispense.

The kettle goes on but the conversation gets no further because we stop it by stopping each other's mouth with our own. Then we are pulling and kicking at our clothes, just like the last, or first, time. We know we can kiss unbroken while getting naked. We are as adept as the juggler who keeps the plate spinning on his forehead while making rabbits vanish with his hands.

I feel us both rushing towards orgasm, as if the endless replaying of the last time, hour after hour, minute after minute, has brought us to the brink, when we have hardly started. Us versus the kettle. We hear the water rampaging in its cheap plastic silo and then the switch clicking off. Kettle wins. No, kettle loses. We slacken a little. I make some poor crack about breaking the habits of a lifetime and going for deferred gratification. She finds this funny, and so goes both up and down in my estimation.

We uncouple for a moment and stroke each other. She says something nice about my hardness, but with the suggestion of surprise on account of my age. I reply that it's all down to her; it's she who's made me able to go up to eleven. This one she doesn't get. I ask her if her father had never had the *Spinal Tap* video - I bet he did - but she's a blank. I try to explain the gag about the volume knob on the amplifier, but this founders like a limp windsock.

We re-engage. It has the thrill of novelty and the comfort of familiarity. Still too the disbelief of fantasy made flesh, the acting-out of thoughts that had been inadmissible in the surgery but which had simply forced their way in with her. Silence settles on us. It feels rather eloquent, although I am not sure what it is saying. Something good, for certain. Before Imogen, I'd only ever slept with three women, and one of the aspects I found hardest was the expectation of conversation afterwards. I don't think it's that I was unfriendly, just that I was no good at it.

So the problem was mine, not theirs. I didn't quite know what to say. Whatever I tried turned into the sort of statement I might have expected from other people - people in books or films. I must have been terrible company, worried that they were going to tell me they loved me (where did I get that idea from?) and that this would trigger a programme of expectations which I could never fulfill.

Serena and I will have to talk of course. She must know this as well as I do, and so we enjoy the not doing it as you enjoy the not getting out of a warm bath. I can already feel the patterns of compulsion forming up in me: the way the street names cause a racing in my blood; the way the outside of this very ordinary building acquires an erotic sheen; the way the number of her room, four, is charged with a huge but private significance; the routine of silence and soft steps, pantomime padding, between the front door and her room.

During these five days, when we agreed not to communicate, like adolescents trying to prove something, I even drove past to score these sensations. The behaviour of an addict? Oh probably, but then the nature of an addict, particularly one in so-called recovery like me, is to spot addiction hiding behind every tree. It's a deeply annoying tendency, as though our defeat of a nasty habit gives us the right to pathologize everyone's excesses.

We are so zealous in this that we do not even spare ourselves. Addiction? Me cruising these mundane roads to quicken an erotic impulse? All I know is this: if you go on doing the same thing over and over again, and this thing damages you, and the only way to feel all right is to do this thing again, then you are probably looking at addiction. So says the extensive personal research of Dr. William Newgate. Seeing Serena does not fall into the category of addiction since there is no damage coming from it. Yet. Quite the reverse. Unless this is the classic denial strategy of the multiple addict. Sometimes I wish I could shut up; the private Dr. Newgate, whose sole patient I am, as well as the public one.

On the way back down the road towards the bus stop, I see a familiar face in a car windscreen. It is fleetingly lit by oncoming headlamps. It is wearing a sour, narrow-eyed expression. It is set on a thick neck and powerful, jacketed shoulders. Maybe it is because I see it like this, briefly and through glass, that I take it to be Serena's father, Brian Miller; because of associating such a face with the viewing window at the squash court, and because of his many recent appearances in my head.

None of which means that it is not him. It plainly is. He has an expression that does not harbour good intentions towards the rest of the world, or towards me in particular (why should it?). I am sure he sees me as he passes. Hard to be a hundred per cent on this. He might just be raising his eyes to the rear-view mirror. I could confirm whether it is or is not him by waiting to see if he parks near the house and goes in. I decide not to. He might see me.

I try to forget about him, but this sighting is like the wind of a horrible dark wing past my face in the night. I daren't even savour the relief of it having just missed me. I had also forgotten that he wanted to see me. I would like to go on forgetting if I could. I do ask myself what I have to fear from this man, whose daughter is not even my patient, and the answer is everything.

October 25th. Maurice says 'Squash,' and I hear myself answer: 'Yes. Sure. When?' The inside voice is going,'Oh Maurice, why don't you just leave me alone and stop trying to set up these little arenas in which you then set about besting me. Why don't you stop looking at me as if you are the world's foremost expert on the secret life of Dr. William Newgate. In fact, Maurice, why don't you just cease to be by getting tragically snatched from your adoring patients by a wholly unheard-of strain of the African Marburg virus.' He says: 'Tuesday. Nov. Nine. After work. Got the court.'

'Terrific,' I reply, already dreading the thought of the game-within-the-game, not to mention the shortening of the odds on running into Brian Miller. But that's that. Squash with Maurice. Tuesday, week after next. He's wanting to chat generally, probably with some purpose in mind, some newly acquired specialised knowledge towards which he will steer, or wrench, the conversation.

HGV puts his head round the door and asks for a moment of his time. Maurice obliges and leaves me alone in his room. I look around. I can't help it. The silver frame with him and his wife Emma looking back out from their 'little place in Provence'; her and their two daughters, all much sweeter and prettier than he deserves; the well-ordered reference books and papers; *Guardian*, *Lancet*, *BMJ*, a powder-blue wallet file.

I flip the top of this open. Can't think why. Just because it's there, I guess. As am I. Or because I'm getting the taste for surreptitious action. Whatever. A substantial wad of plain A4, covered with handwriting. Plenty of crossings-out, asterisks and bendy arrows relocating paragraphs. Stone Age cut-and-paste. Surprisingly low-tech. He couldn't have left the clues more obligingly on display if he had tried: 'Katjana/Mila; Dr. Threapleton/HGV; Hilton Palmer/William.' There are other names, other characters twinned with their real-life counterparts, but the references elude me.

This is a *roman à clef* in progress, and I have just stumbled on the *clef*. I quickly leaf through a few sheets, just to see if there are any pointers to the nature of my own *alter ego*, Hilton Palmer (what a horrible name. I don't want to be Hilton Palmer). Again, Maurice is most helpful, putting the names in capitals for some reason. Here we are: 'The years had not been kind to

Hilton Palmer. He was a doctor with a great future behind him, now trapped in a bleak marriage, with a son who was rejecting him and an au pair who, in common with many in the town of Middleford, found him ridiculous.'

Oddly, my first reaction is one of relief. This is so badly written that it will never find a publisher. 'The years had not been kind… great future behind him,' cliché after cliché, as you would expect from a man with no imagination. Even Middleford, which is presumably meant to be some sort of Everytown, thereby broadening the appeal of Maurice's 'urgently relevant anatomy of Middle England today,' telegraphs its punches pretty crudely.

What about Dr. Threapleton/HGV? How does he come out of it? Here he is: 'I must say,' said Dr. Threapleton, a silver-haired veteran of the old school, 'this is not how things were done in my day.' Martin Amis can relax.

So who is Maurice? I can see no references to a fearless reformer who enjoys the universal respect and affection of colleagues and community alike, but I assume he must have staked himself either of the two identities in the title, *The Good Doctor's Disciple*, which looks almost competent enough to have been stolen.

I put the sheets back. Better thwart my curiosity than be caught snooping. I pick up his *Lancet* and read until he gets back a few minutes later; an article by a former hospital administrator from Lincolnshire arguing that it is time we re-appropriated the overused word 'holistic' to define the way in which our public health services should be run.

Maurice comes back in. He wants to resume our conversation and, I imagine, take aim at one of my sensitive areas. I look at my watch and tell him we've got people coming round. This violates his idea of me and he looks startled. Well might he; it violates my idea of me as well. We haven't had people round for about ten years, and I have lost count of the number of invitations we owe. They are like student loans, never going away, but too big to look at closely. The only positive consequence is that we're not incurring any more. These days our incoming social traffic is restricted to businessmen bearing flowers, and they don't even get past the door. At least, I don't think they do.

October 30th. Whatever it is at the house has come to a head. I am in my study, doing this into the small hours, thinking about Serena and trying not to, or else not thinking about Serena but unable to keep that up for long. We have yet to spend a night together, and I wonder how and where we will go about it. The thoughts should not be in my head, which is why they are levying so much of my attention. They are not to be ignored, any more than burglars in the bedroom are to be ignored.

There is a scuffling sound against the door, like a tall vertical dog. It is Ricky. He has been back on both weekends since the start of Michaelmas. He is knocking without wanting to disturb me, and the result is a series of scratches. He is very drunk. His manful efforts at pretending not to be remind me of my own at his age: the willing of the mouth into coherent action; the mouth's point-blank refusal to sculpt these fussy word-shapes for you; its preference for animal sounds and sudden yelping hiccups; the ankles as a fulcrum for the great floppy could-go-either-way lever of yourself; the shooting of tears from the eyes for no reason and yet every reason the world has to offer. Projectile blubbing. The whole spilling mess of you. Please God, don't let him have to take the same dreadful road to sobriety as mine. This would be no inheritance to lumber him with, no matter what our differences have been.

'Sorry to bother you,' he manages.

'That's quite all right, Ricky,' I say, meaning it. 'Come in. Can I get you anything?'

'Thanks but no. I'm not actually drinking at the moment.'

Insofar as nothing is going down his throat while the words are coming up, you can't fault him for accuracy. But he's got a bottle with him, a brown miniature of something which he thinks he is hiding from me in a clenched hand. 'Thought it best to knock it on the head.'

'Well, Ricky, you'd get no opposition from me, as I'm sure you know.'

'You did brilliantly there. Hats off I say.'

'That's very kind of you. It means a great deal to me to hear you say that.'

'Yup.' These Yups are sounding like hiccups. That's what they technically are, but he is managing to surf his voice onto the wind of them and convert them to affirmatives. He must feel their waves begin to break at the foot of his throat. Considering the state of him, that's some timing.

'Women eh,' he says.

'Ah yes. Tell me about it.'

This phrase must have passed from currency and become as dated as the volume knob going up to eleven. Ricky takes it as a straight invitation to tell me about women, and starts to do so. Well, one woman.

'You know Inez, right?'

'Well yes. Up to a point.'

'What do you think?'

'In what way, Ricky?'

'You know.'

'Do you mean, do I find her attractive?'

'No. Yes. No.'

'I make that a no.'

'What do you reckon?'

'Of.'

'The flowers and that.'

'The flowers are very attractive.'

161

'Come on Dad.' Dad, instead of William. He hasn't called me Dad for years, and his use of it now is a delightful surprise. I wonder why this should have happened just now.

'Yes,' I say. 'Well, to tell you the truth, I don't really know what to make of the flowers. I mean, she is a young woman of, what, twenty-two.'

'Twenty-nine.'

'Surely not.'

'Yup.'

'Goodness. I'm sure she told us.'

'I'm sure she told you a lot of things.'

'Not that many actually. She dealt with Imogen, with Mum. As they tend to.'

'Twenty-nine.'

'You said. Does this actually matter?'

'Saw her license, right.'

I think about telling him that nosing in other people's documents is not a good way of going on, but I can't do it. He starts to lean forwards. He is almost at the angle of a flying buttress and I am worried he is going to head-butt the wall. Then the self-righting mechanism kicks in miraculously and he somehow dances himself upright like a juggler catching his own upper body as it falls from the sky.

'Those men, yeah?'

'Well,' I say. 'I only saw one.'

'Yeah but.'

'How many actually?'

He spreads his palms and gives a don't-know pout. 'Depends if you count me.'

'How?'

'If you count me, then it's one more than if you don't.'

'I don't think I understand, Ricky.'

'I think you do understand, Dad, but are pretending not to.

Which I'm not saying is anything wrong or out of order. Thing is, she's a hooker.'

'Surely not.'

'Oh yeah. Website and all. Want to see it?'

'I don't think so, actually, Ricky. But thank you.'

'La Passionara. Bilbao Babe. The Full Flamenco. Photo and all. Plus her mobile.'

'I see. Well, listen Ricky. Does Imogen, does Mum know?'

'No and you're not to tell her.'

'Of course I won't. Of course I won't. This is just between us.'

'Yeah, you, me, and the business community of Greater London.' Not bad for someone this drunk.

'How did all this, you know, how did you find out?'

'The blokes, Dad. The blokes. Come on.' Yes. Come on William. The strange thing about getting older is that you think you will come to know more because experience will educate you. How quaint. I now find my mind chasing cumbersomely after the implications of what Ricky has just told me. For example, has this house become a, technically, well, brothel as one of its occupants offers sex on a commercial basis? Would this mean that I was, technically and partially, if not actually, living off immoral earnings (though God knows I sometimes feel I am), then at least admitting immoral earnings into the economy of the household? Has the sex actually taken place here?

It has.

'The thing is, Dad, right, I thought, you know, she was OK and quite fun. And serious with it. Doing the Spanish conversation with Mum very conscientiously. Plus, interesting about the politics. ETA and the PNV and that.'

ETA I'm all right on, but PNV stumps me.

'Basque Nationalist Party,' he says helpfully. 'How Greenland's the way to go.'

'Greenland?' I'm aware of sounding like the parody of a

flummoxed listener. Which is what I am. Echoes of Edith Evans saying 'A Handbag?'

'Yeah. Basically, Spain granting autonomy like Denmark has.'

'To Greenland?'

'Right. Anyway, good political nous, I thought. Which I like. And then also, she's sending money home to her people, who are dirt-poor. Grannies and that. Well, she seemed to like me, and we joked about a bit, like there was nothing in it, but then one night, when you were up with Grandad, she starts coming on to me. And the thing is, Dad, and this definitely is just between you and me, the thing is I've been what my friend Sean, my Belfast friend Sean whom you've met, what he calls a bit of a let-down in the trouser department.'

It's not an entirely straightforward image, with suggestions of Brian Rix, and men's clothing shops. But I get the picture, and I feel a bad hit of pity for Ricky for accepting this description of himself.

'Anyway, Sean said to me to go on a run with him and his brother when he was over.'

'Well, that sounds healthy enough.'

'No. A run. In Maida Vale or somewhere. With prozzies. And I bottled it.'

'There's no shame in that, Ricky,' I say, a little too ringingly. 'No shame at all.'

'I know, Dad. But it kind of put the idea into my head. And in my you know.'

I know only too well. 'Yes.'

'And it wouldn't go away. So, when Inez's coming on to me, and like teasing me because I haven't got a girlfriend so I must be an English Nancy Man, and that's her word, I say do you want to make something of it, and then one thing leads to another, and you know, she's actually more attractive than you think, and then, when we are almost, then she says 'For you, Ricky, only one hundred quids.' '

'I see. That sounds like quite a lot of money actually.'

'Yeah. In terms of baked beans, it's well over a term's subsistence.'

'That's an interesting way of looking at it.'

'There's this economist, oh never mind,'

'No go on, I'm interested.'

'Rodriguez. Spaniard as it happens, who takes food staples as an index of personal wealth. He has this formula, oh sod it.'

'Yes. Some other time. And did you, if I may ask,' Without finishing the question, I realise I have in fact asked two.

'Yes. I did. Oh Dad.' He aims himself at me like a scarf. I field him with a hand on his chest and he unwinds again.

'You know, Ricky, I don't like to be too much of a liberal, but I don't think, from what you've said, there's too much to take exception to. From your point of view, I'm thinking. Nothing, as they say, is here for tears.'

'The thing is.' And here he is coming to the point-beyond-the-point. 'The thing is, I can't afford it.'

'No. No. I quite understand. That is the frustration of being a student. As I well remember, good God, you know it's an investment but you wonder if you'll ever see a return on it, and for the time being all you know is that there are things you want, crave even, but just can't afford.'

I wonder if this is the time for a quick canter through the merits of deferred gratification, but decide to defer.

'So,' I say, without anything particular to follow it up with.

'So I paid her.'

'Ah.'

'I thought it was the only proper thing to do.'

'Yes.' Proper is an interesting word here.'

'That is, I... '

'There was a problem. Please Ricky, you can tell me. You can tell me anything. It's important we both know that.'

'Right. The thing is, I said I would pay her.'

'But you haven't actually done so yet.'

'No. The wall turned me down.'

'The wall.'

'Yeah. Service Till or whatever they call it, which is no service at all. Nat West, eh. Promise you the earth if you're a student, and then when you really need them…..'

'So you owe Inez a hundred pounds.'

'That's right.'

'I see. Well, Ricky, thank you for telling me.'

Projection time again. Surely I can be forgiven. It runs like this: I bail Ricky out as any good, well-resourced father of a student son would want to do. At the same time I do my bit to help an extended family in the Basque region of Spain and, for all I know, to fund the resurgence of separatist terror. While I'm at it, I finance the dumping of my son's tiresome virginity while risking the loss of this house's good name, which I have done so much to… '

'I'm so sorry,' says Ricky, as if he can pick up something of my mental drift.

'Oh don't be sorry. Really no need.'

I mean it. It strikes me that the immoral-earnings charge levelled at and by me loses its force since the sole domestic customer is funded by me. But then, does this mean that I/we are 'keeping' her. I give up and fumble around for something light. There is a gag forming in my head, something to do with the appeal of Fair Trade. In the end I don't need to make it, thank the Lord, because at this moment we hear the front door open and close, and then Inez's brisk strides up the stairs. Ricky's eyes well again, and I can see that his distress has nothing to do with the money. Of course it hasn't.

November 3rd. St. Stephen's Wednesday evening. A storming Chair from a New Yorker called Chuck. Thirty years around and literally back from beyond, after lying in the State Morgue with a dead-on-arrival tag round his toe.

'Well, see, I woke up and looked around and I said, Hey Guys, but no-one wanted to know. Told them they were a bunch of stiffs.'

He's got the captive audience in the palm of his hand. Bellows of laughter. Not quite a sell-out crowd, but he'll have had worse.

'And y'know, not one of them disagreed. Just kinda took it lying down.'

We're loving it. He's as good as Mort Sahl or Lenny Bruce, just about the same vintage as them, a bit younger, and he's done this before. Oh boy, has he done this before. The result is that we get a comic routine of professional standard while having sobriety powerfully re-affirmed. No-lose. One of the reasons it's all so joyful is that this is the ultimate club performance. He can't quite resist a variation on the gag about AA being the most expensive club in the world to join, on account of the decades of contributions across the bar - 'drip feed got fixed in the wrong direction'; he says he thought it was the most expensive club until he enrolled in the Fairlawn Country Club, South Connecticut.

He can't really go wrong, any more than Jackie Mason can go wrong with a Jewish audience in Manhattan. 'Guy Fawkes Day, right? After four hundred and five years, maybe give the guy a break. No, but seriously, y'know, for me, by the end, I identify, because I was nothing but a burnt-out case. But hey, what I say now, half a lifetime on, is, when your arse is on fire you sure as hell know you're going forwards.'

He winds up. Too canny to throw in a sales pitch for the Lord, and yet too damned Saved not to. 'I owe it all to the Lord.'

Then a nimble hop towards bathos: 'But then I used to owe it all to the Revenue man. And I know who I'd rather be indebted to.' It turns out he's the founder of something called Bankers for Jesus. I think that was it, although I mishear slightly because at this moment Serena arrives. She is slightly flustered and out of breath. She takes a seat at the back. We manage to avoid each other's eyes. I notice Clive look over at her, then at me. He notices me noticing.

I wonder if Bankers for Jesus is another joke, right on the edge of our sensibilities, but apparently not. It does unspeakably good work in Africa, as well as spreading the word about alcohol and drug abuse in the sprawling cities of the Third World. We all nod in approval, me included. Chuck is burning up his modesty credit with every second that he dwells on Charity, or Cherdy as he pronounces it.

He stops just in time. I find myself getting that dull old pissed-off feeling. It is the same feeling I've had for more than a quarter of a century. This is just the middle-aged version, therefore more wearing but less surprising. It does not direct itself at him, but at me, just as it used to do when I, for example, met a young graduate medic who was turning down the option of a safe career like mine in favour of a job with *Mèdecins Sans Frontiéres*. Guaranteed to revive the old Underground dream at any time and set me aggressively on my own case.

After we've stacked the chairs and washed up, Clive goes assertive and tells me he is giving me a lift. Not to my house but his. Serena went straight off after the meeting, with, I think, Spiritual. I can't log her movements and I must let go of the urge to try. Silence all the way back. Something on his mind, we both know what. Something on mine too: him.

It's chilly in the front room. The temperature makes me think of a morgue. No no, it's not the temperature but the presence of the undead Madge in surround vision. He doesn't offer coffee, just sits down and motions me to the facing chair. In the range of possible words to start such conversations, there's one front-runner. Out it comes. 'So.'

There's Madge earwigging heavily from every available surface. In fact I think she has proliferated since I was last here. He may be driving this interview, if that is what it turns out to be, but she is riding shotgun. Her expression manages to ape his, from fraternal concern, through slighted friendship to, God help us, tough love. And if one of her photos isn't getting it quite right, there'll be another that is, and you only have to flick your gaze a few centimetres to find it. Madge is moral armament in photo form, and Clive is packing heat.

I hear him start to talk. I can hear all right, but I can't quite listen. From the tone of it, he's flaunting tolerance and liberalism, but he is wearing the unmistakable word-clothes of the sermon. My thoughts are away, but I tune hard in for a few seconds to get a flavour. 'We all have it in us to take the right course and the wrong course.'

Both the next two sentences begin with 'We all,' which I always hate because it assumes common ground between the speaker and the listener. It's almost bullying.

I sit and take it. I keep myself busy with translation exercises. 'It's not that I mind you keeping your personal life to yourself' means 'I bitterly mind you not letting me in to your secrets, above all in the area of adultery.' Not just any old adultery either. But adultery with a newcomer, which is the ultimate abuse. You're not meant to get 'too close' to another member until they've been around for twelve months. People do, of course, but they get disapproved of. As I am being now.

Technically, Clive is being very respectful. He's not actually accusing me of anything, he's not mentioning the word Serena, and he's not even lecturing me. He only sounds as if he is. What he seems to be saying is that when he got married to Madge, they agreed that that was it; no more hankering - I think that's the word - after other people (a picture I just can't square with him.). As in hankery-pankery, I suppose. No acting out of carnal thoughts towards third parties. Those are his actual words. As if he's been handcuffed to an insurance clerk.

I can't help looking back at Madge. As I do so, I'm wondering whether the marriage was the idyll he now insists it always was. I mean, it's too easy. If you're married, but also dead, nothing you can do breaches the arrangement. So if you're the one who's living, you're in an inviolable contract. Brilliant. No sulks, temper, boredom, meanness, inexplicable bursts of contempt, farting, PMT, never mind the contract-killer adultery, to ruffle the silk of perfection. Alan Ayckbourn gets this; in a play of his called *Absent Friends* the only happy one in a landscape of collapsing marriages is the sanctimonious Colin, whose wife was drowned.

I'm being hard on Clive. But then Clive is being hard on me. Or is just about to be. He says: 'I suppose it's the deceit that I find hardest to take.' But here, unless I'm badly mistaken, he's not talking of my deceit towards Imogen, but towards him - Clive. Translation: 'When I became your sponsor, William, it was understood that you would share with me, honestly, openly and fully, bearing in mind that we all - or rather you, William - are as sick as our secrets.'

This is reminding me of something else - another time, another place, as the song has it. Several times and several places. Clive - and here he is to be pitied - has become the girlfriend that I don't want to have. We have met at a student party and got drunk on dire red plonk. We have snogged and been to the cinema and tried to discuss Truffaut and decided that we must have some interests in common, if only we could find them. But already I'm struggling; we're off at a pace I can't sustain, the intimacy is irking me and I am, to borrow my own son's chilling expression, a let-down in the trouser department. There is nothing for it. I am going to have to jilt Clive. It will break his heart. But it's him or me.

I start: 'I'm sorry you feel this way, Clive.' It is one of those commuted apologies which is not really an apology at all. But I've got my hands dirty, that's the thing. More: 'The point is, Clive, to come to the heart of the matter, I'm not really good enough for you.' I don't know how he interprets this, but my own translation would be: 'If you think I'm going to tell you all about Serena and me, and then ask for your advice, you're seriously off the pace, Sunbeam.'

Sticking with the language of the jilt, I even say: 'I think we want different things.' He is genuinely confused by this and says: 'All I want for you, William, is continuously good recovery. And we've made such a good start.' First person plural always a problem for me. William as a project under joint management. No.

'And as you also know, William, good recovery depends on keeping open a line of rigorous honesty to a sponsor whom you trust.' So he is raising the stakes, daring me to tell him I don't trust him. I look at his lumpy beige form, slumped there dejected. Rejected. I wish I could abort this jilting, because that is what it is. With Fiona I managed to put it off for months. This was a cruel cowardice as well as a counter-productive ploy. I must not repeat that error here.

Then something occurs to me. I would even say it comes to my rescue, falling into my stalled head like a bright coin into an arcade game. It sets me whirring. The Lord has arrived, and without the breath of a prayer from me. Unless you count desperation and vague begging as prayer, as many do. I suppose that if the Lord is going to drop into my head, Clive's house would be as likely a place as any, seeing as how He is round here all the time. He's probably bagsied the spare room. As Princess

Diana said to Charles of Camilla Parker-Bowles, there are three of us in this marriage. If I hadn't brought Him up, Clive would have.

'When I say I'm not good enough, Clive, I mean that I simply don't have the Lord in my life, or in my heart, in the way that you do.' Clive nods. He likes the fact that I am acknowledging the Lord, and His immanent presence in him. He wants to say we can soon put that right - I know he does - but if I give ground here, I'm sunk. So I harden up, feel somewhere in my head - temples, jaws, nostrils, not sure - for the physical sinews of resolve. Another job for the musculus buccinator. Firm in the face, I state: 'It is for that reason, Clive, that I feel you must do it your way and I must do it mine. And having said that, I want you to know that I can't express my gratitude strongly enough for everything you have done for me.'

He smiles and says: 'It isn't me, William. But I hear what you say. And thank you. Thank you for your honesty.' I try to keep the formality going by standing up, looking at my watch and saying: 'I've taken quite enough of your time.' When I did finally pull the plug on the Fiona relationship all those years ago, I truly felt she was better, morally healthier than me. I feel the same about Clive. I also feel mean-spirited in assuming that what he wanted from me was the detailed politics of my marriage and my affair (I have to call it that, I suppose, and even savour its frisson), with Serena. Serena, the contraband newcomer.

His phone could not time its ring better. I thank the Lord. Sometimes I do love Him, even though I'm no good at showing it, and even though I do my loving for all the wrong reasons. Serena? Surely not. Not this time. No, it is another of his sponsees (what kind of word is that?).

Clive lights up. Unfortunate phrase for an ex-drunk, but that is what he does. As if a current has been fed into him, making him beam as a headlamp beams, taking the rumple and the beigeness from him and turning him smooth. Very nearly sleek. Do I feel a twinge of envy that Clive is two-timing me? I do not. Just gladness that he is loved and needed by someone, even if that someone could not be me. Who knows, if I hadn't let Clive go as I just have, he might have sacked me for my behaviour. We will never know.

November 6th. Weakness. That's the word of the moment. It is more or less permanently in my mind, and just behind the tip of my tongue; ready to translate itself from thought to speech at any minute. It is in my surgery and my caseload, my privacy and my profession. It is in my conversations with patients and, cautiously, in my associations with colleagues. Everywhere. It is even in a paper that I have been preparing.

How pompous a workaday word like paper can sound when given a swanky context. I am to give a paper to the West London Association of Addiction Counsellors, sponsored by a new and rather good quarterly with the forthright title of *Addiction*. Two issues and you're hooked, as Maurice said to Joan the other day, having nicked the line from me. I have no doubt that he will come along to my talk all topped up with cutting edge data from the lavishly funded research industry of Californian campuses.

I have some notes somewhere. These could be anywhere; on my desk at work, at the mercy of Maurice's shifty forays, or filed in the lining of my semi-retired tweed jacket.

I think I have a thesis, or at least a gist, and my life now strikes me as an enactment of the research. Most of the people in the counsellors' association know something of my history, and they are clearly expecting a generous helping of autobiography, however I might choose to cloak it. Intending a pun, which I don't think they got, I've promised them I won't be too dry.

November 7th. Got the notes. They were scribbled on the back of a Pfizer press pack. I remember making them during the drug lunch presentation at that hotel in Sunningdale. Everyone thought I was being diligent when in fact I was in the terminal stages of boredom, could have gone at any moment, and needed an emergency diversion.

Weakness, I shall say, is one of those words whose accuracy is often obscured by the frequency of its use. We hear that so-and-so has a weakness for liquor; or the horses, or for other men's wives. Or other women's husbands. It can be a gentle, euphemistic way of describing a bad habit. It also starts to align the condition with a medical liability such as aneurism. You have a vital artery with a point of fragility along its wall. If it is played upon by certain factors, it is liable to burst, with catastrophic results.

This parallel will bring us, or me at any rate, to the illness concept of addictive disorders. People and societies can have great difficulty with this as it puts physical susceptibility in the place of moral contempt. So we are presented with an endless roll of individuals who must now be considered as victims of a condition rather than as monsters of greed or fecklessness. It's most inconvenient. Can we really afford such an epidemic of unhealthy dependence, such a plague of need? Are we in fact a sick society, and if so, how are we to heal? Who are we to heal? Thank you so much, Dr. Newgate. That was bold and enlightening. Anyone wishing to contribute to the discussion, please raise your hands so that the chairman can see you. I say, a forest!

November 8th. Over the phone I try the argument on Serena and she is commendably robust. Not to say, dismissive. If we all blame our compulsions on illness, she says, then we will never take responsibility for our actions, nor acquire the agency needed for self-healing. I'm quoting her verbatim here. I can think of many responses to this; too many, so I funnel myself down into a single thoughful Hmmm, as neutrally as I can, and change the subject. Or try to. She wants to know when I'm delivering my paper - 'it makes you sound like a news boy' - as she feels sure she can make a contribution to the debate. I feign memory loss and she tells me to relax.

November 9th. 'What's the matter,' she says. We are sitting in her room. Most of our clothes are still on the floor. They fell in such a hastily made trail towards the bed and now they're not sure what to do with themselves while they await collection. I make to reply 'Nothing,' which would routinely buy me a few seconds to think of something to add.

The 'matter' she senses is my self-reproach, which has been swift and violent. No stay of execution during this supposed honeymoon period. I can see Imogen and Ricky in the air before me. Transparent, and removed from the ground by several feet, yet there they are. They are not their present versions, but come from the early days. Ricky can't be more than six. He is holding a little motor boat with pride. I remember it. The blue hull and white deck. We took it down to Pen Ponds and navigated it by remote control all round the island in the middle. He looks less solid; less fixed than his mother. This is only because she is standing in front of Serena and so acquiring some substance from the other woman's form.

Then Ricky starts growing, outwards and upwards, with the speed of a pantomime beanstalk. As he does so, Imogen is matching his progress through the shifting and shading of years. They focus on me, like the press waiting for a statement. Dark-haired women come in towards them from either side and some of them I recognise, including the first Inez and the last. Serena talks softly at me through them and they vanish.

'So, are you beating yourself up?' she asks with a smile, aping one of the many forms of words that she says are my signature queries. Before I can think how to answer, she carries on: 'Because you shouldn't. All right, no shoulds. Therefore no shouldn'ts. But still, in my opinion, you shouldn't.'

'Thank you,' I say. It's thoughful of you, even though it's a statement that carries a world of self-interest. Who would want to get involved with someone who sees her as a cue for guilt?

'I mean,' she goes on. 'It's not appropriate, is it.'

'No. I suppose not.'

'I expect it's learnt behaviour, isn't it.'

'Yes. No. It's what?'

'From patterning that was probably… '

'Well, you know, most behaviour is learnt.'

'But you know what I mean.'

'Yes, of course I do.'

I rather wish I didn't. It's getting harder every day for men and women to conduct any form of relationship without it being subjected to the language of psychological scrutiny. I decide that Serena has had more therapy than she is letting on; as vocabularies go, hers is on the expensive side.

'It's not as though you didn't try, is it?'

'No. It's not.'

'You did go and see someone.'

'Yes. That's right.'

'But she didn't want to know. Did she, William?'

'Not really, no.'

'So, what is that telling us?'

The turn of phrase amuses me and she can see this. 'Us' is the giveaway. It has become a staple word in certain therapeutic transactions, with the counsellor and the client standing back and observing the picture they have been creating between them.

'Well,' I say. 'I think I'd rather hear your views on the subject.' Of course I would. Her view is that since Imogen aborted our marriage guidance sessions, I have the right to behave as I have been behaving with Serena.

This she now reiterates. 'What more were you meant to do, William? For Heaven's sake. By stopping the process she was almost saying she preferred the status quo, which was the failing of the marriage.'

I say thank you, even though I find her familiarity with the politics of my marriage a little strange. Yet when she's on someone's case – someone other than herself, such as my wife – you wouldn't guess there's much the matter with her. She's quick, sharp, even formidable. It's as though she is drawing alertness from the fears of others, help from their challenges, increase from their deficits.

I suppose you could say the same of some very good doctors, and perhaps all one is doing here is defining the nature of a vocation. Some whom I've known are at their most effective when their own lives are in dreadful disarray. Take Dr. Newgate for example. Marriage in a mess, son in revolt, professional life in chaos and yet quite devoted to one of the trickiest cases in his experience; totally committed to two very different courses: healing the sick and asking for trouble.

It is in the rightness of it all that the wrongness lies. That is Newgate's diagnosis of his most untreatable patient, himself. I knew this in my surgery when her kiss accidently went off in my ear. Accidentally, my eye. Its illicitness was the essence of its appeal. If it had been anything else, like formal or restrained, it would been merely clumsy, awkward, like any number of goodbyes when you don't know what the physical drill is and dread the moment when one of you has to make the move; handshake, nothing, harmless kiss in the air.

All this she knows. She reprises our social foreplay and is shameless in the quest for details. 'So when did it first cross your mind that I might be coming to the practice just to see you?'

'I can't be certain.'

'Didn't you make a note?'

'What?'

'Some people do.'

'Do they?'

'I wasn't faking, you know.'

'I do know.'

'You mustn't ever think that I was.'

'I will try not to.'

My protectiveness towards her is subject to a similar ambiguity. Caring is good. Seeing a friend as a creature in need of your support is fine. Outlaw those impulses and the species is done for. But when the creature in question is this particular young woman, then my altruism is made null and void by my desire. Oh yes, and by my fear. How could I forget fear? Of what, I hear myself ask. What've you got, I reply.

It's then that the image of her father arrives, yet again, this time standing there in the space occupied a moment ago by Ricky and Imogen. Brian Miller at the wheel of his horrible car, his huge head and shoulders hunched forward into the windscreen and catching sight of me in the split second of the rain wiped away. The headlamps pinning me against the houses and fixing me in his retina. Filed for future action.

She senses his presence and says: 'He was a dreadful, dreadful man, William.' I guess she uses the past tense because present is exactly where she doesn't want him. I can feel her wishing him away with words. I can see competence draining from her, poise and adulthood under attack. She is once more the battleground of then and now; forces locking back into conflict and her having to host the event. The struggle in her face is plain. As if she is trying to bite and swallow some feature of it.

This could be the moment when I ask her if she can be specific about her father's behaviour towards her. Then again, it could not be the moment. When I ask no such question, I can feel that line of inquiry recede like a speeded tide. It is not that the question is unimportant. Quite the opposite. But because of its very importance, the asking of it cannot help but be intrusive. Therefore it might become one of those questions - more numerous than we know - which continues to go unasked for fear its answer will bring with it more conflict than resolution. I don't say this is the right course of action, or inaction, just that I am aware of some protective silence settling over the area. It might be she who one day breaks it, or I, or neither.

A huge sigh comes out of her like a great wind blowing away her resolve. Her whole body shrugs and then surrenders to the occupation of weeping. It is at this moment that I believe I have never felt such tender concern for any living thing since Ricky's tiny back fitted into the cup of my hand and I could feel his entire being made over to the production of tears. The plain animal grief of him. Of her now.

I remember these feelings of care being called up in me by the very ill and the very old in my St. Thomas days. I experienced them as an affirmation of my calling. That was such a long time ago. Then I remember her mother and her cradled drink in the corner of the squash club bar; how it was really she, not the glass at all, that was the damaged bird, and the glass that was doing the damaging.

The poor woman's husband is still here in the air. He is reminding me of how much he terrifies me. One of those ex-rugby players who is furious that life no longer throws up legitimate openings for clawing opponents to the ground or stamping on their heads in the secret jungle of the scrum. Whenever I fear someone, it is almost always for psychological reasons. I suppose this is because of the nature of my work. But in the case of Brian Miller, the anxiety is purely physical. The kind you would experience if you were just about to be hit by a lorry.

I would ask Serena how far away he lives from here, but caution puts its hand over my mouth. I fear her answer too much. So here too is a growing silence. I don't know how long it lasts, but it seems to take us well into the evening. I might be dozing. I am talking to myself, literally I think. I am giving myself some instruction. I can only hear the back end of it. The word 'heart.' My mind tries to run, to catch up with the preceding words. It is laborious, like running level with a leaving train. The dogs of my trade, I say. I must call off the dogs of my trade from the something of my heart. From the business of my heart.

Next to me, Serena shakes herself awake. Brisk and energetic like a dog getting rid of the pond. She puts her dressing gown on, and her slippers, and slopes absently towards the door. Her eyes are still half-clenched with sleep, as if she is not entirely here. Then she is actually gone, through the door and down along the passage. I hear her bump into something and laugh lightly. There's another voice, from another girl, but a much younger one. I can't think what she's doing here unless she is someone's sister, visiting. I go to the door to see, but then think better of it. It feels like spying, and I've done enough of that in my own home. The words are indistinct but I sense an altercation. Then the younger girl's is the only voice I can hear. There's a silence, then more doors, and Serena comes back in, looking as if she has indeed been in an argument. I ask her who the other person was and she says there was no one else, I must be imagining it.

Nov 9th. Squash with Maurice. How do I write Aaarrrggghh in such a way as to give an inkling of the roar being made by my stomach voice; the don't-do-this-to-me-again roar which it produces as I reach the club and am wrapped in that basement smell of permadamp towels and unfixed drains.

Something has changed. It is not Maurice, but me. Maurice is as Maurice always is, stinking of his poncey embrocation and limbering around the court like a dud Kossack. No, it's me. Something has gone. It feels like my patience. If I haven't been aware of it, that must be because I've had so much else on my mind. Now that I think about tapping that patience in order to get through the next hour without - without what? Just fragmenting all over the court like a grenade in order to not be present; drastic but effective. I realise I have no patience to draw on. Nothing in the account. Request rejected.

Maurice sees that all is not as it should be, and I spot the gratifying glint of anxiety in his eyes. He says 'warm-up' as competitively as he can, and I reply: 'Yes, fine, Maurice. As long as we use the warm-up ball for the match.'

'Sure,' he says, as if any other strategy would be unthinkable. I win the toss, get serving and proceed to beat the living crap out of him. Oh, it's so good. Everything clicks. The wheels of the universe mesh sweetly to flight my untouchable lobs, to inform the perfect angles of my scything boasts and to power my wicked forehand drives an inch above the tin. A deeply unfriendly backhand arcs over his head and sends him rushing back to dig it out of the corner. I say rushing but it is really nothing more than a forced waddle. Digging is accurate though; he could be a man trying to shovel compost. His feet tangle and brake but his head carries on like a thrown ball to ricochet in the nest of concrete right angles. I pretend not to have noticed.

I take the first game to love, no problem, and get straight on with the second. Maurice has no idea what's happening. He tries a line about how I must have been practising, but he's already too out of breath to speak properly. For a second, no more than that, I worry about the colour of his face, and reckon there's bound to be a defibrillator on the premises. Early in the third, two games and three points up, I send him back in pursuit of an inch-perfect lob. It does a dead-spider fall to the foot of the back wall. There is a noise of splintering wood, as if a model plane has pranged into a house.

Maurice lies splayed in the angle. His back is leaning against the wall so that his body is at ninety degrees to his legs. His racket is aping the posture by having an L-shaped shaft. An almost clean break, with just a few fibres in the hinge between the two parts. I offer to lend him my spare one but he has had enough. I have turned into a monster, and he is as much confused as defeated.

Before the guilt comes to seek me out - which it will, it will - I wonder why I never did this before. Like all the best ideas. Instead of patronising him with the illusion of equality. For a start it would very likely have got me out of subsequent encounters. I might even have let my club membership lapse and hence not run the risk of seeing Brian Miller. Which of course I now think I do as the profile of his big head moves across the viewing window. I keep repeating in my own ear that I have not actually done anything wrong - not to him at any rate-- and fall well short of convincing myself.

Considering Maurice has taken such a hammering, I have to admire his manner. I think it comes from denial of some sort, as so much obduracy seems to. He is simply not accepting the reality of what has taken place. Like that spokesman of Saddam Hussein's, Tariq Aziz, dismissing talk of an invasion even as the US tanks were swarming into Baghdad.

So, no post-match analysis, no comparative study of our well-matched style, not a word about the undoubted improvement in my ground strokes. Nothing. Instead he regroups, buys a round - 'still off the sauce then?' - and shifts the competition to a more cerebral court. Crisis in the health service is his chosen pitch. Long-term funding of care for the elderly his preoccupation, holism his theme. He throws the word in as if it has only now occurred to him.

I can see where he's heading, of course I can. It's as plain as a road on a map. Along it he duly goes, and then: 'You know, William, I sometimes think it's a rather overused word.'

'Holism?'

'Yes. It strikes me we would do well to re-appropriate the term in order to define the way in which the NHS should be run.'

'Funny you should say that,' I reply. 'Just the other day I was reading an article in, *The Lancet* I think it was, by a former hospital administrator, in Lincolnshire I think it was, and he was saying very much the same thing. And I can remember thinking what a load of glib and modish old nonsense it was.'

Maurice silenced. For now. I've non-plussed him. Even done something similar to myself while I'm about it. Next time perhaps I should murder him. Just play him along with crucifying rallies that eventually do, physically, kill him. When has anyone ever been charged with murder-by-squash-match? For now, I go all cool and say 'Shall we call this one a draw Maurice?'

The back of Brian Miller's head brings me back down to earth. He is going down the exit steps into the car-park. I feel the same chill I used to feel when a very overgrown boy (forgotten his name, which must be significant) used to fling me around and sit on me in the mud of the playground. Identical fear. No negotiation possible. The language of cicvil resolution simply not spoken here. The terror passes as Brian Miller vanishes.

Still a good day for me. Good results, good outcomes. As Clive says - no, as Clive used to say - the best thing about recovery is that it becomes interesting to be ourselves. We surprise ourselves. We want to hang around and see what happens.

Nov 14th. Dad on the phone. Imogen passes it over as if it is something not very nice that she is holding in tissue. One of those calls I'd rather take at surgery than at home, but he's too old now to start thinking it is all right to disturb a man at his place of work. He's got the funereal tone on. Telegraphing that there's bad news coming by the downturn in the voice. Like the news readers. I can hear it as soon as he says 'Hello William.'

Imogen leaves the kitchen. I don't know - I never do - whether it's out of respect for my privacy or despair at who I'm talking to. The perishing old chill coming off the in-laws. She didn't deserve that. Just another perishing old chill from another set of in-laws behaving disgracefully. The oldest narrative going.

'Duggy's gone.'

'Oh Dad, I'm so sorry to hear that.'

'Aye. Late last night. Peaceful in the end. No struggle.'

'That's good, Dad. I'm glad of that at least.'

'Aye.'

'I hope you are too. That he didn't have to struggle any longer. And so, in that respect, nor did she. I hope. Nor did Mary.'

'She's here if you want.'

'She's very lucky to have you, Dad. I mean, to have you living down the Row. And you're lucky she's there too, I'd say. I know how close you were to Duggy.'

'I'll put her on now.'

He does so, and Mary Garside says 'Hello William,' quite bright and firm considering.

'Oh, hello Mary. I'm so sorry.'

'Aye.'

'I have very good memories of him, you know.'

'Aye.'

I don't. He was just another of the old boys, and had been there forever. On the earth, under the earth, up in Highmoor. To my shame I can't summon up a distinguishing feature. Something to do with dogs, I think. Whippets. Or hound trails. It all blurs.

'It was good to see you, William,' she goes on. 'Don't leave it too long now.'

She then says something about the funeral, and how he's not

expecting me to come for that, it's such a distance, but folks like to be told. I don't listen too carefully as I am already thinking the outlandish thoughts of, I suppose, love. They are out of order and out of place here, but I cannot keep them away and nor, honestly, do I want to.

Madness has now officially got control of my behaviour. It's a very old, very well attested form of madness, and I'm in good company. Not that this makes it all right. I will take Serena with me to see Dad. I will do what? Yes, why not? I will capitalise on this new, welcome goodwill between us. He won't mind, I feel sure he won't. I can't go on seeing Serena only in her room. We'll get caged. We should have a life beyond those walls, but how?

These streets feel thick with danger. Her father not that far away, albeit in a very different neighbourhood. People everywhere. People who know me or know her. Perhaps she should have moved far away, as young women do. But she hasn't. Deal with what's there. I love those moors and I would love her to see them. To be with her there. We could stay at the Pitman's and to hell with what anyone thinks, myself included. Life is short. Surely Dad wouldn't freeze and outlaw her the way he froze and outlawed Imogen.

That was just his misguided loyalty to Mum, surely; carrying on the rejection that was born of her jealousy, her hot blind hatred at the first sniff of another woman around her son. At the risk of heresy, stupid Mum. What a dreadful legacy. Dad might just be delighted to see Serena. Sometimes the old outgrow the straitness of an earlier morality which was never really theirs anyway; it takes too much energy to keep the rest of the world in order.

For all these reasons, I find myself thinking 'Poor Imogen.' But I can't afford too much of that just now. I should, but I can't. Serena. How could anyone not be glad to see her?

Nov 19th. Her room again. This time the knowledge that I am

185

due to see her has made me unable to think of anything else. It is an almost total disability. For the past few days my patients come in and become her as they sit where she sat. The transformations are beyond implausible. Mr. Blain with the cold he's had for two years (Chillblain? Not funny) acquires her face; Mr. Glazier whose middle fat will once again tumble over his pants and fall down to his thighs like a circular pelmet when we have his top off - he acquires the taut curves of her waist. They are the briefest of metamorphoses, but I am toxic with her images and they glaze my retinas whenever they choose. And they choose all the time.

After morning surgery I am talking to Joan, our brilliant new practice manager, about something. I can't remember what, but then instant amnesia is a symptom of my condition. Total non-storage of data. Big, round, pub landlady Joan. I want to put my hand on her back and pull her towards me and send my fingers into her blouse. Sacking offence, don't do it.

My first visit to Serena is replaying and replaying. I can click on another title for my projector, but the same sequence occupies the screen. Our mouth-joined bodies fighting themselves to be free of clothes. The animal snorts, better than the smoothest cocktail compliments; the inevitable victory and triumphant tumble. The unbelieving yells and the grounded riot.

There is nothing that does not point me at this room and the action in it. I am as priapic as a weather vane. The cock is determining the direction of travel rather than following the pull of a superior force. There is no superior force. I don't know how I sustain it. I feel it exhausting me, levying all my blood to maintain its standing while the rest of me fights it out for what's left. Like the starving Catholic village that still boasts its single, solid spire.

This time we demolish it and wait with an almost Christian certainty for its resurrection. Or reserection as she calls it. We will it up. No problem. There it stands, proud and plain, miraculous as the early monoliths. Goodness, how did they do that? Sleep lies patiently in wait and then takes me down into the Underground. All the usual frames: train in, passengers out, cluster of new ones pushing themselves and each other into the doors; the buggy going on, the boy getting separated from his mother and sister; the train moving; the boy yanked into a fast walk, a trot.

Then something different, something new. Instead of falling and being scraped along the platform to the tunnel's murderous mouth, he is calling out. It is my name: 'William, William. You must help me, William.' The noise pulls me awake and I see Serena's lips, barely six inches from my face. They are moving in sync with these words, as if she is reciting my interior script. She says it again: 'You must help me, William, I am only small.'

When I realise that the words have come from Serena, I take it as a joke, guessing that this is some, I don't know, larky persona that she has adopted with other lovers; one that comes out in the unguarded loopiness of the post-coital moment, before we are reclaimed by the day in progress, the alleged adults within. Yet there is an urgency in her pleading. She is looking directly upwards, at the ceiling and yet not at the ceiling. She is mouthing the words with the intensity of here-and-now.

If there is an absence here, it is merely an absence from the usual manner of communication which people have in the wake of such passion. It is only when she turns her face left into mine that I catch the mix of terror and reproach in the fierceness of her look. I feel the chill of lying with a complete stranger, someone who has come to take Serena's place while she is, what, not being Serena. I can't think of a comparable panic in my experience except the time I attached myself to strangers at a funfair because the man had the same coat as my father.

The wrongness arrives again. This time it feels more visceral than before, something as acute as a gut illness. Well, I would not be the first to pathologise love, nor to find in it all the menace of serious mood-changing materials. Poets have been doing it since Sappho, all the way through to the Jacobean dramatists and on to the more enlightened of the agony aunts. Maybe the grim and joyless theory of the air bubble is valid after all. This holds that if you are an addict then you will always remain one, no matter how much you alter the details of your behaviour. There is an air bubble in a bottle. You rotate the bottle into a different position and the bubble vanishes. But's it's only out of view for a short time before rising back undaunted to the surface.

I ask her if she is all right. Sometimes the best questions are the least original, and she gives a slightly shirty yes, as if resenting the inquiry. The moment goes. I follow her lead and behave as if nothing has happened. I shouldn't, but I do. How often have I said those words.

November 20th. Another dilemma which I have no training for. I owe Inez £100. Or rather, Ricky owes Inez £100. But Ricky isn't here. And Imogen has gone to Oxford so that he can show her round and introduce her to the alleged magic of the deer park, the river, the dreaming spires generally. She's up for it as never before. Apparently her brother Jay has been on at her again about the need to get out and enjoy herself, and she has paid attention.

She and Ricky then plan to carry on to her sister in Banbury, the one who was always suspicious of me and I could never work out why. I admire Ricky; after a rapprochement with me, away with his mother. Very even-handed and diplomatic, but loving too. I must phone him and see how they're doing. Also establish when they're back. I see the chance of a whole night with Serena open up in front of me like a clear, dangerous page in a diary.

First though, the (totally platonic) prospect of a whole night with Inez. That is, no-one but the two of us in the house to-gether. So, how to handle the case of the hundred pounds. As far as I know, Ricky has still not paid her, although he might have scraped the money together without my knowing. I doubt it, and will proceed on the assumption that she is still owed.

If I have such a thing as a moral compass in my emotional hardware, the needle is being flung all over the place, from the magnetic north of settling your debts, even if they are your son's, to the far contrary south of withholding funds because payment would sanction the transaction between her and Ricky. Am I against it? If so, why? No longer drunk and maud-lin, Ricky's mood is improved beyond recognition. Young men do change when they have broken their sexual duck and gained their first experience of, well, of an innings. Yet he was in se-vere turbulence that night a few weeks ago. Understandable, what with the challenge of confession and the horrors of debt. Mounting debt, you could call it.

But now, with his system clear of all that alcohol, he seems to have a new confidence on him, a sense of his own viability. I go to the cashpoint and get out a hundred pounds. I carry it around in my trouser pocket so that if I decide to settle with her instantly, I've got the wherewithal. The money can just change hands, no questions asked. Or perhaps I should put it in an en-velope and leave it out for her, no explanatory note or anything. While I'm deliberating, Inez's bedroom door opens and she is standing in front of me on the landing.

'Hello Inez, I say.'

'Hullo Docktor Neeyoogate,' she replies, using the formal address rather aggressively, it seems to me. She looks as if she is dressed for something, I have no idea what. She is wearing a dark silk dress with thin shoulder straps, a mid-thigh hem and a silky sheen that is responding to the light on the landing. It re-minds me of a nightie that Imogen used to have many years ago.

It is a nightie. In fact I think it is Imogen's nightie, the very one it is reminding me of. She smiles. Not unfriendly, more canny. The smile of someone who wants you to know they know what you are up to. I wish she'd let me know, because I'm not sure myself.

She says something by way of explanation, but I can't make head or tail of it. She's emerged as one of the au pairs whose English has got worse during her time with us. In fact I'd say none of the others ever matched these levels of deterioration. It's possible she's making it sound even more unusable than it is, so that she doesn't have to give an account of herself.

I am trying not to stare too hard at her, but at close range it is hard to pretend to someone that you are not looking them up and down if that is what you are doing. I have to say she is looking more alluring than I have ever seen her. I lose the plot again. First I try to think of the Spanish for nightie, in order to explain my interest. It comes out like *noches* - night. I repeat it, trying to make it sound more authentic, this time putting *bella* in front of it. She gives a slightly bemused grin.

In order to change the subject, I take the little roll of five twenties from my pocket and hold them out for her. The grin turns to a nasty grimace. She flings the notes to the floor, spits at them and lets fly a fusillade of Spanish invective. I understand not a syllable, but the meaning is all too clear. Or is it? Does she think I'm acting on, or trying to act on, Ricky's recommendation? Or is she objecting to the mere fact of his telling me what he did? I'm not only clueless here, but also operating well beyond my linguistic, cultural and moral competence. I go into our bedroom, she into hers. Even through the two doors I can hear a blurr of what must be expleting on the phone. Who to? A friend? A fellow erm, what, escort, is that the word? Another dreadful one. To Ricky? Whoodooyoothinkingyoooareyoo-neeyoogaytes. Fortuately I can't understand a word. This one's well beyond me. Why this pitch of rage? Is it because Ricky has blown her cover? And if so, what cover was that anyway? Or is it because she thought I was fancying myself as a, what, client, now that there was no-one else in the house? What sort of man does she think I am? Don't answer that.

I decide to leave the money out for her, somewhere, so she can do with it as she wants. Then I cancel the plan and decide to give it to Ricky when he gets back, so that he can settle the debt himself. This is what I should have done in the first place.

Nov 21st. Serena taken aback by my suggestion of a trip to Highmoor with her. No sooner have I made it than I think it's a dreadful error. But then I think how easy it is to interpret surprise as disapproval. The first faces they cause can be so similar. Like laughter mimicking tears.

But it's out now, which is where I wanted it. Dad, against all the odds, has become the man I am most likely to confide in. I ask myself if this dash towards intimacy with him is an attempt at compensation for years of awkwardness, and as usual I come up with no answers. Serena embraces me with everything she has, and says she would love to come with me, please forgive her if she didn't seem enthusiastic straight away, just that she wasn't expecting such an invitation and had to absorb it before she could respond.

Like me, she had wondered whether our relationship was to conduct itself forever in this one small room, but didn't want to raise the matter for fear of seeming pushy.

I stay over. She says she has been dreaming of this. When the guilt and anxiety threaten to take her place in my arms, like cold-eyed professionals in an excuse-me dance, I cling to her even harder to rebuff them. Everything in the evening and the approaching night is new. As far as I can tell, there are no carpets or rugs in the building. You can hear people walking across the floors overhead, a toilet struggling to flush, a fire door banging shut down at the far end of the corridor. The whole structure has a percussive acoustic. It auralises the spaces around us, similar spaces above, beside, below declaring themselves through the darkness. A tap goes on upstairs. The water slaps around with the washed hands. The plug gives a muted hiccup, and after a pause of a few seconds you hear the water going down into the ground at the foot of the outside pipe. Nothing insulates the act of being in this place.

We lie there and talk as the sounds alter. A sudden disembodied yell, as if someone has scalded themselves on a cooking ring; the spring-creak of someone else, or maybe the same person, sitting on the bed to undress. A running tide of young drunks as the pubs chuck out. Down the back of the building they come, picking fights with the dustbins, then blowing off down to the station and the all-night liquor shop.

Then nothing but a lone straggler taking issue with something in the sky. And off into the long dark watches. Four, five, six hours, I lose count, between the very last of the night creatures and the crinkling of plastic as some fresh foxes truffle at the rubbish bags.

The only other sound of any consequence in that period is the voice from inside Serena. When I first hear it, I think it is a component of some dream that I have found myself in. Therefore I think it is I who have woken myself with my own talking. But the voice is following me into my consciousness. It is hers, even though her rhythms, her sounds and her scents are those of a sleeping person.

It is the small girl again, calling out for help. Same as last time, except that now she is even littler and there is a stain of something or somewhere different in her accent. The vowels have the flatness of the Midlands, the East Midlands I would say, not unlike Imogen's Leicester aunt. She is sounding desperate. There is something about lambs and chickens, but the words don't come properly into focus. I wait for her to wake herself, just as she woke me, so that I might find out what's been going on. But the episode passes like a wave going overhead, and she lapses into calmness again.

When it's six, and we can hear the radio pips from another room, she wakes up and smiles. I ask her if she slept well and she smiles and asks for some tea. She approves of what I bring her and cups it cosily. I'm waiting for the hangover that must follow the zeal of my idea. For the moment there's just joyful anticipation. I feel ecstatic, literally standing outside myself and looking back into a place of alarming happiness.

Nov 22nd. Phone Dad to say I'm going to be up that way again. With someone else. A friend. Would he like a visit. Only six weeks since the last one, I know, but that was so enjoyable I'd love to repeat it. If he fancied it. He says yes, instantly and enthusiastically, adding that Mary Garside would love to see me again too. I tell him the friend is a female one, and considerably younger than me. Why bother with euphemisms like colleague, assistant, god-daughter? Life is indeed too short and we're all too old.

He's known for a long time, probably as long as I have myself, that Imogen and I are in poor shape. He even asked me about it once. I couldn't discuss it then, and he drew the right conclusions.

There is a brief pause and then he says: 'That's nice then.' The words are neutrally spoken; no judgement in them. No disapproval. If I detect anything, it's the hint of interest. Mischief even, not just on my part but on his as well.

'What did you say her name was?'

'Serena.'

'Well, that's a nice name.'

'She's a nice person, Dad.'

'I wouldn't doubt it. We look forward, I look forward to meeting her. And to see you again, William.'

'Sorry it's a bit like the number eleven bus.'

'What's that then?' He raises his voice as old people do when something confuses them over the phone; a hangover from the years of bad lines.

'You know, nothing for a long time and then two in a row.'

'Is that right? Two in a row would be a fine thing up here.'

'Yes?'

'It's coming off altogether. No more buses to Highmoor. That's it.'

'But they can't do that.'

'No, you're right, but they have. Well, not yet. Next September.'

'But there's people there that depend on it.'

'There is. You're talking to one of them.'

'I don't think they can get away with it.'

'Oh, there's a great deal of opposition to it. Hundred per cent, I'd say. But what's a hundred per cent of Highmoor to the fellows in the transport offices? Might as well be the bleating of a few sheep on the fellside.'

Nov 24th. Imogen totally understanding. I hate writing this. Not just understanding but almost glad, which does relieve me. 'Of course you must go and see him again if you want to. That man was a very close friend of his, wasn't he. And particularly if your father's not well himself.' I have manufactured a lung condition about which he is wanting my advice, so that I'm touting a double motive: bereavement and infirmity. 'He's lucky he has you,' she adds with great civility, 'particularly as he doesn't trust the doctors up there, does he.'

'I'll only be gone a couple of days,' I say.

'It's very good the two of you are getting on. It's just a pity that,'

'Yes.'

'Never mind.'

'No.'

The phone rings with impeccable timing and keeps us from the looming awkwardness. It's her brother again. She asks me with her eyes if I mind her taking the call and I shake my head amiably. Even so, she turns away, squirrelling the phone into her shoulder and lowering her voice. The old exclusive way she has with Jay. I can just hear her end of the conversation. It is to do with some song, which you wouldn't expect from him. Unless I've always got him wrong and failed to acknowledge his hidden depths. She's humming some notes, apparently in response to what Jay's singing. And I had him down as tone deaf.

Nov 29th. Haven Park Monday evening. A bit further afield than my usual. I've come here because it's a different crowd. I've been open with Serena about it, and it's not a problem. I bump into Clive, who happens to be having a meetings binge, trying out new ones for the sake of it. He shakes me rather stiffly by the hand and asks how I am. No malice here. No festering resentments. He has, as they say, moved on. Respect to him. In the meeting I step up as close as I can towards the plate of honesty and share about our, or rather my imminent visit. In the end I am so economical with the truth that it could pass for a court circular.

Wednesday Dec 1st. East Coast main line again. City and suburb and light industry to within twenty minutes of Peterborough, then the flat infinity of Lincolnshire passing to the right. Empty country but crowded train. In Serena's case very crowded. The man next to her is so vast that when he sat down he failed to fit, spilling powerfully over the top of the arm rests on one side, and into her on the other. I catch her eyes and we start to laugh. No hope of self-control. I try to manufacture a cough for myself, but it is swamped by the tears of juvenile hilarity. The enormous man says to Serena: 'I think there's something the matter with your father.'

She apologises for me, says I need a glass of water, and we

escape down the train and into the buffet. Somewhere in my head I'm computing the chances of our being spotted. One in I don't know how many thousand. Spotted by a hostile party who would then blow the whistle on us? Multiply by two or three. Spotted by someone who knows her father? Multiply again. Spotted by her father, the way Imogen's father once spotted us going to the cinema when she was meant to be at choir practice? I call a halt. My heart's not in the game. There's a risk all right, but it's only spicing the journey. When did I ever think otherwise?

We find ourselves talking of our shared friends in AA. It is the first time we have done so at any length, but not the last, I feel sure. She has the unfakeable enthusiasm of the newcomer who realises that this way of life is for her. She even lists a number of women's names and asks me which, if any, might best suit her as a sponsor. I answer that she must find one to whom she feels she can say anything at all, however shocking it sounds, without fear of being misunderstood or harshly judged. She nods at this in a way which makes me think she has already seen the importance of such trust.

Before the end of the journey we come back to the subject. I can feel the urgency in her, but I can also sense her reserve in talking about it. It is less reticence than diplomacy - not a quality I had spotted before - as if she does not want to crowd me with questions or take my supposed expertise for granted. I think she is also keen for me to notice this sensitivity of hers. It was only the other day that I feared she might be coming to meetings in order to stalk me. It couldn't have been a more unfounded worry. I am embarrassed by such a self-centred diagnosis of another's condition. Her desire for the meetings — it's truly a thirst -makes perfect sense to me. Her mother died of alcohol, and although I'm not allowed to say these things, or even think them, I do find myself wishing her father would go the same way.

With other travelling companions, I would probably be apologising. Sorry about the train, sorry about the stations, sorry about the buses, sorry about the moors, sorry about the village, sorry about my father, sorry about the old woman who lives up the Row from my father. Sorry about sorry about. With Serena I don't feel the need. She gets it. She flies wide-eyed over the railway viaduct at Durham, with the solid fantasies of cathedral, castle and palace going past on their promontory in the loop of the Wear. I look at her eyes being flicked rapidly from side to side as they try to keep pace with the view.

She rattles and floats across the majestic slow approach into the city. She looks slightly dazed as the train emerges from its high bank and strides in across the Tyne like an arriving army, flights of bridges, sky and water to the right and left of it. Then the outrageous awning of the station, all that volume of air staked out in stone and glass by unstoppable Victorians. Rather than forcing age into the fabric, the impacted grime gives it the power of the national high noon from which it came.

Just down the road is the old Lit. and Phil. Building, part of the same socio-geological stratum. We've nearly an hour until the Hexham train, so we go and have a look round. My father brought me here when I was nine or ten. The idea was to put me into direct contact with knowledge, rather as you might take a boy to the zoo if you wanted to nurture in him a fondness for wild animals. The smell is unchanged. It is the now rare smell of print asleep in old pages, and old pages bound into an entity by their spines. Broad, proper spines with here and there the vertebrae of raised leather tooling. Up and up the wall they go, climbing on each other's shoulders in a high ladder of aspiration. Serena takes in the air approvingly as if she has found herself in a secret autumn valley, and says she wished her parents had brought her to places like this.

The old pram of a train strikes out for Carlisle, amplifying each uneven joint in the track. Into the countryside of the Tyne and the wall; solid farmhouses composed of its plundered length; bits of outpost masonry re-knit from Roman to yeoman. The abbey tower and the grim old keep arriving to the left. The Station Hotel and the bus depot.

Three of us this time for the ride up into the half-wilderness of the moor; Serena and me and the same woman as last time. We acknowledge each other. She probably thinks I'm bringing old Jack Newgate's granddaughter on a visit. But when Serena nestles into my side as the bus growls its way up, she has to have a re-think.

The slow climb into the sky, the air between the ears starting to push and pop. The crown of the ground, England's secret top. Then the small descent into Highmoor. The bus's knees going. The triangular square. Dad coming out of his front door in response to the high tone of the motor. Him standing there like the welcoming committee.

He looks with warm fascination at Serena and says 'You must be Serena.' They both laugh at the thought she could be anyone else, or that anyone else could be her. I can feel him scanning my face as I look proudly at her and hopefully at him.

Mrs. Garside is sitting in the front room. She could have been there at the table all the while since I was last in the house. She has taken charge of the tea operation, which Dad would only cede to the most trusted of allies.

I say, 'Hello again, Mrs. Garside,' and she says 'Mary, please.'

'I was sorry to hear about your husband.'

'I know you were, and bless you for it. We all were. He and your father were very close. Went back further than time. This must be Serena.'

'I'm so pleased to meet you, Mrs. Garside.'

'As I say, it's Mary, and I'm pleased to meet you too. We're a little out of the way here, so it's a treat to have people come by.'

'Depends on who they are,' says Dad.

'His father is more sociable than he lets on,' says Mary to Serena.

'I'm glad someone's spotted that,' I say.

'He's been ever so good to me.'

'Nonsense,' says Dad.

'Then he's like his son,' says Serena to Mary.

'That's just as well then,' says Dad.

'Because he's been very good to me as well.'

I say 'Nonsense,' and then we all laugh, all four of us. And down we sit as if we've been doing this forever and have no plans to get up again. Do I at some point, privately and invisibly, fret for the older woman not being my mother and the younger one not being my wife? If I do, I keep it so tightly contained that it has no access to my conscious attention. When regrets choose to tyrannise me, I will know about it. They will probably do as they have done before, jump on the wagon of me and freight it down so hard that nothing can shift it; unless they get me on the downward gradient, hurtle me to the buffers and crush me there.

No stirring of such a thing just now. We sit there in our sad happiness, all curiosity and strange familiarity. So much to disapprove of in this world. So little of it going on in this house.

'More scones, love?' says Mary to Serena.

'Thank you. They're the best I've ever had. So light and, yes, so light. Perhaps a little less of that delicious cream.'

'Don't tell me you're watching your weight now, love, or I shall despair. Slip of a thing you are.'

'Tell us about yourself, love.' says my father. So she does. A little bit. The convent school, the horse-riding, the relatively late discovery that she wanted to act. It's a brisk canter through the course of her brief life, and it dodges the five-bar gates of her dead mother, her dead sister and her unthinkable father.

'I take my hat off to you,' says Mary. 'I'd have loved to do that but I never had the courage for it. Still, I'd have had a struggle, wouldn't I, as we're a bit short of professional theatres in Highmoor, isn't that right Jack. My parents took me to *Cinderella* in Carlisle and that was me gone. Well, for a year.'

'What happened then?' asks Dad.

'Boys, Jack, boys. Do you have family, Serena?

'Yes, more's the pity.' I try to come to her rescue by saying lightly that it's a bit of a sore point at the moment. Both Mary and my father nod firmly at this and we never touch the subject again.

'Grew up in London, did you?'

'Leicestershire,' says Serena, providing information that is new to me.

'In the countryside. Middle of nowhere really. We came to London when I was four or five.'

'And the two of you met,' says Mary. It started out as a question but then thought itself out of order and demoted itself to a statement. A slightly obvious one. I think about interjecting 'through work,' but quickly decide in favour of 'we have a number of friends in common.' True.

Serena asks Dad about his work. When he sees that she is interested, and not just going through the motions, he answers her fully. The call-up by lottery, his moving away from home for the first time, the darkness and the sheer strangeness of it. He enlarges in a way he never has to me. It reminds me how children lack the distance from their parents to know them well.

'The darkness,' he goes on, wrapping his arms around his ribs and concentrating. 'What can I say? All the days were dark. There were these men I didn't know, just the flash of their faces in the torchlight. Old enough to be my father, some of them, which is not to say they were old men. What must they have made of whippersnappers like us? Oh yes, and the roofs so low. No higher than this table, some of them. As I say, what with the dark, it was all a journey into an unknown place. My life, I mean, not just us going into those tunnels. I couldn't pick one from the other. It must sound odd, but I can't say it any other way.'

'You don't have to,' says Serena.

'That's right,' says Mary. 'And you know, Jack, that's how Douglas used to look at it. Not that he did say much in that line. But what you just said, that could have been him talking.'

'Is that right,' says Dad. He looks affected, as if he is remembering him hard. Maybe he feels he is wearing the conversational equivalent of dead man's shoes, or regretting that he and Duggy never shared these thoughts and images with each other when they had the chance.

We lapse into silence, each of us surely focusing ourselves and our memories on dear ones who have gone for good, whether husbands or wives or parents or siblings. Armistice Day just a few weeks back, when silence was turned out in industrial quantities. No awkwardness about silence. No necessity for smashing it.

December 2nd. Josh and Graeme most welcoming at the Pitman's Arms. Not that I was expecting otherwise. They know little of me beyond the fact that my father lives in Upper Level Row. My marriage? My history? My present? All blank, I expect. They take an instant liking to Serena, and she to them. The menu has proliferated, even in the few weeks since I was here. Filet mignon with sage cream and ratatouille, boeuf bourguignon, a brioche called Crown of Epiphany, and plenty besides.

From the snug bar an oblong of smoky air is coming from the old serving hatch, clear as a projector beam. The same faces in the same hats, at the same game. One of them, the same one as before, breaks cover across the restaurant floor to the Gents and re-emerges a couple of minutes later hauling his fly back up.

Same laughter from one of the tables, American again.

This time though, the table is full of heavy and dark-suited men, in the Al Gore mould but much younger. I count five or six of them, sitting there shoulder to shoulder and so broad that they are having to draw their elbows in to eat, projecting their forearms almost daintily. They make Graeme's boeuf en croute look no bigger than petits fours. They could be linebackers from the Boston Red Sox except that they are too watchful, too much at work in their faces to be sportsmen.

With them is a young woman and an older couple. They have their backs to me but I take them to be her parents. 'Steve was right about the food,' says the man, silver-haired and with a Southern state in his drawl.

'So, Chelsea,' says his wife to the young woman, 'who did he say he was approaching?'

'He talked about Travolta.'

'Uh-huh?' says her mother, waiting.

'And Kathleen Turner.'

'Okay. Would she take weight off?'

'I guess, if necessary.'

'Okay. Except Travolta already did Pa.'

'Well now, honey,' her husband comes in, 'that's only if you accept that... *that* book contained a portrait of me.' The *that* is pejorative, used in preference to the title.

'Aw, c'mon Billy,' says his wife.

Their daughter comes in again with the skill of someone used to defusing potential stand-offs. 'He also mentioned Colin Firth. And Gyllenhaal for the Oxford years. Oh, and Kylie for Mom.'

'Kylie would be far too old,' says Hillary.

'Seymour Hoffman was begging to do Dad, but Steve said no.'

'That's good,' says Bill, visibly relieved. 'Say Chelsea, did you mention Hillary's idea to Steve?'

'Which one? She has so many.'

'That we play ourselves.'

'I'm too busy, Billy. You know that. I have a career.'

'I have a career too, honey.'

'I didn't mention it to him,' says Chelsea. 'I thought that should come from you guys.'

'We're a long way from Oxford here,' says Bill. 'Can you remind me what we're doing here?'

'Steve said we had to come,' says Chelsea.

'Right. Right. Y'know... ' He sits back, expansive and anecdotal now, the old dog charm still alight, the head woggling and the eyes twinkling shut - practised modesty doing its thing. 'I remember Aaron telling me one day,'

'Aaron who, Pa?'

'Spelling. *Dynasty* man. Used to live in Crosby's mansion, remember honey?

'Crosby like in Stills and Nash?'

'Stop it. Bing. I remember him telling me the British royal family was the ultimate soap. He even got around to casting it. Let me see. He wanted Liz Taylor for The Queen, until he read up on Princess Margaret. So Lee Remick got the Queen. Beatty got Charles, which I have to say did surprise me. I thought Dustin, but there you go. Eastwood for Princess Anne. I said, I think you mean the Duke of Edinburgh, Aaron, and he said OK, so who gets the Duke, and of course it was Heston. Now, I guess, it would be Gyllenhaal for Prince William.'

'Oh come on,' says his wife.

'On the grounds that if it ain't got Gyllenhaal, you ain't got a movie. And then he said, no, forget all that, we'll get them to play themselves, sure it'll cost but they got all those palaces to maintain and their country's broke, so; do you know what new roofs cost these days, and I mean we're talking ten-acre roofs here. Billy, he says, if anyone wants to do a movie of you and

Hillary, and hell who wouldn't, then play yourselves. You're a fine actor.'

His two women laugh at this, a little too enthusiastically for his liking.

'Be yourself,' he winds up. 'Ain't that the name of the game? Be yourself. That right, boys?'

They nod in unison. He gets up and stretches his legs. There is a small explosion of laughter among the boys. They control it. It has been caused by one of them spotting Cockermouth on the map and wondering if they would be heading there. He walks over to the mining photos. *Déjà vu* takes me over and I suggest to Serena we go upstairs. I don't think Dad is ready for a visit from the forty-second president of America and his family.

Serena soundlessly happy. Concussed with disbelief about everything, but then so am I. As if she is carrying on from the conversation downstairs, she says the thing she most loves about being with me - it embarrasses me even to write it privately - is the knowledge that she is known; that she is with someone who has been where she has been.

I hear the words and am glad of them, even while I am wishing that I could be with her more thoroughly and not get stranded when she reverts to the sound, and presumably the place, of her infancy. Yet her words do bear the unmistakable stamp of recovery, and are none the worse for doing so. I reply that her joy and her reasons for it are in that case identical to mine. I say I didn't know about Leicestershire, and she says 'oh yes' without wanting to enlarge.

She leaves this for later, hours later when she stirs in her sleep and starts speaking in that voice again. The same accent, girlhood Leicestershire, and with the same urgent note of fear. As if something unspeakable is about to happen. I wait for the wave to pass and the sea of her to settle. I'm not the best of Freudians, but I like the old boy's point about the brain never sleeping, devilling away at the stuff of the day, breaking it down and processing it, no less than the gut and the liver process what goes down our throats, poor buggers.

Instead of coming up with excrement and urine, the brain does its less guessable trick of converting the data of our days to the illustrated stories of our nights. But with such a range of styles, from punctilious reportage, as in my Underground dream, to postmodern collages that make Resnais look as plain-dealing as Elmore Leonard.

And so I lie next to her, also on my back, the brass-rubbing spouse, waiting for her recycling plant to do what it has to do. This only becomes a problem when her status moves from asleep to awake but the voice stays put inside her. Not just the voice but the persona that goes with it. The little girl somewhere in Leicestershire.

She sits up, swings her legs out and sits on the edge of the bed. She is talking quite fast. I try to hang on to the words as they fly past, but I can only grab the tails of them. Oddly appropriate since many of the words seem to concern animals. These creatures themselves are passing in such a way as to make it impossible for her to hold them, or have them, or keep them. Whatever it is she wants to do.

The lisp I thought I detected before is now more pronounced. I think this is because she is, as it were, younger than on that occasion. To say it is convincing would be to patronise her. True, whenever the voice comes, I start thinking it must be an affectation, the very committed pretence of a very gifted actor. And so again I wait for the function, whatever it is, to be performed, and for normality to be resumed.

But today the little girl - I put her at no more than three or four - is hanging on. A rabbit comes into her speech, and a farmer, and a gun. She is rummaging with bits of *Run Rabbit Run*. Then she puts her hands dramatically over her ears as the thing goes off and she screams.

The problem becomes social, adult, administrative. How to contain this quite loud and very distressed noise. How to explain it if someone becomes curious. How to have this companion with me at breakfast.

Most of the building is still asleep, but the very first smell of Graeme's expensive bacon is curling its way up the stairs, a more effective summons to the day than any alarm clock. She paces round the bedroom with a splay-footed gait that is new to me. She covers her face with her hands, then removes them and looks at the door as if she is going to have to make a break for it. I am waiting for her to turn and look at me, knowing that this will be a make-or-break moment. She does. Who am I? Friend or foe? Comfort or threat?

I wait to find out. I smile at her and see her return, coming back into herself through her face. Her mouth lets go of its lisping shape, and her shoulders pull back and grow. It is the current returning to a shorted appliance, the lifeblood heating on again in a chilly house.

I put my arms out just as if I am welcoming a stranger back. She takes it as a routine hug and joins in enthusiastically. 'What a beautiful place this is, William,' she says. 'What a beautiful smell and what a beautiful day. Thank you so much for bringing me here.'

I reply that it is a pleasure, which it once more is. She looks so right, so balanced, sorted, all those things, that I even find myself questioning the actuality of what I have just seen. Certainly she is not acknowledging it, and I would love to join her there if I could.

December 3rd. Up well before it's light to write these pages. These days they take far less time than they used to, even though the long entries run to two or three hours. Not such a problem when I'm at home as I can settle into my study and

206

get scribbling while everyone is asleep. Late into the night or from the very early morning. It has become a compulsion. Surprise surprise. If I can't do it, I start to feel void and panicked. Is this therefore another addiction, to which I have transferred my always-present needfulness? The first answer is that I am past caring. The second is, probably not. If you accept that damage must be done by the process which you then repeat until you have the illusion of contentment, then the paradigm doesn't hold. Yes, I evidently need to do this writing, but no, I can't, really see any damage in the activity.

Strange though, to be writing up the previous day's observations while Serena lies asleep a few feet away, harbouring whoever she is harbouring. I have my strategy ready in case she wakes suddenly; the broad spread of a newspaper which I would simply put over the top of the notebook; and then, when I could, I would put it back down into the expansive folds of my briefcase. Well, Jane Austen had her knitting. Excellent, but not for me.

Outside the air is dark and cold with the recent snow. Between sentences I go to the window and focus hard on the land in the far and middle distance. With no light to pollute those long slow lines, the tops of the hills begin to declare themselves and start the act of separation from the sky. Soon this big book will be full up and I shall have to start another. Even the thought of letting go of this one, all scuffed and roughed and squiggled to death, fills me with ridiculous fears of abandonment. For heaven's sake.

Goodbye to Dad and to Mary Garside. 'I'm so pleased to have met you, pet,' he says to Serena. The use of this word, always and exclusively for Mum until now, moves me so much that I'm worried he will see my eyes mist. Since he's got the hugging habit, there's no stopping him. Or Mary. I'm wondering what they think of it all - of me and Serena.

In the end it stares me in the face. Or rather, I stare it in the face, his face. All he ever wanted for me was that I should be happy and fulfilled. For some reason he and Mum must have seen something in Imogen - or more specifically in Imogen and me - that was going to be an obstacle to that objective. I can't think what they knew or how they knew it. I don't think I would have a clue about who or what would be the making or the ruining of Ricky. We think we're smarter than our parents but it isn't always so.

Mary Garside says, 'If you're passing,' and we all laugh. They come to see us off. Same driver as before. Bob. He welcomes us like regulars. Through the routine of gears and gradients we go, up and over, the grey of the sky above us, the dark green of the ground below, the snow breaking up on the tops, the shaky ribbon of road feeding itself through.

We're lolling and bumping and looking at the bigger view forming when we hear the driver call out 'God!' and we feel the bus brake sharply. He's not the sort of man to call out like that without a good reason. No collision though, just a reflex response to something he's seen up ahead, or down ahead. I stand up to have a look. In the bottom of the steep trough of ground a vehicle is facing back up at us. It's at the wrong angle though, because we can see its roof. It's a big vehicle, without being a bus. White roof, quite broad. A Land Rover perhaps, or an aged jeep.

It is facing us in this way, as if we are vertically above it, because the nose has gone down into the deep cleft of the stream beneath the road. Even from here, more than a hundred yards away, I can see the impact must have been big because there is a concertina look about the front of the bonnet. One of the doors is open, but there is no sign of anyone using it. I think it has been opened and crumpled by the crash.

Our driver accelerates down. I try 999 on my mobile but there is no signal. Not so much as the fraction of a bar. On the road just behind the vehicle is a dark patch, like a big disturbance in the surface. Maybe the jeep caused this as it crashed. No, we're almost at it and I can see it is a crater, a big bugger of a thing, taking in more than half the road width.

The side of the dry stone bridge has been blown apart by the force. Its pieces have been flung across the open moorland for twenty or thirty yards. Just like an explosion.

Our driver points up left at a chimney just visible behind a stone barn. It's a farmhouse, he knows the people. There's a track up to it, but the bus would never go. And he's a heavy man, is Bob. Serena leaps out, sprints up and out of sight, her heels going like a two-stroke. I grab my briefcase with its habitual but tiny stock of first aid. I should have checked it. I always forget what I have.

I run down to the stream bed to reach the open side of the jeep. I strain and struggle to get in. The door has stoved its own hinges in. I can see no-one. This should be a relief, suggesting that whoever was in it has walked clear. It is no such thing. Looking down through the shivered windscreen and over the crumpled front, I can see a form in the stream.

The driver, of the no-seat-belt persuasion, was flung through the screen and into the cleft. I squeeze back out and down. He looks remarkably relaxed, curled there like a child. Asleep, you might think, except that his eyes are as wide as the moors. Zero pulse. The blood from beneath his hair is now falling rather than gushing down his temples. Nothing pumping it. It carries on down the side of the big round stone which now pillows the head it smashed.

I clamber back up and into the jeep to make sure there's no-one else. I can hear laboured breathing. The out-breaths shade into a moan. More blood, dark deep stuff, is coming down the casing of the transmission shaft. Its source must be behind the second row of seats, the storage bit at the back of the vehicle. At such a tilt, the seats are like the steps of a big soft ladder in a play area. I get to the top. The boy is lying in the angle between the floor and the rear chair-back. Boxes have been hurled everywhere by the force of the crash. Boxes and sports bags and loose kit. A football coach maybe, with the last boy left in it. And the father driving?

He has lost consciousness. He looks about nine or ten to me. I scan him quickly for injuries. Only one that I can see, but it's a grave one. An obvious fracture of the right shin, which must have been caught between the seats somehow and snapped by the wrench. He is wearing shorts, and I can see the immediate problem is the massive haemorrhaging from the anterior tibial artery. While I'm looking at this and pulling a length of bandage from my case for a tourniquet, I reach my other hand carefully up to his neck to locate a pulse. Into the ridge next to the Adam's Apple for the carotid. It feels good and strong, until I realise that I was using my thumb, which registered my pulse and not his. Schoolboy howler.

Forefinger and index. It is here I realise how woefully out of practise I am. Time and rust have made a novice of me. Either that or I am panicking. Rich, considering how I felt myself wilting under the load of failing bodies on my books, all moving like tortoises to oblivion; how I have longed for action and emergency.

I locate the carotid pulse. It is only just there, the mildest hint of a life current. I wind the first length of bandage round his leg, just above the knee, and make the first half-knot. Then a pencil, no, biro, less likely to break. Through it goes, and the second half-knot on top, and twist and twist. Gently but firmly. It tightens. I note the time and scribble it on the back of my hand. Should I have used my belt for the tourniquet? People do. No, too abrasive, isn't that the objection?

Keep him with the damaged limb up. Not too hard, given the angle of the jeep. He was more or less on his side already, so not too much shifting of him needed. I think about a splint. I should have had an inflatable with me, and must remember for the future. It has even come up at the practice, with Joan strongly in favour. The breathing first though. I fish my finger down into his throat to make sure the tongue is pulled up and clear. So long since I have done this. I take my air in and fix my mouth round his. Did I ever ask Imogen to volunteer as a patient? I believe I did.

Breathe out, right into him. Again. Pause. Again. Wait for his little chest to reply with its own exhalation. How it used to hurt me directly whenever Ricky got the slightest knock at this age. Vulnerable little men. Nothing. Pinch his nostrils with my left hand, at the same time keeping pressure on his forehead so it stays tilted back. More breaths and still nothing back. CPR it will have to be. Have I ever done that? Of course, of course. Heel of the hand just above the junction of the breast bone and the ribs. Interlock fingers, arms straight and push down. Harder than feels right. Who said that to me? Harder than feels right. Yes, but not too hard. So, how hard is that? I feel the tiny rack of his frame give and spring, give and spring. I could break it like a quail. But it holds. The maleability of childhood.

I take in his face and his head properly now for the first time. He reminds me of someone and yet I don't know him. Someone other than Ricky at the same age. The fair curls against the dark floor. Of course, the boy in the Underground, on the platform after the tunnel mouth has socked the life out of him. I haven't room for him now. I am losing another. His life is passing away through my hands. I am violently cajoling him to stay. It is seventy years too early for him to go. Stay, little man, stay.

Fifteen hard thrusts and then the breathing again, my hand keeping his head back and his nostrils pinched, and my mouth airtight on his. One breath every five seconds. I remember the counting method: 'One-five-thousand, two-five-thousand,'

and so on up to five, and then the breath.

What was the advice we used to give when we did those first aid sessions at the community centre? If this fails, seek professional medical help immediately. I always loved that one. The thought that some poor sap at a road crash has been struggling in vain to stop the victim exsanguinating while all the while resisting the temptation to alert the nearby doctor. It's like the small print on medication: if symptoms persist, consult your doctor. If death occurs, slow down. I'm the final longstop, landlord of the last chance saloon. I'm the one I have to call.

Then he starts again. Something has got through to the half-dead bird of a heart in the cage of him. He works. I feel his chest answering my input with a gentle fall, and I feel and hear with my cheek and with my ear for the air that comes out of his nostrils. He has his own now. The heart is up and going, as if it never rested. Independence compressed. You support them and keep them and do what you can for them, long for their self-sufficiency to kick in and take over from you.

I turn my attention back to the wound. What have I got? A small quantity of water-and-iodine solution and, for heaven's sake, a tube of Savlon. I start to take my shirt off for use as a makeshift dressing, but then I see a sports top spilling from its box. Moor Top Juniors on the front, the number ten on the back. Brand new, cleaner than clean, perfect for the job.

As the boy stirs, I can see shock beginning to telegraph its presence. Sweating, fast breathing, paleness. How I sympathise. Identical symptoms to mine. I wonder about a jab of morphine. For the boy, not me, although God knows.

Through the rear window, which is above level with the road, I see the flashing lights of an ambulance. And then another behind it. Disbelief at first. Their presence looks incongruous, miraculous, conjured out of the empty hills against all odds. The country working, just when you were despairing.

Like the boy. Serena is standing on the road. She is with the farmer whose house she ran up to. Two big children have followed them down, but the parents, seeing the gravity of the scene, are trying to shoo them back. The mother has a thermos and some cups.

The two paramedics from the first ambulance stop briefly to speak to me. I point them on towards the stream. The two from the second assess the boy. He is conscious and confused, his eyes beginning to search nervously around him. With the rear end of the jeep at such a considerate height, we manage to get him onto a stretcher without too much trouble, then into the ambulance and off. I offer to go with them, but they say there's no need.

Then off goes the second one, quick as it came, with its sad cargo. Serena sees I'm shaken, comes to my side and hugs me. She asks me if the boy is all right and I nod. Our bus driver, Bob, same one as before, takes some photos of the scene - the hole in the road, the smashed bridge and the nosedived jeep. Everyone thinks the drivers exaggerate the bad state of the roads, he says. Perhaps they'll listen now. Let's hope so, I say, privately thinking it will have the effect of closing the services all the sooner on safety grounds.

December 4th. Beaumont Hotel, Hexham, looking out at the abbey and the municipal gardens. Train to Newcastle and the East Coast main line back down. West Tyne General phones to say the boy's fine. Someone (the chief administrator, I think) thanks me for having saved his life. It was indeed his father driving, and yes, he had just been dropping off other members of the team after training at Brownheads. The mother would like to thank me, but is too distraught to speak to anyone.

Everything flat outside. The dull prerogative of the return journey. Literally back down, like descending a ladder, all the expectation spent and the map-height surrendered. Serena sweet and attentive. Reading me unerringly, every moment of the day, every mile of the way. What next? And how?

December 6th. Joan and Mila to see me. They ask for fifteen minutes and suggest my room, half an hour before surgery. Why no Maurice, I'm wondering, although always happy not to see Maurice. And why no HGV, although again, more than happy to keep dealings to a minimum.

The two women look as serious as I have ever seen them. Not exactly hostile, but challenging all right. Something more than challenging, actually. No need to ask them anything as they come straight to the point. This they do by placing an A4 sheet in front of me. It is a print-out from the web. A big monochrome photo, slightly smudgy in the reproduction, but quite decipherable. A document from the borders of the new technology and the old. It comes from the *Hexham Courier* and is displayed beneath the headline: Holiday Doctor Saves Soccer Boy's Life.

I scan the brief report and it all looks quite accurate. Can't always say the same of the national press. Certainly not where medicine is concerned. Even as I'm looking at it, I feel something give inside of me. I don't know what it is. Self-diagnosis will have to wait. All I know is that it is major and structural, both physical and mental, and that as a result of it my life is once more being taken into an entirely new place and can never return to what it was. That is my initial diagnosis. There is not the faintest sign of anything to suggest I have got it wrong. How I would love a little of my usual inaccuracy.

The photograph shows the jeep standing dramatically on its nose in the stream cleft, surrounded by the stones which used to be the bridge. There are people in the picture, including the family with the big children. Slightly to their right, in the background, is Serena. She has her arms tightly round the waist of Dr. William Newgate, whose quick thinking and expertise saved the life of eleven-year-old Peter Mannion from Hartside.

His father, also Peter, was killed instantly. 'Local drivers have called for an urgent programme of road repairs to prevent such accidents happening in the future. 'It's a disgrace the conditions we're having to drive in,' said a spokesman,' and it's a wonder this kind of tragedy isn't happening every day of the week up there.'

I look again at the photo, this time squinting as I always do at something I would prefer not to take in too accurately. Wishful squinting. When I unclench my eyes, as you always have to in the end, I can see that although Serena and I are only a detail of the bigger picture, there is no room for doubting our identities. None whatsoever. The faces, the hair, the clothes, the plain us. Then I see the small print of the byline at the top right hand corner of the picture. Robert Armstrong - Bob, the driver of our bus. In the caption she is described as Dr. Newgate's partner, Serena Miller, a London-based actress.

All very straightforward in our instant world of digital ligatures. The paper sees his images. Bob Armstrong probably takes photos for them regularly. They opt for this one. Good choice actually. Dramatic prang, doctor with local connections, stunning young woman. Newgate, says Bob; son of the old boy in Highmoor, give him a call; that's right, says Dad, I hope he's all right, hold on a second, I say, Mary, what was the girl's name? Miller? Aye, Serena Miller. Into the online edition, and then off into the public air it floats, hooked down by anyone with a passing glance.

Even without googling on Newgate (don't do it, William), it could drift into your window at any time on a current of some-thing else. Country buses, potholed roads, soccer boy, long wheelbase jeep.

It isn't taking me long to track the story across its myriad likely synapses, but long enough for Mila and Joan to look as if I might be puzzled by some aspect of it; mistaken identity, coin-cidence, something of that sort. They hear my train of thought, which can be summarised as 'Maurice.' His name comes so heavily into my mind that I can't hold it, and it escapes through my mouth.

'Why do you mention Maurice, William?' Joan asks politely.

'No reason,' I lie.

'Is better, William,' says Mila, 'if you say what is going on. Last thing we are wanting is for you to be villicated for something not yours. Not right, Joan?'

'No, that's absolutely right, Mila. William, we just thought it would be a good idea for the two of us to speak to you informally, before anything else.'

'Yes. I see. That's actually very decent of you. What sort of anything else did you have in mind?'

'Not us,' she says, 'so much as'

'Ah.'

'It's a matter of the practice. Whether one likes it or not, it's not something the practice can ignore.'

'Yes. I see. The practice in the form of, I mean, have you discussed with HGV? If I may ask.'

'Not yet, no.'

'Any other members? If I may ask.' Meaning, of course, Maurice. They look at each other and are silent.

'Actually,' says Mila with a steeliness which I'm aware of but have yet to experience directly, 'actually William and with great respect to you, I don't think you are in position to interrogate us. BMC is mentioned.'

The sound of these initials falls onto my desk like an axe. Terrible stories of the British Medical Council sacrificing good GPs' careers on the altar of their petty moral prejudices. Here I realise how far I have strayed from the field of acceptable behaviour; how I have been made over to another system - call it love as I can find no better shorthand - with its wayward logic and wild rationale. Actually, logic that is no logic and rationale that is no rationale. Answerable only to its mad autonomy.

I cannot expect my life, my mind, my actions, anything to stay compatible with the laws of the GP's adult order. And so I am not in that order any more. I have gone another way, and very dutifully too, carrying out the demands of love unquestioningly and unconditionally. The shocking thing is that I have defected so fully that from my new vantage point I cannot even see the moral objection to my behaviour. And yet I must, as these two fine, strong, well-meaning women are reminding me.

I reach for the defence of Serena, the mere fact of her, since my justification flows from her existence. But that is inadmissible here. So I say to them, as Serena said to me, that we haven't actually done anything wrong. I must be mad. They're not having it. Both of them look at me as if, regretfully, they also have no choice but to question my sanity. I embark on the argument that since my marriage is a private affair, it follows that the effects on that marriage of my behaviour outside it is of no concern to anyone else. If we dwelled on this, I have no doubt they would disagree vehemently. But it is not their concern, and is of no consequence at all compared with the offence which they perceive.

I try another form of the Serena Defence, namely that she is not actually a patient of mine. This has no effect on them. 'Crucial thing,' says Mila, 'would be that she has been. Therefore has had the dependence of patient on doctor.' I want to ask what about the dependence of the doctor on the patient, can we please not hear it for that. But naturally this is so far out of order that the phrase 'out of order' comes nowhere near covering it.

One of Mila's words went off like a fire alarm in me just now. It was the word 'would.'

'Crucial thing would be that she has been.'

'Will you tell him or will I?' Mila asks Joan.

'I don't mind,' Joan replies.

'I think is best coming from you. Practice manager.'

'Very well,' says Joan. She sounds sad and tired. 'The point is, William. You say she is no longer your patient.'

'That's right. She left, oooh, some time ago now.'

'Do you have a date for that?'

'Not in my head. No.'

'But it would be on the practice records, wouldn't it?'

'Yes, of course. I'm sure it would.'

All these conditional verbs knocking around, littering the floor with anti-personnel mines.

And then, suddenly, a bang, brisk and brutal, from Joan.

'Except that it wouldn't, because she is still on our books. On your books, William. She is still your patient.'

I thank them both for taking the time and trouble over this. What I don't manage is an apology, or anything resembling a promise to do something about it. I feel my tone become formal and remote, my head go muffled through bombed hearing. This is the formality and remoteness you can only impose on people with whom you were once both easy and close.

December 7th. Alone in the house with Imogen. Ricky back from Oxford again, but he and Inez both out just now. Whether separately and together, I don't know. Nor does Imogen. Their dealings are beyond me. My own dealings are beyond me now. They conduct a virtual life in the eyes and on the screens of others and soon, no doubt, in the dull machinery of retribution. We sort of bump into each other in the kitchen, both saying 'after you' with the kettle.

Imogen pre-empts anything that might be coming from me by saying, 'I'm sorry, William.' She puts her hand tentatively on my forearm. It is a very long time since she has touched me purposefully in this way, or in any way, the only other contact being the chance bumpings in the night.

What is she sorry for? For me? For her? For both of us? For

everything? It is a strange and tender gambit. I shrug, which is an honest response, and say 'Yes.' A self-adjusting Yes, which could have any number of functions, depending on what she is looking for.

'No, no,' she goes on. 'I'm sorry. I mean, for me.'

'Yes. Absolutely. You don't deserve this.'

'Oh but. I did, William. I did. That's the whole point. It was bound to happen, wasn't it.'

'I don't know. I don't know.'

'I'm only surprised it hasn't happened before. Or at least as far as I know.'

'No. It hasn't actually.' Salvaging some dignity from an unlikely place.

'But it could have done.'

'I suppose so.'

'I just want to say that I don't actually blame you. I thought I was going to. Because obviously it's not easy, this. Not for any of us. I don't suppose it ever is.'

'Ricky?' I ask.

'You'll have to speak to Ricky yourself. He's his own man. As we want him to be.'

The absence of information about Ricky and his response is ominous. More music I will have to face.

'As I say, William, I thought I was going to blame you. And so I tried it out, but it wasn't working. So I stopped. You haven't that to worry about. If you were.'

I was. Of course I was. Or was about to. I just hadn't got round to it yet. Too much else to worry about. I can't say how grateful I feel to Imogen. I can't say because I don't have the words for it. If I had, I would put them here, as I have tried to put everything else. When I think of what I might say, I have to stop myself. I can feel the emergence of a version in which she is not just the stoical spouse, but a fellow conspirator in the venture.

It's a good thing I savour this feeling as it is short-lived. One day only.

December 8th. The kitchen again, both of us smiling sheepishly at our elaborate good manners in the queue for the kettle. Strange that neither of us offers to make a pot for two. Strange but habitual.

For twenty-four hours it has felt like a free pardon, something which we all know I have no right to receive. It couldn't last, and it hasn't. Yesterday was not a free pardon at all, nor even an expensive one; it was a gambit, an introduction to what she really wanted to say. Now she says it.

'As I say, I thought I was going to blame you.'

Well go on then, I'm thinking.

'But there is no point. Is there?'

'Oh?'

'Yes, oh, William. That's about it, isn't it.' She makes the sound again, emphatically.

'O'

'How is that? If I might ask.'

'A circle with nothing in it. An empty shape.'

'Ah.'

'Holding zero.'

Meaning what? That I contained nothing? Or nothing of substance? Or, worse, that when I held her - or rather, had held her, then - it was as if I held nothing by virtue of having voided her, us.

Long ago, in what seems like another life, Imogen had written an essay on zero as part of her Elizabethan Studies course. It was all about how the Romans had had to do without it, and the Mayans not having invented it until the tenth century; then nullity as a blasphemous concept, with Shakespeare quotes about nothing coming from nothing. And of course the wooden O of the Globe Theatre, packed with its plentiful metaphor. These snatches of thought and image come back into my awareness, like dinner guests from a quarter of a century ago turning up again, all altered and yet the same.

Imogen owes me an explanation, or at least an enlargement on Zero. This she knows. She doesn't summon Shakespeare for any old grievance, busy man that he is. When she does, you know the stakes are high. Five-star bollocking on its way.

'It looked,' she begins, 'so open.'

What is this It? If she means me, as in William, perhaps she should be saying so. Or does she mean Us, that old concept? I don't ask, just wait. She must be reading my first question on the air because she says: 'You, William. So open.'

It sounds as though it might be a compliment so I prepare a thank you of some sort. I can see this is not what's wanted so I let it commute to a mild rumble of assent.

'So much possibility. And yet, and yet... '

Go on. Say it. You'll do so far better than I can. Maybe I'll even learn something of myself, late in the day. No, perhaps better not.

'I remember, when I asked Mummy... '

Now there's a chilling word.

'... what she thought - and I don't think I ever mentioned this to you,'

Almost certainly not.

'... she said, well, Imogen, the thing about that young man is... '

Yes, that was her all right.

'... that he doesn't know who he is,'

How kind of her.

'... and he's looking for someone who will help him to find out.'

And this role, presumably, was to fall to

'Whoever he ends up with will have that not entirely enviable task.'

So the big guns are out today. First Shakespeare and then Mummy. That word, the M-one, becomes once more what it always used to be, a license to abnegate judgement and hand that responsibility over to a power greater than herself, her mother. It always used to strike me as ironic that Imogen, so intellectually self-sufficient, should devolve such power, in the old, old manner of daughters and mothers, to the generation above. But never mind how we got there, William had nothing to him, nothing in him, and his fulfilment, in the literal sense, would fall to 'whoever he ends up with.' The very construction of that phrase makes it sound like the last halt on a dire track. Virtually indistinguishable from 'ending up in jail.'

'I'm not saying Mummy was always right.'

No need to.

'But I think, William, that she was correct on this. And that, you see, is why I am not blaming you. I thought then, and think, still, now, that you were unwell.'

She can see my face stirring like the doctor I am, bridling as she strides onto the very turf of my professional identity, but she puts up a hand to stop me interrupting.

'I know this may sound presumptuous of me, but I don't care. Not any more.'

She thought then and thinks, still, now, that I was unwell. As I wait for next the words, I replay the last ones, scrutinising the tenses to see where it leaves me in her diagnosis, here and now. Week in, week out, in the meetings, people like me sit and acknowledge certain inconvenient truths about our condition. These include the presence in us of a threefold illness from which we are never, technically cured. Imogen knows this and is exercising her right to remind me of it, in her own terms. I wait for her to invoke the image of the circle once more - that is, the circle with the section missing from its perimeter, always a popular way of defining the malaise of the practising addict. But Imogen is moving on.

'Her however I do blame.'

I guess she must mean Serena. No prizes here.

'I mean,' she begins. 'Of all the, of all the...'

Say it. Say it.

'Say it,' I say.

'Of all the cheap, deceiving little sluts in the history of the world...'

This is Imogen as I have never seen her. Or if I have, then I've forgotten. The content is, what, bracing, to say the least, and there's obviously more where it came from. But it's being up-staged by the delivery, which is declamatory, passionate, magnificent in a way which, again, I have forgotten. It transfixes me.

'I mean, how dare she? How dare she feign illness in order to take advantage of a weak, libertine, addict of a GP.'

Weak. Libertine. Addict. They fall like the blows of a pile-driver some way off across a beach. You see the weight falling but your ears don't register the impact of it for fully a second or even more. Late deliveries of sound. She draws breath as if she is winching herself up for the next hammering.

'How dare she plonk the whole sick baggage of herself on your doorstep and lumber you with her spoilt and self-indulgent whingeing?'

Because this comes in the form of a question, I find myself re-flexively scrabbling for an answer. She doesn't want one, even if I had time to come up with something. 'How dare she flaunt her tawdry self before a man who is, and always has been, a weak apology for a professional carer and a slave to his own appetites?'

The 'always has been' is ominous. It makes me think she has

been going back into the past, the distant one before we were to-gether, trawling for further evidence of my moral and emotional emptiness. I even wonder whether she has been using Maurice as a consultant. I have to steer myself away from that route of inquiry; not so much steer as wrench myself away by the neck as if I have become a bareback runaway.

'I suppose she told you she loved you and… no, don't answer that… got you to tell her the same thing back.'

She makes a face of the deepest disgust. A sort of wretching noise comes out of her throat, which I don't think was meant. 'You know what makes me sickest of all… '

There's no longer even the pretence of a question, and even if there were, I'd get it wrong.

'… is the way a woman professing to care for you should lie and lie for her own selfish ends and to hell with everything else. I said everything, William.' There's a fluency that I haven't seen for a very long time, and I suppose it is coming not in spite of but because of all those years of forbearance.

She fixes me with her eyes as she says my name. I return her look but can only hold it for a split second before flinching away, aware she is still staring at me hard and steady. 'Not just your good name - which was good, which was good, despite what I may think of you - but your job, your career, your livelihood. Therefore mine too. Mine too.'

Does she know something that I don't? Has she been speak-ing to someone else at the practice? Not just Maurice. Maurice, who must be enjoying this unfolding story more than he can say. Not a story any more. Something much more than that. A scandal.

From the behaviour of her mouth, she is about to shout. 'I said mine too!' She throws her head back. The set of her jaw, the line of her neck, the drawn-back shoulders… all these are lending her a presence and yes, a handsome dignity which I thought was gone; terminated by me. She has become fearsome and formidable. Public even. And magnificent, there's no denying it. How ironic that she should be finding this manner in the very moment I lose any last lingering illusions about her opinion of me.

'I am,' she announces, with a rallentando that signals an end, 'I am no longer the wife of a doctor.' She can't know - surely she can't - that this statement echoes Serena's to me about no longer being my patient. Both were made with the air of a game-changing announcement. Yet there's an ambiguity about what Imogen has just said. Does she mean she is no longer my wife, or that I am no longer a doctor, or does she mean both? I don't ask. There are times when you can find yourself knowing too much, and I think this is one of them.

In the silence, bleak and floor-staring, her phone goes, as if on cue. It must be her brother again because she darts me the same look as before, almost as if she is asking my permission to take the call, then lowers her voice and goes out of the room. So, not her brother. Someone else. How she used to inflame me with that unavailability of hers.

December 9th. Still no sign of Ricky, yet I'm sure he's here. Imogen either ignorant too or sworn to secrecy, which I of course respect totally. I have to face him, there's no question about that. The more I try to predict his reaction, the further I get from it. Could be anything from mournful solidarity with his errant father to, at last, the cue for that Oedipal killing.

Waiting up for him, all ready with my contrition, I catch Paxman giving some RC spokesman a horrible time about priests who abused children. The man is looking all fugitive and Paxman's face is twisting about like some aristocratic racehorse appalled at being fed Kennomeat. I try to savour the *schadenfreude* of someone getting a moral bollocking but then realise that I haven't taken in a single word.

December 10th. St. Stephen's Wednesday evening. I try to read the faces in the room for evidence of the public knowledge about my private life. What a ridiculous game. I suppose this is what happens when the wheels start coming off the whole sad project of yourself and you assume others are as obsessed with your plight as you are. Perhaps a few of them are. For example, the Maurician tendency with its insatiable appetite for the misfortunes of others. But for the rest, they've got their own movies to make, as Martina Lubasz would say. Perhaps she's the one I should be speaking to. Or rather, should have spoken to.

It's too late now. Too late for everything. Re-grouping, working on yourself, starting over and all such shiny, generally American offers of a New You are for others only. For the Old Me, consequences are all that remain, nasty and overdue.

However; I'm out. The thought hits me as I sit down and Spiritual Sally does the welcome. Outed. Gone public. And since, as every person in this room knows so well, you're as sick as your secrets, goodbye sickness. In theory. I should have been a Catholic. One of those ones who only takes one half of himself to confession; the half that owns up to the naughty stuff and takes the rap for it, leaving the other half free to carry on sinning. Like having a bent accountant who's well in with the Revenue.

I expect the door to open and Serena to walk in. But then I cannot be in a place that has associations with us, and not see her. That's the very reason I kept going to such places, driving along the roads near her house with the specific aim of conjuring her image.

A priest from north London does the chair. A priest for Heaven's sake, a Catholic priest. If the medical laity of the fellowship get some strength from knowing there is a doctor in the house, I suppose I draw some comparable comfort from sharing my club with a spiritual pro.

He's good - one of those priests who doesn't wear his trade

on his sleeve. Or collar. Plenty of saucy asides about his con-freres, and language that flirts with profanity. He first came to his drug of choice as an altar boy handling the wine - a common point of entry, this - and took it on from there. As for his church of choice, as he calls it, the habit was on him from the cradle.

And then off he goes: some of us have the horses, others the hooch; some go for the High Street, others for the lowlife. It has the ring of a secular sermon. The circle is incomplete, he says, as we have been left unfinished. We set our eyes on the missing segment and must have it at any cost, up to and includ-ing our lives. He does not omit religion from his list of destruc-tive essentials, and considers his own church toxic (his word) with addicts in chronic denial.

Fine, thoughtful stuff, which raises the tone of the sharing. I shall have to come in; share with all the honesty I can muster. I go out through the side door for the toilet, and for a few mo-ments in which to think about what I might say. Forthrightness is of course the only route. A desperately rough one though, since I am as much in breach of a moral code here as I am at the practice. Serena is a newcomer. She's not meant to get emotion-ally involved for the first twelve months, and certainly not with a married man. I decide to open my mouth when it's my turn, and see what comes out.

As I am about to go back into the room, I can see that some-one has arrived. I have a good view through the little glass porch. He has his back to me. He looks unsteady, flapping in his coat like a newcomer still under the influence. A huge, ground-ed, appalling bird. Movements of blind anger, the rage of a man shouting at the darkness. He wheels round, raking the chairs with his squinty-focused eyes. It is Brian Miller. He is bellow-ing. From outside the porch I can't quite hear whether he is say-ing 'Where is he?' or 'Where is she?' I don't think I could be sure even if I were back in the room as the esses are eliding drunkenly.

I hate looking at him for fear of seeing his daughter's features contorted there.

He strides down the brief aisle in the middle, staring down each of the rows. If he were a regular, it wouldn't be so bad; relapse we can cope with, even habitual relapse. At least the man would be in touch with the programme, however shakily. No-one is past redemption. Our own stories are proof of that. But this man is different; alien and unbiddable, wild in the shoulders and the staring, snorting face. A vertical bull, sending the literature flying as he barges the table with his burly hip.

'Excuse me,' says Spiritual Sally.

'Friend,' says the priest.

'Don't you fucking friend me,' Miller roars. The priest stands. He is a slight, ascetic man, probably no more than half Brian Miller's bulk. He barely comes up to his shoulder. Miller goes close up to him and lowers his big face until they are nose to nose.

'Did you hear me?' he says in a deafening whisper. 'I said Whereisshe?' The priest stands his ground and says he's sorry but he can't help.

It is Clive who makes the incident pass. He goes past Brian Miller towards the door, thumbing at his mobile. Before exiting, he turns back to the room and says 'Just entertain him till the police get here, would you. Easy on the custard creams though.' The whole room laughs and Clive throws in another one: 'Oh and don't let him leave without a starter pack.' More laughter. Miller glares down at the table, where the titles are staring back up at him: *Alcohol Problem? Me; How To Stop Drinking Before It Kills You*, and so on.

Miller looks around him, fear in his eyes now. The bull at bay, humiliatingly pricked by the banderillas. He sees the laughing faces in front of him, the slogans on the wall, the photos of the wartime Americans with their Eisenhower buzzcuts. It is too much for him, and he stumps out, stiff-legged with drink. Another victory for the Lord, you'd have to say. With a little help from Clive, which He appreciates more than I did.

Fuckshitfucksjit, shittingfucking sdit. Gone it's gone. No other word for it. Effig gone. Couldn't have but has. Tip everythig up Would tip the whol fucking room up if I culd and bang it by the flor. I do ths to my briefcase even though its as empty as ascooped shell. Bang it like it is a keeping a scret compartmentto itself that it hasn't told me about, hiding my big hardbook notebook like some recusnat priest.

Slow down. Type proprly. Properly. I do the same with the right-hand drawer of the desk where it has sometimes lived. Again nothing. I do the other drawers, even though it has never lived there. I go out of the study, into the hall, turn round and come back in, hoping to find everything like I expected, the notebook still there in the top right-hand drawer. Under some practise documents. Like re-booting the computer to give it another go at the starting sequences.

No go. Gone. Think back. Click back and then back again, and again; the screens of my last few days in reverse order. The practice. Ah yes, of course. Phew. It has been there with me. Panic over. Don't do it again. Ooooo, what a sobering second. Learn from this, Newgate. Caution with it at all times and in all places. You were going to get it photo-copied, remember? Spread by spread at the chemist, ten pence a sheet, so that something like this couldn't happen.

Round to the surgery. So weird to go there out of hours. The counter and the scrip box, our names on the unlit panels. Past Maurice's room and into my own. The big comforting shapes of the books on my desk. The books and the book, black and red, A4 hard cover, reassuringly scuffed and worked-in. Surely. Except that not. Same routine with the drawers. Total scooping out. Even banging the empty ones on the underside. How mad is that. Emptiness comes for me. Everything falls out of my head and I am as void as an empty drawer. Passers-by. I could try them. Have you seen a book passing this way? Big, red and black, definitely not new. No? Oh.

The metal file with the old records. Could it have got in there? With something else? When I wasn't thinking? This has been happening quite a lot. Can I have left it somewhere? Try lost property. It's of no use to anyone else. It will filter back down to Baker Street or wherever the centre now is. How joyful to be reunited.

First, back home. Inez is in the kitchen, looking surly. Of course she is. She's got material now. No matter. I can't be bothered with her boring surliness. And while we're about it, screw Spain. Polite as I can do, I ask her if she has seen a book on my desk? I describe it. Quite thick, A4 etc. I draw the dimensions in the air with my hands. 'No print. Just writing with hands.' I try to make it sound less vital to me than it is - just something which I might have mislaid and which it would be nice to have back, but not that urgent, honestly. She sometimes offers to tidy up for Imogen, and it's possible her writ took in my study, or she thought it did. Or she wanted it to.

She shakes her head poutily, sniffing accusation. Yes, well, God, what if? The mere thought is a sliprail onto MadTrak. What if what if what if it's got into her hands. Then to Ricky. Imogen even? What if it's gone another route, a Maurice route? (I should have looked in his room, except it wouldn't have been open) - then to HGV, Mila, Joan... BMC? All that stuff about, well, where to start. Maurice, Imogen, me and Serena, the practice. It's an endless list. To say nothing of the AA entries; good God, all the broken anonymities there. As hostages to fortune go, this would be the most reckless consignment ever lodged with hostile powers. Wikileaks looks like a mild indiscretion over the embassy port.

I focus on Inez again. I am aware of scanning her. I try not to, but do not succeed entirely. She is looking extremely, the word expensive comes to mind. Her coat alone would probably feed a Bradford family for three months. Not bad for an au pair, albeit in Richmond. Aware that these calculations are deranged and unacceptable on too many counts to enumerate, I try to stop them.

Beside her, at her feet, is a bag which must also be described as expensive. 'A haaandbag?' Not exactly, no, just a shopping bag. But a Russell and Bromley one. Ignorant though I am about such things (R and B is still rhythm 'n' blues as far as I'm concerned), I do remember, from hearing the Sloaney girls who came to the commem balls, that this was, and presumably still is, at the posh end of the retail outlet spectrum.

Amazing how mere cardboard and paper can exude class when it puts its mind to it. I can't see what the bag contains and am not going to demean myself by peering. Instead, I hear myself saying to her: 'Ricky settled up then' It comes out without any help from me, like a hiccup. Too late to take it back in. She looks at me and this could go either way, cosy alliance or nuclear showdown. I'm in luck. Her face slips back into a Manuelesque *Que*-setting and it's clear she's stumped by the idiom. 'Yes,' she says, on the haughty side of civil, 'he much better now.'

The Lost-notebook problem swarms back round me. How can such a catastrophe have happened? Convene a quick inquiry. I'm the suspect here. Not impossible that in my distracted state of recent days I have simply chucked it out. I can do this, am quite capable of blithely dropping the house insurance schedule into the rubbish, while carefully retaining the empty Chicken Kiev pack. This from the man who also brings you: pouring Listerine in the bath and mouth-rinsing with Radox.

Growling outside, reminiscent of the Highmoor bus. I go

out and see two men hooking our big green wheelie bin onto the gear at the back of the rubbish lorry. Naturally I am certain I see the red/black binding of my book flash out a last appeal to the indifferent world before vanishing for ever into the scary innards of the beast. Up goes the bin, vertical as the jeep on the moor. Shake shake shake, and down again empty. I go right out onto the pavement and see the bar pushing everything in tight with the power of a dozen rugby scrums - move right down the car please.

As the lorry crawls on down the road, I catch up with the driver's window and beckon to him - any chance of being able to retrieve something? I start signing, like language for the deaf, then dive and rummage with my hands. He gets the idea. He's never been asked anything like this before and so he has no reaction to offer. That's what it looks like although I realise when I try again that all we have here is a good old-fashioned language problem: my total lack of Estonian. If that's what it is.

Into the car and down to the depot. Park round the corner and wait. Feel like the strangest of loiterers. An anti-robber. What's my story for when I'm challenged? Glad you arrived, officer. Just waiting for some rubbish. True. Waiting for the big hulks to come and then, then what? Search them? Pull rank as a doctor? Climb into their great iron bellies and start picking through the crushed detritus of our local households?

Hope to find my chronicle of a life - a life which, it must be said, is going down its own equivalent of the refuse chute - somewhere among the flattened cartons, the humiliated packagings, the knackered Jaycloths? Bill Clinton turns up in my thoughts, doing his waggle - headed old dog charm-smile. What's he doing here? I'm envying him for his ability to function publicly while the walls of his personal life are ripped down like shower curtains; for managing to live apart from the catastrophe of himself. To inhabit Elsewhere.

I wait and wait for the big land-borne shapes to loom through the fog of refuse, proclaim to the world their intention of reversing, a man to dismount from one, recognise me and approach me courteously, carefully blowing the dust off the red and black binding of my priceless (literally) book and apologise on behalf the borough's waste disposal services for having picked it up in error.

None comes. After ten minutes a single vehicle limps into the scene, then two more of a similar shape. They are about a quarter of the size of the lorries. Has there been some weird process of shrinkage between the pick-up and the drop-off? Has my reason been taken away and dumped? These are builders' vans and this is where they bring their waste. I think I see the crude logo of Brian Miller's firm on the side of one of them, but am no longer trusting my cognitive powers. Him I would recognise, if a van door opened and he got out of it and strode towards me with that stiff-legged gait of rage. Please let this not happen.

I have come to the wrong place. One of the supervisors has seen me from his prefab office and is definitely coming in my direction. Not hostile at all. Eager to help, in fact. I explain to him that I have lost something. He has no English at his command. Just enough to explain to me that the refuse lorries don't come here.

He mimes such a lorry as it scrunches up its domestic takings, then he points up and over the trees with his fingers, to denote their destination. 'Very long, yes. Is far.' It's a virtuoso performance. He could be a mime artiste. I explain to him that I have lost something. I'm aware of doing what Englishmen are said to do when failing to make themselves understood by people not blessed with their tongue, and increase the volume. I'm headed for eleven on the knob. It sounds sad and demented. Laughable too because of its incongruity. As pitiable in its own way as

Brian Miller bawling at the meeting.

The man now looks me up and down in the way officials do quite openly when they are seeking sartorial proof of madness. He has no choice. He sees nothing there, but finds plenty in my face to be going on with. He has one last shot at explaining; these big lorries that go far away; the things in them get put into the ground. This he denotes by vigorous digging motions. There's a little crowd of birds over from the Urban Wetlands Trust to see what's doing at the depot. He points to them and then to the dug ground at his feet. I say Landfill and he nods triumphantly.

From his own face, this sort of thing might have happened once or twice before, but no more than that. Of course people get pushed into distraction by loss, but it can't happen often to this extent when nothing more than a notebook is involved. I thank him for his help and walk back towards the car. Past the dunes of casual discards; old packaging that once thrilled children with the thought of the toy it contained; a quadruple amputee of an old chair, nothing but back and seat; steep slopes and shifting shoulders of post-life matter, shrouded by the dust clouds of their own making. As I go, he opens his palms in sympathy. It must look to him as if I have lost nothing less than my life. Which is precisely how it is striking me. Industrially done away with, cancelled with no record, like an untended child taken off to a centre of extermination. A mass burial site. The blind disproportion of the consequence. Happy now, Higher Power?

Whenever.

Well, I'm carrying on with the keyboard, the freeze and flicker, flicker and freeze of the digital way. Look Mummy, no hands. Presences wave their arms in the margin to get my attention. No-one polices them. They see I am here and act as if they have the instant right to gatecrash my schedule. I can feel the whole picture strain and tense as they bust through the frame of it and into the burnt-out privacy of my head. All the world on record, every texted aside and twittered banality everywhere, all locked down forever in the bunker of virtual memory, while the writing that came out of my veins and onto those pages is singled out for the dustbin of ephemera. So cope with it, Dr. Newgate. Turn to life. Day at a time and all that. Live with it. Save and store.

Ditto.

When I wake in the night and wonder what on earth comes next for us all, I find myself pulling back from the certainty that the book somehow got binned and destroyed. It's very possible. But a certainty? No. Then, in the small, endless, technically growing but still stunted hours, I once more imagine what would happen if it has found its way into certain hands. Hands whose owners appear in its pages, and in the ugliest of lights; trashed, some of them.

Again I start going through the list of names, round and again, like sheep being counted, then checked, and re-checked, as they bunch towards the gate of daylight - Maurice, Clive, Ricky, Inez, Imogen, even Brian Miller. Brian Miller, Clive, Ricky, Maurice, Imogen, Inez. Imogen, Maurice… but the appetite goes and I have another go at re-entering sleep. At least the suburbs of it. Nearly there, so nearly savouring that saintly thing, the tip of oblivion, but then: still so many ways in which the book could have fallen into hostile and vengeful hands. Not exterminated, but kidnapped and held, for reasons that have yet to be revealed. We shall have to wait for the demand.

I start imagining that whoever's got it will mind it carefully, just for these few days, then wrap it in festive paper and let me have it as a gift. Poor choice of words there, let me have it. Christmas has already got us all in its chilly vice-like. Goodwill, fresh starts, heavenly babes, love, our best selves, healing redemption, red-nosed fucking reindeer, I could go on - all being force-fed into the air from every screen and speaker and station forecourt. Generations making common cause in the joy of it, shoulder to shoulder in the countless choirs. Robust old boys all glowing red with piety as the singing of the ancient yuletide carols slips them back to the official innocence of childhood. Let me not be bitter. Hey what, Lord?

I should start another book, another physical volume, get back onto the horse you have just fallen from, and all that. But the fire has gone out of me. I suppose this really is a kind of bereavement, bringing shock in its wake. I feel for it, reach for it, like a familiar jersey or a privileged memory, but I embrace only air with my hand or with my head. I am as amputated as the chair in the depot. I now realise that while I was wondering whom I should confide in, I was continuously selecting myself for the job by virtue of writing. Self-help Through Story-Telling; Let Dr. Newgate sort your life out with the miraculous power of narrative. The diary entries were the subscription to the support centre of Me. Enough for now. I have supported myself as the rope supports the hanging man. No more diary-keeping. Not for now. The days are coming at me too hard. The shots of them fly past me into the back of the net. I am losing. The game, which is no game at all, will soon be over. That's something.

THE NOTES OF DR. NATTRASS

Dr. Nattrass had a guilty secret. He was sicker than the people he treated. This meant he was very sick indeed since his patients, who had the highest average age of any GP's practice in the country, were falling apart. He was approaching fifty himself, which had always sounded old when he was far away from it, but now seemed really quite young. However, he was old enough to know that his career was never going to fulfil him. He would carry on servicing the failing bodies and minds of his London constituency until he too fell into obsolescence.

He could still be pricked by reminders of his youthful ideology. He felt personally diminished by references to Red Cross workers, *Mèdecins Sans Frontiéres* or even to English GPs who had gone to practise in the most deprived communities of his own country.

Technically he was a baby-boomer, although he disliked being bracketed with the Beatles generation. He always had done, first as a boy and then as a young man. The Mop Tops already seemed quaint and historical, while the Stones, who were meant to be the real, feral alternative, had turned into wrinkled curios; dirty old men, even. New Romantics, early U2, Elvis (Costello) and Smiths had been the soundtrack of his student years at Barts. 'I'm the m on the end of boo,' was his line.

Andy, his twenty-year-old son, laughed at it the first time, even though he suspected it wasn't original. He did continue to laugh at the man though, either covertly with his student friends, or else with Gabriella, the young student from Portugal who was staying in their house.

Dr. Nattrass's sickness was an addictive disorder. Though outwardly opposed to the libertine manifesto of the original Boomers, he had managed to develop a nasty little alcohol habit. He knew in his heart and in his medical mind that ethyl alcohol was a drug just as devastating in its own way as crack cocaine or heroin, but one which escaped banning through the accidents of social history and successive governments' own unhealthy dependence on its excise duty.

An objective outsider hearing just the beginning and the end of the Nattrass tragedy would assume that drink was at the heart of it. But the objective outsider would be wrong. It was something else entirely that drove events towards their terrible conclusion - if conclusion it was. He or she would have to think again and face the possibility that the real culprit was love.

Mark Nattrass had been married for twenty-five years to Deirdre, a former languages teacher at an independent school round the corner from their house. After the birth of their son, three years into their marriage, she spent most of the next year in a state of exhaustion and despair. She loved the baby - of that she was fairly sure. At the same time she was terrified by the responsibility of looking after him. In the worst darknesses of the night she wondered whether the giving of life to another had in some fundamental way pulled her own from her.

Where other young mothers seemed to find an all-embracing fulfillment in this act of production, she feared - no, she knew - that such a process was not working in her. So strongly was she experiencing the pain of subtraction rather than the joy of addition that it was only a matter of time before she became, physically and emotionally, a husk. Then there would only remain the question of how she was to be disposed of.

The slightest snuffle or cough from his cot was enough to make her think he had developed a terminal condition. If the child died, what? Would she have her old self returned to her? Probably not. Even though she hated to bother her husband at work, and knew it infuriated him, she could not prevent herself from phoning him. She would have one hand on the phone, try to remove it with the other, and fail.

She found herself unable to deal with the world beyond the

four walls of their house. She was aware of being trapped in it and even recognised a certain safety in her situation, just as prisoners overwhelmed by liberty recognise the security of their accommodation.

At first her husband thought she was suffering from postpartum exhaustion, and put it down to the usual combination of hormonal changes and sleep deprivation. Little Andy suffered from colic and so her twenty-four hours were no longer ordered by the technical divisions of night and day. Waking took place at any time. Sleeping, less frequently.

When the symptoms persisted, Dr. Nattrass decided it must be PPD. After all, he reasoned, up to twenty five per cent of women suffer from such depression in the wake of childbirth. Wake; what a morbid word to use after one so full of life as childbirth. Deirdre was displaying the classic signs. She was moody, short-tempered, over-sensitive, particularly if he asked her how she was feeling and wouldn't take 'fine' for an answer. As the months passed, she seemed to dislike herself more and more, avoiding eye contact with everyone, including herself. Particularly herself.

He saw how her eyes dipped and her head turned in order to avoid the big mirrors in the hall. She had low self-esteem long before the term was everywhere. For what it was worth, Dr. Nattrass diagnosed anhedonia, the state of not being able to experience pleasure. She seemed dogged by emptiness and wrongness. He could find no other words, scientific or otherwise. It was, he reckoned, some non-specific guilt. Remorse for a crime never committed and not even contemplated.

He thought about consulting his own partners at the practice, but decided against. There was a problem there too, in the form of Greg. The two had been contemporaries at Barts. Deirdre had been going out with him. It was through Greg that she met Mark. Greg was tall, broad-shouldered and athletic, with gentle grey eyes and a manner which invited confidences without being obtrusive. Everyone knew he would become an outstanding GP, and so it proved. Mark joined the practice a year later than Greg, and was taken on largely because of his friend's recommendation. They were, in the stolid words of old Dr. Claude Harrington, the Young Turks.

Mark was privately grateful to Greg, but had trouble displaying this. He had never stopped wondering whether he had in fact stolen Deirdre from him, that long vacation when Greg was away in the Karakoram with the Mountaineering Club. When he got back and learnt that Mark and Deirdre were an item, he put a brave face on it, found someone else, a newly qualified family lawyer called Anunciata, married her and started having children - pink, bouncy, blameless and compliant.

Whenever Mark saw melancholy settling on his wife, he always assumed it had to do with the loss of Greg, easy, generous, outgoing, popular, squash-playing Greg, and the 'gaining' of himself - dark, difficult, private Mark. He even wondered whether Greg had helped him join the practice so that he could re-acquaint himself with Deirdre, while knowing in his heart that the man was as honourable in his private dealings as in his professional ones.

Morality for him was indivisible. Moreover, Greg was not a holder of grudges. The time for airing these anxieties was past, if there had ever been a time for such a private, some said diffident, Englishman as Mark. The friendship had shifted into an association, and in the place of intimacy came competitiveness on Mark's part. This showed itself most explicitly on the squash court, where he charged and ranted but could make no impression on Greg's stylish and effortless stroke-play.

Just before Andy's first birthday, Deirdre's mood began to brighten a little, although Dr. Nattrass feared he would never again know or see the wife he had once had - the hauntingly beautiful young woman who had so obsessed him and any number of other young men. Whenever Greg's name came up in the course of a conversation about work, Mark saw the weather change on his wife's face. It really was as if a cloud had settled on her brow and imposed the conditions of wistful reflection. As time went on, it became increasingly hard even to consider the possibility of talking to her about this, of asking whether she regretted the choice she had made and perhaps even resented him (Mark) for pursuing her with more passion than he could sustain.

As with the two men, so with the man and his wife. Because it was something that wasn't discussed, you didn't talk about it. And because you didn't talk about it, it was something that wasn't discussed.

Gabriella brought her food, drink and music from Portugal. They supped on *caldo verde* soup, and ate the sausages called *chourico* and the fish dish called *bacalhau*.

Gabriella made her try to pronounce the words and they both laughed and agreed that it was not a very good effort for a languages teacher. They sang along to the *fados* with Amalia Rodriguez, Chabuca Grande and the young sensation Mariza. They sat together in the kitchen, caterwauling of love, separation and the cruelty of the high seas rocking the baby between them as if he was a tiny boat on a mighty swell. Dr. Nattrass would return from work to find them pulling his son backwards and forwards like a Christmas cracker, their faces blotchy with tears and make-up.

When Gabriella went back to Coimbra to look after her widowed father, Deirdre was broken-hearted. She tried to replace her with other Portuguese au pairs. Sometimes it worked. Give these young women a chance and they became trusting and expansive. For most of them it was their first extended time away from their family. There were only a couple of disasters; one when the girl stole all the jewellery she could find (not much fortunately) on her very first day; and one when another girl set up an escort agency and they got a visit from the vice squad.

Mostly though, whether they were talkative or silent, outgoing or introspective, their presence became a necessity to her, and the necessity became an essential. The girls got a good deal. Andy was not a demanding boy. He was not even spoiled, although there was just the one of him and so the temptation of indulging him was strong. And as his mother was always there, their evenings were free. It was such a good billet that they told their friends or younger sisters about it, and recommended them to the Natrasses.

When Andy was five, Deirdre went back to work, teaching part-time at the same school. She wished she hadn't returned. The children seemed louder, as though their playful calls were being fed through amplifiers and coming out as siren wails. The innocuous tennis court mesh of the playground became the watched fence of a prison yard. Even the head teacher, benign and committed as she had always been, morphed into a bullying, irrational tyrant. It was she who one day had no choice but to phone Dr. Nattrass at work and gently tell him that his wife had locked herself weeping in the toilet for over an hour.

And it was this same head who suggested that the three of them - herself, Deirdre and Dr. Nattrass - should have a private chat in her study to try and see what was for the best. It was the politest dismissal ever. It needed to be nothing nastier since everyone present had come to the same conclusion, which was that Deirdre would be better off not having to work there 'for the time being.'

The time being became the time future, and then more of the same. And then more after that, so that the settlement hardened into permanence. It was not until Andy was a teenager that the presence of the au pair struck anyone as eccentric. For the family it was a case of 'if it ain't broke, don't fix it,' to borrow from the wisdom of the fellowship which Dr. Nattrass was to join.

How Dr. Nattrass got into that fellowship was a story in itself. It can be told and read in a number of different ways. One version is that as his relationship with Deirdre became distant and formal, so his drinking worsened. Infidelity never entered his mind, not yet at any rate. He was a well brought-up boy, the only son of a working-class couple from the far north-west. He had a moral compass and, despite his anxieties over Deirdre and Greg, had never truly experienced the turbulent effects which the wrong sort of magnetism can have on the needle.

Besides, he couldn't imagine himself in bed with another woman. It would be awkward and embarrassing, a bogus intimacy, and it would violate his idea of himself as a basically good man - honest, hard-working, caring, the best GP it was possible for him to be. That is why it is tempting to see his deepening dependence on drink as a kind of affair. A liaison with Ethyl Alcohol. It bore the hallmarks. He became furtive in his pursuit of it, dishonest about the extent of his contact with it, even blushed when the subject of it came up in conversation. Like a boy caught stealing sweets.

He began to feel guilt when he saw patients who were worried about their own drinking. The words 'Physician heal thyself' kept finding their way into his thoughts. Several had less pronounced problems than he did. He nodded and noted with his face down. He suggested they try attending meetings of Alcoholics Anonymous, which he had heard were very good. Some of them came back weeks or months later to thank him for his advice. They got under his skin with their healthy glow, their sudden positivity, and their distinctly American embrace of the programme's spiritual dimension.

Dr. Nattrass found himself asking after their progress for his own benefit rather than theirs. He persuaded himself that these

243

inquiries – they were almost interrogations – were quite in order as they added to the sum of his knowledge, and therefore to the practice's knowledge as well, on a notoriously difficult condition. One satisfied customer, incontinent with zeal, even suggested he try the rooms himself, just to see what went on. Dr. Nattrass blushed and gave an amused smile of thanks.

It tightened its grip until it became part of him, the convolvulus wound around the flower's stem, leeching off him while appearing to sustain him. Normality shifted its position in him. It was only attainable after a heavy intake – about two bottles of wine now, or a third of a bottle of Scotch. Without that he was beached, hollow and desperate. He knew what was going on. That was both the advantage and the liability of his profession. You know what's going on, but the knowledge is inconvenient.

He still managed to give his patients the benefit of it, explaining to them that hangover and withdrawal were largely the result of depleted serotonin levels. He would hear himself as he might hear a lecturer: 'When we use alcohol repeatedly to alter our mood, the brain assumes we have no further use for its own natural opiate and so it stops manufacturing the stuff. It concludes, quite understandably, that we have contracted out the job to some industrial supplier.' All this delivered from the depths of the predicament he was describing so well.

He started waking at all hours, sweating when he was cold and freezing when he was hot. He curled into a foetal ball and howled silently. He nosed out the all-night garages and general stores that sold liquor. With the off-licences, you had to wait until 8.30 or nine in the morning. He tried not to wake Deirdre in his night ramblings. He looked at her sleeping form and wondered if he was giving himself a sympathetic illness. The symptoms of worthlessness and self-contempt were, after all, the same as hers.

Then he was off and out. Careful at the wheel, never parking in a garage, but leaving the car round the corner and walking up to the window. Him and the vagrants and the brown-baggers, queuing incongruously next to non-stop men with company Daimlers and expensive PAs.

He did the off-licences too. In rotation so that they wouldn't know how frequent his visits were. No-one was fooled. Quite soon the men behind the counter would see him coming and be ready with the half of Johnnie Walker before he was at the counter. He feigned surprise but stopped short of asking them how they had guessed. He took the bottle and unscrewed the cap. It gave a small reassuring rasp as the seal broke. By now he could no longer be bothered to go to the public toilet or slide down an alleyway to drink the stuff.

That was how the affair worked. It had to be here and it had to be now. He might once have minded being caught in the act - who knows who might have seen? - but no longer. Such concerns were overridden by the need to do as Ethyl dictated, and get her down you.

One day during this time, he found himself at the scene of a terrible accident. A young boy's anorak cord got caught in the doors of a tube train and he had been pulled along and smashed against the tunnel entrance. Instead of rushing to the aid of the boy (who died), for fear he would give his condition away if he intervened, he left the station as fast as he could. The incident was to play again and again like a tape loop in his head. He would have classified it as a recurrent dream, except that it was not really a dream at all, more a recollection replayed in his sleep with punishing accuracy.

The self-anaesthetising became chronic. Eventually Greg persuaded him to seek help. He was in no position to refuse since two patients had already said that he was slurring his speech and falling asleep during their appointments. One of them claimed he was so bad that when he said 'cancel,' meaning it was time to stop her course of medication, she took it to mean 'cancer' and became enraged when he wouldn't, or couldn't enlarge. Another alleged that he had mistaken him for another patient, and prescribed haemorrhoidal suppositories for bursitis of the elbow.

His time in the Priory was hell to begin with. He was told what to do and what not to do, by men and women who looked like boys and girls and whose medical training was not a fraction of his. He suffered agonising withdrawal symptoms which the Heminevrin and Librium did little to relieve. He kicked and he bucked and he denied, and knew better than everyone else, and was an arrogant and dismissive member of the therapy groups.

His fellow patients included a High Court judge with whom he argued competitively, a famous actor whom he tried to out-declaim and a controversial bishop whom he attempted to debunk. Anything but look into himself for the source of his illness. He loathed the counsellors, never more so than when they beat him on his own field of play and suggested to him that he might compare his problem with an aneurysm; both were weaknesses which, when played upon, could give way with all the devastation of a flood wall breached.

Some time in the third week the fight went out of him, and he understood the argument of constructive surrender; don't get in the ring with Mike Tyson and you can't get beaten up. Simple but unassailable logic.

He had a vision. Later he even admitted as much. It was of a plant growing in a desert under a ferocious sky. A boot stamped it out and it started growing again. With it came the green shoots of his own recovery. When the plant faltered in the vision, so did his own progress. When it prospered again, so did he. It was the visual counterpart of his striving. He craved its success because he knew his own depended on it. He had become, as the founding fathers of AA had put it seventy years before, sick and tired of being sick and tired.

He went to the meetings. Sometimes he saw his own patients there. He flinched, but they smiled back encouragingly. He became a pillar of his local group. He got himself a sponsor, or mentor, called Christian, who was as his name suggested. Deirdre told him she was proud of him, but as distantly and as formally as before.

He suggested they might go and see a counsellor together. The mere idea showed how far he had come, since he had always been sceptical about such services. She agreed, but reluctantly. The counsellor was called Bella Russell-Hart and she worked in the cosy attic of a large north London house. There was a pleasant, civil, professional foreplay, in which Bella outlined the kind of service she could offer - basically helping the two of them to communicate more fully with each other.

But the frankest exchanges were between Mark and Bella, and when Deirdre saw her husband and this strange woman opening up a line of conversation about intimate things, she withdrew from the process before she had entered it, and well before she would have to give an account of herself.

When it came down to it, she had no idea what was wrong with her, and was embarrassed by the thought that she was in some way defective. Perhaps it was nothing. Perhaps she and Mark were just another of those couples who discover that they are not right together; that they get in each other's way, with the result that both are diminished. Perhaps she should have stayed with Greg. Whatever it was, she didn't really want to find out since she was sure it would result in more difficulties than she had already. Mark went on seeing Bella for a little while, but this too became furtive and undisclosed. Besides, said Bella, it's hard to improve a marriage with only fifty per cent of its membership. And so his visits lapsed as well, and he and Deirdre returned to their familiar discomfort of distance and formality. If they didn't know who the other one was, then at least they might live in hope of the comfort of strangers.

Stella Hunter was not quite the stranger Dr. Nattrass had in mind. She had been registered with the practice since she was a child, but she had not until now been one of his patients. Before him, she had seen Olga Pietrowska, the only female doctor there. But there had been some sort of falling-out between them. Then a friend of hers, an admiring patient of Dr. Nattrass, had suggested she see him instead.

He recognised her, remembering her family from the days when she and her sister went to the squash club and watched their father's games through the viewing window in the bar. Barry Hunter was a big, raw-boned and truculent man who ran a successful local building firm. Dr. Nattrass had played against him once and been outclassed. He could remember Hunter loving the humiliation of the scoreline. 9-0, 9-1, 9-0. He still went to the club, although his daughter, who was now twenty-three, had long since stopped going. Nor did Dr. Nattrass play him these days as Hunter, though carrying too much weight, was fiercely competitive and had risen to the top rungs of the premier division.

Stella was a tall, outwardly healthy woman who reminded Dr. Nattrass powerfully and painfully of Deirdre at the same age. Both in the face, which could verge on handsome, and in the voice, soft and low, she struck him as almost identical to his wife. She was a drama student. When she came to see Dr. Nattrass, she was suffering from depression.

That is what she said herself, and he had no reason to disbelieve her. She spoke of nameless fears that locked her into inertia, of her physical inability to get out of bed. While such symptoms were becoming more commonplace nationally among young women - and men too - they rarely presented in the body of his clientele; most of them would have barged such things aside, much as they had barged cancer or pneumonia aside, and got on with the business of getting to one hundred. How refreshing to have a patient young enough to be the great granddaughter of these estimable, interminable people.

He remembered rumours of the father's violence, the sister's tragic death in circumstances he had never learnt, and also the mother's death in circumstances that were all too plain - liver cirrhosis. He recalled a small, anxious woman always nursing a drink like a damaged bird in the far corner of the squash club bar. She was nursing it and it was nursing her. She was the damaged bird too.

No sooner did Dr. Nattrass ask Stella whether she too had a problem - issue was the word he used out of deference to her youth - with alcohol, than she sighed with relief and said she had known all along that he was the one for her. When she said 'one,' he assumed she meant 'doctor.' She did, but she meant more besides.

She started coming to his surgery more often than was necessary. She ingratiated herself with one of the part-time receptionists and occasionally sneaked herself in without an appointment. Dr. Nattrass made an outward show of disapproval but this did not persuade her to change her behaviour. Nor was it meant to. She knew him, she argued. It was not her fault that she did. She and her sister had said he was the kind of man you could trust, all those years ago at the viewing window in the club.

She started going to AA meetings. He could hardly object since it was his idea that she should. What he didn't suggest was that she should go to the same meetings as him, and befriend his crowd. He took himself off to other meetings for a while, but his resolution foundered on his wish, his need, to see her.

People around him became suspicious. Particularly his sponsor Christian and his old colleague Greg. He told himself they were merely jealous. Nothing was beyond that kind of rationalisation, now that she had turned into this imperative in his life. He should have cared what people thought. He should have cared that his behaviour was out of order. He tried moral opprobrium on like a garment but it got in his way and he cast it aside.

After their first night together at her student lodgings, the opinions of the world beyond were a matter of sublime indifference to him. Besides, as she told him herself, his wife was more in breach of the marriage than he was. And, as she also told him herself, she had stopped being his patient. Where was the problem?

Everywhere. In the rooms, at the practice, in the neighbourhood. Although she never saw her father, and said she didn't even know where he lived, Dr. Nattrass was apprehensive. The anxiety infiltrated his recurrent dream about the Underground, with a figure identical to Barry Hunter grabbing him at the exit and forcing him back down to the platform and the fallen boy.

The most serious grounds for worry were to be found in Stella herself. A voice started coming out of her that was not hers but that of a small girl. It seemed to him that she had a West Country accent. She was not always comprehensible as much of this talking was done in her sleep. Dr. Nattrass wondered if it was the knowing idiosyncrasy of an aspiring actress, but when he asked her about it, she looked at him strangely and said she had no idea what he was talking about. Then, while they stole a weekend away together in Cumbria, the voice came out of her as she was lying awake. He might not have worried if she had not sounded so distressed or cried out so hard for help.

Then it fell silent and passed from her. Until the next time. And on each occasion it happened, it became younger and younger, smaller and smaller. Dr. Nattrass felt the chill of panic. It threw him as nothing had thrown him since his student days. As the voice became tinier, so its vocabulary reduced from audible words, through half-formations, down to squeaks and whimpers. The first calls had been concerned with chickens and foxes, rabbits and guns, like scenes from a violent countryside recalled in fragments. But now they had become howls which came nowhere close to specifics by their lack of language. Yet they could have not have been more articulate in expressing the terror of something imminent and, in every way, unspeakable.

This terror was transferring itself across the air to Dr. Nattrass. He grew certain that unless something was done, this girl would continue hurtling into her infancy and beyond. It was a journey which had to end in her absence. He knew this diagnosis would bear no rational scrutiny, but since rational scrutiny had never gained a foothold in the field of Stella Studies, this made no difference to him.

But what to do with her depression, anxiety neurosis, regression, and all the related words of the medical lexicography that mocked him and his trade with their inadequacy. He picked up his *Oxford Book of Clinical Diagnosis* and cast an eye down the index for something that might spark an initiative. There was nothing; a desert without a plant. She was approaching the moment of her arrival in the world, but moving in the opposite direction, labouring herself into nullity.

He might have decided it was too much for him and sought help from Olga Pietrowska, whom he both liked and trusted. The risks of such a course were obvious, but not necessarily greater than the risks of doing nothing. He might even have had a change of heart and asked Greg for help. Impossible to say, because it was barely two days later that everything was dramatically torn from his control and he became even more powerless than he had thought possible.

The best way, probably the only way of establishing just how these events unfolded is to do as the jury did in Court Thirteen of the Old Bailey on June 20th the following year, and review the evidence. The most important item, but also the most tantalising one, was the CCTV footage from the number 452 bus running south from Kensal Rise into the centre of town on the evening of December 11th.

The members of the jury were also issued with a booklet containing a chronological selection of stills, each one accompanied by the time it was taken. The young police officer who had compiled it explained his methods. When asked anything by the prosecution counsel, the defence or the judge himself, he would look in the direction of the questioner, then turn his head to aim the answer at the jurors. It gave him the look of a professional toady, one whose delight was to catch people in the act without risking his own safety. 'Yes sir, no sir, that is correct m'Lud.'

He talks them through the footage, explaining that what they have is an edited version of the material recorded by the eight cameras distributed through the two decks of the vehicle. The first images are of a man boarding the bus at Kensal Rise and then sitting at the front window seat on the top deck. The time is 11.08 pm. There are five other passengers on the deck, including a young couple at the back who are oblivious to everything except each other. A few frames later, but still before the bus has set off from Kensal Rise, the man appears to have nodded off.

As the bus moves, two more men come up the stairwell. They are both tall, with big shoulders and heads. One of them is middle-aged and the other between ten and fifteen years younger. They look around, then go and sit directly behind the dozing man. They have almost certainly been drinking. It is hard to be absolutely sure because the half-second jump between the frames imposes a loss of control on their movements.

You see them looking one way, and then in the next instant

their face has shot through a hundred and eighty degrees and a leg has flicked itself into a different shape. It has the other-worldly look of digital puppetry. The two appear shifty but also full of purpose.

The bus crosses the lights at Harrow Road and carries on into the northern stretches of Ladroke Grove. A mix of council blocks and Victorian terraces diced small into flats. There is not much traffic about and the bus travels fast. Even from the imperfect footage you can see the passengers being nudged about by its motion. Under the Westway, and Ladbroke Grove becomes a different street, entering the province of affluent Kensington. Left into Elgin Crescent, then up again towards the Gate, all mansion blocks and smart communal gardens.

Now the bus passes the stop where the two are evidently expecting the man to get off. This is the closest one not only to his practice but also to his large, comfortable house in one of the borough's choicest parts, with its still undivided family homes and cake-icing stucco. The older one gets up and is about to shake him by the shoulder. The other dissuades him with a down motion of his hand. They wait and the bus goes on.

They have grown restless, alternately cajoling and restraining each other. At one point the older one again stands and looks as if he is finally going to attack the dozing man where he sits. Again the younger one pulls him back down by the shoulders. On and on, all the way up to Notting Hill Gate, then down Church Street and its big lurching S-bend, and left again towards Knighstbridge with the open darkness of the park on the left.

Suddenly the man wakes up, looks around and realises he has overshot his stop by miles. Kensington Palace has been and gone on the left, the Royal Albert Hall on the right. He is at Knightsbridge barracks. Glassy faces of big new buildings opposite. He clatters down the stairs and into the street. The two men follow.

The footage now cuts to the lower deck camera sited opposite the exit doors. It catches the back of the lone figure and then the pair. From the look of the older man in the final frame, he is breaking into a run as he steps down. It catches the pale sole of a shoe, like a moth in a milky dusk. Then nothing but the gap between the doors, and the back of a vanishing head, and everything is gone from its purview.

Nothing more, not even in this city of prodnosed public lenses. Not for a full two minutes, during which time the man and his pursuers go the three hundred yards east along the north pavement of Knightsbridge, with its closed shops and big flat-blocks. He might go into the station entrance up ahead, by the big road junction.

Instead, he crosses to the southern entrance, which means negotiating the busy lanes to the east of where Brompton Road forks into the two prongs of the A4. At the start of the trial the judge apologised for the likely length of the eye-witness accounts. Here - in the temporary loss of automatic surveillance - is the reason. He also suggested they might keep in their minds the possibility of joint enterprise, meaning that a person could be found guilty of a crime even if he did not seem to be its main perpetrator. Encouragement of the protagonist, even complicity, could make him equally culpable of the offence.

The jury waits for the men to reappear on the big court screen. They duly do, flitting two steps at a time down the escalator, then being picked up by a platform camera as they spill into its expanse. The two men are right at the other one's shoulder, talking to him with animated gestures. He looks confused and frightened. Their exchanges must have started back in the street. They are stabbing their fingers at his chest.

Hard to say for certain why he has come into the tube if his aim was to return to his house in W11. Perhaps he is thinking of getting back up on the Underground; Earls Court then Notting Hill Gate. More likely he is just trying to get away from these men; to put ground between them however he can. Aggressive though they are, they have yet to attack him physically.

This now changes. One of them is pushing at him and he is recoiling. The view is partially obscured by more people arriving on the platform. He walks briskly away, but they follow him and the routine starts again. They have their faces close to his. He reverses, with his palms opened into a show of innocence.

The lights of the next train come into view. At first just the tiniest of pin-prick stars low in a night sky, but quickly the whole of the train front filling the tunnel, and the first carriage flicking along the station's track. The soundlessness of the scene and the lack of a warning boom make its emergence more threatening. It slides along jaggedly.

The jury sees the man totter back from the force of the push from one of the men. Possibly from both of the men. They will be divided on this point for several hours. He is in the air, apparently launched up and arching like a backwards diver, with the tip of one foot just leaving the white line of the platform edge. Then he is on his back. He is lying horizontally at about the level of the driver's face. This face becomes dominated by the dark hole of a mouth wide open, as if he is yelling at the man to get out of the way.

These frames are played and played during the early days of the trial. Even on the second and third and subsequent viewings, there are jurors who can't take in the enormity of what is happening. They still harbour the hope that the event can be cancelled by being wound back and held there in the time that preceded it. That way, it need never happen. The whole world will not, after all, be compelled to change and cope. The shock need not go through the ground of people's lives. The court need not sit.

Some, the younger members, are thinking of all those cartoons and video games in which a figure would lose his life, loads of lives, then reassemble himself after a few seconds and rejoin the fun. For all of them, the sequence downloads itself into their heads for ever, and will play more or less as it pleases for the rest of their lives.

After the lying-in-the-air frames, the man vanishes. He has been consumed by the train as a mouse is consumed by a snake. He was there and now he isn't. Nothing to say. A killer? Me? goes the train. It is hard to know if he hits the track before the train hits him. It hardly matters. Passengers on the platform are about to react in all the ways that shocked bystanders do, but the court has no time or brief to dwell on them.

The footage shifts back to the escalator in its diagonal shaft. The two men are flitting and flapping hard up it and out into the night.

This is what the jury sees in Court Thirteen of the Old Bailey. What Deirdre Nattrass watches is the ending of the life of her husband, Dr. Mark Nattrass, aged forty-nine, of Kensington Park Close, London W11. She does so in the same suspended animation as the rest of the court, and as silently as the footage itself.

What her son Andy, sitting next to her, sees is the ending of the life of his father, Dr. Mark Nattrass, aged forty-nine, of Kensington Park Close, London W11.

What Dr. Olga Pietrowska sees is her colleague, what Greg sees is his college friend and squash partner, what Gabriella sees is her employer, what Christian sees is his friend from the fellowship, and so on. What Stella sees is the life of her lover ending at the hands of her father and an accomplice, Geoffrey Reynolds of St. Charles Avenue, London W10. She recognised Geoff. Of course she did. He had been one of the younger directors in her father's firm, as well as his most regular drinking partner.

She had wondered whether to come or not. The man whose advice she would have sought, Mark, was dead. There he is, time and time again, dying before the court, giving it another go, and another, to help them come to a conclusion. Hardly his fault if each showing hardens their uncertainty. As it happened, his absence did not stop her asking him what he reckoned about her coming here. It was quite straightforward. She just tried to imagine what he would have said. From her knowledge of his responses to such questions, she borrowed his reasoning and found herself travelling to the Bailey on the strength of it.

She sees everything through gauze, hears it through wool. It is happening and yet not, just as Mark was still there but then not. She still feels his presence as you do the sensations of a severed limb. Her circuitry was too much aligned by the current of him to deal with such a disconnection.

To say that when she half-turns her head in the direction of her father she sees him through glass is only the truth. He and Geoff Reynolds sit impassively in the dock, either side of the constable. They never acknowledge each other. They have separate counsels. Reynolds's will argue that Hunter was the ringleader from first to last; Hunter's will maintain that his client only wanted to speak to Dr. Nattrass in order to ascertain from him certain facts pertaining to the welfare of his daughter, while Reynolds incited him to action. For all the world - the court being all the world just now - these two men are complete strangers to each other.

Hunter did take in his daughter's presence on the first day. They didn't catch each other's eye; either would have looked away before such a thing could happen. Instead they swallowed the plain brute fact of the other being there and then waited to see how they felt after it had been ingested. This was the inescapable arrangement with feelings and emotions of every class. Too many facts to process for the moment.

Time would have to pass before you could establish how you felt. For that reason the unthinkable fact of Stella Hunter and Barry Hunter being in the same room together, and in such circumstances, looked as if it was having no effect on either of them.

So too with Deirdre and her son Andy. Mark's son Andy. They had looked at her - closely, she thought - on the first day. But she could see no strong signs of hostility in either of them. More a certain social awkwardness, which she reciprocated. She could certainly see the resemblances between the young man and his father, but thought the mother's genetic input had the upper hand. Besides, he could not compete with his father as he lacked the years, which was no-one's fault.

Judge Cantwell knew very well what happens when tragedy is opened up and anatomised. It wasn't pleasant. That would not be the word for it. And yet it had its patterns, and humanity was at the heart of their revelation. These patterns were complex, but within them were to be found certain regularities which did acquire an almost aesthetic appeal. In this respect, he would not have bridled at a comparison between his relationship with tragedy and a cardiologist's with the heart.

At the bar he had a distinct reputation for being a juridical conservative but a social liberal. He had handed down stiff sentences to the MP found guilty of perjury and the TV historian who had plagiarised his students' notes; but to the countless men and women overtaken by their passions in matters of the heart and the family, he proved alarmingly lenient. Scandalously so, the *Daily Mail* kept saying.

They looked so harmless in the dock, the two defendants - suited, sober, modest - straight from the virtuous heartland of small-firm Britain. Quite different creatures from the two being assembled by word and picture for the benefit of the jury. It was the eye-witness accounts which took the time. The camera may not exactly lie, but its accuracy is also its defect since it reproduces the ambiguity and the veiled actuality of a particular deed. In this case: which of the pushes could be taken as, in effect, fatal? And which of the two accused administered it?

Witness statements by contrast are forever contradicting each other, so that an action described by one onlooker might have absolutely nothing in common with the same action described by another. A white man becomes a black one, a bald one acquires a mane of hair, a woman becomes a man. People are turned into shapeshifters by the disparity of their viewers' accounts. What you hope for, if you are interested in a just outcome rather than a freakish acquittal, is some form of consensus; the secret democracy of narrative.

A dozen eye-witnesses were called. On their evidence hung the fate of the two, since they had what no camera had produced, evidence of intention or the lack of it. Several said they had clearly heard the older man abusing Dr. Nattrass. One whom they passed on the pavement on their way to the tube told the court he had heard the same man repeatedly calling Dr. Nattrass a you know what. Not just that, but a f... but here the witness, an elderly librarian from Dulwich, stalled on good manners and upbringing.

Judge Cantwell helped him with the utmost care and gentility. 'I believe, Mr. Wilkins, that you are telling the jury that you recall the older of the accused calling Dr. Nattrass a cunt.'

'I am, my Lord, yes.'

'And that in addition to this he also called him a fucking cunt.'

In any other setting it would have been comical, this handling of such coarse verbal material with such civilised inflection. It very nearly was.

And then, later: 'Can we be quite clear, Miss Snelgrove. It was the younger of the two men whom you heard say to Dr. Nattrass: (consulting his notes) 'We're going to do you proper, you piece of fucking shit.'

259

'That's right, Sir.'

'And this was delivered with the menace one might associate with such language?'

'It was, Sir, yes.'

'Thank you, Miss Snelgrove.'

Even with their old technology of memory and account-giving, these exchanges delivered a drama of the stretched moment no less mesmerising than the TV footage. Jolyon Chambers QC filleted their words deftly to convey the intention of serious assault, the consequences of which were of no concern to either man. He had put away some thumping frauds and professional liars who had been in the public eye far too long for the health of the public. He was quite happy to sink his teeth into these more obscure but still lucrative gobbets of rotting flesh.

For Reynolds, James Bainham QC tried to find no bones of intention, but rather the evidence, in the bus footage, of a restraining hand. 'A restraining hand which he boldly continued to exercise until, as we have all too vividly seen, his associate moved beyond the point of restraint.' He was seventy now, an old radical who had come up through the Neighbourhood Law Centres, but was privately tiring of arguing the innocence of nasty men; and of helping them to drop their friends in it. When his mind wandered, which it did increasingly these days, he found himself wishing he'd gone in for a different and more useful game. Medicine for example. He might have done some good in medicine. Dr. Bainham. Call Dr. Bainham.

During his summing up, Judge Cantwell asked the jury to bear in mind the legal principle of a drunken intention being an intention nonetheless. 'The Carouser's Curse,' he called it, 'but the Juror's Friend.'

Out they went and sat in their room for the rest of the day and the whole of the following one. There was a red pig of a man called Claude, a former mayor of his borough who declared himself foreman and told the other eleven it was their civic duty to find both men guilty of murder, particularly since neither of the accused had said anything in their own defence except that the other one did it.

There was a young social worker from Cricklewood called Fiona who said you couldn't possibly convict someone of murder if you couldn't be sure he had caused the death himself. Since the footage had been inscrutable on who had given Dr. Nattrass the fatal push, she argued, it was not possible to convict either of them. Speaking under the pompous influence of courtroom procedure, she reminded the others that guilt had to be established beyond reasonable doubt.

Suddenly finding themselves looking at the unthinkable idea of a double acquittal, they rounded on her as if she was a personal friend of Hunter and Reynolds. Her worst mistake was to be the only smoker among the twelve. Whenever she exercised her right to have a cigarette, it meant they all had to file out of the building into a yard at the back in order to comply with the rule of not breaking into groups.

One of them, a large man, was in pain from a recent hip replacement, but no-one managed to interest Fiona in his right to stay put and not have to hobble in agony along the corridors.

The pig-mayor rode the swell of feeling against her. The old town hall politicians of his youth would have had her for breakfast. With his special-occasions council chamber oratory he said best be on the safe side and send both the buggers down, then declared the meeting closed and rang for the clerk. A packed gallery saw him stand and deliver the jury's verdict. A wince passed across Hunter's eyes. He had taken the dart but was yet to feel the pain of it.

Not much moved in the gallery, except for Andy's face clenching and his right hand gripping his mother's arm in bitter triumph. Everything else had the look of a sports crowd wound down to minimum volume, minimum movement. Some faces of grief and relief can briefly be taken as their opposite. Later, out on the pavement, Greg did punch the air, but it was more of a jab really. And Christian did offer a prayer of thanksgiving to the Man Upstairs, even though this vengeance was a thin substitute for the life of Mark Nattrass.

Both Miller and Reynolds were found guilty of murder and sentenced to fifteen years each.

Then there was Stella. She went back to her room and got into bed and waited for the emptiness to make itself known to her. This it did, wrapping her and rolling her about in its mocking embrace. She acknowledged its power and she wept. She asked it what it wanted from her but got no answers beyond its continued presence, night after night.

Disbelief arrived and struggled with it for control of that side of the bed. For a while they shared grudgingly, all elbows and cussing. Still she spoke to Mark, sometimes softly and evenly, full of gratitude, sometimes angry and abandoned. Through him she began to see that she need no longer live in fear of her father. It was so obvious, but it took these conversations with Mark to reveal it to her. No more tyranny of Daughtergate, he said. This had become his shorthand for all her troubles with the thought and the fact of him. He had coined the term as a humorous device with a serious purpose. Through Mark she gradually began to feel that she could act again. It took months to get to this point, but she now felt ready to let the principal know her situation and see if she could resume the course.

She was doing so already, Mark reasoned with her. If she doubted it, she only had to look into her own head, her own larynx, to see that she was being him; look, she was doing it now, even as they spoke. Listen, she was supplying his thoughts and then articulating them with his words and his voice. She was conducting this process so thoroughly and so, yes, professionally, that she was doing everything in the limited power of a human to bestow revenance on him.

In this condition he appeared soundlessly at her window in the liminal watches of the night, between the last ragged call of a vanishing stale carouser and the appearance of the first fox nosing at the bins. He came in through the window, straight through the glass and lay down quietly beside her. He placed his face close to hers so that he could feel as well as hear the rise and fall of her breathing and know whether the old interloper was scavenging into her throat to seize the passage of the air from her.

Once or twice he thought he heard the creature - the old, pleading noise to begin with, but then, by degrees, the softer sounds of resignation. Finally there was a low gutteral shushing tone followed by the sound that nothing makes when it is leaving. It was like the exhalation of a self, of something properly expelled, and after it had passed, her breathing resumed, safe and regular, unmolested. It was, to his ear, nothing less than the sound of false infancy returning to the darkness of no existence. When he was satisfied that it was gone, he did as he had to do, and went the same way, leaving the light to come up.

The rail journey from London to Chesham is almost comical. For the last five miles you're on a single-track country railway, contouring high on the slopes of a lovely rural valley. Fields and spinneys run off down towards the babbling Chess and its beds of water cress. But you're on the tube. Between you and these views are the window logos of London Underground, yet the endless tight tunnels of the capital could hardly be further.

The train has come up from such deeply urban places as Aldgate and Farringdon, taken nearly an hour to pull through north-western suburbia and Metroland, under the great belt of the M25 and into the golfing country of Chorleywood. At Chalfont and Latimer it's done a bold right turn across the serious tracks of the Aylesbury trains, and then pootled on to the Chesham buffers. You're in the otherworldliness of Zone Nine, a designation of remoteness shared only by the near neighbour Amersham. It's a sub-region where toilets work, heaters heat, waiting rooms have rail heritage posters and piped classical music laid on by the local user group. You've come thirty miles but gone back several decades.

No wonder Emily Chatfield chose such a place. Proper library, pedestrianised High Street, solid history of furniture-making, real hills, big green Chiltern ones, rising above the higgeldy roofscape. Coffee shops as well as Greasy Spoons, so that when BMPC (British Medical Publishing Company) wrote on its thick old-fashioned paper to say that *The Notes of Dr. Nattrass* was a 'powerful, mature and timely' piece of work which they wanted to publish in their forthcoming collection, *Physician Heal Thyself*, Emily was able to meet their representative in the weekday civility of an upstairs room.

Of course the representative had wanted to know the provenance of this 'astoundingly vivid' story. She was an eager young Scotswoman called Cynthia Rattray-Dixon, with little dark eyes that were on the alert behind the round-rimmed glasses and the library pallor of the young woman.

Although her questions about Dr. Nattrass's origins were pertinent verging on sharp, she was scrupulously polite throughout. She couldn't help wondering, nothing more than that, whether the story had been inspired by real events; whether Emily had known some actual counterparts to these people - the ones in the practice, the troubled young patient, the boy, the wife, the horrid violent man and above all, the doctor himself. The poor doctor, even though, no, his behaviour was at times very wanting. And all of them so thoroughly believable. Had she - had Emily - come across such people? It was a perfectly fair question, if an unfashionable one.

Also, had she, Cynthia, missed some event, something in the news perhaps, that had informed Emily Chatfield's fiction? It was hard to say. So much of the previous year had been taken up by Datagate15 and the havoc caused by such massive, running quantities of private information flooding freely - and for free - across the gaze of anyone with a computer, phone, pad or CHF (Cranial Hyper Feed). That had been an all-trumping story in a wholly different league, upstaging the combined atrocities of paedophile priests, MPs on the fiddle, hacking hacks, bent bankers and all other criminally greedy professionals. Like a Black Hole, it had drawn the light and life not only from the rest of the news agenda but also from the daily simplicities of private lives. If private lives could still be said to exist after that.

It was now the autumn of 2016 and even the events to mark the centenary of the Battle of the Somme had been going by almost unnoticed. Datagate was suffixed with a 15 because that was the year it broke, yet the fall-out had dragged on, even deepened, in the course of the following year. Still no human agency really mastering it. Plenty saying they had the answer but none demonstrating it. Therefore no real end in sight, just as there had been none for the poor bloody soldiers bogged down in the Pas de Calais a hundred years before. Unless they were among the million-plus who never came back. A million-plus. Say what you liked about Datagate and the lives it trampled, as godless catastrophes went it was not fit to lace the Somme's boots.

Cynthia Rattray Dixon had to ask the question she asked all the authors. It wasn't quite as hard as it used to be. Out it came and the world did not halt. 'Tell me, is *The Notes of Dr. Nattrass* based on real events?'

Emily Chatfield fielded the question with a neutral face and gave her reply. It was the standard defence of the fiction-maker; no, these people are themselves and nothing more; they are not cyphers or portrayals of others; I don't even know who they are myself, or what they will do, until they let me know, and so on. While she was saying this, she saw Cynthia Rattray-Dixon's face lose its tension and realised that the question which this earnest young woman was really asking was: Will anyone sue us for defamation? Because we're a small company and couldn't afford big libel settlements.

'No danger of that,' said Emily. They sat back and smiled. Cynthia then asked what had given her the excellent idea of coming to live here and she replied that it was her husband's idea. Good childhood memories of the area. Cynthia asked what her husband did, but as Emily made a misty, unforthcoming motion with her hand, didn't pursue it.

She was a cryptic one, this Emily Chatfield. Some of the other writers selected for *Physician Heal Thyself* had barely managed to stop to talking about themselves, their work and the relationship between the two. They seemed to be loving the opportunity to do just that - and be listened to; and paid into the bargain. Dr. Hugo Bell of Ludlow had said his novella *Accident And Emergency* was a personal howl of protest prompted by the closure of so many rural support services. In fact the words of his title were meant as a description of the crisis.

Muriel Weston, a consultant paediatrician, had made no secret of having based *Babes and Sucklings* on elements of her own caseload; but then if that was good enough for Anton Chekhov, it was surely good enough for the rest of us. And there was always the routine disclaimer, wasn't there - any resemblance between the characters in this book and real people are entirely accidental, or whatever the form of words was.

The conversation between the two women ran back down towards a genteel close. No unseemly cadences, although Emi-

ly Chatfield did sense Cynthia's mild disappointment that more
had not been exchanged. She was right. Cynthia had not been
long at BMPC and she longed for some significance in her role.
She wanted to mean something to her writers; to be encouraging, critical if necessary and protective at all times. Protective
above all, given the way in which the supposed fire walls of the
web had burnt down like paper and left every man woman and
child as bare and exposed as naked couples on the road ahead.
And if no-one knew, really knew how this had happened,
wasn't there always the danger it could happen again?

'I'm sorry I haven't been more informative,' said Emily as
they stood to go.

'Oh not at all, not all,' Said Cynthia.

'You see, I suppose… no, it doesn't matter.'

'No, do go on. Please.'

'Just that, well, when it's done, when it's written, there's really not much more to say.'

'Yes. Of course.'

'Because what's happened is, it's all been said.'

And it had been. Hadn't it?

December 18th (???????or 19th??????) 2010. Desperate. No. Beyond desperate. To Mila's on the bus, but don't go in. Light on in her living room. Probably listening to music. Bartok, Scriabin, one of those. Jagged but comforting. I loiter at the door, and wonder what I might say if she opens it. Help, I suppose. Help and sorry. Help for everything and sorry for everything. Me, my behaviour, its effect on the practice. As I say, everything.

I rehearse the catch-all apology/appeal but stand at the gate and never go up the path to the front door. This is like the last days of my drinking - priming myself for conversations that never take place; conducting them minutely, exchange by exchange, word by word. Why did I come up this way? No interrogation necessary. Mila is only a couple of stops further along from Serena on the 33 bus route. Closer to Twickenham than St. Margaret's. That's what I'm doing here, once more savouring the streets and the systems that lead to Serena. They are all still infused with her - mundane names made magical, even the plonking old christenings like Harris Gardens or Wilson Close, named after long-dead aldermen who did some good locally. Which is more than I've ever done. Newgate Terrace? They'd have to strike it off.

I walk a few hundred yards down the road so that I can use the stop I have sometimes used when visiting Serena. A bus comes along. As I get on and go upstairs, I am aware of a large and out-of-breath man behind me. He has got on immediately after me. When I see who it is, I realise he must have been waiting for me here. But for how long? And how regularly? This was always going to happen. Quite how, I never knew. Until now. It makes sense. Horrible, unwelcome sense. I was expecting it to happen at the practice, where he knew I would be. He probably thought about it, but preferred getting me on my own, as he just has.

I go to the front seat on the right of the top deck. Miller

comes and settles himself on the edge of the left seat. He sits at right angles to me, his legs in the gangway, his hands on his knees and his arms straight. He is striving with everything he's got to appear businesslike and resolute through a skinful of booze. God knows how much of the stuff he has shipped over the past few hours. I am tempted to ask him, as I would a patient. But, as with patients in that state, I'd only get a lie in return, the laughably deflated estimate that all drunks try to fob you off with. 'Ooo, a couple of sherries, I suppose.'

I wait for him to say something if he can. He has put on a good deal of weight since I last saw him close up, and he can now accurately be called out of condition; one of those former sportsmen who reckon a few sessions in the gym would return them to their mid-twenties peak any time they chose. Still useful though. Brutally useful, not one to be against in a neighbour dispute or a row over parking.

I should be more shocked than I am, looking at him straight in the face like this. But because I have envisaged the encounter more often than I can count, always with a (for me) terrible outcome, the reality of this moment has a long way to go if it is to match these imaginings. I am seeing his daughter's eyes, but then, behind them, the monster of his own hideous temperament. This is turned into something even more foul by the drink he has shipped. No wonder they called it the Demon for all those centuries. No wonder they were flummoxed and floored by the way it gathers itself, as it has done just now, in the wings of a man's head and morphs him into a mutant. Another useful practical for Dr. Newgate; a salutary reminder of the gravity of this condition.

It is not only his beautiful daughter who I see coming and going in his face, but me as well. Even there in his hooded, slow-blinking, undredged eyes.

And now here comes the pity, as I knew it would. Here also

comes the sympathy. They show up like a couple of nice old bores at a meeting, and I let them in. Miller is in misery. A terrible man for sure, but in misery nonetheless. Probably even more misery than he deserves. It is the misery of himself, of being locked into the stinking jail of his body and his mind, but it puts a standing army of ill-feeling at his disposal. This he will deploy against anything or anyone that thwarts him. Such as his daughter, or more particularly the man who has the nerve to do with his daughter as the one facing him has done.

I look at him and see he intends to say something. My God, does he intend to say something. First though, he must get the wind to fill the bellows to power his cords.

'Newgate,' he says eventually. It's a quiet intonation, the result of a struggle to appear reasonable against the promptings of everything in his make-up - the temper, the flair for retaliation, the build of a lock forward.

There are four or five other passengers on the deck, and they know nothing of what is passing between us. After 'Newgate,' he slumps, physically and facially. A little burst of effort in the first round and he is practically out on his stool. Dear God, he's plastered. Hip-flask plastered, I'd say. He must have spent hours, even evenings in this neck of the woods, just waiting for me to show. Me or his daughter, or both.

'Newgate,' he says again. Then something which is fluency itself by 'I'm not known as an unreasonable man.'

'No,' I lie.

'But what's been going on here is, is... '

He hangs his head and lets it swing from side to side like a bucket. I suppose this is meant to denote that the matter is beyond words. It is, for him at least. The bucket is for receiving his own incomprehension. I do have words, but I don't use them. They are: 'What's been going on here is actually none of your business.' I wish I could get myself to use them. I might yet. For the moment, watchful silence will have to do. Hell, was I like this when I was drinking? Yes, I suppose I was. When people tell me about that time, carefully and gingerly, there is no suppose about it. So thank you, Brian Miller, for the invaluable loan of your distorting mirror.

I try to think of him as a patient who has ground to a halt in front of me; like any number of patients reduced to this inertia by the knowledge of death, the gallop of rheumatoid arthritis, the loss of a wonderful wife.

The bus goes on. Sharp cornering, big road works, angry driver. Miller rides the bumps like a sack. I'm about to get off. He senses this, as drunks do (I've never been able to explain it), and wakes. A bear now, with the dart wearing off. A new clarity in his voice, an awful new competence in his bearing.

'Not yet, Newgate, not yet.' He shifts his bulk on the seat so that his big legs are blocking the gangway. I suppose I could climb over them, but what if he decided to stop me? So I stay sitting and let him say what he wants. Better out than in, I reason. Not that it exactly pours out, but emerges in small dribs separated by blockages. These are some of the snatches. A few of them recur several times, like components that can be slotted in anywhere: 'Never thought I'd have to say this to another man.'; 'Always been led to believe you were a man of honour'; 'Find it difficult to keep a civil tongue in my head'; 'What would you do if you were in my situation?' (Burp and fall over, I imagine); 'There's ways you'll be paying for this' (I know, I know); 'Can you imagine if it were a child of yours?' (Better than you know, actually).

At some point during this, those forbidden words of mine start mustering themselves again in my throat. Those largely true but wholly dangerous words: 'I'm sorry, but it's really none of your business.' Before I can stop them, they're out. Cats through a flap. They take a while to affect Brian Miller, passing

271

through his various blocked lobbies of registration before getting to his chamber of consciousness.

When it hits, it goes off with a bigger bang than its size and weight would have suggested. It explodes him into a sort of life. It was a slight, a very serious slight. That's what it was. I can see him trying to compute the offence. He can't get there, but he's fairly sure he's been struck by a hefty insult concerning him and his daughter.

With alarming speed he's on his feet. Words have done their stuff. Now all the articulacy is passing to the limbs. The man who has never been called unreasonable has moved beyond reason. It has happened with the swiftness of a dinking fly-half. It leaves the gangway unblocked. I am off the deck and down the stairs, waiting for the huge foul tackle of him to fall on my back.

Amazingly we are at a stop. A big one. The station. The exit doors are open and I hop off. Him too. It is not until much later, like now, that I realise we could have been spared everything that followed if the doors had been closed. Miller's drunkenness would have got him thrown off the bus, and we could both have walked away - at least for the time being, although I suppose the events had gone too far for there to have been anything except a brief respite.

Over the zebra and onto the far pavement, right outside the station. My plan, if it can be called that, is to shake Miller off. I've thought none of it through, but it strikes me as a good idea to be where there is light and other people. In I go, and down the stairs. Him too. I catch a glimpse of him in one of the bulbous mirrors on a corner of the passage leading to the platform.

He has become a bull - huge head, mighty torso, down to little tapering legs and almost dainty feet that fairly trip him along.

Now I am on the platform. I turn round and there he is too, emerging from the low archway. He is pointing at me and bellowing. People are looking. We are going public. I catch two lights like cats' eyes coming out of the dark. They are approaching fast and the train comes loudly into the little valley of the station.

Brian Miller is still roaring and pointing, but the train drowns the noise of him and he becomes a fierce cartoon without a caption. The train's exchange of passengers comes between us. I board the train and then, just before the doors close, jump off again. He has seen me doing this and remains on the platform, which is now empty except for us. I can hear every word, every one of his curdling expletives, all horribly fit for purpose after decades of use in the shower room and the clubhouse.

Then it's all over and he stops. No more words. Just the echoes of the last lot dying away with the train, and silence. He's said what he had to. He wanted to speak to me, and now he has done so. Better out than in. Still he points at me accusingly. An entirely new expression takes hold of his face. If not surrender, then truce possibly. Two men trading through their difficulties.

But then he calls back his pointing arm. It is needed closer to home and it clamps hard against his chest, where the pain is coming from. Now it is not clamping any more, but scrambling like a stuck crab on his black coat. His mouth wants to do or say something, even if only to communicate that what is happening is an outrage. He is being murdered from the inside and his hand is trying to finger the culprit, his heart. Better still, get it in his hand and give it a good talking-to; what does it think it's playing at.

Nothing. There's no playing. It's stopped, and no-one can stop it. It is beyond intervention. He can get no purchase on the air with anything in his face - not his nose nor his grabbing mouth nor, soon, his eyes or his ears. But his final face, the one before he falls back in defeat, tells me deafeningly that this is a man who has been felled, and probably fatally, by rage.

If symptoms persist, contact a qualified medical practitioner without delay. (If possible, make sure you notify him before he is struck off.) I go to his big slumped form with its dreadful head and its face made unspeakable by the encroaching blueness. Sometimes, when you are watching sports, you know at once if an injury is serious rather than an Oscars entry.

I remember in the small hours of a boxing show seeing a Mexican boy caught on the jaw by a mighty swing and being dead as he fell towards the canvas. I remember too a huge prop forward lying motionless on the ground as the scrum broke up and the players moved away. Motionless as Miller is now. Paralysed or worse. I don't enjoy being right on these things, but I swear Miller left the world behind just now, along with his consciousness. I could be mistaken. It has been known.

I lean over his face and lock my mouth around his. It is a similar pose to the one his daughter and I have made so many times, though never on a station platform. I get the rasp of his stubbly chin on mine. The fumes of spent alcohol are gathered round his mouth in such concentration that I am probably running the risk of relapse through passive intake.

No excuses. No trammelling games by the imagination. Just get on with it. Be grateful for your recent experience of the procedure on the way back from Highmoor. Also, Dr. Newgate, have you not said repeatedly how much you regretted the tedium of your normal round? What would his daughter think if you let him die? Worse, what would she think if you let him live?

I give it my best shot. I more than go through the motions. Anything else is no option, and I am glad to be reminded of that enduring clause in my moral constitution. Having said that, dead meat is what we have here. Starting with the static muscle-pump in the core of him, lying there doing nothing. His visible self doing likewise and being a beached and unmoving hulk. Without this just-finishing life there would have been no

Serena. Even this thought cannot make me see him as anything other than a rather nasty corpse who has at least had the grace not to string himself out for another fortysomething years.

Two St. Johns ambulance men arrive. Did they get here faster than the vehicles on the moor? I don't know. Time dies in these moments. What I do know is this; despite Dr. Newgate's repeated attempts at resuscitation, the deceased will be found to be dead on arrival at Charing Cross Hospital, Fulham, as Westminster Coroners Court will be told.

September 20th 2017. I love the route. Addicted to it? Oh yes, probably, but boring question. All I know is that it's in my life like a pattern or a rhythm. The pattern of the map with its stations growing further apart as the train pulls clear of the ribbon roads; the rhythm of the wheels, shifting from the syncopation of town junctions to the silkier run of country rails. I breathe more easily as the roads give up, a last big one flashes beneath us like a border river, and the little hills get their chance. Set-back, blameless Betjeman houses with their blameless Betjeman girls, decent as the Fifties. A golf club, a green, a bunker, a retired consultant rehearsing his swing.

It feels like an afterlife. Familiar if not entirely real. But good. Plenty of reassuring presences in the side-by-side worlds of the built and the unbuilt. Certainly a different life from the one that went before.

So, I seem to have started again. Scribble scribble. Late at night, early in the morning, on the trains, same as before. Scraps of notes and reminders on envelope backs, dashed off when I was doing something else, then folded into the book. No idea how long I will continue. From the size of this volume, which is almost as big as that old one, I'm intending to dig in.

Off we go, swinging away from the main line and contouring along the curve of the wooded hillside. Magic valley below us to the right. The simple things that denote light, even lightness, the possibility of more days in this vein. A whole stock of them. The recurrent surprise of this. Predictable yet somehow always fresh when you get to it.

And if I really have started again, one is bound to ask why? Reading the stuff back, I suppose; that's what did it; revisiting the end of my life - it felt no less than that - but from a place, here, now, moving, where I am safely beyond its grasp. It has been made powerless. Next job is to get everything back in its proper order, check the dates and the chronology. Like tidying up before you leave somewhere. For some reason that last entry, where I'm on the tube platform with Brian Miller, the late Brian Miller (whose name no longer frightens me) slipped back in the file to the wrong side of Emily Chatfield's Dr. Nattrass story. As if it didn't belong with the rest of the entries, on account of all that striking-off and reproach and dying. As if it knew itself to be in a terminal place and wanted to stand apart as a codicil, when it is in reality no such thing.

Ten minutes on and the train starts its slow, that's-your-lot halt and gives one of its shivering electric noises. Down in the square, next to the war memorial and the café with the upstairs room, the buses are looping round as ever, going off again to Wycombe, Berko, Wendover, Missenden, Aylesbury. You can smell the wind as you never could in London. Well, you could, but by the time it got there, other things were riding on it and turning it bad.

Up past the park and the pond. Leaves everywhere. Glorious natural litter. Right turn into Stanley Gardens. I don't much like it when people say, 'No, no, we've been vehr lucky,' usually talking about the beauty of where they live, or the brilliance of their children. What I dislike even more is hearing myself say precisely those words. Even though I mean them, of course I do.

I go in through the door of number 39 and say 'Emily Chatfield' at the usual volume. I've lost count of the number times

I've done this, but if a line keeps getting laughs, why change it? And this one always works on her. No point in analysing why, beyond guessing that private jokes carry mirth in the same way that smells carry memory.

Sometimes it's not me who says 'Emily Chatfield' on entry, but her. And then of course we fall back into the business of deconstructing the poor woman, trying to establish which of the two of us she essentially is. Or was, now that she's been discontinued. I say it was her because she was the woman in the café with Cynthia Rattray-Dixon that day. She says it was me because I wrote *The Notes of Dr. Nattrass*. I say no, the character was essentially hers as she created it by means of her now professional acting skills. She says she could say the same of me since Chatfield's story was the product of my now professional writing skills.

september 22nd 2017 No-one finds us here unless they really want to. Ricky does come occasionally, which is very good, especially when you think what he's up to. Clive too. He's been twice now and we've talked easily, like the old friends that we're meant to be. Respect to Clive. The Lord comes with him, of course. He has no choice, but Clive manages to park Him outside, either browsing in St. Mary's Church across the park or else monitoring the well-being of the souls upstairs in the café.

Maurice would like to come, I know. He has even asked if I belong to a squash club. As if. That's one practice I'm glad to have surrendered along with all the rest. Besides, my shoulder hurts, and the only thing my self-diagnosis can come up with is Hurt Shoulder. *The Oxford Handbook of Clinical Diagnosis* is silent on the condition. I retain a copy as a sort of souvenir of that other life. It's an impressive work all right, until you need it for yourself. What it should say is: 'Bits hurt as we get older.'

Maybe I should have gone private and charged £400 a go for such assessments. 'Yes, Mr. Snott-Hartley, the thing to bear in mind with HSS (Hurt Shoulder Syndrome) is that it tends to get worse rather than better. One way of telling that it is getting worse is that the pain will become more severe and the movement more restricted. We find these developments often occur simultaneously, four hundred pounds please.'

Mila I could handle. And Joan too. Their last emails were almost friendly. Well, it's been five years. Not an eternity, but generally long enough for wounds to heal, four hundred pounds please. But Maurice. Issues. Particularly since HGV retired and died (they say it was in that order), all within three months, and Maurice has become senior practitioner. As I suppose I would have been, although he'd have fought me for it. Thank God I'm out of it, to coin a phrase.

September 24th 2017. What I am not out of is this. Three entries in four days. I can feel the compulsion starting up again, all this time later. It is like an old heartbeat, without which, writes former Dr. Newgate, the patient runs the risk of flatlining. This can have far-reaching health implications.

One thing we do agree on, Serena and I, is that the day Cynthia Rattray-Dixon came to Chesham was an important one for both of us. Look at us now, we say, with what would probably strike an onlooker as intolerable smugness: Serena unstoppable as a voice-over artiste, one of the most sought-after of the new generation. Country spinster, stroppy teen, titled toff or town tart, she can do anyone to perfection. Children in particular.

Whenever her agent Trudy Dunlop phones with the latest offer, I see her literally throwing herself into the part. That is, she flings her voice at it, like a quoit, and then follows it with the rest of her person. If the role doesn't submit to her immediately, then she will break down its resistance by attrition, wrapping the person into herself and taking her everywhere, down into the Wednesday market, over into the library or the little Elgiva Theatre, which we frequent, into the bathroom, anywhere, until the merger is complete and she has taken possession. Or until she has been taken possession of. Both readings of her process are accurate. She both leases her attributes out for the purposes of impersonation, and absorbs the characteristics of others with a view to altering herself.

Sometimes, naturally, these other people come into the bedroom with her, then into the bed with us. I say I would quite like to know if I'm going to be waking up with Country Spinster or Town Tart, as it would help me to arrange my own behaviour. Her skills are uncanny and, I admit, a little unsettling. Even more so than the college realised at the time. Particularly when she is asked to be a little girl, as she regularly is. How could she not be brilliant at that, and how could I not be troubled by that brilliance, and panic, even now, that she might become so small that she vanishes altogether?

Oh yes, she has also worked up a parody of me, a leering, lecherous quack called Dr. Strukovsky, har har. I say thank you very much but I can write my own lines, hadn't you noticed.

And I can. Since *Nattrass* got optioned, by Canal Numero Cinq of all people, I have had more offers of work than I can take on, most of them adaptations of books or plays with a medical theme as I am reckoned to be sound on the technicalities (if only they knew), but also to have a good ear for dialogue. 'Jean-Claude say only a guy who's saved lives could write so… *confiant*.' That's not my view but, as Serena says, don't do their disapproving for them.

There's also the consultancy work. I must be one of the very few defrocked docs to land this kind of gig, but who's complaining? When Serena came clean about the authorship of Nattrass, after *Physician!* had been such a success, Cynthia couldn't have been more magnanimous.

Instead of getting miffed about being hoodwinked, she said how postmodern it was (or was it post-structural?), and added that BMPC would be delighted to have me aboard. That was definitely the phrase. I like to think I've been of some use to them; so many of the MSS are written by amateurs; I mean amateur doctors as well as amateur writers. Like my patients - I should say my ex-patients - they think they can wikipaediate their way to instant expertise. It would have killed HGV. Perhaps it did.

September 26th 2017. I am not about to fill my professional gap by turning into Arthur Miller, and Serena is not (I hope) about to become Joyce Grenfell. She is better than that. But if either of us had been told back that - what, six years ago - that we would have the life we now do, we would have laughed them out of court. Court is exactly where I felt I lived during those final ragged days, walking around with Guilty branded onto my forehead, each day indistinguishable from a dock, waiting for my prosecutors to feed as fully as they chose on my somehow-still-breathing cadaver.

I keep wanting to let Maurice know all about my success, to patronise him with my (unwritten) thesis on the healing powers of narrative, with particular reference to *The Notes of Dr. Nattrass* (pub. BMPC 2015). Out of the question, but how I would love to see his face contort with the effort of trying not to show its envy and resentment. Yet I feel this desire pulling me back down into the crude politics of the squash court. It is a *schadenfreude* I cannot afford. But then he probably wants me to know all about his own professional triumphs.

I decide that I am not ready to re-admit Maurice into my life. It could go on like this for ever. The years may have been kind to him, but we have not been kind to each other. We think we are men, but are only boys. If ever I tried to broach the subject of regression with Serena, she would have every right to answer that it takes one to know one. And it does. That's why we are together, scrabbling eagerly for the droppings from maturity's table. That's why we go to our meetings in the church halls and community centres of the Chilterns, and see our local counterparts of Frankie the Fish, Spiritual Sally and the rest. All quite unique. Wendover Back to Basics, Monday; Loudwater Discussion,Thursday; Beaconsfield Step, Sunday, and so on for ever, I hope.

September 28th 2017. Extraordinary how the past goes on yielding up its secrets. Like a dig. Here's one from the book itself, the black and red volume I had feared was lost, incinerated, stolen, held hostage, whatever, when in fact it had met an even worse fate, detained indefinitely at the bottom of my squash bag and shrouded by Stinky Pink the Killer Towel. No fate for an innocent (well, not entirely) witness. It languished there for months while my head had gone wild and feverish with the dread of it having fallen into enemy hands. I waited and waited for some dreadful if unorthodox come-uppance beyond the scope of my imagination and grimmest projections. But it never came.

How slack-jawed, infantile, crap but also how reprieved, home-free and lighter than helium I felt when I found it there. I had been drawn by the corpse smell coming from the cupboard in my bedsit.

When I scanned the book again, just the other day, I came across this account of my striking off. This too had been written in another part of the volume, away from the regular tide of entries, as if it was ashamed to declare itself. It's dated April 6th 2011, therefore just over three months after the Brian Miller incident, I mean death. I force myself to look at it, no squinty eyes, and as I read I can feel that odd, slightly toxic sense of weightlessness and abandon entering me:

'Up before a bench of distinguished nobodies. Failed medics of some sort, I imagine, trying to rustle up some status for themselves by the bureaucratic route. Some big room in the horrible

HQ of the General Medical Council up by the Euston Road. Driven past it countless times, but never expected to be visiting it in this guise. Never mind; I feel totally, but I do mean totally absent from the occasion. Like I'm already gone. One of the men on the panel I do recognise, actually. I think I went to his lectures at Thomas's. Though probably not more than once. His voice is one long Edwardian yawn. I hope some of the shame intended for me sticks to him by association.

At some point he asks me to give an account of my behaviour - with regard to Serena, I suppose - and I really can't be bothered. I don't say that. I say something which is probably even more offensive to them, namely that I don't consider it any of their business. Which I don't. That's the heart of the matter. It's also my goose cooked, as surely as if I'd boasted to them that I'd stitched a scalpel back into someone's aorta. It's not just me against them, although it patently is that too, it's a clash of two irreconcilable systems, theirs and mine. Theirs is full of public rectitude, service and accountability - and bully for them - while mine is based solely on the imperative of being with Serena. It's no defence; not legally or morally. I take no pride in defining it, none whatsoever.

I was offered the services of a representative - a legal officer, I think he was called. A very pleasant, earnest young man, whose help I declined as politely as I could. I would explain to him that right flows from my togetherness with her, and that any rule, code or convention which questions or undermines this togetherness has no validity; that official guidelines cannot expect to have currency in the higher moral councils of unconditional love. But of course I don't. Nor do I need to. Everyone's face conveys the clear understanding that I have no wish to defend myself; therefore that I have no defence; therefore that this present business need not detain any of us long. Their attitude verges on the considerate. At least one of them senses that I am in some sort of breakdown. If that's where I am. How dreadful. All those poor men and women I used to treat, or try to treat; quiet, brave men and women who had somehow come to a halt, as cars do, and didn't know how to start again, or even whether this would be possible.

Breakdown. The wonderful, vernacular, to-hell-with-niceties plainness of the word. And the terrible interior of the condition, an old cave of a place with a total and thorough absence of facilities. The thought-trains locking into a loop line that brings them back to what they wanted to escape. Again and again, the switch-points in their conspiratorial network. Left, then left again, then left again and so back where you least want to be, which is this dire cranium of yourself. Well, I suppose there is no substitute for the first-hand knowledge of a condition. I once saw the value of this, didn't I, back when I was practising; I even put the principle to use. Didn't I?

I see the diagnosis appearing in the tribunal chairman's face, whoever he is. I see him enjoying his dawning perception. Sympathy I don't sense, and experience no surprise, nor even wrongness in its absence. Who am I to deny him? As I say, he is very likely correct. Must consult my *Oxford Handbook of Clinical Diagnosis*, for a change. Anyway, I'm out, and pretty soon. Minutes rather than hours. Out in every sense you can give that word, and savouring the weird freedom of the suddenly jobless. I'm faintly aware of the tabloids doing a number on me. 'Naughty Dr. Nibs caught with knickers down - and they weren't even his.' I might be making that up, but who cares.

Quite.'

September 30th 2017. Dad on the phone. He sounds anxious. It's Mary Garside, of course it is. 'Now William,' he says, 'I know you don't go doctoring any more, but I was wondering if I could ask you something. Not for myself, mind.'

'Please, Dad, go ahead.'

'We're not too gone on young Cowgill, I'm afraid.'

'Young' meaning still not fifty, although he must be approaching it.

Dad, bless him, never asks why the doctoring came to an end, just says how proud he is of me for making a go of it in the writing game. Medicine lets people down, is the unspoken message; it's one you can prove because people die when they're not meant to. I ask some questions about Mary, whether she's eating properly, or lost weight, or on medication - the usual chestnuts. So glad I don't do that for a living any more. They'd have fitted well into my old constituency, both the wrong side of ninety now. Or the right side, depending which way you look at it.

Without knowing it, he refers to her as 'your mother' once or twice. I don't put him right. I say he should keep the doctor informed - very original - and if he and she aren't very keen on Dr. Cowgill they can always ask to see another. People do, I tell him authoritatively. He thanks me as if this is the most illuminating wisdom he has ever heard.

I ask how everything is in Highmoor and he says 'very quiet.' That's the news. 'Not a single bus,' he explains. 'That Anne Charlton's an angel, mind, with her volunteer taxi run. We'd be buried otherwise.'

I hear the knocker go on his front door, and reckon it's Mary. 'Hold on, pet,' he calls, and we end our conversation. I think I hear her calling out 'Duggy' through the door. I envisage the two of them shuttling the few doors up and back along Upper Level Row, stepping boldly into a shared state of true senescence.

October 2nd 2017. Imogen round. When I write these two words, I stop in disbelief. As if I have to go back about thirty years to those early days of ours. But no; Imogen comes round to our house. Chiltern Line to Chalfont, country tube, the lot. Not just Imogen, but Charles too. And Ricky with them, a little behind them, demure and patient. I'm at the window, watching for them as they come through the gate. Loitering is the word. Some things you can't give up. I have to say, they make a splendid couple, her as we know her to be when she is well, and him with really quite serious levels of handsomeness; thick dark waves of Iberian hair (you can't beat that stuff) with only the very beginnings of silver at the temples. Nature's aristocrat. His greying will be impeccably phased. Surely I'm not going to dodge jealousy today.

He looks familiar. When I asked Imogen over the phone whether I knew him, she said 'not properly, no,' and left it at that. But he had been in our house, had he not?

Somewhere among the emotional chaos towards the end. If so, what had he been doing there? It is when they are coming through the little so-called pergola on our front path that I get, literally, the picture. It happens in the second or two that his head and shoulders are framed by the woodwork, as if he is the subject of a photo or a portrait. But why Charles and not Carlos - Carlos Adorno - as he was on that CD cover? What was it called? Oh yes, plain *Carlos Adorno*, it being his first album.

And now here he is, apparently walking straight out of our record collection - Imogen's collection - and up my front path. I try to take it in, make it conform to the usual laws that govern perception and reality. I can see how he has made the transition from one life to another - from being a sultry CD cover to being a man coming up my front path. At least I think can see. Inez is the link. Yet it is too early to see quite how he made the crossover. Well, he does have a profile as a crossover artiste, doesn't he? This is a joke I had better not make, even though I'm privately pleased with it. No, *because* I'm privately pleased with it.

I shall have to be careful with Carlos jokes, i.e. not make any. He is emerging as a serious popular singer and, that rare, bold thing, a musical citizen of Europe. Crossover in a border sense. The reviewers have him as a classier version of Julio Iglesias and a more accessible one than Jose Carreras. I patronise this man at my peril.

Besides, I owe him a great deal. If that sounds odd, I can only say he might well be thinking the same of me; me and Serena. We have been the agents of each other's freedom, it's as simple as that. Even in the teeth of Imogen's assault on our behaviour - Serena's immorality and my gullibility - I did sense that liberty was being passed across into my possession.

A huge transaction was being enacted between us. It was happening as we spoke, even if the process was obscured by everything else that was happening. I was being let go, in every possible sense of that usually unwelcome form of words - morally, maritally, socially, contractually, corporately, you name it. More than that, I was being gifted with the power to grant her that same gift of liberty in return. It was a power I was taking and using. This was one of those rare presents whose value lies not in the gaining of an asset but in the losing of a liability - the dogged and hitherto unshiftable wrongness at the heart of my - I suppose I have to call it affair - with Serena.

I can't very well ask her whether she sees it the same way. Not now, anyway. Perhaps there will be a time. But then perhaps I won't need to. Her ease with Carlos, the light of admiration - really, twin beams of the stuff targeting him at point blank range - are eloquence enough. What I would love to know though is, in Van Morrison's words: 'How long has this been going on?'

I suppose the answer depends on when you start the clock. I throw myself back into those end times at the house. Goodness they seem distant from here. The Coalition - how dated the word seems now - was still in. Datagate hadn't yet happened, and no-one had predicted it or anything like it, much as they liked to claim later that they had. The world had gone tense, sure, like the air before a humdinger of a storm. I knew that, but then my view of its outward life had probably been tainted by contagion from my inner one.

Throwing myself back into those end times at the house, I can now see him, Carlos in CD format, making free with the open spaces - the kitchen table, the drawing room window sill, even, once, our bed. I wonder if he knows how much he was putting himself about under our roof. Or whether he knew - this particular penny is only dropping into my head now as I write it - that she was pretending to me that his calls were in fact coming from her brother. I remember that he was a friend of Inez The Last's parents. I believe he came over to England to give some concerts and, while here, saw (small s I suppose) Inez at what used to be our house. I also remember the two women going to a concert at Cadogan Hall. His concert, surely. It all begins to form a… all right, narrative.

In they come, all loud with anxious bonhomie. Except for Ricky, who is watchful, and biding his time. When they take their coats off the air is filled with subtly expensive smells: from the coats, the scarves, the hair, the skin.

When she smiles at us, then embraces us, I can see some county component in her health and wellbeing that I had never noticed before. It gives her the lustre of a high value stranger. I must have lowered her game during our time together. She has become untouchable. To me certainly. I would get a heartstopper electric shock from that shiny green coat. My whole arm would be flung away from it so hard that it would hurl my body into a far corner of the room.

The sight of her brings about three more affirmations in quick succession. The first is that I have no vested interest in Imogen's unhappiness. The second is that I no longer have to see my own failures and shortcomings through the look in her downturned face.

The third is that, just as I had suspected, I had never properly known her, nor made myself known to her in return, while she was 'mine.'

Today that face is as far from downturned as I have ever seen it. It is up, and looking, and sniffing the social air. She has lost weight and you can see the true, graceful shape of her. She has done something new to her hair. It catches the light in a quite spectacular way, to the extent that it seems to be a light source in its own right.

New dress too, and shoes. Everything. There is something unusual in her hand. No, on her hands, both of them. Two rows of long and perfect nails with the colour and sheen of bright plums. New Imogen. The kind of new which makes her look like the old one. That is, the young one. You can go round and round like this for ever. She looks positively forbidden to me, which is just as it should be.

The two women smile at each other in unison. Ricky is observing them. This leaves me and Carlos to our own traffic of glances. I'm not sure what my face is up to, so I offer him a drink, he compliments me on the house, we discuss the benefits of the area, transport, distances, all that sort of thing. He is softly spoken and disarmingly modest. I tell him his English is excellent and he shakes his head in disagreement.

By comparison with our au pairs, he is as native as a Cockney. I ask him whether he is to be Carlos or Charles and he answers 'Charles' emphatically. His aim, says Serena, is to pass for an Englishman in six months, by which time he intends to be resident here. I say that when I heard him singing yesterday I assumed he was an Englishman, but the compliment seems to misfire slightly.

Imogen tells us about his new album. It is called *Descompuesto*, which means Broken, and is a lament for the condition of the world in general. Also for Spain in particular by the sound of it as there is a number called 'Broke.' This national condition is hardly new - just worse. I think about saying, purely as a joke, there's bound to be a *Descompuesto 2* but decide not to. His country, after all. Even a minimal patriot like me would be stung if I was in Spain and someone started dissing Britain.

He is launching the album with a series of concerts throughout Europe and giving the proceeds to poverty relief and job creation in his home region of Catalonia. She is explaining this to us with the zeal and fluency of a totally committed press officer. We nod, impressed and suitably humbled.

I should probably be taking this opportunity of engaging him to perform at our next rally against HS2, the new train line that's ripping chunks out of prime Chiltern countryside so people can get to Birmingham a few minutes faster and begging the question: 'Couldn't they just get an earlier train?'

Ricky is in England on one of his rare trips back from New York, where he is working on the international economics desk - I'm probably getting that wrong - of the *Wall Street Journal*. I'm delighted, in the standard Proud Father way, that he's got this mighty job and can look forward to decades of issuing the world with prescriptions for its redemption. But I'm also privately relieved that he hasn't gone into something so virtuous that it will set off in me another cycle of self-denigration.

He is nearly as intrigued as his mother by Serena's five-month bump.

It has not only changed the shape of her but also that of the whole world. Nothing is now thought or spoken without the close presence of this tiny/huge alteration. Imogen is solicitous, Ricky a little askance. When Imogen offers to give her some baby things and starts reminiscing about her own pregnancy, he becomes visibly uncomfortable. He can't quite work out where he stands on the prospect of a tiny sibling. When he's out of the room, Imogen ventures the unexpected opinion that he is getting broody in his own right. It turns out he is still seeing, with a capital S, Inez. In fact she might turn up here if she can follow his directions. She can't, or won't. The afternoon goes by and there's no sign of her.

He goes outside to get reception (i.e. to speak privately) and I catch him through the window looking thunder-faced. Imogen says she thinks it will end in tears, and I say isn't that where it started. He comes back in and has no appetite for anything - not food, not drink, not conversation, nothing. Love, says the former Dr. Newgate to himself: they were right, all of them, Sappho, the Jacobeans, the agony aunts. Nothing to choose between it and illness. Beyond medicine, like so much else. He'll learn. I fear he'll learn.

Later I try to establish from Imogen whether Inez still lives at our, at her house. She isn't entirely sure, and looks to Carlos for assistance. It seems Inez has become much more interested in Ricky since he got this clearly lucrative job in America. She has even said she wants to look after him. The former Dr. Newgate diagnoses a very late onset of the au pairing instinct.

Before he goes, we do manage to have a conversation of sorts about... I'm not sure what it's about. I ask him to give me an explanation of the world's prolonged economic failure. More than a decade now, something authoritative and easily assimilable, and with a proper villain at the heart of it. A Bush, Obama, Madov, Blair, Murdoch, Soros, anyone, presented in the form of a cartoon monster. I've spent so much energy anatomising my own sins that I'd like a break while we go global and nail the real Bad Guy.

He gives me a weary, aged look, the kind of look I must have failed to disguise when people would corner me at parties in pursuit of a free opinion on their bad back. Still, not a good idea to lighten the mood by asking him if Inez waives the hundred quid these days. So, thank God, I don't.

Ricky launches into an overview. He does this obligingly but mirthlessly; I catch some references to John Maynard Keynes. I'm OK with him - binge your way out of the shit - but not the next one he mentions: Hyman Minsky. Ricky throws his name in as if he is a good friend in the States (he probably is, if he's not dead) even though they have their differences.

By 'endogenous financial instability' I'm struggling. When we get to Basle II rules and the reduction of banks' tier-one capital held against risk-weight assets in order to support triple-A securities, I am, as we say in the fiscal laity, fucked.

I nod intelligently as he proceeds, just as I nodded at my patients when they explained what was wrong with them and the treatment they required from me. I am of course as bamboozled as they looked when I decided it was time to show them who was boss and launched into a heavy doctorish tract about the deposition of monosodium urate crystal, and the vulnerability of the podagra's metatarsophalangeal joint.

Maybe they were reluctantly impressed, as I have just been by Ricky. Maybe they felt that they were at least getting their money's worth. Maybe the posh ones worked it out from their Latin and Greek. I don't know. What I do know is that for all Ricky's and my showy command of the subjects, huge corporations still crash like skyscrapers and big toes swell up like party balloons.

Clive - damn him and bless him - says the only thing we need to know is that we don't know. I suppose it's a variation of his better-known 'the only thing we need to know about God is that we're not It.' This leans him back comfortably into his faith and me forwards and uncomfortably into my doubt. When I was young, yes, I did have faith, small f, in medicine, rather as I can see that Ricky, at the same age, has small-f faith in the international healing powers of economic science. Or, I suppose, as dramatists have faith in the improving capacity of the theatre.

I lost mine. Something went wrong. I started whoring after

toxic gods but I'm blowed if I'm going to write another word about all that. If I hadn't lost it, I wouldn't have found this, whatever this is. I need to do it as much as I have ever needed to do anything. I hate to sound so solemn about it, and actually so pompous, but the doing of it, the writing things down, does make the world seem more whole than it otherwise would. Hubristic? Definitely. Great. And if Clive tries to tell me that only a power greater than myself can relieve me of the compulsion, I shall sack him as a friend.

October 4th 2017. So. I do appear to have started again. More than started. Eighth entry in a fortnight. This almost constitutes a habit. Here I am, downstairs in the small hours, scribbling. Same book. At least, same model, A4 red and black. I was going to say I must remember not to leave this one in my squash bag. But that can't happen again. No more squash-playing (suspected medial meniscal tear, says Dr. Strukowski) means no more squash bag to keep things in - 'keep' here meaning also forget or lose or expose to the risk of detection.

September 23rd. Everyone knows everything about everyone these days. We are experts on total strangers, versed in the minutiae of their lives and work. We cannot help it. Datagate15 saw to that. We will recover gradually, writes Dr. Know-Nothing, although we cannot be sure how. In the meantime our behaviour will be characterised by new levels of mistrust and secrecy. Connectivity will continue to be viewed not as a builder of alliances but as a public thief of private resources. Since the cancellation of privacy, the commodity has gained a scarcity value beyond our wildest imaginings. It is as precious as breath. Perhaps the market will restore its position in ways we cannot foresee.

Meanwhile, I gather (from *The Economist*, no less) the really smart corporate operators have stopped using the web altogether. Even mobiles, some of them. No automatic archive of correspondence. No casual calls packed into someone's aural digibank. Everything back to the low-tech of ink on paper and words in rooms. The younger generation have never seen anything like it. So clean, so radical. These heads are like savvy tribal elders who move across the ground without leaving a footprint, and are no more traceable than the ghosts of their forefathers.

Datagate15 pulled everything inside out like a glove torn off. So much was written about it, so many special issues of this and that, that I've nothing new to say. Yes, all the partitions fell down, the firewalls went up like tissue, we were all there, all of us, naked and visible as lovers, adulterous lovers in the centre of a main road at rush hour. Look at us now, two years down that road, the brave face on, recovery strategies wherever you turn, and yet everyone somehow hushed and chastened. A kind of dumbness, mistrust of words and therefore of their users, ourselves.

People say they saw it coming, but to hell with retrospective prescience. It came when it came. We may have set up the mechanisms by which it turned on us, but when it rounded on us it did so with its own incredible, wayward autonomy. We scarcely believed it; how could it do this to us? We blamed everything and everyone, naturally, all the usual suspects: God, No God, Beelzebub, Lucifer and all other variants of the diabolical, modernity, greed, hubris, the Liberals, the BBC, Rupert Murdoch.

The Government have got MI5 onto it, for goodness sake. Not just them but senior military personnel too. (*Economist* again.) Same old. When they send for the soldiers, that's when you know they're really flustered.

September 24th. For some reason that is way beyond my competence, there has been a contagion from the written, that is the on-line, into the spoken. The paralysis has gone into the fingers and toes of our social manoeuvres. Our dances of love are halting and sclerotic. Maybe this is why my conversations with Serena come to a halt in particular places, even now; the places where I might ask her the questions I never yet have, the ones that still hang in the air between us; the ones about what happened with her father; the ones about the way her voice used to... but I daren't complete the sentence, not even privately, for fear it will go trailing us into the old regression. *Primo non nocere.* The words still hold good beyond the bounds of professional doctoring.

Sounds upstairs. More in morning.

September 25th. Or not. It's a truce, is all I can say just now. A truce based, probably, on the balance of terror between us. Which doesn't make it necessarily a bad truce, any more than Nixon/Kruschev or Reagen/Brezhnev were necessarily bad truces.

Matrimony, eh. If symptoms persist, contact a qualified medical practitioner, i.e. not Dr. Newgate.

September 26th. But definitely get this back into a bit of shape, if it really is the case that I have started again. The big question for me is: 'Why did you kill yourself, Dr. Newgate? Former Dr. Newgate.' It's a fair one. Did it happen just as deaths happen to us - the frequent culmination of an illness's narrative? All I know is that someone had to kill Dr. Newgate. That Dr. Newgate. Literally, figuratively, metaphorically, any damned way you choose. It was clear. He had it coming to him. The someone was me. My accomplice was Emily Chatfield. And Serena.

??? Add date. One of the last of the long days. Everything going gold around the church. The wind waiting to get its hands on the leaves. Dogs flying about on the rising ground between here and there. The light doing a classy fade, silhouetting St.

Mary's little tower with photographic taste. The evening taking possession. Friends round. Hers rather than mine. A Derek, a Joy, a Trevor and a Jean. Plus another man, with another name. I'll get them wrong if I try to use them, so I just sit and look harmless. They are from one of the studios. Nice people. Nice young people.

Interesting professional conversation. About voices, I think. They demonstrate and laugh, demonstrate and laugh. They laugh so much that they look as if they are falling over, even though they are sitting down. Horizontal with mirth on the settee, or their heads landing into their folded arms on the table.

They are very good. So good I could swear the room is more crowded than it is. I smile supportively at her. She is framed in the window with the sun low at her shoulder and I begin to lose her. She does a voice I've heard before, and her visibility reduces a little more, and then a little more.

She leans forwards in laughter and her face is briefly visible against the plain white of the wall. She has that smile, the private but open one she wore in the surgery, and before that at the window of the squash club. Except that now it is not face-on but in profile, and therefore pointing away from me. I follow its line, which I am not used to doing, and my eyes run straight into the face of the man whose name I don't know, the one who has come by himself. The really quite distressingly handsome one. He is looking delighted by what he sees. He says something and she laughs again, close to wildness this time.

Same evening, late. The after-day. The hollowness after the noise. Something ashen and chidden in the night silence. Then the floorboards upstairs. The click of the landing light. Her footsteps, audibly heavier by the week. The toilet. The stairs. Her coming down and the light coming in. Put it away now.